Dear Reader,

I'll never forget my "first" mummies. I think I was about five when we met.

My mom and her family immigrated to the United States from Ireland when she was a teenager. She eventually married my dad, and the two of them made the decision to move to Florida, but my mom's family stayed in the Chicago area. That included my great-grandmother and a lot of my wonderful crazy Irish family.

Naturally, we traveled from Florida to Chicago frequently when I was a child.

And thus—among other great institutions—I was taken to the Field Museum of Natural History with a bunch of inventive storytellers. One example: Nefer-hoho (a made-up name, yes) had been a dancer and a jester, but she had danced too close to a brazier and it had hit her on the head and...next up, mummification. Then there was the mummified cat, who was magical, of course, and came alive in the museum at night. You had to be very careful to be out of the museum before dark, I was told, because the pharaoh would awaken and take his sword and...

As a five-year-old, I was (as an uncle explained to my mother) a wee bit traumatized by all these stories. Nightmares abounded!

But a lifelong fascination was born.

Years ago, my husband, Dennis, and I were able to visit Egypt to see the Great Pyramid of Giza, the museum in Cairo and learn more about the culture.

This is a long and roundabout way of explaining that much of the Egyptology in this novel is true—but then again, I did spend those days with Irish storytellers, so some of what you're about to read is entirely made up.

I could tell you which is which. But maybe you'll want to explore—or maybe you know far more than I ever will about the subject. Anyway, it's all part of a new story, and I sincerely hope you'll enjoy it.

If you'd like to comment on the story (I love to hear from readers!) or learn about upcoming books, contests, etc., please visit my website, theoriginalheathergraham.com. Thank you so much for being a reader!

Heather

New York Times and *USA TODAY* bestselling author **Heather Graham** has written more than a hundred novels. She's a winner of the RWA's Lifetime Achievement Award and the Thriller Writers' Silver Bullet. She is an active member of International Thriller Writers and Mystery Writers of America. For more information, check out her website, theoriginalheathergraham.com, or find Heather on Facebook.

HEATHER GRAHAM

SHADOWS IN THE NIGHT
&
NEVER SLEEP WITH STRANGERS

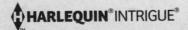

HARLEQUIN® INTRIGUE®

ISBN-13: 978-1-335-14200-9

Shadows in the Night & Never Sleep with Strangers

Copyright © 2017 by Harlequin Books S.A.

The publisher acknowledges the copyright holder of the individual works as follows:

Shadows in the Night
Copyright © 2017 by Heather Graham Pozzessere

Never Sleep with Strangers
Copyright © 1998 by Heather Graham Pozzessere

Recycling programs for this product may not exist in your area.

Printed in U.S.A.

www.Harlequin.com

CONTENTS

SHADOWS
IN THE NIGHT

PROLOGUE

The Mummy
A Year Ago

"Sir!"

The word was spoken softly and with respect.

Dr. Henry Tomlinson, renowned Egyptologist, turned. One of the grad students had just slipped through the inner flap of the air-controlled prep tent and was smiling benignly, awaiting his attention.

He hadn't actually taught in about five years, but he still loved it—and working with students. He'd retired to spend all his time in the field, and he'd recently been hired by Alchemy, an Anglo-American sponsoring company, to head this dig. Alchemy was into all kinds of tech and had become a Fortune 500 company. Every year, they sponsored an exceptional archaeological event, followed by a public exhibit. Recent ones had been centered around the Amazon River, central China—and now ancient Egypt. Their resources were phenomenal and Henry still couldn't believe his good fortune. But no matter what monetary resources had been offered, he was thrilled about having grad students involved.

This one was Harley Frasier. Just twenty-six, she was tall, shapely, honey blonde, with a face crafted in perfect classic symmetry and enormous green eyes that seemed to take in everything. She was serious and brilliant and could nail the crux of information with laser-like acuity. She also had a sense of humor and the most delightful laugh he had ever heard.

Of the five specialty graduate candidates, she was, beyond a doubt, his favorite. He often felt like a grandfatherly mentor to her—and the idea made him happy. He'd had no children of his own. He'd never even had a wife. No time for a family. He hadn't intended it be that way forever, but there was always so much to do. If he'd had the chance to be a father, he would've been pleased and proud to have had Harley as a granddaughter. She seemed to feel the same closeness to him.

Perhaps their bond was odd since, of the five grad students, she was the one who was different, the only one not majoring in Egyptology—though she was minoring in it. She had no plan to go into Egyptology or even archaeology or history for her life's vocation.

Harley was with him, first of all, because of her knowledge regarding the field and her love for it. But she was also there because her work was going to be in criminal psychology and forensic science. Henry had been baffled when he was approached by her university. Professors at the Maryland college Harley was attending—which was arguably the top school for criminology and it also offered majors and minors in Egyptology and archaeology—had explained to him the importance of having a student like Harley on this expedition. He had been on the hunt for the tomb of Amenmose for nearly a decade; for that entire decade, he'd been finding more and more clues about the location—and, of course, with the permission and blessing of the Egyptian government—finding other ancient tombs and treasures in the process. This allowed for his continued excavations. But the discovery of the tomb of Amenmose was the main focus of his work.

Many others had searched.

Some of them had died or disappeared in that effort.

History suggested that Amenmose had been murdered. As a criminology student, Harley was to be in on the discovery and would seek and find whatever evidence those who had managed his secret burial might have left behind.

Not that, to Henry's mind, Amenmose hadn't deserved murder. He had usurped power every step of the way. He'd abused officials below him. It had even been intimated that he had attempted to kill those in power above him.

"I think we've gotten all the manual labor done for the evening and we're going to pack it in, maybe drive to that little town for some dinner. Want to come with us? You should. You'd enjoy it. Or shall we bring you back something?" Harley asked him.

"Next time, Harley, I'll come with you all," he promised. "There's so much in here! I'm not going to go touching anything until we've had a chance to work with the preservation measures, but I do intend to look at everything."

Earlier that week, they had finally discovered the secret site of the tomb of Amenmose. And, of course, since then, Henry Tomlinson had been on cloud nine. This was a dream come true, a fantasy realized, the culmination of a lifetime of love and dedication.

Harley laughed softly. "Yes! You did it, Dr. Tomlinson."

"I did, didn't I?"

The Amenmose find was among the most important

ancient Egyptian discoveries of the past few years; he couldn't have been more excited about being a major player in that discovery. And even now, at the end of an exhausting day—and even though he truly enjoyed the young people working with him—he was far too fascinated to leave. There were a dozen or so coffins to be studied, one of them presumably that of Amenmose; the group wouldn't consider opening them until everyone was back at the museum in Cairo. But he *could* study the canopic jars they'd found thus far. There were also other artifacts that had been carefully moved into the prep tent. So much to observe and to describe! And there were the broken coffins, which had probably been as meticulously set as any of the others, but had been in the section where a partial cave-in had taken place. Several of those outer and inner coffins had split and exposed their mummies. Henry Tomlinson was fascinated to see what study was possible before the mummies were packed and crated and prepared for the trip to Cairo, where options for preservation were far more sophisticated, and where the mummies could be X-rayed and DNA could be tested.

Oh! It was all so monumental.

Amenmose had been a priest in the days when another priest, Ay, had ruled Egypt as regent. Ay had done so for a well-known pharaoh, the boy king, Tutankhamen. As regent, Ay had wielded immense power. He'd gone on to become pharaoh in his own right—after the death of Tut at the age of nineteen.

Amenmose, according to ancient texts, had tried to usurp some of that power. And he'd had his own followers in the court, making him a dangerous man. Because of this he had feared for his immortal life—and his wife had kept his burial plans a complete secret, shared only with members of his family. Naturally, legend had it that many of his most loyal followers—rather than give away any secrets—had been willing to die with him, sealed alive in a grave for eternity.

"Dr. Tomlinson, you worked so hard. And wow! You triumphed. You should celebrate. Come out with us. Is there nothing I can do to convince you?" Harley asked. She still had that wonderful smile, as if she were the one who was far older and wiser. "Nothing's going to disappear. We'll go have some dinner and drinks and come on back. There are plenty of men on guard here. And," she added, "you really deserve a little celebration with us. Think of it—you researched and imagined and looked into the ancient Egyptian mind and you made the discovery. It's your shining moment. You're another Carter with his Tutankhamen, Dr. Tomlinson. Do you realize that?"

"Oh, no, no," Henry demurred. He shook his head firmly. "A celebration is tempting, but I couldn't leave. I couldn't. I do promise that I'll come with all of you on another day. Harley! Look at this! I feel like, as the song says, I have treasures untold."

Harley laughed. "You saw *The Little Mermaid*?" she asked.

He stared at her, feeling a bit chagrined. "Oh! Yes, I get it, you wouldn't think that I'd see a children's movie…" He laughed, too. "Remember, I do have great-nieces! Anyway…"

He started walking as he spoke. "Harley, these are such treasures! This broken coffin." He gestured at it. "Damaged by time and by that cave-in, however many centuries ago. And this fellow, Harley. It almost looks as if he was buried alive. Wrapped up alive and screaming."

"I don't think you can embalm anyone and have that

person come out of the process alive," Harley reminded him, amused. "That's only in fiction. We both know what was involved in Egyptian embalming, and just how many factors could've had an effect on the mummy's appearance. Screaming mummies belong to B movies, right? And when you think about it, weird mummies are all the more reason you should come with us."

"Why is that?"

Harley didn't answer. The flap opened again and Jensen Morrow, another of the students, poked his head in to answer.

He'd obviously heard the question.

"Ooh! 'Cause you shouldn't be alone with scary old stuff when you have cool kids like us to hang out with!" Jensen said.

They all laughed. Jensen was a good-looking, dark-haired young man who loved the study he was involved in, and Dr. Henry Tomlinson liked him very much, as well. Jensen played hard, but he worked harder. He came from money; his father was an inventor who'd come up with a special cleaning product. And yet Jensen never acted like money, never acted pretentious or entitled the way some rich kids did.

"Tempting, tempting, tempting," Henry said again. "But I'm going to stay."

Jensen raised his eyebrows at Harley. "Hey, girl, then it's you and me heading out. The old man here isn't coming. That's okay. We're bringing back the goods. Just the two of us, since Belinda Gray is waiting for a video chat with her fiancé—military, as we know!—in Iraq. Roger Eastman agreed to help one of the tech guys investigate some computer info they're picking up. I hate to say it, but we're getting chatter about an insurgent group starting up. And Joe Rosello said he wants to learn more about the excavation equipment. He's working with that pretty Egyptian girl, our translator, and learning about hoists."

"Hoists? Yeah, right!" Harley said. "Satima. She *is* pretty, and thank goodness we have her. I'm just grateful she filled in at the last minute when the older gentleman we'd hired wound up ill. If I know our friend Joe at all, I know he's very happy!" She said to Henry, "We won't go far, since we seem to be feeling a wee bit nervous! And we won't be late. We'll bring you something to eat and see if you want to be social when we get back, okay? If, and only if, you're absolutely positive you don't want to take a ride with this handsome, if ridiculous, guy and me?"

Henry laughed. "Oh, Harley, you're a sweetheart, but give it up. You know I'm not coming."

She grimaced, a delightful movement of her face. "Yes, I do," she admitted. "But we—your devoted students—have to try. I'll bring you a special treat for dinner."

"Don't worry about me, guys. I'll be fine."

"Sorry, we *will* worry about you. At least we can make sure you eat. I'm willing to bet you're going to be up all night—and you won't even notice that you haven't slept," Harley said.

He smiled and made a shooing motion with his hands. "Go! Get on out with you. Be young and have fun and don't become an obsessive old curmudgeon like me. Jensen, get her out of here!"

"Yes, sir!" Jensen said.

Harley still hung back. "You're neither obsessive nor old," she insisted. "Okay, wait. Maybe you are obsessive. Anyway, we'll be back by nine or so, and like I said, I'll bring you something delicious."

"Sounds lovely! See you soon."

And at last, Harley and Jensen left.

Dr. Henry Tomlinson turned his attention back to Unknown Mummy #1 for several long moments. Many pharaohs and royalty and even esteemed but lesser men, like Amenmose, ended up with unknowns in their tombs—servants needed in the next life.

Almost the entire lid of the coffin had been torn open. That afternoon, two of the students had painstakingly cleared out the rubble around the mummy. But Henry felt as if he was indeed looking at remnants featured in a B horror flick; the thing really did appear to be a man who'd been wrapped up with his mouth open in horror, left to silently scream into eternity.

Mummies weren't wrapped like this alive. Unless, of course...

He'd never been intended to be a mummy?

He'd been a murder victim.

Could this unidentified mummy be Amenmose himself? he wondered excitedly. They hadn't identified the man's tomb.

Great question, but it wasn't scientific to jump to conclusions. X-rays would give them an image of the insides—and that would probably tell them if the facial contortions had happened because of some accident in the drying process or if he *had* somehow been wrapped alive!

No, it couldn't be Amenmose, Henry decided. According to the ancient texts and all the information at his disposal, Amenmose had died before burial. Besides, they'd discovered one coffin in an inner tomb, deep in a hidden recess—again, just as the ancient texts had said. Amenmose's enemies might have defiled his tomb if those who loved him hadn't concealed his remains. The mummy here, found in the outer chamber, couldn't be Amen-mose—not unless there was a great deal they were miss-ing! "Sorry, old boy. Lord only knows what happened to you," Henry told the mummy.

"Hey!"

The inner flap to the preparation tent opened again. Henry looked over to see that it was Alchemy's director at large, Ned Richter.

He was smiling. As he should have been. Their day had been fantastic.

"Hey," Henry said. He liked Richter okay. Although not an Egyptologist himself, the man was studious and yet always ready help out with manual labor when needed.

Henry didn't like Richter's wife, Vivian, so much. She was an Egyptologist, too—at least in her own mind, he thought with a snort. Okay, so she did have her master's degree from Brown; she was just annoying as hell and she didn't think clearly or reason anything out. She was an attractive enough woman with short dark hair and dark eyes, and she claimed the maternal side of her fa-ther's family had been Egyptian.

She liked to pretend that she knew what she was talk-ing about.

She seldom did.

"Just checking on you!" Richter said.

Henry heard Vivian speaking behind her husband. "Tell him to come with us. We'll get some food and drinks."

"Hey, Viv!" Henry called out. "I'm good tonight. Going to work. And a couple of the students are pick-ing me up something to eat. Listen," he added in a more affable voice, "can't wait till you and I have a chance to talk tomorrow. We can compare notes then!"

"Can't you make him come?" Henry heard Vivian whisper.

"No," Richter said flatly. "He's head of the examination and prep all the way through the removal to Cairo—by Alchemy and the Egyptian government. As you know," he muttered.

"See you in the morning!" Henry called pleasantly. Yes!

But he'd barely turned around before he heard the inner tent flap opening again.

This time, it was Arlo Hampton, the Egyptologist who'd been employed specifically by Alchemy to watch over their investment.

Arlo was young—tall, straight and a little skinny. He preferred his thick glasses to contact lenses. Good thing for Arlo that nerds were in; he was, beyond a doubt, a nerd. But a friendly and outgoing nerd. He loved Egyptology, and yet, unlike certain other people, he wasn't full of himself or convinced that he knew everything.

"Hey, I knew you'd be alone with the treasures, snug as a bug in a rug!" Arlo told him cheerfully. There was something slightly guilty in his voice. "I wanted to make sure you were okay, though."

"I'm great. And, of course, if you want to join me…"

"I'm beat, Henry. I'm what? Thirty years younger than you? I don't know how you do it. I'm going to have a sandwich with the grad students when Harley and Jensen get back, and then hit my bunk until tomorrow. If that's okay. I mean, I should be like you, hard at work… Oh, I did just meet Belinda's fiancé on Skype. Seems like a decent guy. So Belinda, Roger and Joe are taking care of their personal business, and then we're all going to meet and after that—"

"I saw Harley and Jensen. They'll bring me food. You're fine, Arlo. Have a nice night."

"Yeah, thanks. Strange, though. Something doesn't feel right this evening. Am I just being paranoid?"

"Yes. And shoo. Go on, Arlo. You worked hard today. And I'm an obsessive old bastard. Get out of here!"

Arlo grinned. He lifted his hands. "I'm gone!"

And, at last, he was.

Henry was thrilled. He even began singing Ariel's song from the Disney movie *The Little Mermaid*.

He walked back over to Unknown Mummy #1. "Strange," he said, shaking his head with perplexity as he studied the mummy. "Just who was he? And what brought him here in this state?"

But then he shrugged. He'd found "natural" mummies at other sites—servants who'd stood guard after burial rites and died where they collapsed after the tombs were sealed and they slowly asphyxiated.

Henry walked back over to his desk to dictate notes into a recorder for the exhibit, which would one day be based on this project. "The earliest Egyptians buried their dead in small pits in the desert sand. The sand and the heat naturally 'mummified' the dead. Later, to prevent animals from digging up the bodies, they resorted to creating coffins. Coffins kept out animals, but they didn't allow for the natural mummification that had been occurring when the bodies had gone straight into the sand. So the Egyptians began to learn the art of embalming. They quickly discovered that the 'wet' parts of the body needed to be removed. That included the heart and lungs, brain and liver and other organs. These were stored in canopic jars, where they were guarded, just as the body was guarded, so the dead were protected and ready as they entered into the afterlife. The process became forty days of drying with natron, a form of salt. Of course, a body was never simply dried. It was adorned with oils at various stages and also treated with religious rites."

Henry stopped speaking; he thought he'd heard something moving in the preparation tent. That was odd. The local guards and the staff who worked for Alchemy were weary and bored with the findings. Egyptians had been unearthing mummies forever and ever, and even the security force of Americans and Brits was more bored by the ancient than intrigued. Most of them had worked around the world. They were, in a word, jaded—and far more interested in the pay scale than the work itself.

He looked around the tent. Nothing. Everything as it had been. Crates and boxes and mummies and treasures!

He shook his head, impatient with himself. He was incredibly lucky to have this time alone in the preparation tent. He'd been the one to do the research and the calculations; he'd been the one who'd garnered the sponsorship that had provided the money for this expedition. His papers had raised significant interest. It was—yes, indeed—his baby.

But eventually Dr. Arlo Hampton would want his time here, his chance to study these mummies, these treasures. So would Yolanda Akeem, their liaison with the Department of Antiquities. Then, of course, there was Ned Richter…and his wife. He'd bet that Richter couldn't care less if he got any time with the mummies and ancient treasures or not. Richter was there to guard Alchemy's interests and, Henry suspected, to ensure that they looked as if they were being incredibly magnanimous to the Egyptian government. After all, Alchemy financed these expeditions, he was almost certain, for tax breaks—and the media attention and promotion they provided.

Fine. The excavation was a great success. And this was *his* time. His time alone with all his treasures!

He started to go back to his work, but he could've sworn he'd seen movement from the corner of his eye.

He stood up and walked around.

Nothing.

Henry sat back down and continued his recording.

"Ancient Egypt—"

There *was* something behind him!

He tried to spin about.

And he saw nothing but binding, the linen binding that had been used on the ancient dead, saw it wrapped around fingers and a hand, saw the fingers and the hand circle his neck and—

Fingers, like wire, clutching his throat, so powerful, so strong...

He fought their hold. Wriggled and squirmed. He tried to rise; he couldn't. The pain was terrible. The world began to blacken before him; little dots of light exploded in the darkness. And all he could think was that—

The mummy!

The mummy had risen to kill him!

It was impossible. Impossible. Impossible...

He was a scientist. Rational. He didn't believe.

He was a scientist...

And as the last electrons exploded against the stygian pit of his dying mind, he couldn't help but think...

He was a scientist.

Being killed by an ancient Egyptian mummy.

It didn't make sense. It wasn't right.

CHAPTER ONE

One Year Later
The New Museum of Antiquity
New York City, New York

THE MOON THAT shone down through the skylights in the temple region of the museum created a stunning vision. Opalescent light shimmered on the marble and made it appear that the ribbon of "Nile" river by the temple was created of crystal and glass. The lights in the area were dim, designed to look as if they were burning torches set along the walls.

The exhibit in the New Museum of Antiquity was impressive—even to Harley, despite all the time she'd spent in the real Sahara. In designing this space, the organizers had also borrowed heavily from another famous NYC museum, all to the benefit of the Egyptian displays. Harley felt a sudden breeze from an air-conditioning vent, and she shivered.

"Mummy thing getting to you, huh?"

"Pardon?" Harley turned quickly to see the speaker. The words had been teasing; they'd also been spoken in a pleasantly deep, masculine voice.

The voice aroused a strange memory she couldn't quite reach—and seemed to whisper to something inside her, far beneath her skin.

She hadn't seen the speaker before, despite the fact that his voice seemed oddly familiar. Here, on opening night, she should've known most of the invited crowd. But she didn't know him, and—as her chosen field of criminology had taught her—she studied anyone she didn't recognize in a situation such as this evening's event.

A soiree to celebrate the exhibition. This was opening night for the traveling exhibit that would, in the end, return to Egypt, where the precious artifacts of that country would then remain. But tonight they celebrated the very first time the exhibit would be seen! It would open to the public in the morning. It had, quite properly, been named in honor of Henry—the Henry Tomlinson Collection of Egyptian Culture and Art.

There would be toasts in his honor, of course.

This phenomenal display would not have been possible without him.

But Henry was gone, as much a part of history as his treasures.

She sensed that this man—with his deep, somehow familiar voice—was connected to Henry.

She definitely hadn't seen him before.

He wasn't the kind of man you forgot.

He was tall—well over six feet, she thought. Because she'd recently taken identification classes that taught criminologists to look for details to include in descriptions, she also noted that not only was he about six foot three, but he had excellent posture. Nicely muscled, too. She had no doubt that he was the kind of man who spent time in a gym, not to create impressive abs, but to train the complex human machine that was his most important tool.

How could she be so sure of this? she asked herself. And yet she was.

He wore a casual suit, no jewelry. He was freshly shaven, and kept his dark hair cropped close to his head.

Someone's bodyguard?

Beneath the glimmer of the moon that showed through the skylights, she couldn't quite ascertain the color of his eyes. She had a feeling they were light, despite the darkness of his hair.

Thirty-three to thirty-six years old, she estimated. Carefully nondescript clothing—dark blue suit, dark blue shirt, pin-striped tie in shades of blue and black. Sunglasses resting on head.

He moved closer to her; she was certain he'd been doing the same kind of study on her that she'd nearly completed on him.

No, she'd never seen him before, but she *had* heard his voice.

"Sorry. I didn't mean to interrupt. You're not afraid of mummies, right?" he asked again, his expression quizzical.

"No, not at all," she assured him. "Ah, well, that's a bit of a lie. I might be afraid of some of the bacteria that can be found in old tombs, but as for the mummies themselves…no. My dad was a cop, a very good one. He taught me to fear the living, not the dead."

"Sounds like a bright man," he said. He stepped toward her, offering his hand. "Micah. Micah Fox."

She shook his hand. "Harley Frasier. How do you do? And pardon me, but who are you? Do I know you?"

He smiled. "Yes, and no. I'm an old student of Dr. Tomlinson's," he said. "I was at Brown when he was teaching there. About twelve years ago, I was lucky enough to join him on one of his expeditions. Back then, he was looking for the tomb of a princess from the Old Kingdom, Fifth Dynasty." He paused, still smiling, and shrugged. "He found her, too—right now she's in one of the display cases in a room not far from here, near the temple." He stopped, studying her again, and asked, "Are you surprised by that?"

"No, no, I'm not. You don't look like an Egyptologist," Harley said. "Sorry! It's not that Egyptologists look a certain way. I just—"

"It's okay. I'm not an Egyptologist," he told her. "I meant is it surprising that he found his princess? No, of course not. Henry was the best. But even though I began in archaeology, I changed my major. I'm with the government now."

"FBI?" Harley guessed.

He nodded.

"Something seems to be coming back. I'm not sure what," she said. "I know your voice, but I don't know *you*. I mean—"

"Yes, you know my voice. I guess I should start over. I called you soon after the incident when you were staying in Rome. Your group was shipped from place to place, and we were trying to get a handle on what happened. I'm the Fox from those phone calls. Special Agent Micah Fox—though I admit, I was working on my own, and not as assigned by the bureau. And I apologize, because I do know a lot about you, although it wasn't appropriate to bring that up at the time. You're Craig Frasier's first cousin, and Craig and I have actually worked together. Of course, we're in different offices now. Naturally, you've met a number of the men and women with the New York office. Craig told me you finished grad school, and you're deciding what to do with all your education—join up with NYPD's finest, remain with the private agency employing you now, or go into a federal agency. But tonight, you're here for the same reason I am, honoring our old professor. For one summer, you were an unofficial Egyptologist. And, as I just explained, you recognize my voice because we spoke on the phone. I'm Criminal Division, FBI. Right now, I'm assigned down in DC. I've taken some leave to be here."

"I...see," she said.

Did she?

No, not really.

Wait. Fox—yes, that was the name of the man she'd spoken with about Henry Tomlinson, just once, what now seemed like a lifetime ago.

These days, that time was mostly a blur. Maybe because she didn't *want* to think of it. But she couldn't stop her mind from rushing back to the night they'd returned to the camp, laughing and loaded down with food and drink for their professor, only to find him on the floor, along with the broken coffin and the "screaming" mummy. He'd been garroted by his own belt, eyes open and bulging, throat blackened and bruised, a swatch of ancient linen wrapped around it.

There'd been an immediate outcry. Security was convinced that no one from outside had been anywhere near the expedition tents; they kept a tight perimeter around the work area, which included the tents that had been set up for the staff. Egyptian police had come out, ready to help with the investigation.

Then, all hell had broken loose. The computer had picked up more chatter. And word had come that the fledgling, unaffiliated militant group calling themselves

The Ancient Guard was bearing down on the expedition. Perhaps they intended to steal the artifacts to finance their cause. Not an uncommon scenario… It meant that everyone and everything needed to go as quickly as possible. Government forces were being sent out, but no one wanted scientists from around the world caught up in an exchange of gunfire.

Security forces from Alchemy, along with the Egyptian police, did their best to preserve what they could from the expedition, as well as the body of Henry Tomlinson so they could discover the circumstances of his death.

Much was lost. But at least no one else was killed. The final inquiry, conducted by the Egyptian police and the Alchemy security force, concluded that the brilliant archaeologist Dr. Henry Tomlinson had driven himself mad and committed suicide. According to their conclusions, he believed a mummy had come to life with the intention of murdering him… It was suspected that some unknown bacteria had caused the temporary fit of insanity, and everything from the expedition would be scrutinized using proper precautions.

Harley had fought the verdict—vociferously. She was a criminology student; she knew what should have been done and a lot of it wasn't. Pretty much nothing had been done, really, not as far as a crime scene examination went.

Not in her opinion, anyway.

How many men committed suicide with their own belts in such a manner? She sure as hell hadn't seen or read about any. And she was *studying* criminology.

Nope, never heard of it!

Her friends backed her up, at first. And then, one by one, it seemed, they all decided that the poor professor—

so caught up in his love and enthusiasm for his work—had gone mad, even if only temporarily. No one could find a motive for murdering him. Henry Tomlinson had been respected and dearly loved by everyone. No one could find a clue.

The police assigned to them had been incompetent, to Harley's mind. Authorities in Egypt and in the United States hadn't done enough.

And the Alchemy people…

They wanted it to be a suicide. They didn't want to deal with a murder. They accepted the verdict without a whimper.

They were so sorry and sad, they'd claimed, and in hindsight, they could see so many mistakes.

They should've known to be more careful!

Henry should've known to be more careful!

But in fact, they said, the professor's enthusiasm for the project had caused them all to bypass modern safety regulations that might have kept him alive.

A great company line, Harley thought in disgust.

And what was the matter with her? They might all have been killed by a crazy insurgent group that hadn't defined exactly what it was fighting for or against. It was a miracle that they'd gotten out, that they were all alive.

Well, most of them. And Henry, poor Henry, he'd done himself in—according to the authorities and to Alchemy, who went on to say that now they'd never completely understand the biology of what had gone on. They weren't allowed back on the site; the Egyptian government had stamped a foot down hard.

And that night…

First, they were shuffled to Cairo, then, almost immediately—on the orders of the Egyptian authorities and the

US State Department—they were put on planes to Rome, and from Rome they were flown to New York City.

But, thinking back, Harley recalled that it was while she'd been staying at the little Italian hotel near the Spanish Steps that she'd spoken with this man. Fox. He'd wanted to know whatever she knew about the situation, and she'd told him everything, adding that she didn't believe a word of the official explanation.

There was no way Henry had killed himself.

Special Agent Fox had seemed to accept her version, but apparently he'd been just as stonewalled as she had.

Like her, he'd been forced to realize in the end that no one was going to believe him. Or her.

And even if the authorities had believed him, they didn't care enough to make a killer pay!

Here, tonight, for the first time in a year, everything about that horrible occasion was suddenly coming back.

Tonight was about honoring Henry Tomlinson. This would be an event during which people would shake their heads sadly, missing the professor who'd done so much, declaring it tragic that he'd lost his mind because of what he'd loved so deeply.

"Ms. Frasier?"

She blinked, staring at the man in front of her, wondering how long she'd been lost in her own thoughts.

In a way, she did know him. They'd just never met in person. She'd left the Sahara before he reached it. Then she'd been flown out of Cairo, and soon after that she was back in New York.

"I'm sorry!" she said softly.

He shook his head. "Hey, it's all right. I know you really cared, and that you tried to do something. It must have been hard to maintain your own belief that he'd been murdered when everyone else was telling you otherwise," Micah Fox said.

It had been and still was. "Oh, don't you know?" she muttered. "'Henry went crazy. Bacteria in the wrappings. He just *had* to dig in before proper precautions were taken. It's so tragic—don't make it worse by rehashing every little thing!'"

Her tone, she knew, was heavy with sarcasm.

They were alone in the temple area—or so she believed. Still, she looked around and repeated, "I'm sorry. I tried… I do believe he was murdered. They did find bacteria, but not enough. Henry was murdered. And I couldn't do a damned thing to prove it."

Micah nodded at her. She liked his face. Hard-jawed, somewhat sharp-boned. His eyes, she saw now, were actually blue—sky blue—and they seemed to see a great deal.

"Remember, I was a student of his, too. And now I'm an FBI agent. And I couldn't do anything, either. You have nothing to be sorry for." He paused. "I should explain. I knew about you through Craig, of course. And also through Henry. We kept in touch when we could—he'd let me know what was up, what was going on. I went into law enforcement, but I still love Egyptology. Henry thought the world of you." He shook his head. "I can only imagine what it was like that last night. I hope you're okay now. Time…heals, so they say."

"So they say."

"It heals when you're at peace with the past."

"And I'm not," she said grimly, and added, "And neither are you."

"No. Anyway, I'd like to find out about the last time you saw him. If you don't mind."

"There won't be a chance tonight," she said.

"I know. At a later date."

Harley nodded. "I'll be happy to speak with you. I'm not sure what I can tell you, though."

"You found him."

"Yes."

"I'd just like you to go over it with me. I realize it's painful, but…"

"The verdict was ridiculous! You know what the ME said! That he killed himself."

"An Egyptian ME, who wanted out of there as quickly as possible, with armed insurrectionists about to attack the place."

True!

But then…

"The company, Alchemy, brought in a medical examiner, too. He agreed with the Egyptian ME's findings."

"I'm sure that all happened in about two minutes in Cairo or Rome. And as soon as they made their decision, Henry was shot through with preservatives and packed into a box. So anything that could be construed as evidence was compromised. I could be way off base. *We* could be way off base. Thing is, I'd feel better if we could talk."

"Yes, of course," she said.

Of course?

She didn't want to remember that night!

And yet, here was someone—someone in law enforcement—who agreed with her, the only person who did. Like her, Fox believed there was a truth out there that everyone else had denied.

They looked at each other awkwardly for a moment.

"Well, a pleasure to meet you in person. I guess I'm

going to head over to the party area," Micah said. His voice softened. "I didn't mean to interrupt you. You might want more time here. On your own. By the way, as I said, I really do know your cousin fairly well. We worked together years ago on a case in DC. He's a great guy."

"Yes. Craig's great," Harley agreed.

She sensed that he wanted to say more.

Like maybe when or where they could meet again?

But he didn't speak. They weren't alone anymore.

Jensen Morrow came striding through the temple area. He apparently saw Harley, but not Micah Fox, probably because he stood in the shadow of a carved obelisk.

"I knew I'd find you here!" Jensen told Harley, heading toward her for a huge hug.

He'd written his thesis, gotten his graduate degree and taken a job here as an assistant curator, making use of his doctorate in Egyptology. He'd been her friend through her suspicions, her anger, her demands—and her final defeat, when she'd realized that nothing was going to be done.

No one was ever going to make her believe that Henry Tomlinson had been convinced that a mummy was attacking him—while strangling himself with his own belt.

Jensen, she was certain, had just given up. He'd been told the lie so many times that to him, it had become truth.

Harley accepted Jensen's hug; she still cared about him. When they'd first met, they'd hit it off as friends. They might have become more at one time; he was fun, energetic and thoughtful, not to mention tall, dark and handsome. But everything had changed the night Henry Tomlinson died.

Even though she didn't see the friends she'd made in Egypt very often—they were all busy working, getting on with their lives—they had all stayed friends. They were, in fact, oddly close; they had shared the experience of the dig, Henry Tomlinson's death and the escape from the desert under dire circumstances in the middle of the night. All of that meant they had an emotional bond few people shared.

And yet it was a closeness stained with the loss of the man they'd all adored. Stained, too, by the way they'd fled on the very night he died, swept up in a reign of terror.

She'd gone on to finish her own graduate work, head bent to her studies, and had taken part-time work with a prestigious investigation firm in the city so that she could still take classes when she chose while deciding what path to take for her future. It felt right, for the time being. But she had to make some real decisions soon. And yet, even as she'd worked toward her educational and career goals, she had felt that she was waiting. A temporary post—with flexible hours!—was all she'd been willing to accept at the moment.

"They're about to start," Jensen said, pulling away from her to study her face. That was when he rather awkwardly noticed there was someone else in the temple exhibit.

He offered Micah Fox a hand. "I'm sorry. How rude. I didn't see you. I'm Jensen Morrow."

"Micah Fox," the other man returned. "And actually, we've spoken. Over the phone."

"Oh! Hey, that was you?" Jensen said. "Wow. Was I vague when I talked to you? Or worse, rude? If I was, I didn't mean to be. It's just that…well, you had to be there that night. We found Henry—or, I should say, Harley found Henry—and by the time the medical examiner arrived, they were screaming that the insurgents were a few miles out and we had to break camp ASAP! I know Harley and I were going crazy with concern and disbelief and…well…hey," he finished lamely.

"There wasn't anything you could have done to change the situation," Micah said.

"Well, you're FBI, right? I guess if you couldn't prove anything different from what was said or get anything done, Harley and I, who had no law enforcement power, couldn't have done more than complain and question. Which we did. Who knows? The thing is—thing that got me, anyway—we weren't in a closed or confined space. I mean if bacteria were going to get him, you might've thought someone else would've had a reaction or… Anyway, had you been assigned to the case—officially? The FBI works in Egypt? Or does it?"

"The FBI works all over the world, as necessary," Micah replied. "But… I was there because of Henry."

"Special Agent Fox was another of Henry's grad students, but years ago," Harley quickly explained.

"Ah," Jensen murmured. That was obviously enough of an explanation. "I guess you were crazy about him, too."

"I was. Brilliant man. Horrible circumstances."

Jensen glanced at Harley. "I think we were the last people who saw him. Alive, I mean. Harley was trying to get him to come out with us. But you knew him. There was no way he was going to leave his work that night."

"No, Henry wouldn't want to leave his work." He paused, clearing his throat. "Well, I think they must be about ready to start."

"Let's go." Harley slid her fingers into Jensen's and they left, nodding to Micah. It was ludicrous, but she was suddenly afraid to be too close to the man. He not only projected strength—he was someone warm when the world had been cold. Too confident, too attractive…

She could easily give in to her feelings of sadness and loss and even anger on a night like this. With a man like this.

She was aware of Micah watching them leave.

And she wondered what he was thinking.

HARLEY FRASIER, CRAIG'S COUSIN, was certainly a beautiful young woman, Micah thought, watching her leave, hand in hand with Jensen Morrow. He'd been studying her intently for some time before he'd spoken with her. It was evident that she had really cared about Henry. And he knew how Henry had felt about her.

According to Craig, she had wonderful parents and a great older brother, living grandparents, all kinds of family life. Micah's parents had been lost in a bridge accident when he was a child; his aunt had raised him. Auntie Jane. He loved her and she was a talented and compassionate woman. But she was it as far as family went. He had no siblings, no cousins—no one else anywhere that he knew about. His family went far back in Virginia history; it had simply winnowed down to him and Jane.

His father had been FBI. People had feared the dangers of his job. They'd never imagined that he might die young because of a bridge collapse.

Henry Tomlinson had treated him like a son or grandson. He'd shared his enthusiasm for Egyptology with Micah. Henry had a family he adored. He hadn't married, but he had a loving niece and nephew-in-law, and he was crazy about their kids.

He'd send Micah pictures of an unusual canopic jar

right alongside ones of the kids with their new puppy.
That was Henry.

Micah followed the pair who'd just left, wondering if
he was indulging himself in an exercise of futility. Was
the truth about Henry Tomlinson's death ever going to
be uncovered? Henry had been murdered, which was terrible enough, but it had happened on a night when both
the Egyptian government and the US Department of State
had been determined to get all the workers away from
the site and out of the country. The group who'd planned
the attack had called themselves The Ancient Guard.

Apparently, they hadn't believed that Alchemy intended that the treasures they'd found would merely go
on loan to the United States and other countries—and
that they'd remain Egyptian property. Maybe they hadn't
cared. And maybe, like most militant groups, what The
Ancient Guard wanted, religious and political ideology
aside, was a chance to fight and stave off frustration.
And probably steal the treasures to finance their fighting.

They'd either been beaten back or dissipated quickly
when met with armed resistance.

Micah had gone to Cairo to investigate Henry's death
on an unofficial basis, and then to Rome, where the Alchemy crew had briefly stayed. Their communication
had been by phone—he'd been a day behind each time
everyone had moved on. And by the time he'd reached
the States, it had all been too long.

Henry had been cremated, just as he'd instructed his
niece to arrange in the event of his death. Then, of course,
it was too late to bring in any experts.

But Henry had never suspected that he might be murdered.

And why would he?

Why the hell kill an academic like Henry? The man had never wanted or kept anything for himself—he'd never tried to slip away with even the smallest, most insignificant artifact. His work had always been about sharing treasures with the world.

Tonight... Well, tonight, Micah could watch. He could see the people who'd been close to Henry in his last days.

The grand foyer of the museum had been chosen for the site of the private gala opening. The center monument here was a massive replica of a temple from Mesopotamia that sat in the center of a skylit rotunda. The museum was beautiful, and just down the street from its larger cousin, the Metropolitan. Many design ideas that worked well in the first had been used in this newer museum. The offices were deep in the basement, for the most part. The museum was dedicated to the ancient world; it was divided into sections that concentrated on the earliest humans to the rich, ancient civilizations of Greece, Egypt, Persia, Mesopotamia and more.

The exhibition hall that would open to the public in the morning was an admirable addition to the museum. Exhibits didn't stay forever, but the hall itself would continue to thrive because of the work of Henry and other archaeologists and scholars; right now, however, it was all about Henry.

Men and women in pairs and groups stood around the room, chatting, while waiters and waitresses in white-and-black attire moved about with trays of hors d'oeuvres and flutes of champagne.

Many of those invited were here because they were sponsoring patrons of the museum. There were also a number of politicians, including the mayor.

None of them interested Micah.

He scanned the crowd, taking note of those he did find intriguing.

Arlo Hampton, young, pleasant, eager. Tall and slim, but handsomely boyish-looking in a suit, speaking with an Egyptian dignitary. Ned Richter and his wife, Vivian. He so robust, she so tiny, both smiling, standing close, chatting with the mayor. And there—between an aging Broadway director and his latest ingenue—Belinda Gray, sans her fiancé, who was still serving in the military. He saw Roger Eastman, wiry and lean, wearing thick-lensed glasses, talking with his hands as he loudly discussed a technical innovation for dealing with the security of priceless historic objects. Across the room, in the midst of a few young female museum apprentices, was Joe Rosello. Joe seemed electrically energetic; he was a square-shouldered guy who could've been a fullback. He had a full head of curly dark hair and a very white smile.

Micah had done research on everyone involved with the last stages of the dig. Every one of the workers who'd had access to the tent. It hadn't been easy finding out about the Egyptian workers. Since they weren't archaeologists or preservation experts, they hadn't been allowed into the inner sanctum of the camp, where the preparation tent was located. Still, he'd done his best. But everything in him screamed that the guilty party was not Egyptian, but someone among those who should have loved and honored Henry.

Why? he asked himself again. Why the hell would anyone kill Henry? If he could come up with a *why...*

"Micah?"

He turned. He hadn't expected to know many people

here tonight. His name had been softly voiced by one of the few people he did know, and he knew her fairly well.

Simone Bixby, Henry Tomlinson's niece.

Simone was in her midthirties, a sandy-haired woman who looked eternally like a girl. She was small and slim and wide-eyed. She was accompanied by her husband, Jerry, a banker, who was equally slim and wide-eyed.

Micah greeted them both.

"Thank you for coming. And thank you for caring so much," Simone said. "It's still so hard to accept what they say."

"Yes, it is," Micah agreed.

"But tonight," Jerry said brightly, "tonight we honor his body of work."

"Yes. An incredible body of work," Micah said. "How are the girls?"

"Getting big!" Simone answered. "Ten, eight and five now."

He nodded. "I've seen pictures. They're beautiful."

"They are. Thank you. They loved their uncle Henry, too," Simone said.

"We all miss him."

"Oh, look—there's Arlo Hampton," Jerry said. "Micah, we'll talk later? Simone, we need to find out what he wants us to do when he speaks."

"Excuse us," Simone said.

"Of course!" Micah told them. They moved on.

He continued to survey the room.

Hail, hail, the gang's all here. Grad students. Administration staff. Egyptologists. City officials. Museum people. And there…

An exotic woman with dark skin and almost inky

black hair was speaking with Simone and her family. Arlo stood beside them.

Yolanda Akeem. They'd met briefly—very briefly—in Cairo. She was the Egyptian liaison with the Department of Antiquities. Naturally, she'd be here tonight.

She saw him looking at her. She elegantly lifted her glass a few inches in acknowledgment.

She'd given him whatever information she'd had in Cairo; it hadn't been much. A two-second autopsy report and a lecture on the dangers of the Middle East. He didn't listen to much of it. Henry's body was gone by then and the members of the expedition had been shuttled off. He'd been ready to follow them as quickly as possible when they'd been in Egypt—and through their escape from the trouble that had befallen the expedition that night.

Tonight, they were all here.

And there was Harley Frasier. She had a smile on her face as she spoke with Gordon Vincent, director at large for the museum. Her smile was forced. Jensen was with her, smiling and chatting, as well. He seemed to be putting a little too much effort into being charming.

Which didn't seem necessary, since he was already employed by the museum.

Harley didn't; she worked for Fillmore Investigations, a large security and investigation company that served the civilian market, but was known for its close affiliation with the New York City PD and other law enforcement agencies. The founder of the company, Edward Fillmore, had barely survived a kidnap-for-ransom scheme as a child. He had founded his company on the premise that all agencies, public or private, should work together for the benefit of victims. Since Micah's job with the FBI had come about because of similar circumstances, he liked the man without even knowing him. Micah was pleased that Harley Frasier had chosen such a reputable company. None of his business, of course. But…

He'd felt something for her, just from hearing her voice over the phone a year ago.

And now…he'd seen her.

Anyone awake and breathing would find her attractive and charming.

He was certainly charmed by her and impressed by her—and so much more.

Even though he hardly knew her…

He forced himself to look away from Harley and objectively observe the other people in the room.

He was standing back, watching, when he became aware that a friend had arrived.

"I have to admit I was definitely expecting you to be here," Craig Frasier told him.

Micah smiled without glancing over. "And I guess I'm not surprised that you're here," he said.

"I can't let you get into too much trouble," Craig murmured.

"I'm just here to honor an old friend," Micah said.

"Like hell." Craig smiled grimly, studying the crowd milling in the foyer. "But I don't know what you think you can discover at this late date."

Micah turned to face Craig at last, a rueful half smile on his face. "Right. Well, it would help if someone suddenly had a guilt attack and admitted going crazy—from the bacteria in the wrappings, of course—and murdering Henry."

"Not going to happen."

"I know."

"So?"

"Don't worry. I'm not going to harass your cousin," Micah said.

"I'm not worried. I think you two can actually do each other some good it you get a chance to really talk. Maybe you can figure something out, late as it might be. There was so much done so quickly and so politically. State Department, international bull. A cover-up. Yeah, it'll be good for the two of you to talk."

"You say that as if you doubt the official line, too," Micah said quietly.

"Because I do. I believe it was a cover-up."

"Not by the government," Micah said.

"By?"

Micah looked at him and said, "By Alchemy."

Craig didn't get a chance to respond.

Arlo Hampton took the microphone on a small portable dais set in the center of the foyer. He cleared his throat, then said, "Ladies and gentlemen, friends of the museum, friends of science and exploration, and friends of the City of New York!"

It took a moment for everyone to stop talking and start listening. Someone tapped a champagne flute with a fork or spoon. Then the room fell silent.

"We welcome you to our amazing new exhibit, brought to us through the genius of the man—the brilliant, kind, ever-giving man—whose name will now grace our museum walls, Dr. Henry Tomlinson. Those who knew Henry loved him. He was a scholar, but he was also a very human man who loved his family and friends. No one knew Egyptology the way Henry did…"

A sudden gasp from the crowd silenced him. Everyone turned.

Someone had come up from the basement steps, and was now staggering through the crowd.

Someone grotesquely dressed up in a mummy's linen bindings, staggering out as if acting in a very bad mummy movie.

A performance for the evening?

No.

Because Arlo grunted an angry "Excuse me!" and exited the dais, walking toward the "mummy" now careening toward him.

"What the hell?" Micah and Craig were close enough to hear Arlo's words. "Richter, is that you? You idiot! Is that you?"

It wasn't Richter; Micah knew that right away. Richter was far too big a man to be the slight, lean person now dressed up.

Or at least Ned Richter was!

Micah burst forward, phone out and in his hand. As he neared the mummy, he was already dialing 911.

"Get those bindings off her! Get them off her fast!" he commanded.

The mummy collapsed.

Micah barely managed to catch the wrapped body sagging to the floor.

As quickly as he could, he began to remove the wrappings.

He heard the sound of a siren.

Then Vivian Richter looked up at him, shuddered and closed her eyes.

The wrappings, Micah knew, had been doused in some kind of poison.

CHAPTER TWO

CHAOS REIGNED.

Harley was stunned and horrified that Vivian Richter was so badly hurt—so close to death.

She was wrapped tightly. The outer wrappings were decayed and falling apart; they'd come from a historic mummy. The inner wrappings were contemporary linen, the kind the museum used in its demonstrations, made to look like the real deal.

Vivian was gasping and crying, completely incoherent. One woman in the room was a doctor—a podiatrist, but hey, she'd been to medical school. She was kneeling by Vivian, calling the shots, talking on the phone to the med techs who were on their way.

Special Agent Fox had already taken control of the room. No one was to leave; they were all in a lockdown.

She was incredibly glad that Craig was there. And, of course, he was with his girlfriend or fiancée—Harley wasn't sure what Craig and Kieran called each other, but she *was* sure they were together for life. Kieran was standing near Harley, ready to comfort her, as the slightly older and very protective almost cousin-in-law. Harley appreciated that, even though she didn't really need it. She worked with criminals all the time, as well as people who weren't so bad but still wound up in the criminal justice system. She was calm and stoic; Micah and

Craig were questioning people, grouping them, speaking to them, both digging for answers and assuring them all that they were safe.

"She's going to die! She's going to die!" Simone Bixby, Henry Tomlinson's niece, cried out. Harley saw that Micah Fox hurried over to her, placed a comforting arm around her shoulders and led her to a chair.

By then, of course, museum security had arrived. So had the police—New York City and state police.

People were talking everywhere. Micah and Craig had herded everyone into groups, depending on their relationship to the museum. Some were employees of the museum; some were special guests. The people who'd been on the expedition were in a corner. Harley was with Belinda Gray, Joe Rosello, Roger Eastman and Jensen Morrow, as well as the Alchemy Egyptologist, Arlo Hampton.

Ned Richter was crouched on the floor, at his wife's side.

All of this seemed to go on for a long time, yet it was a matter of minutes before more sirens screamed in the night and the EMTs were rushing in. Ned Richter was allowed to go with his wife; Arlo Hampton and others more closely associated with the exhibit were now gathered together in a new group. Guests who'd only recently made it through the doors were questioned and cleared.

Anyone who had anything to do with prep for the evening was in another group; every single person would be questioned before being permitted to leave for the night.

Officers and crime scene techs were crowding through the museum, heading to the Amenmose section—and to the staff office and prep chambers beyond.

"Too bad we couldn't continue the celebration," Joe

said, hands locked behind his back, a look of disappointment on his face. "What a waste of great food and wine."

"Joe! What's the matter with you?" Belinda chastised.

"Come on! Vivian Richter's a drama queen," Joe said.

"She might die," Roger said very softly.

"You mark my words. She will not die," Joe insisted.

"They're saying it's poison," Roger pointed out. "Some kind of poison on the wrappings."

"She's going to be very, very sick," Jensen said. "Those wrappings decaying and falling all around her... Who the hell knows where they came from—or what might be on them?"

"Or if something was *put* on them," Roger said. "That's how she would have been poisoned."

They were all silent for a minute.

"And then dead—like Henry Tomlinson," Belinda said.

Again, they were silent.

"Great. But at least now, maybe someone besides me will start fighting to figure out what happened to Henry," Harley said quietly.

She'd actually discovered that night that someone *was* on her side. The agent with the great voice. Craig's friend. Micah Fox.

"Okay, okay," Belinda said. "I didn't push it a lot at the time. I mean, it didn't make any difference, did it? The cause of death—two medical examiners said—was the fact that bacteria made him crazy and he killed himself."

The reaction to her comment was yet another bout of silence.

"What were we going to do?" Belinda wailed. "We had no power. Insurgents were bearing down on the camp, and everyone wanted us out! So, what *could* we do? Henry was dead," Belinda said.

"And back then, none of us believed he killed himself," Jensen said at last.

"But we all let it go." Roger sounded sorrowful as he spoke. "Except Harley, and we all kind of shut her down," he added apologetically. "But, seriously, what were we going to do? There were some whacked-out insurrectionists coming our way. I'm sorry, but I've got to admit I didn't want to die. I really didn't care if anyone was collecting evidence properly—all I wanted was out of there! And in the end, I guess we bought into the official—" he made air quotes with his fingers "—version. It was just easier and—"

"Ms. Frasier!"

Harley was being summoned. She saw that it was the plainclothes detective who had apparently been assigned to the case. He was lean and hard-looking; his partner was broader and had almost a baby face and a great smile. They were McGrady and Rydell, Rydell being the guy with the smile.

She wasn't going anywhere alone. She was never sure how Craig could home in on her problems so quickly, and tonight he was with Micah Fox, the agent who had called her before—and approached her at the beginning of the evening. What if she *had* talked to him when he'd wanted to?

Could tonight's disaster have been avoided?

Did it have anything to do with what had happened before?

She was led into one of the museum offices that had been taken over by the police. She felt, rather than saw, her cousin Craig and the enigmatic Micah Fox come in.

They didn't sit; they took up stances behind her.

McGrady took the seat behind the desk and asked her sternly, "Ms. Frasier, what exactly is your association with the museum, the expedition—and the injured woman?"

"I was on the expedition. I don't really have an association with Vivian. It's not like we have coffee or hang around together and do girls' night," Harley said. "Vivian is married to Ned Richter, the CEO of Alchemy. Alchemy financed the expedition. Alchemy is the largest sponsor for this exhibition. We were all pretty close in the Sahara—not that we had much choice."

"So you did know her well!"

"I didn't say I knew her well. We were…colleagues."

"But you like mummies, right? All things ancient Egyptian?" McGrady asked.

"Yes, of course. I find the culture fascinating."

"And it would be a great prank to attack someone and lace her up in poisoned linen. Like a mummy?"

"What?" Harley exploded.

McGrady leaned forward, wagging a pencil at her. "You were the one who discovered Henry Tomlinson—dead. Correct?"

Harley had never thought of herself as particularly strong, but his words, coming out like an accusation, were too much.

She heard a guttural exclamation from behind her. Craig or Micah Fox, she wasn't sure which.

But it didn't matter. She could—and would—fend for herself. She leaned forward, too.

"Yes. I found Henry. A beloved friend and mentor. I found him, and I raised an outcry you wouldn't believe. And no one in a position of power or authority gave a damn. First, it was oh, the insurgents were coming! Saving our lives was more important—and yes, of course, that was true—than learning the truth about the death of a good man. I could buy that! It's an obvious decision. But then, no decent autopsy, and his niece, bereft, had him cremated. And now you're asking me about Henry—and about Vivian Richter. You have nerve. I was here tonight in honor of Henry. I didn't see the exhibit before tonight. I haven't been associated with Alchemy since we returned. I suggest you speak with the people who *were* involved there and worked on the exhibit."

McGrady actually sat back.

Everyone in the room was silent.

Then Harley thought she heard a softly spoken "Bravo."

McGrady cleared his throat. "Sorry, Ms. Frasier, but you do realize that Vivian Richter is dangerously close to… Well, we might have a murder on our hands."

"You *do* have a murder on your hands. Dr. Henry Tomlinson was murdered. Now we have to pray that Vivian comes out of this, but still, you've got a killer here. Do you have anything more to ask me?" Harley demanded. They did need to hope and pray for Vivian, but by now, surely they had to recognize the truth of what had happened to Henry!

"Did you see Vivian this evening?"

"No."

"But you arrived early, didn't you?"

"Only by a few minutes. I walked out to the temple area."

"Which is off-limits until after the exhibit officially opens tomorrow."

"I was allowed to go back there because I'd been on the expedition."

"And you were close to the backstage area where exhibits are prepared?"

"Yes."

"Where Vivian would have been?"

"Possibly."

"But you didn't see her. Who did you see?"

"Just Jensen. Jensen Morrow. He's working here, with the exhibit. This is actually his field of work. I saw Jensen—oh, and Special Agent Fox." She glanced back at him. He and Craig were flanked behind her like a pair of ancient Egyptian god-sentinels. They almost made her smile. Not quite. She couldn't believe that this detective was quizzing her—when she couldn't get any help before, no matter how she'd begged and pleaded!

"Special Agent Fox?" McGrady said.

"I arrived within minutes of Ms. Frasier. I was told she'd just headed for the temple. I wanted to speak to her about the death of Henry Tomlinson. I went straight there. We were speaking when her colleague Jensen Morrow appeared. Exactly as she indicated," Micah Fox said.

McGrady stood up. "Fine. Ms. Frasier, you're free to go."

Harley stood up and glared at him. "I'm delighted to leave. But perhaps first you'd be kind enough to let me know how Vivian's doing. We might not be close, but we were serious associates."

McGrady sighed. "She's holding her own. The doctors are combating the effects of the poisoning."

"What was the poison?"

"It's an ongoing investigation. That's information we can't give out right now, even if we had it."

"I see. Thank you."

Craig opened the door; she marched out. He and Micah

followed. She thought she heard McGrady mutter, "And take your Feds with you."

"Not the usual helpful attitude, at least not in my association with the NYPD," Craig said. "Usually, we have an excellent working rapport."

"Maybe he's resentful because he's not sure what this is yet. It's impossible at this time to say what happened," Micah said.

Harley spun around to stare at him. "What are you, a fool?" she snapped. "We both know—not suspect, but *know*—that Henry Tomlinson was murdered. Then Vivian Richter comes out wrapped in mummy linens, screaming and poisoned with some kind of skin toxin, and we don't know what happened? Obviously, someone tried to kill her!"

Craig grabbed her by the shoulders. "Harley! Stop. Micah's on your side. What are you?" he asked. "A fool?"

She flushed uneasily. They were just outside the door. The nicer cop, the quiet one with the baby face, Rydell, came out and approached Jensen Morrow. He was next on the block, Harley thought. And how stupid of the cops. Jensen had been with her, away from the camp, when Henry Tomlinson was killed. They just didn't seem bright enough to realize that there was a far bigger picture here. They needed to see it—before someone else died.

But Craig was right. She shouldn't be taking it out on Micah Fox.

Why was she being so hostile, so defensive?

Pushing him away on purpose.

He was trying to help her. He was…

He was a promise she was afraid to accept. He claimed he wanted the truth, and he seemed to have all the assets needed to get at that truth. He was too damned good to be true, and she didn't dare depend on someone like that when the very concept of an ally, someone to depend on, was still so…

Foreign to her! He was law enforcement—and on her side. It was good. After all this time, it felt rather amazing.

"Sorry," she murmured.

She'd barely spoken when Kieran Finnegan came hurrying up next to her. "I have a car outside. Come on, I'll get you home."

"But—"

"There's nothing else you can do here tonight, Harley," Micah said.

"Remember, you came to me."

"Yes. And there's nothing else you can do here tonight," he repeated.

Harley stiffened.

"Let's go," Kieran said gently.

So she nodded. "Thank you," she said to Craig and Micah, and then she allowed Kieran to lead her out the door, to the front of the museum.

A light-colored sedan was waiting, just as Kieran had promised. Kieran wasn't driving; Harley assumed the driver was FBI and that Micah or Craig had made the arrangements.

Once in the car beside Kieran, Harley regretted the fact that she'd already left. "I should still be there. I should be back with the exhibits. I should see the prep rooms. I was with them on that expedition and I know what we discovered. I saw the tomb when it was opened. And I… Lord, yes, I'm the one who found Henry."

"Logically, there isn't a damned thing you could've done tonight. They won't let anyone back by the exhibits, the prep rooms, the offices—anywhere!—until the crime scene people have gone through it all. Naturally, everyone's hoping that Vivian Richter pulls through. If she does, maybe she'll be able to remember something that will help. For now, well..."

"McGrady is NYPD. He isn't letting Craig and that Agent Fox in on anything."

"They'll get in on it. Trust me. Craig will talk to his director. His director will call the chief of police or the mayor or someone, but they'll get in on it," Kieran said with assurance.

Harley leaned back for a moment, suddenly very tired. She closed her eyes and then opened them again, looking over at Kieran. She liked her cousin's girlfriend. Really liked her. She wasn't sure why they weren't engaged or married yet, but...

Kieran, of course, knew all about what had gone on during and after the expedition out to the Sahara in the search for Amenmose's tomb. Considering what she did for a living—a psychologist who worked with law enforcement—nothing much surprised her or rattled her. Besides, she'd met Craig during a period when the city was under siege with a spate of diamond heists.

"So tell me—what's your take on this?" Harley asked Kieran. "Who would kill Henry Tomlinson? Or rather, who'd dress up as a mummy to kill him, and then dress Vivian Richter like a mummy to try and kill her?"

"The incidents might not be related," Kieran said.

"Oh, please! Don't tell me Henry wasn't murdered! Don't tell me I want that to be the case because I don't want to believe he went crazy and committed suicide."

"I'm not saying that at all. Here's the thing. You were in the desert, so it had to be someone there. Henry's dead and maybe this would-be killer is playing on that. Or maybe the two are related. The problem is, I don't know anyone involved. It's hard enough to make judgment calls when you've had a chance to speak with people and question them."

"Yeah, yeah, I'm sorry."

"That said…"

"Yes?"

Kieran smiled and shrugged. "You've had as much education as me, if not more."

"Ah, but in different courses! I need more in psychology."

"Specifically in human emotions. Like jealousy."

"Jealousy? As in…someone who wanted to be a famed Egyptologist?"

"Possibly. Some people kill because they're deranged. They're psychotic, or they're sociopaths. Then, of course, you have the usual motives. Love, greed, hatred…jealousy. Think about everyone involved if you're convinced that the two situations are related. The rest of us weren't there. Only you know the dynamics among all the people who were on that expedition."

"I can't imagine anyone who would've wanted Henry dead. I just can't."

"It's not that you can't. It's that you don't want to," Kieran told her.

They'd reached Rector Street and the old warehouse apartment that legally belonged to Harley's uncle, who was mostly out of state now and had generously given the large, rent-controlled space to Harley while she finished her degree and decided on her permanent vocation.

The driver hopped out of the car, opening the door

for Harley. Kieran leaned out to say goodbye and thank the man.

"Get on home, get into bed, go to sleep," Kieran said. "Much better to start fresh in the morning."

Harley gave her a quick hug and a peck on the cheek. "Thanks. Thanks for getting me here. But... I'll be back on it in the morning."

Kieran grinned. "We'd expect no less." She leaned back in the car and the driver shut the door. He offered Harley a grave nod, and waited until she was safely at the door to her building.

Harley keyed open the lock and waved to the night clerk on duty at the refurbished twenty-floor building. Then she took the ancient elevator to the tenth floor. It wheezed and moaned, and she wondered if Mr. Otis himself had seen it installed in the building. However, it worked smoothly, and she was soon on her floor and in the spacious area she knew she was incredibly lucky to have in New York City. The building had once housed textile machinery and storage. She had over a thousand square feet with massive wall-length windows that looked out on the city with a special view of Grace Church. Harley knew she was blessed to have this space, and reminded herself to send Uncle Theo another thank-you. A counter separated the kitchen from the dining area and living room, while wrought iron winding stairs led up to the open loft space that was her bedroom. Her mom had told her that the apartment had once been Uncle Theo's bachelor pad, but at the ripe old age of sixty-five, he'd met Helen, the love of his life, and they were happily enjoying the pleasures of Naples, Florida, year-round. Helen, a spring chicken of fifty-five, was delighted that Harley was watching over the place, just so they'd have a place to crash when they came up to see friends.

Harley found herself staring out at her view of Grace Church.

Home, bed, sleep.

Impossible.

Henry Tomlinson, an Egyptologist by trade, had loved Grace Church. The church itself dated back over two hundred years, although the current building went back to the 1840s, with new sections added along with the decades. Gothic and beautiful, it was the kind of living history that Henry loved.

She wondered if Vivian Richter was still hanging on. She thought about calling the hospital, but they probably wouldn't give her any information.

Home, bed, sleep.

She could try.

Climbing up the stairs to her bedroom, she quickly changed into a cotton nightshirt and crawled beneath the covers. She realized she hadn't closed the drapes.

She stared out at the facade of Grace Church.

Yes, Henry would have loved a view like this.

What was Henry's niece, Simone, thinking tonight?

And Micah Fox? How had he arranged time off? How had he managed to be there? Would he figure something out?

She prayed for sleep, but her mind kept returning to that time in the Sahara. Being part of the expedition had been such a privilege. She remembered the way they'd all felt when they'd broken through to the tomb. Satima Mahmoud—the pretty Egyptian interpreter who had so enchanted Joe Rosello—had been the first to scream when the workers found the entry.

Of course, Henry Tomlinson was called then. He'd been there to break the seal. They'd all laughed and joked about the curses that came with such finds, about the stupid movies that had been made.

Yes, people had died during other expeditions—as if they *had* been cursed. The Tut story was one example—and yet, by all accounts, there had been scientific explanations for everything that'd happened.

Almost everything, anyway.

And their find…

There hadn't been any curses. Not written curses, at any rate.

But Henry had died. And Henry had broken the seal…

No mummy curse had gotten to them; someone had killed Henry. And that someone had gotten away with it because neither the American Department of State nor the Egyptian government had wanted the expedition caught in the crosshairs of an insurgency. Reasonably enough!

But now…

For some reason, the uneasy dreams that came with her restless sleep weren't filled with mummies, tombs, sarcophagi or canopic jars. No funerary objects whatsoever, no golden scepters, no jewelry, no treasures.

Instead, she saw the sand. The endless sand of the Sahara. And the sand was teeming, rising up from the ground, swirling in the air.

Someone was coming…

She braced, because there were rumors swirling, along with the sand. Their group could fall under attack—there was unrest in the area. Good Lord, they were in the Middle East!

But she found herself walking through the sand, toward whomever or whatever was coming.

She saw someone.

The killer?

She kept walking toward him. There was more upheaval behind the man, sand billowing dark and heavy like a twister of deadly granules.

Then she saw him.

And it was Micah Fox.

She woke with a start.

And she wondered if he was going to be her salvation...

Or a greater danger to her heart, a danger she hadn't yet seen.

CHAPTER THREE

MICAH DID HIS best to remain calm and completely in control. That was definitely a hard-won skill from the academy.

It was the crack of dawn, the morning after the event, and he'd been called in to see Director Richard Egan. Alone.

Egan was Craig's immediate boss. The man was Hard-ass, Craig had told him, but in a good way. He had the ability to choose the right agent for the right case in the criminal division.

He'd also fight tooth and nail when he thought the agency should be involved. He'd take a giant step back, too, when he thought he'd be interfering with the local authorities.

They were often part of a task force, but it didn't seem there was going to be one in this situation. Hell, there might not even be any official FBI involvement. At the moment, they were looking at what might have been a murder thousands of miles away, and what might have been an attempted murder at a museum opening. It might also have been some kind of bizarre ritual or prank.

Several morning newspapers—among the few still available in print—were on Egan's desk. The front pages all held stories with headlines similar to the first one he'd read: Mummies Walk in New York City!

Egan glanced at the papers and shook his head, dismayed, Micah thought, more by people's readiness to believe such nonsense than he was by the disturbing headlines.

"You see? Everyone will be going crazy. Thank God that woman didn't die—thank God she didn't die, no matter what—but with this mummy craze…there'll be pressure. The press will not give it up. So. Let me get this straight," Egan said. "You have lots of leave time?"

"Yes, sir. I'm on leave now."

"But you started off taking some of that leave and traveling to Egypt."

"Yes, sir." He hesitated. "That was a year ago. I took several weeks then, and I'm taking several more now. I'm never sick. I've accrued other time as well and work with a great group. So, last year…"

Egan was waiting.

"I came back. I'd heard that Henry Tomlinson, an old friend, had died under unusual circumstances. I tried to reach the site, but when I got there, it had been cleared out. I tried to track down his body, but I was behind by several steps. But you know all this." He hesitated. "I'm a bit of a workaholic, sir. Like I said. I put in a lot of time, and wind up owed a fair amount of time off."

"And you use your leave working, I see."

"I flew all over last year, being given the runaround. Our people in Cairo helped, but they were stonewalled, too. And a lot of the time, certain Egyptian officials acted as if I was an idiot and an annoyance. According to them, they were trying to keep people alive and I was making waves about a dead man. It was too late for them to do anything, of course. I pursued it as far as I could, but Henry's niece had been told that her beloved uncle had died in a horrible accident and, abiding by his wishes, had him cremated. Can't autopsy a pile of ashes."

"Our people in the Middle East would've done exactly what you did," Egan assured him.

"Yes, sir."

"But?"

"But I knew Henry Tomlinson," he said. "He was a friend. He was also a good man. His death deserved a decent investigation, which—due to the circumstances, I know—he did not get."

Egan was quiet for a minute.

Then he said, "And you just happened to be at the museum last night when a woman, wrapped in would-be old linen tainted with nicotine poison, came crashing into the ceremony."

"So that was it, nicotine poisoning. Hmm. But I didn't just *happen* to be at the event, sir. I was there purposely. As I said, I knew Henry Tomlinson. I loved the guy. I was there to honor him."

"But Craig Frasier has an involvement because his cousin Harley was on the expedition."

Micah shrugged, but kept his eyes steady on Egan's.

"You're a good agent, Micah," Egan said after a moment. "I've seen your service record. I know your supervisor."

Micah lifted his hands. "Sir—"

"Yeah, whatever, forget about it," Egan said flatly.

"Begging your pardon, sir, but—"

"I heard the cop on the case is a dick." He grinned. "In more ways than one."

Startled, Micah raised his brows.

Egan laughed. "The guy's partner, Rydell, actually called me. He wanted to apologize for McGrady's behavior. I guess the guy was hoping it would turn into a murder case and that it would be his—and he wanted the FBI out of it."

"I see."

"Don't worry. The FBI is in. Taking lead."

"Really?" He'd decided to stay calm, so made a point of not betraying his surprise and delight.

Egan leaned back, studying him. "The case began in the Middle East. It entails far more than the City of New York."

Micah felt his pulse soar, but he still maintained his composure.

"That's excellent, sir. And…"

"Yes, I've spoken with your office. You and Craig can take lead on the case. Mike—you know, Craig's partner, Mike?—he needs some vacation time, and if you're here and we're taking this on, I'm going to go ahead and give it to him. So it'll be the two of you. Work with the cops, though, and any other agencies that may become entangled in this. We'll have State Department and embassies involved, too, I imagine. Anyway, our victim from last night regained consciousness thirty minutes ago. I've asked that they let you and Craig do the talking. You are no longer on leave. I suggest you get moving."

"Yes, sir, absolutely. Thank you."

"Just get the son of a bitch," Egan said.

Micah nodded and started out.

"Hey!" Egan called, stopping him.

"Sir?" Micah walked back.

"I didn't hear much about that whole mess in Egypt. What ever happened with the insurrection?"

"Over before it began, from what I understand," Micah

told him. "By the time I landed in Cairo, the expedition people were on planes headed out. And the military had routed the coup—it was more of a student protest than anything else. Sadly, it's a fact that there's a lot of unrest in the Middle East, for various reasons. Anyway, it was over, but the expedition was gone. I went out to the site, but…by then, there was nothing to find. Everything had been cleaned out."

"And the insurgents?"

"A few arrests. Most of them dispersed when the military came on the scene."

"In retrospect it might look like overkill, but better safe than sorry," Egan said.

"Of course, always," Micah agreed.

But as he left Egan's office, he found himself wondering, for the first time, whether the insurgent event had been planned to ensure that Henry Tomlinson's death wasn't investigated.

Maybe he was pushing it, getting paranoid.

Maybe he was taking a conspiracy theory too far.

And yet…

Had there been some kind of conspiracy?

"WHAT DO YOU THINK?" Jensen asked Harley.

She was back at the museum, in the Amenmose exhibit; she hadn't been able to resist. Jensen had called her, saying that with Vivian in the hospital, he could use some extra help, so she'd come.

"They've delayed the opening by a day," he'd told her over the phone early that morning. "But with Vivian out of the picture—temporarily, of course!—and especially since you were there and have a memory like a camera, you can help me with loose ends, tying things up, paperwork."

She'd assured him that she'd be there.

Jensen had told her he'd never left the museum the night before. He didn't look tired, but he was one of those people who could work for days, then sleep twenty-four hours, party a night away, and work a full load again. Jensen could be absolutely tireless.

"I think the exhibit is so special. Just like Henry," she said quietly.

They were standing in the temple area, right where she'd stood the night before when Micah Fox had come upon her. But she wasn't staring at the exhibit, which was surrounded by the glass-and-concrete walk and the "river"; rather, she was looking back at the hall that led to the temple.

One broad corridor led here, with six smaller chambers off the main hall. The temple faced east, in the direction of the sunrise, since it was dedicated to the sun god, Ra. It wasn't filled with statues. Instead, it was open to the glass that revealed the sun.

"The earliest known temple to Ra," Harley said, smiling.

Jensen nodded. "Info on Ra, on Tutankhamen, Ay and Amenmose are on the side there. Near Amenmose's mummy." That was on display in a small room, which it had all to itself. "The hallways feature a lot of the fabulous funerary art we found," Jensen continued.

"Which is surprising, don't you think?" Harley asked.

"How do you mean? That we have anything left—after running out with our tails between our legs?"

"Running out with our tails between our legs was the only thing to do," Harley replied. "No, of course, the historical assumption is that Amenmose was murdered. By someone under Ay, who knew that Amenmose wanted to usurp his power with the boy king, Tutankhamen. Our discovery proved that he *was* murdered, once we were back in the States and the body was properly identified through the DNA testing."

"He'd been strangled!" Jensen said.

"Like Henry," Harley murmured.

"Well, we don't really know about Henry."

"I do."

Jensen shrugged. "In this case," he said, "when it comes to Amenmose, X-rays that show fractured hyoid bones don't lie."

"But we have no clue who did it."

"I'm willing to bet Ay did it himself."

"Oh, today, in one of our courts, Ay would be guilty. He'd be guilty of *conspiracy* to commit murder. It was his idea, I'm sure. But that's just it. Somehow, Amenmose still ended up being properly mummified and placed in an inner coffin and several sarcophagi and laid to rest in his tomb. So who killed him? And who got the body and managed to bury it with such honor?"

"Hey, I'm the Egyptologist here!" Jensen reminded her.

"Yes, and I'm the criminologist. We've got to know who did it and why," Harley said lightly.

"I think we can rest assured that the murderer has long since gone to his own reward," Jensen said, grinning.

"Amenmose's murderer."

"Ah! But not whoever murdered Henry, right? Is that what you mean?"

She nodded.

"Your cousin's FBI and that other guy, Micah, he is,

too. They'll get to the truth. And now, because of what happened to Vivian, they'll keep going," he said with confidence. "And guess what? We sold out. We didn't open today as planned, obviously, but we will tomorrow…and it's a total sellout. Not that sales weren't good before, but now that we have mummies walking around, we're a real hit."

"I've seen the news and read a few of the papers. Yeah, what a great story. But there was no mummy walking around. That was Vivian. And speaking of her, how's she doing? Have you heard anything?" Harley asked.

"Doing well, I understand. Awake and aware and lording it over the hospital staff. She's going to be fine."

"Thank God. But what's she said?"

"Nothing. She remembers nothing. Who knows what'll happen eventually? They'll have shrinks in there and everything. At the moment, though…nothing."

"But she'll be okay. That's the most important thing."

"Of course," Jensen agreed. Then he said, "So, what are you doing tonight?"

"What am I doing?" Harley repeated. She felt a strange tension. She'd almost dated Jensen when they were on the expedition. Almost. There was nothing to dislike. He was good-looking, he was smart, he was alpha-fun and…

She did like him.

But she suddenly dreaded the fact that he might be asking her out. There wouldn't have been anything wrong with dating Jensen. They'd teased and they'd flirted and come close. But now she wanted to retreat; she wasn't sure why. It must be everything that had happened, that *was* happening…

She didn't want to turn him down. She wanted to be

friends. Maybe she even wanted the relationship option left open.

"I'm, um... I'm not sure," she said. "I came here this morning because you said you needed me, and I want to help."

"This is social."

"Oh. Well, um—"

He laughed softly. "Don't worry. I'm not putting you on the spot. Not tonight. We wanted the whole group to get together. Those of us who were the last people with Henry," he added.

"Oh. Okay. Well, you know that my cousin's girlfriend owns a place and—"

"Yes! That's right. What a great idea! Finnegan's on Broadway. We were planning on meeting somewhere midtown, but once you're on the subway, who cares? We talked, Belinda and Joe and Roger and I. And we thought we owed it to ourselves and to Henry to have our own private little event. Can you get us a corner at Finnegan's? A reserved corner?"

"Anyone can make reservations. But—"

"But you'll be someone they care about when you make the reservation."

"It's a pub. That means hospitality. They care about everyone."

"But more about you."

She gave up. "No problem. I'll make the reservation."

"Cool. So you'll join us all?" Jensen asked her.

"Sure. It'll be great."

Would it be great? she wondered. What was going on with Vivian now? The woman hadn't died; she was doing well. If that had changed, surely they'd all know.

And the majority of the museum was open, although there was a little time left for the cops to come back and look over the new stuff for the Henry Tomlinson section. Still…

"Love ya!" Jensen said, grabbing her by the shoulders and planting a quick kiss on her lips. "I'm so glad you're in for tonight! I was afraid that you wouldn't be."

"Nope, I'm in," Harley assured him. "Anyway, I thought there was work you needed me to do?"

"Yeah, look around the exhibit. Some of the work here is yours, like the prep stuff you were writing up before we even found the tomb. For someone who was going into criminology, you were quite the Egyptologist."

"Hey, lots of people do more than one thing in life. I love Egyptology. It was my minor, just not my major."

"That's my point here. Thing is, check it all out. Make sure there are no imbecilic mistakes."

"Okay. But I'm not the most qualified person to be doing this."

"Oh, come on! You *should've* been an Egyptologist. You were so good at all the stuff we delved into. You knew who thought what, all about the argument over the gods, everything. And you cared about what we were doing. You just wanted to do more with fingerprints and DNA and the detecting part of it. But this exhibition is your baby, too. Check it out for me. You're going to love it!"

He waved and started walking in the direction of the temple, then apparently decided he should go the other way. The temple was a dead end, except, of course, for museum employees. There was a back hall that led to the stairway and a number of museum offices.

"Where are you going?" she asked.

"To clean up—after the cops!" he told her.

"Clean up what?"

He didn't hear her or pretended not to. But he wasn't heading to his office. She had no idea what he was up to.

She glanced at her watch.

That was all he wanted? For her to verify exhibits? He'd said he'd needed help because Vivian wasn't there. And yet he didn't really need much.

Did it matter? She'd never get a chance like this again.

She wasn't even part of it all anymore; she was Jensen's guest and she was a guest because once, she *had* been a part of it all. She didn't embrace Egyptology with the same wonder that drove some of the others, but she did love ancient Egyptian history.

Nope, she probably wouldn't have another opportunity to wander the exhibit entirely alone.

For a moment, she stood still, and then she smiled. She hurried to the right, slipping into one of the rooms where the social and political climate of Amenmose's life and times were explained. She'd done a great deal of the research work and prepared a number of the papers from which the story in the exhibit had been taken.

Entering the first room, she looked around. Display cases held many items of day-to-day life; sure, there were fantastic necklaces and beautiful jewelry, but Harley had always been most fascinated by the storage jars, the pans and other cooking implements that told more about a basic everyday lifestyle.

The center in this exhibit was an exceptionally fine statue of the god Ra, depicted with the head of a falcon, the sun disc above him.

She read softly aloud. "'Ra—ancient Egyptian sun god. By the fifth dynasty, in the 25th to 24th centuries BC, he had risen to prominence, and would be joined by others at various times. Tutankhamen's great changes after his father's reign and his own ascension to the throne involved bringing back the old religion. Under Akhenaten's rule, the old gods had been disrespected; many statues and other honorary sites were destroyed. His dedication to his religion—he wanted to see the deity Aten, the disc of Ra, the sun god, worshipped above all else—caused a weakness in the Egyptian military and a lack of action that was seen as a betrayal by a number of the kingdom's allies. Tutankhamen meant to undo the harm, as he saw it, his father had done. He wanted to bring back all the old gods, including Amun and Mut and others who made up the hierarchy of ancient Egyptian power. Amun-Ra, as Ra was often called, and the others would return. Tutankhamen felt his father's legacy was one of destruction, and under *his* rule, the world would improve. To that end, he looked to the priest Amenmose, despite the fact that the priest Ay was in power as the boy king's regent.'"

She let her words settle in the empty room. "Pretty good," she said with satisfaction.

There was an inner sarcophagus of a handmaiden, buried with Amenmose, in the last of the horseshoe-shaped displays. The woman, at least judging by the artist who had painted her face for the sarcophagus, had been beautiful.

"What do you think?" she asked the image of the long-dead woman. "The New Kingdom, Middle Kingdom, Old Kingdom—it can all be so confusing. Not to mention the dynasties! Anyway, I think the display works, and I had a lot to do with that. It's simple enough to be understood, without leaving out any important facts. Of course, in my view, young King Tut was probably murdered, too. But we'll never find out now, since Howard Carter found that tomb so long ago!"

She read the little note beneath the sarcophagus. The young woman's name had been Ser. She'd served Amenmose in his household. She hadn't been killed for the purpose of being placed in his tomb. She'd succumbed to a fever before his death, and had been moved here to lie with the man she had served so loyally.

Next to her was a servant, Namhi. Like Amenmose, Namhi had been strangled. There was no explanation anywhere on his wrappings or in the tomb. From all that she had read, Harley suspected that either Namhi had been used as an instrument of murder, or he had belonged to the cult of Aten-Aten, a secret society pretending to agree with Tutankhamen's return to the old religion while trying to undermine it at the same time. It had been suspected during Amenmose's lifetime that Namhi was a leader of the cult. That alone would make Ay want to murder him, as well as Amenmose. But Amenmose might also have been murdered by Tutankhamen's half sister or brother-in-law.

Ay had actually been the grand vizier. And, upon Tutankhamen's death, he would become pharaoh.

"You all had motive," Harley murmured.

Yes, just as it seemed everyone did today in the murder of Henry Tomlinson and the attempted murder of Vivian Richter. No one had a solid motive—or, rather, they all had the same motives! Fame, position in life, in society. But...was that enough to make someone kill?

Harley turned to look at the case where mummified animals were displayed. She was staring at a mummified cat when she heard the bone-chilling sound of a cat screeching as if all four paws and its tail had been caught in a car door.

She froze; she felt goose bumps forming all over her body.

There were no cats in the museum. Not living cats, anyway!

A complete silence followed the sound. And then Harley became certain that she heard movement in one of the side rooms off the Amenmose exhibit main hall.

She remained still, listening.

She'd spent her life priding herself on her logic. Obviously, a mummified cat had not let out a yowl. It was more than possible that someone else was in the exhibit. And possible that a cat had somehow found its way in. There might well be police in the prep areas and in the offices behind the public areas of the museum.

Despite her logical reasoning, there was no way to explain the sensations she was feeling. They were different from anything she'd ever known.

She quickly slipped from the side room where she'd been, the first one next to the temple. She thought she saw movement at the end of the hall.

A person, wearing something dark.

That hall was a dead end for visitors. There was a magnificent podium that held the giant-size lion sculptures that had guarded the inner door to the Amenmose tomb. You walked around it and saw the second side of the exhibit before exiting to the rest of the museum.

She told herself she had no reason to be afraid that someone was there. People worked here, for heaven's sake! The cops and crime scene techs were probably still trying to figure out how Vivian Richter had been assaulted with nicotine poison.

But…

There'd been something furtive about the dark figure.

Well, at least it hadn't been a mummy walking around. The person had definitely not been in decaying and frayed linen wrappings.

Whoever it was wore black. Head-to-toe black. Slinking around.

Crazy!

The room she was in displayed different stages of mummification. There was a life-size display in which a mannequin was being dried with natron on a prep table, while priests said their prayers and sprinkled him with some kind of herb water or oil. In the next window, the wrapping process itself was displayed.

The next room was filled with sarcophagi and mummies, wrapped, half-wrapped and unwrapped. And among them…

She paused again, gazing at Unknown Mummy #1. She suddenly, vividly, remembered the night Henry had died. She could see the interior of the prep tent, could see Henry, his face reflecting his enthusiasm.

Somebody brushed by something out in the hallway.

Anyone might have been there! Working, investigating, exploring.

No. The person was moving…

Furtively.

She hurried to the door and looked outside. She could run back to the statues and escape into the back to the offices and prep rooms behind the scenes.

She could demand that whoever it was show him- or herself.

And wind up with a belt or other object around her neck, or poisoned linen wrapped around her body?

She realized that her heart was thundering. In a thousand years, she could never have imagined being so frightened in the middle of the day in a museum. She wasn't sure she'd been this frightened even when they were forced to flee the Sahara.

Harley flattened herself against the wall, waiting.

She was startled to hear the scream of a cat again.

That was no damned mummy! There was a living cat in the museum—fact!

But she wasn't staying to search for it.

She burst out into the hallway, racing toward the exit.

"Harley!"

She heard her name; it was a heated whisper. She sensed somehow that it wasn't a threat, but by then she was propelling herself forward at a frantic pace.

"Harley!"

That whisper of her name again.

She wasn't going to make the exit.

She turned and saw Micah Fox standing there.

One minute she was running, her feet barely touching the floor.

The next…

She'd fallen flat on her back, blinking up at the man straddling her.

"Harley! Damn!"

Fox. Micah Fox. Special Agent Micah Fox.

She stared at him blankly. For a moment, she wondered if *he'd* been stalking her through the Amenmose exhibit.

"There was someone in here!" she said. "Watching me."

"Yes," he said flatly. "And thanks to you, that someone has gotten away."

Micah rose to his feet and helped Harley to hers. "What?" she demanded. "How?"

"I had him—or her. I don't even know which it was. Then you made enough noise to raise a legion of the dead—"

"Oh, no, no, no! *You* were the one making the noise!" Harley told him.

"Harley, if you'd just stayed where you were…"

"And let someone get me? What a bright comment from a law enforcement officer!"

"Harley," he began, then broke off and halfway smiled, lowered his head and shook it slightly. "Sorry. I guess I think of you as Craig's cousin, and as a student of criminology, and I suppose…"

"You suppose what?"

"That you'll behave as if you were trained in criminal behavior and…well, working a case."

She stood there, still staring at him, pursing her lips. Then she offered him an icy smile. "Okay, let's put it this way. Take doctors. Some are great practitioners and others are diagnosticians. My training helps us to figure out what happened—not to bulldoze our way into a situation with guns blazing!"

He listened to her speak; his reaction was undeniable amusement.

"Okay, whatever. Let's go to the offices here and see who we can see, yes?" he asked her.

She turned and headed for the doors marked Cast Members Only—as if they were at a theme park rather than a museum—and pushed her way in. She feared for a moment that the doors would be locked. They were not.

A long hall stretched before her. To the left were offices; to the right were the labs and prep rooms.

She could see that one door was marked with the name Gordon Vincent. She hadn't really met him, she realized, and he wasn't just in charge of the Amenmose exhibit, but the entire museum. His appearance was perfect for the part; he was solid, about six feet even, gray-haired and entirely dignified. The office beside his bore a temporary name; that was obvious from the way the name placard had been slipped over another, the name being Arlo Hampton. Next to his office, the jerry-rigged nameplate read Vivian Richter.

Jensen Morrow had his own office, since he was now an employee of the museum.

No one was in the hall. Looking through the large plate glass windows to the lab, they could see that Arlo wasn't in his office; he was in the lab. He was working with one of the unnamed mummies they'd found in the tomb, running the X-ray machine over the remains. Harley waited until he'd completed his task. Then she tapped on a window. Arlo raised his head, startled. He saw Harley and offered her a large smile—then noticed Micah and didn't seem quite so pleased. He disappeared for a moment as he walked through the changing area and then opened the hallway door to let them in.

He beamed; in fact, he seemed to come alive as he met Harley's gaze.

He did not seem concerned that a woman, a colleague, was in the hospital. That someone had attempted to murder her in a particularly grotesque manner.

"Harley, nice to see you. Jensen said he asked you to

come in. I believe he was going to ask you to work with
him on a few last additions we're thinking of adding. I'll
tell you the truth, I wish you'd been one of ours. I want
a room on what we've discovered from the mummies—
and what we know about their deaths. Oh, the whole
Tut thing is still speculation, and that's not ours to tear
apart. This is!"

"Thanks," Harley said, wondering why Jensen hadn't
mentioned that. "I'm happy to help with…whatever's
needed."

"Great. And you, Agent Fox." Arlo turned to him.
"Are you part of the police investigation? They were here
all night. They found nothing. Of course, they still have
Vivian's office closed off and we won't open this section
until tomorrow, but…wow."

"Yeah, wow," Micah said, his tone flat. "So, what do
you think happened to Vivian Richter?"

"Her husband's with her now," Arlo said. "I mean,
needless to say, we care most about the living. It's just
that…well, the world can't stop because something bad
happened to someone."

"Yeah, but that bad thing happened right here," Micah
reminded him.

"Of course," Arlo said. "But…it had to be a prank,
right? She didn't die. I'm thinking some college student
who suffered some kind of slight at our hands was in here
and played a prank on her."

"Nicotine poisoning is no prank."

Arlo looked truly perplexed. "Someone definitely
came in through the back, to get to her. Otherwise,
whoever it was would've been on the cameras. The only
people picked up on the security video cameras in this
section were the two of you and Jensen Morrow. But, of

course, there are entrances from the basement on up—a few secret entrances. Did you know the building itself was originally erected by Astor as a bank? That's why there's the gorgeous foyer and all. But speaking of secret entrances, the cops are looking at everything. Oh, yeah, you're a cop. Okay, sort of a cop. Do you want a tour?"

"I would love a tour," Micah told him. "But first, who else is working today?"

"Well, define 'working.' I think everyone's been in. The only one not really part of the new exhibit is Harley. Belinda, Joe and Roger have been giving it about ten hours a week. Jensen is here full-time, which I'm sure you know. Joe and Belinda both have full-time jobs with two of the other major museums in the city, and Roger is teaching now. They were all in at one time or another this morning, checking out their space. The cops tore through everything, looking for the source of the wrapping and the poison. But honestly, I don't think we even have any natural linen back here. And any idiot knows that's not how you make an ancient Egyptian mummy. But—"

"So who else was here this morning, Arlo?"

"Let's see. Ned Richter was in. Left the hospital, popped over here and went back. But he was here."

"And the others?" Harley asked.

"Yes, like I said, at one time or another. I've been busy, as you can see. We still have a wealth of remains and artifacts. There was the mess with that so-called insurgent group, but then the company and the government sent guys with big trucks and equipment, and they emptied the tomb—including all the mummies—before thieves could. Oh, yeah, some people see the Western world as one giant thief, but everything we have is cleared through the Egyptian government and will be returned, and that was common knowledge from the get-go."

Arlo seemed to consider it more important to honor international agreements than to worry about anything else.

Admirable.

But Henry had died. And Vivian might have died, too.

"I'd love that tour now," Micah said, smiling. Harley saw the way his face moved when he smiled. Obviously, despite his work, he smiled a lot. He had the kind of smile that made her wonder what it would be like if they were just talking together at a restaurant, in a class…

"I can't give you a tour of the entire place. We're going to concentrate on this exhibit. You'll notice that our offices are in this section with the directors, with Gordon Vincent. He's a very smart, well educated and supportive guy. He purposely keeps his office over here. That way, whatever is new, he's in on it."

"So he might have been in his office before Vivian came out screaming?" Micah asked.

"I suppose so," Arlo replied. "But are you suggesting Gordon was involved? Really? I don't think so."

Harley didn't, either. He hadn't been on the expedition. She could tell that Micah didn't think Vincent was guilty of anything, either; he was just covering his bases.

"Show me around, please. That would be great," Micah said.

"Okay, let's go!"

Arlo ripped off his paper lab coat and set out. "As you can see, that's a lab—a 'clean room' lab, if you will. You have to coat up, glove up and mask up before going in. You never know what might've been in the ground for millennia! And over there, the museum offices. Now, we're on the ground floor, or so you'd think. Directly beneath us is the cafeteria and there's another rotunda-like area for international exhibits. That one's a bit different. International, of course, but Egyptology has always had a place in the higher echelon of what people find fascinating in a museum. And, sadly, museums are bottom-line—everyone needs donations and funding and numbers—and mummies are a draw. Always have been. Even though they were so plentiful in Victorian times that people used them for kindling! Yes, those good religious uptight folk used human remains as kindling."

He kept talking, pointing out different research rooms and more offices. Then he came to a staircase. It was an old stone circular staircase, high and steep. "This led down to the vaults at one time. It wouldn't have been easy to steal from this place when it was a bank!"

They followed him down to the basement and then the subbasement.

"Does this bypass the actual basement?"

"Yes, these stairs do. And…" Arlo turned, shining a flashlight at them, although they were still receiving ample light from above. "It'll get dark in here!" he warned.

Harley took a penlight from her purse at the same time as Micah drew one from his pocket. She was rather proud of herself for never leaving home without one!

"You can still kind of see. There was emergency lighting put down here before the place went belly-up during the Great Depression," Arlo told them. "As you can tell, the design of the hallways is almost like a perfect cross, and each of them opens out to five vaults. The elite of the elite had their treasure down there. The museum will use the space eventually, but at this stage, it's not really needed yet. Anyway, the quality of the exhibits means more than the quantity."

Arlo was quite happy to keep talking. They saw what he meant about the cross design, and each section held vaults of slightly different sizes.

"And there's a way out?" Harley asked.

Arlo didn't get a chance to answer. There was a narrow area that simply looked like an empty space at the end of the vault area facing Central Park. Micah headed that way.

Harley followed Micah, and Arlo followed her.

"What's going on?" Arlo asked when Micah came to a stop.

Micah had found something. Harley could hear metal grating and squealing; she realized he'd come to a door. That he'd gotten it open.

She came up behind him and looked over his shoulder.

All she saw was black.

"Abandoned subway tunnel. They're all over the city," he murmured.

"I guess that's one way out. Or you can just walk out the door that leads back up to the park and picnic area at the side of the museum," Arlo said, pointing to the right. "But an abandoned subway. I think I'd heard rumors, but never really knew if they were true of not. Cool!"

"Yeah. Cool," Micah said wryly. "So, does everyone know about that way out—to the park area?" he asked Arlo.

"Oh, I wouldn't think so," Arlo replied. "Just people who work here. And maybe people they've told."

"We might want to get a lock on the door to that exit," Micah said. "And to the subway tunnels. The info could easily have been tweeted across the country. Maybe it has." He paused, studying Harley. "We'll get a few of our people down here," he told her. "I need to go over to the hospital. I've been told that Vivian is conscious and speaking. But I'll need to find you later. Do you know where you'll be?"

Harley hesitated. Then she shrugged. "Finnegan's," she told him. "Finnegan's on Broadway."

"Kieran's family's place?" he asked her.

"It's the only Finnegan's on Broadway."

"You'll definitely be there?"

"Oh, yes. I'll be meeting my colleagues from the expedition."

"Including me!" Arlo said happily. He sighed. "Well, we won't have Vivian there, and I doubt we'll have Ned Richter with Viv in the hospital."

"Henry. We won't have Henry," Harley said.

"No, we won't have Henry," Arlo agreed. He tried an awkward smile. "But at least we won't have any mummies running around at Finnegan's. A banshee or two, maybe, but no mummies!"

Neither of them managed even a small smile for his attempt at humor.

As they left, Harley remembered the cat she'd heard earlier. There'd been no further sound after Micah had appeared—claiming she'd frightened off the person who'd apparently been stalking her. The person he, in turn, had followed. And lost.

CHAPTER FOUR

"I was in my office," Vivian Richter said. "I was in my office…"

Her voice trailed off. Her face was set in a concentrated frown.

"In my office and then…"

"And then?" Micah pushed gently.

Vivian was in her hospital bed, in a seated position. Craig Frasier and Micah stood at the foot of the bed, patiently waiting.

Micah knew that the local cops had already been in. But it had only been a short time since the lead on the investigation had been handed over to the federal government. Vivian had let them know that she'd spoken with McGrady and Rydell. The nurse in the hallway had informed them that McGrady had brought Vivian to tears, demanding that she remember what she just couldn't.

Micah had received a call from Rydell, since it was still a joint task force, if a small one. Rydell had apologized for his partner.

For the most part, I work with great people. No one is better than the NYPD, Rydell had assured him.

Micah had told him not to worry; any agency in the world could come with a jerk or two—and McGrady was that jerk. He hadn't said that in so many words when he'd spoken to Rydell, but they both knew exactly who he was talking about.

"I'll bet you were excited about the exhibit," Micah told Vivian. "All the work that had been done. And then the discovery—and the terror in the desert, with Henry Tomlinson dead and the fear of armed rebels coming at the camp. But now, here, you have the culmination of your dream of getting the Amenmose exhibit up!"

"Oh, I was excited. So excited. And we were going to have all our grad students and Henry's niece and her family at the opening. And…oh! Those children. Henry's great-nieces. And there were probably other children there. And they saw me coming out like—?"

"A mummy. Vivian, think. Did anyone come in to see you in your office when you were getting ready for the grand celebration?"

Her frown deepened.

"Everyone had been there. Everyone. Ned, of course. We were excited together. He's administration and I'm an Egyptologist, but we're a married couple, and that made it an incredible night for both of us. Arlo, darting in and out with last-minute things. The grad students… they were all there. Belinda wanted me to look at her dress and Joe—that boy is such a flirt!—asked if he looked both dignified and handsome. Let's see, Jensen. He's full-time here now, you know. He was in more than once. And then…"

She went silent, dead silent, her mouth falling open in an awkward O of horror.

"What?" Craig asked.

"One of the mummies came in. It was walking. Yes, yes, that was it! There was a mummy. Oh, my God! A mummy… I remember now. It…stared at me!"

She began to shake. Micah and Craig glanced at each other, deciding it might be time to hit the nurse-call button.

But first they both moved close to her, each man taking one of her hands.

"It's going to be all right," Micah said in a soothing voice.

She shook her head. "Mummies don't walk. Except in really bad movies. Okay, even good movies... *The Mummy* with Brendan Fraser was good." She paused. The shaking had stopped, and she looked at Craig. "You any relation?"

"I'm afraid not. My last name's actually Frasier," Craig told her.

Vivian suddenly stared hard at Micah. "That was it, yes. I saw the mummy. I stood up—I'd been at my desk. I stood up, and I couldn't believe what I was seeing. It had to be a joke, a prank...but then the thing came at me and I tried to scream, or I think I did, and it kept coming...and..."

"And?" Micah asked.

"That's it. That's all I remember. A mummy came to life," she whispered.

"Vivian, you of all people know that a mummy didn't come to life. Whoever was pretending to be a mummy wrapped you in linens that had been soaked with nicotine. That person wasn't a real mummy," Micah said.

"But...it seemed so real. Or surreal. But terrifying!" Vivian said.

"Vivian, someone who was in the museum at the time dressed up as a mummy to attack you. Do you have any idea why? Were you having an argument with anyone?

Is there any reason— Well, I'll be blunt," Craig said. "Is there any reason anyone would want you dead?"

Vivian gasped. "Oh, God!"

Micah glanced at Craig. She must have just realized that someone had tried to kill her.

"No, no, no!" Vivian said. "I know I'm not the nicest human being in the world. I'm not a Pollyanna of any kind, but… I don't hurt people. I've never fired anyone, not that I have that kind of power. I'm not mean to people, I don't scream at them to work harder. I'm a decent person, damn it! No, there's no reason anyone would want to kill me!" she declared.

"Did you have a fight with anyone—anyone at all?" Micah asked.

She sighed. "Every once in a while, I get into it with Arlo. But that's just because…well, when Henry was alive, we all acknowledged him as the real guru. He had the experience. He was chosen by Alchemy to head up the exhibition, and he was chosen because all his research on Amenmose was so good and so thorough. With Henry gone, I think maybe Arlo and I have a bit of a rivalry going. But a healthy rivalry!"

"Arlo was working today."

"Of course he was. There's still much to be done. You have to understand that the tomb was *filled* with mummies, including that of Amenmose. And, as with Tut, some of the funerary objects appear to have been reused. We have every reason to believe that Amenmose was murdered—and it must've happened quite suddenly. He was entombed with all the rites by someone who really loved him, but it was all hush-hush and under the radar. Ay did become the ruler after Tut died. Anyway, there's still so much to determine about our find! I'm sure everyone's working." She was quiet for a minute. "Including my husband. Bless Ned. He was so torn! But I've assured him that I'm on the way to being just fine and that the museum—at this moment—is the most important thing in our lives right now. And I'm getting great care here, so it's fine that he's gone."

Micah wasn't sure she was telling the truth. He wasn't convinced she didn't feel hurt that her husband wasn't with her.

But he didn't want to rub salt into any wounds.

He glanced at Craig. They would move on. Craig was probably doubting her words, too, but they wouldn't get different answers to what they'd asked—not at the moment. Time to ask other questions.

"What about the grad students? Any arguments with any of them?"

"Well, they're not grad students anymore, are they?" Vivian asked a little sharply. "I told you, I saw Belinda and Joe and…" She paused, sighing deeply. "I was a bit worried about seeing your cousin, Agent Frasier. She was so committed to Henry. We all loved him, but it was as if he saw her as a grandchild and she saw him as a wonderfully brilliant grandpa. She never got over his death. Then, of course, there's Jensen, and he's taken a permanent position with the museum. He helped her fight for Henry up to the end, and then… Henry was cremated. We had two different medical examiners give verdicts that suggested suicide, possibly brought on by a delirium caused by bacteria. Anyway, we'll probably never know just what was going on in Henry's mind. And…" She broke off again, looking from Micah to Craig. "Someone wanted me dead, too. But how did I get out in the foyer? How did I get help? Oh, it's all so terrifying!"

She began sobbing quietly.

Micah squeezed her hand. "Hey, you're going to be fine. So if there's anything, anything at all, please call one of us. We intend to find the truth. We *will* find the truth."

She nodded and squeezed his hand back. "Thank you," she said.

"Of course," he told her.

He thought she smiled.

THERE WAS A lively crowd at Finnegan's on Broadway that night, but then again, it was Saturday.

New Yorkers had a tendency to be "neighborhood" people. On the Upper East Side, you found an Upper East Side hangout. There were lots of bars and pubs around Cooper Union, St. Mark's Place, the Villages, East and West, and any other neighborhood you could think of in the giant metropolis.

But Finnegan's drew people from everywhere. For one thing, it was one of the longest-running pubs in the city, dating back to pre–Civil War days. For another, it was run with a family feel, and somehow, people knew the right time to bring their kids and the right time not to. The kitchen was as important as the bar. It was simply a unique place, and Harley was delighted with Craig's association with the Finnegan family—and through him, her own connection to them.

She'd been able to reserve a corner near the entrance, against the wall and across from the actual bar tables.

Jensen got there first, greeting her with a hug and a kiss on each cheek. She wasn't sure just how far he would have gone; a waitress—a lovely girl who'd just arrived from Ireland, came by to take their order. That was when Joe Rosello walked in.

He had to flirt. But he couldn't seem to decide whether to flirt with Harley or the waitress.

He opted for both, which got him a punch on the shoulder from Jensen. "Hell, you can't take him anywhere."

"You are atrocious," Harley told him, shaking her head.

"Hey! I just admire people and make them happy. I don't do anything evil!" Joe protested.

"We'll let it slide this time," Jensen said. "Lay off Harley, eh? She's seen you with the ladies. She knows your MO."

"Harley, do you really mind me telling you that you're gorgeous and mysterious and desirable in black?" Joe asked, sounding wounded.

"No, just don't slobber on my hand, please."

"Slobber? That was an elegant kiss!"

"Aha! A very wet and elegant kiss!" Jensen said. By now, Roger had come in; he listened to the ongoing conversation, rolling his eyes. "And every one of us has a doctorate!" he murmured. "Pathetic. What is this world coming to?"

"I think the world was a mess long before we came along!" Belinda said, joining them.

It was then that Harley noticed Micah Fox; she hadn't seen him come in. He was standing at the bar with her cousin Craig. The oldest Finnegan, Declan, who ran the family establishment, was talking to the two men.

She had a feeling they were all watching her and her friends.

A minute later, Micah walked over and joined the group.

Harley wasn't the first to greet him; Belinda was. Harley was busy greeting Arlo, who had just arrived, and Ned Richter, who had apparently chosen to join them rather than stay with his wife at the hospital.

They were seated around two of the big mahogany tables in the corner, Ned Richter, Arlo, Joe, Roger and Belinda crowded in against the wall, and Micah, Harley and Jensen perched on the chairs across from them. There was ordering of drinks and meals, with casual conversation at first. And then Ned Richter raised his glass and said, "In memory of Henry Tomlinson, the greatest Egyptologist I ever knew and one of the finest men to have ever walked this earth, as well."

"Hear, hear!" the others chimed in.

They all raised a glass to Henry, and then Ned continued with, "And to the bastard who hurt my Vivian—may these agents and cops find him, and may he rot in hell!"

"Hear, hear!" another cry went up.

"That's harsh," Jensen teased. "At least you're among friends."

"That's what an Irish pub is all about," Richter reminded them all, drawing a round of laughter. He went on, saying, "Sorry, I can't help it. I hope the bastard dies a hideous death."

Harley wondered why he wasn't with his wife, since he was so devastated by what had been done to her.

But she was wedged between Jensen and Micah, and she was very aware of both men being so close to her. She found herself wondering, too, just what connected people. She was seated between two very fine men. Both exceptionally good-looking and bright—and both engaged with the world…in completely different ways.

She liked them both.

And yet, sitting there, she knew why she wasn't with Jensen, why they hadn't gone out. Each man's interest was unmistakable.

But only one man's seemed to matter.

She was attracted to Micah Fox. She barely knew him, and yet when she'd seen him again, just the sound of his voice had aroused her senses.

"Seriously, who would've done such a thing? Harley, what do you remember?"

Harley realized that her mind had completely—and inappropriately—wandered. Belinda was staring at her, brown eyes wide, and waiting for an answer.

Harley took a sip of her drink—a Kaliber nonalcoholic beer by Guinness, since she'd decided she couldn't risk losing an ounce of control tonight. She hoped someone would say something that explained Belinda's question.

She felt Micah's eyes on her. Maybe he knew she'd been distracted. Hopefully, he didn't know that her mental absence at the table had been due to him.

"About that night…that night in the Sahara," he said.

"We were all so excited," she began, and around her, Jensen, Joe, Roger and Belinda all nodded.

"And we were rewarded!" Ned Richter said.

"A find beyond measure!" Arlo agreed.

"We'd started to bring some things from the tomb into the prep tent," Harley said. "It's a special tent, temperature-controlled. Everyone's careful there. Amenmose's tomb turned out to have more than a dozen mummies and sarcophagi—all in different states of disrepair and decay. We've proven that Amenmose was murdered, so after it happened, someone who loved him borrowed—or stole—funerary objects from the dead who'd passed on before him. They also brought together people, dead and alive, who'd served him."

"Why would they do that? Why go out and find people who'd already died to bury with him?" Micah asked her. "I studied Egyptology," he said sheepishly, "but, I don't understand—taking people who have already died and their things. It's like robbing the dead. It *is* robbing the dead."

"He would need servants in his next life. Servants, women… He would need people and animals, just as he'd need his bow and shield," Harley explained.

"I know about objects needed for the next life. I guess I never heard of them being taken from somewhere else… dead, or still alive."

Micah seemed to move even closer to her. She could feel his eyes; she could almost feel his touch. His elbow was on the table and his fingers dangled near her lap.

She forced herself to concentrate. "We worked really hard that day—for hours and hours. I'm pretty sure it was close to eight o'clock. There was a little village not far from the dig and the people there were incredibly nice. We'd go sometimes to have dinner and maybe sit with coffee at a place there, something like a family-run restaurant or cantina. But we decided in the end that Jensen and I would go by ourselves and bring back food. Jensen came to get me while I was trying to talk Henry into coming with us. We were all tired, of course." She glanced over at Belinda who was still watching her with wide brown eyes. "Belinda was Skyping with Al. he was in Iraq at the time, I think."

"Iraq, yes, just about to leave," Belinda said.

"And Roger was working on tech and communications because we were hearing rumors about an upstart hate group, so he didn't go." She turned to Joe and couldn't help grinning. "Joe was still moving some of the artifacts. We had a lovely young Egyptian as our interpreter. Satima Mahmoud. They were…working."

"Working, right!" Belinda mocked, then laughed affectionately. "Joe was flirting."

"What? I don't flirt!" Joe protested.

"You're a flirt!"

Harley was sure they all said the words at the same time.

Joe flushed and shrugged. "She's really pretty. And smart."

"That she is," Harley agreed.

"So, Jensen," Micah said, looking past Harley, "you and Harley went out together that night. How long were you gone?"

Jensen thought it over, raising a brow at Harley. "Hour and a half maybe?"

"Somewhere in there. An hour to an hour and a half," Harley said.

Micah nodded, then swiveled around to look at Ned Richter and Arlo Hampton. "Neither of you checked on Henry during that time?"

"There was no need to check on Henry!" Ned Richter said. "We had security on the outskirts of the camp. Henry was completely in his element, like a kid in a candy store. I wouldn't have interrupted him."

"And you?" Micah asked Arlo. "Shouldn't you have been in there with him?"

"No, because I—"

Arlo turned beet red and stopped speaking.

"You what?"

"I was working," Arlo said.

"On what?" Ned Richter demanded.

Arlo looked guiltily around. "Well, I had one of the funerary tablets in my tent."

"You took a tablet from the find into your tent?" Ned repeated, his tone grating.

"Well, you see, I was interpreting, trying to figure out just what had happened at this site and how. It wasn't usual, having that many dead in a tomb. I was transcribing the tablet."

"What did it say?" Harley asked. She'd never heard about the tablet.

Arlo flushed miserably again. "I don't know."

"No artifacts in private tents," Ned told him, irritated. "I'm not going to fire your ass or anything over it, but damn it, that's the last time, Arlo. We follow the rules at Alchemy."

"What did the tablet say?" Harley persisted.

"I don't know," Arlo said again, his expression peevish.

"You didn't translate?" Harley asked.

"I didn't have time. I got through a zillion lines of how wonderful Amenmose had been and then...you started screaming."

"I'd just found a friend—dead!"

"Well, yes, you screamed, and then everyone had to come and look at Henry. Then we heard we were about to be attacked, and *then* we were all helping when it came to loading up what we could, trying to get to the airport in Cairo."

"Yes, but where—"

"Harley, I haven't the faintest idea where the damned tablet ended up!" Arlo said. "I thought we were getting together tonight to be supportive, and you're all accusing me of terrible things!"

"We didn't *accuse* you," Ned pointed out drily. "You admitted you took an artifact."

Arlo sighed. "Where were *you*? What were you doing? Why wasn't Vivian with Henry? She's the one who loves it all so, so much!"

"I had gone to get dinner to bring with Jensen. And, then, of course, when we got back, we were busy making plans to get everyone and everything out of the desert! That was a nightmare. What the hell? We're going to attack one another now?"

"Hey, guys, you all came here to honor Henry!" Micah reminded them.

Jensen laughed. "You're the one who started this."

"Yes, I am," Micah said seriously. "Henry died out there that night. Now Vivian's been attacked. I wonder if you realize just how lethal nicotine poisoning can be."

"I certainly realize," Ned Richter said hoarsely.

"We all do. It's just that…we wouldn't have hurt Henry!" Belinda said. "And… I have no idea what went on with Vivian. No idea," she repeated softly.

"Nor do I. She was in her office," Jensen said.

"And you last saw her when?"

"I told the police—I told anyone who asked. I saw her about an hour before the celebration started. She was in her office, said hi, then waved me out. She seemed too busy to worry about the opening ceremonies, although she definitely showed up later. She loves the exhibit, you know."

"The rest of you? Did anyone see her before the celebration?" Micah asked.

"I saw her at about four o'clock," Ned Richter said.

"She came to my office. She wanted permission for more expensive testing. I told her we had to hold off for a while." He paused and then added, "Every once in a while, I have to make her understand my position. I'm a CEO. I can't give in to her just because she's my wife. *Especially* because she's my wife. She's a highly qualified Egyptologist, but she didn't even work for Alchemy at first. She has her position due to me, so…"

"I waved to her," Arlo offered. "I was working in the lab. She didn't wave back. She was concentrating on whatever she was doing. Then again, that's Vivian's way."

"I didn't see her at all," Belinda said. "You know, not until…"

"Me, neither," Joe said.

"Nor me," Roger chimed in.

"Thanks." Micah lifted his glass. "So, to the evening, then, huh? To Henry, our mentor, a man we all loved dearly… I assume?"

Assent was quickly voiced by everyone in the group. "To Henry!"

Their waitress came by; Harley noted that Micah made a point of dropping any questioning at that point. Instead, he ordered the pub's very popular shepherd's pie.

He clearly had the ability to be very charming when he chose. He got Belinda to speak about her upcoming marriage—she was supposed to have a Christmas wedding—and he got Arlo talking about the way he'd fallen in love with mummies at the Chicago Field Museum as a kid. Joe, in his turn, became enthusiastic and wistful talking about the beautiful Satima Mahmoud and what an excellent interpreter she'd been, helping whenever anyone needed it. They'd come this close to having an affair, he admitted, and then, of course, everything had gone to hell.

Roger talked about his love for the desert—and his happiness over the fact that they were home. There was no place like New York. He loved being home, he said; he loved his job.

Ned didn't stay more than an hour, since he was going back to the hospital to be with his wife.

No one else seemed to want to break up their get-together, but it was growing late. The fine Irish band playing that night announced their last number.

The evening inevitably came to an end.

"So who sees to it that our lovely companions get home okay?" Joe asked, rising and indicating Belinda and Harley.

"No need to worry about me," Harley assured them. "Seriously. The tall, dark, handsome and deadly-looking guy at the bar is my cousin."

"Oh, Craig's here! I didn't realize. He should've joined us," Belinda said.

"Maybe he didn't want this to look like an inquisition," Jensen said, staring at Micah.

"Maybe," Micah said casually. The two men were almost the same height, both about six-three. Micah was smiling, not about to get into it—and not about to back down.

"If you're tired, I can take you to your place," Jensen told Harley.

"I'm fine, really," she said. "My cousin, remember? Craig is my cousin."

"Yeah, he is," Jensen said. For a moment, his eyes fell on her, and she thought he might be feeling something like jealousy over her preference for Craig's company rather than his. But although they'd teased and flirted, they'd never dated; they'd never been more than friends. She liked that he was protective. However, he didn't have any grounds to be jealous. At least not of Craig…

"Fine. Belinda?" Jensen said.

She laughed. "I'm a native New Yorker. I've been taking the latest subway most of my life. But sure."

"Your fiancé is a man serving his nation, Belinda. It's my privilege to see you safely home. And," he added, "I'm damned good with the subways myself."

"Okay, thanks. Come on. I'll make tea when we get to my place—so you can get yourself safely home after that!" Belinda left with Jensen's arm around her.

Harley realized that, as the others trailed out, she was still standing near the exit with Micah.

"Strange," he muttered.

"What is?"

"He's the one person who can't be guilty."

"Who? You mean Jensen?"

Micah turned to look at her, studying her eyes thoughtfully, his own pensive. "Yes. He was with you in the desert. The two of you saw Henry alive together, and then you left together, and when you came back, Henry was dead."

"Yes. Why do you find Jensen suspicious?"

"Something about him."

"They teach you that at the academy?" Harley asked.

"Actually, yes. But never mind." He took her elbow. She was startled by the way she reacted to his simple touch.

"Shall we join Craig?" he asked.

They did. Craig stood politely to offer Harley his bar stool, but almost on cue, the cuddling couple who'd been taking up the seats next to him rose, hand in hand, seeing nothing but each other. They began to wander from the bar and toward the exit. Craig gestured at the three stools conveniently left for them and they all sat down.

Micah went over the conversations at the bar and Harley knew that Jensen had been right; Micah really had been grilling all of them.

If Craig had joined them, it wouldn't have been a get-together.

It would've been an inquisition, just as he'd said.

Kieran came from the back office, sliding in comfortably with her back to Craig's chest, leaning against him on his bar stool.

"Make any headway?" she asked.

"Ah, yes, Special Agent Fox has had a gut feeling," Harley replied.

"I don't trust the guy," Micah said mildly. "Jensen."

"Hmm," Kieran murmured.

"The psychologist's deep, dark 'hmm'!" Craig said. "There must be a Freudian meaning there!"

"No, I don't think there's a rational explanation for a gut feeling." Kieran shook her head. "But perhaps if there's dislike involved…"

"Don't dislike the guy. He seems okay. But I sense that he's not quite trustworthy," Micah said.

"Ah." Harley shrugged. "I have a hard time seeing Jensen as a criminal. And in our group, Joe's the one who tends to go off on tangents, not that it means he's guilty of anything. But he's easily distracted."

"By the beautiful Egyptian girl," Micah said. "Satima Mahmoud."

"Yes, and she's still in Egypt, so I doubt she had anything to do with last night," Harley said.

"You know for sure that she's still in Egypt?" Micah asked.

"I, um…"

Harley was forced to pause. "No. Of course I don't know *for sure* that she's in Egypt. I assume she is. It's where she lives and works."

"Worth checking on," Micah said. He was, however, aiming the remark at Craig, who nodded in agreement.

"I think I need to go home." Harley stood up, yawning.

"I've got a car today. We'll get you home," Craig said. "Kieran? You ready?"

"You guys go ahead. I promised Declan some help figuring out an invoice."

"No, it's okay! I go home alone all the time," Harley said. "You—"

"Micah, you take the car," Craig interrupted. "Pick me up in the morning. I'll wait here with Kieran. Declan can drop us off or we'll grab an Uber."

"I can grab an Uber, too. I'm really close, just by Grace Church," Harley said.

"No," Craig insisted. "Let Micah take you, please. This whole mummy thing is…creepy."

"I'm not afraid of mummies."

"You should be. But only of the living ones," Kieran said. "Living people who are pretending to be mummies. Or having other people dress up like mummies. Anyway, get home safely, okay?"

Arguing would make her appear…argumentative, Harley thought.

"Thanks," she said simply. She turned away, aware that she was trembling slightly. It was a ride—a ride home. She wasn't afraid of Micah. She was afraid of herself.

She felt intensely attracted to the man. She'd sat at their table in the bar, wondering how she could be seated between two men with all the right stuff—and feel such an attraction to one and not the other.

She knew nothing at all about Micah Fox, except that he was with the FBI, that he'd worked with Craig and that Craig seemed to like him. And that he'd also been a student of Henry's.

That was the sum total of her knowledge. Was it enough of a basis for…anything?

Or had she spent the past year drifting, trying to develop an interest in someone, and not managing to find any kind of spark, any reason to pursue a relationship, even just a sexual one?

But if this was sexual, did it matter?

It did! He'd loved Henry, too. He was friends with Craig.

What if she threw herself at him, and he turned her down?

She was afraid her thoughts were making her blush, so she kissed her cousin and Kieran good-night and led the way, with Micah right behind her. She explained that it was ridiculous that he felt he had to drive her; it was maybe a mile away at most.

"Yeah, but it's late," Micah said.

She knew that the cars Craig used that belonged to the bureau could be parked just about anywhere. Except that parking wasn't easy in Lower Manhattan—or pretty much anywhere in Manhattan!

"You can drop me off in front of the building, and thank you again," Harley told him.

"I don't think so." He gave her a smile. "Sorry, even if you weren't Craig's cousin, it wouldn't be my style."

"You'll never find parking."

"Yes, I will. The academy also taught us how to summon our individual parking witches," he said, his tone droll.

She pursed her lips and sighed. "Great. Witches? I thought people had parking fairies."

"Not in the academy. Witches are scarier. They get rid of the other cars, frighten them off, you know?"

He did have a parking witch—or damned good luck. She was surprised at how close he got to her building.

He walked her there, and stepped inside with her. He saw the security guard and nodded in approval.

And, of course, he could leave her right there. She was obviously safe; her building had keyed entry and security! The push of a button summoned the police in the event of any trouble.

She found herself staring at him, waiting.

"Good building," he told her.

"Thanks."

She hesitated. She wanted to kick herself. She was standing here so casually—surely she was standing casually; surely she could speak casually!—but she didn't want to let him go. Something was alive inside her, something burning, hot, shaking, nervous...something that made her feel as if she was in her teens again. She'd done very little except study and work over the past year, trying to struggle up from the strange void Henry's death had created.

"Did you want to come up for...tea?" she finally ventured. "Or something stronger? And a view of Grace Church?" she asked. She had to sound like an idiot. "I'm keyed up tonight. I don't know why. I keep thinking we should all be exhausted..."

"Yes."

"What?"

"Sure, I'd love to come up."

"Oh! Um, great." She turned and headed for the elevators, praying that her flushed face wouldn't betray the way she suddenly longed to forget every propriety, every word, and just fall into his arms.

Preferably naked!

CHAPTER FIVE

"THIS PLACE IS INCREDIBLE!" Micah said, looking around her loft. He glanced at her with a curious frown. "Did I miss something about you? You're a trust fund baby?"

She laughed. "I happen to have an uncle who isn't living here right now. He was a snow bird, but these days he's spending most of his time in Florida. He's had the place for fifty years, and I'm pretty sure his dad had it before him. They were both in construction, so they did a great job with the space. However, only in NYC, Tokyo, Mexico City and a few other cities around the globe would this be considered a big space. You must've tried to rent in New York at some point."

He nodded, staring out the windows at Grace Church.

"I went to Brown, and then to Columbia University, so I lived here for a while," he told her. He grinned drily. "I think I lived in a closet."

"Ah, Columbia," she murmured. "But you knew Henry at Brown, right?"

"Yep. I knew Henry. I went on to Columbia, where I was a grad student. I didn't particularly intend to be an Egyptologist, but I was considering anthropology or archaeology. And then…"

His voice trailed off. He shrugged and then turned to look at her again. "My senior year as an undergrad, a friend of mine was kidnapped. The FBI tracked down the kidnappers. My friend's family was rich, and yes, they were going for a ransom. But…well, one of the guys admitted after they were caught that they hadn't intended to let him live. I guess I kind of fell into a bit of hero worship for the FBI. So, I switched to criminology. I knew I wanted to do what those agents had done."

"I'm sure you made a great choice. I know how Craig feels. Of course, my whole family worries about him, but we all believe he made a great decision."

"Yeah. Sometimes, though, the bitter truth is that you lose, too. Things don't always work out the way you want them to."

"You didn't lose with Henry. You were never in the fight," Harley said quietly.

He nodded. "Yeah? Thanks. Well, I suppose I should get going."

"I'm still wide-awake. Um…can I get you something to drink? I was going to make tea. Oh, it's not decaffeinated. I mean, that's never made much of a difference to me, but…"

"Caffeine. Sounds good."

"Okay."

She turned in her little kitchen area and put the kettle on. He perched on one of the bar stools. Facing her, he also faced the kitchen. Spinning around on any of the stools, you'd still have the great view of Grace Church. She waited for the water to boil, aware that he watched her as she got out mugs and tea bags.

She needed to let him go. And she needed to let go of her interest in him—emotional and physical!

"How's it going with Officer Friendly?" she asked.

"McGrady?" he asked. "He's kind of irrelevant. The powers that be have gotten the NYC office put in charge," he told her. "Henry's death may not be related to what happened at the opening ceremony, but on the other hand, it might have been. That makes this not just national but international, and luckily the FBI does work out of an office in Cairo. It was my first avenue of investigation last year when I heard about Henry. I wasn't officially on the case, but I went to Cairo. I knew our guys would be sympathetic. This might be a terrible thing to say, but I think Detective McGrady might've been disappointed that he wound up with a live victim. He wanted a murder case."

"You still have to deal with him, though?"

"Yes, but he's not really interested now. Rydell's a good guy, and he keeps apologizing for his partner. We haven't made any complaints. We're trying to keep it all copacetic."

"Where would someone get nicotine for a poisoning like that? I gather the linens were soaked in it and only the fact that they got them off her so fast saved Vivian's life, right?"

"Right."

The kettle whistled, and Harley poured the water into two mugs. Their fingers nearly touched as she pushed his toward him, as they both dipped their tea bags in the hot water. She flushed, catching his eyes on her.

She really, really needed to let him go.

That or...

Give in. Spit out the truth that she was incredibly attracted to him. Totally inappropriate under the circumstances, but they *were* adults, after all. It could just be sex; she could handle that. And they could try to figure out what was going on between them after this case was solved.

"We have people looking into large purchases of nicotine, but—"

"Insecticide," Harley interrupted, thinking of the most obvious place to buy commercial nicotine.

He sipped his tea and nodded. "I forgot. Research for an investigation agency is what you've been doing."

"Part-time. I've been trying to sort out what to do with my career. And this job pays well." She shrugged. "Only a few of the cases I've worked on have actually been criminal. Mostly civil suits. A lot of my time's been spent monitoring bad behavior. People trying to get a relative to leave money to one person or another, husbands and wives behaving poorly and, very sadly, in one case that did become criminal—stopping a blood relative from preying on a young boy. The job's been interesting, but I haven't been sure what I want to do, which way I want to go. But since I met Kieran, I've come to like the psychology part. I think I'd like to get into profiling."

"You certainly have the right degrees."

"It all looks good on paper. I'd have to see how I do in practice."

"Want to practice?" he asked her.

"What do you mean?"

He was suddenly very serious. "Think of all the people you know who were involved with the Amenmose expedition and exhibit. Who would have a reason to kill Henry? Was money ever an issue?"

"Not that I know of—other than the fact that an archaeologist's prestige means more money the next time he or she wants to go out on a project. But I'm sure you're aware of that."

Harley realized she was leaning against the counter. He was seated in one of the stools, so that meant she was leaning closer and closer to him. Their fingers, wrapped around their mugs, were only inches away.

It was hardly champagne and strawberries.

It was...

She needed to move back.

"Ye olde process of elimination," he murmured, apparently unaware of their closeness. "So, who can you eliminate?"

"Everyone!" Harley said.

He shook his head. "That won't work. You most probably know the killer."

"Any of the students would benefit from prestige. It would make a radical difference as far as their careers in Egyptology, archaeology and anthropology are concerned," Harley said. "It was impressive to work with a man like Henry, but to take his place would be even more impressive. Still..."

"Process of elimination," he repeated, then abruptly stood up.

"I have to leave."

"Oh. Okay. If you have to."

"Yeah, I do."

But he was still standing there. He smiled suddenly. "Yeah, I have to go," he said again.

"You really don't."

His smile deepened. "I do."

"Because I'm Craig's cousin?"

He shook his head, his eyes never leaving hers. "Because you're you. I don't know what it is... I guess we can't define attraction, but... Anyway, I'm being presumptuous, but—"

"No, actually, you're not," Harley broke in. She wondered how you could *feel* someone so completely when you weren't even touching that person.

"We have to give it time and thought."

"I wasn't thinking everlasting commitment. I'm not FBI, but I can help a great deal and we're going to…be together. Differently. I—"

"That's not what I meant," Micah said.

"Yes, okay. I guess I know what you mean. I believe… I believe we'll see each other tomorrow and the next day, and if…"

"Yes," Micah said. Then, neither spoke; they looked at each other.

"We're adults," Harley whispered.

"Yes, and so… I'm heading out."

He walked to the door. Harley followed him, ready to lock up when he left. She stayed a short distance behind him. She felt as if her flesh and blood, muscle and bone, had come alive, as if neurons or atoms or other chemical entities were flashing through her system with tiny sparks of red-hot fire. He had to leave; otherwise, she'd embarrass herself.

But she didn't really care.

Still, he was right. They needed time. Just because they could hook up didn't mean they should forget that there were consequences to any deed, even if neither had any expectations.

At the door, he turned to her.

It could have all ended there—as it should have.

She could've stayed where she was.

But she didn't. She walked forward, her eyes on his, until she was touching him, and when she did, he backed into the door. At the same time, his arms came around her.

She touched his face. Stroked his cheek, felt the power in his arms as he drew her close. She let herself shudder with a delicious abandon as she felt the heat of his body, the texture and strength in his muscles. And then she felt his mouth, crushing hers, and she returned the kiss with equal openmouthed passion. They stood in the doorway, fumbling with each other's clothing. Micah pulled away for a second, removing his holster and Glock from the back of his waistband, setting them down on the occasional table.

Then he paused, breathing heavily. "Wait. Is there… someone else? Is there that kind of reason?"

She shook her head. "No. No one else. There hasn't been anyone else in well over a year." She felt her cheeks turn a dozen shades of red. "But it's all right. I'm on the pill."

He drew her back into his arms for a very long, very wet, hot kiss.

Then they moved through the apartment, half disrobing themselves, half helping each other.

They stood in the center of the loft, next to the plate glass windows looking out on the night, on the Gothic structure of Grace Church. They both hesitated a minute.

Not that anything was wrong; rather she felt blessed.

The light that came in and bathed them together was beautiful and romantic. Micah smiled and said, "I have this great image of me sweeping you into my arms and carrying you up the stairway…but it's winding and it's iron and…"

Harley laughed. She turned and ran up the winding stairway to the loft. He quickly joined her.

The loft seemed to be aglow with light in the most glorious colors—pastels with bursts of darker blue and mauve, probably from some vehicle moving down on the street. They found each other's mouths again, kissed forever, and then Harley rolled over and straddled him. They twined their fingers together and looked at each other

again, and she couldn't help wondering if it was possible
to not really know someone—but to believe that you did.

You could be fooling yourself! a voice nagged.

But she didn't care. She'd been spending the year since
Henry's death biding time, waiting…

For what, she hadn't known.

Until now? Until this? And maybe it was just sex…

But at this point in her life, that was fine, too!

She felt his hands moving over her body, touching and
teasing, exploring and giving. They turned on the bed,
facing each other, laughing, kissing, their lips roaming,
intimate. They shared kisses that caused sensation to
soar, cries to escape into the night…

Then at last they were together, moving with the brilliant colors of the night. She caught his eyes and they
were beautiful.

His hands were electric, his movement fierce and
erotic, and it seemed that they'd joined in something
wonderful that captured the pulse and beat of the city…
agonizing in its wonder, lasting too long, and yet over
too quickly.

She lay beside him, breathing desperately. She could
hear her own heartbeat as if it shook the very founda-
tions of the building.

And she felt his knuckles, gentle on her cheek. He
pulled her to him. She prayed her heartbeat would slow…

"What are you thinking?" he asked her quietly.

For some reason, she couldn't resist being honest.

"That you're very, very good. Or that everyone else
in my life of the boyfriend variety has been bad. Disap-
pointing, anyway. I mean, as a lover…"

He laughed. "I'm going to take the 'very, very good.'"

He hesitated, drawing a line gently from her face to her collarbone. "Why?" he asked.

"Why are you good at this?" she murmured, perfectly aware that wasn't what he meant.

"Why have you been…alone?" he asked her.

She shook her head. "I haven't been alone. My world is very rich with family and friends. I'm lucky. I've been out there. I've even waited tables a few times at Finnegan's when they were short on people. And I actually like working for Fillmore Investigations. I'm not out on the street much. I like to think I'm kind of a little like Sherlock Holmes. Field agents with the company bring me information and I figure things out from the bits and pieces. I often talk to Kieran, and discuss my people with her, put them in hypothetical situations."

"That's work. Not personal."

"Yes, true. I've been to Florida to visit my family. And I've gone to tons of shows with Kieran's family. Her twin brother, Kevin, is an actor and—"

"I know. So why did you suddenly need me so badly?" he asked her.

She turned toward him, drawing the sheets to her shoulders as she answered the question. "Why are *you* here—needed or just as needy?" she asked.

He laughed softly. "Ouch. Hmm."

"It's a fair question. I was in criminology, probably because of Craig. I've lost family members, but I hadn't ever seen anyone die the way Henry did. And I was so crazy about him, as if he'd been a relative. You know… yeah, you know what he was like. Anyway, I tried to do something about his death. I failed. I never expected this, though!"

"You mean me?"

"No, sorry! No, I meant Friday night, at the gala. Vivian! Why kill Henry and wait all this time to attack Vivian?" Harley asked.

He rolled onto his back and stared at the ceiling. "Maybe the killer's triggered by events."

"You mean—"

"Henry died the day your team made the discovery. Vivian was attacked the day you were all about to celebrate that discovery."

"The mummy's curse?"

He groaned.

"No! I don't believe it, but… Micah, there were Egyptian workers who told us we were going to be cursed."

"None of the Egyptian workers were here at the gala," Micah reminded her.

"Yolanda. Yolanda Akeem," Harley said.

"Ah, Yolanda."

"You know her?"

"I do. I met her in Cairo."

"So…would you say you're friends?"

"Oh, I don't think that word describes our brief time together. No, she got me out of Egypt, helped me chase after you guys," Micah said. "We're having some problems reaching her, although I assume she's still in the country. McGrady tried to get her to stick around after the night of the celebration, and he managed to talk to her for a few minutes, but in my mind, she hadn't been properly questioned yet."

"What? Why?"

"She has some kind of diplomatic immunity. And, of course, she had nothing to do with what happened to Vivian."

"How do you know that?"

"She was always within range of cameras," Micah said. He smiled. "The FBI's taken the lead, so we have footage, prints, you name it. Sadly, even with all the crime scene evidence that was collected, we don't have answers. But as far as Yolanda goes, we're almost positive she wasn't anywhere near the museum before the gala. She arrived just in time for the party, and she was on camera the entire time. She didn't even take a trip to the ladies' room."

"Why do you think she doesn't want to talk to police?"

"Apparently, she believes that the entire expedition was run by a bunch of idiots, and she's tired of all the bad press involving archaeological work in her country." He grinned suddenly, and ran a finger from her collarbone to her abdomen. "There's something wrong with this picture. I'm lying here, next to you, seeing you, feeling you and…"

"And we're talking about work. But with your kind of job, it's what you do all the time, right? Is that what you mean?"

"No," he said, laughing. "What I meant is that I'm obviously not so good or you'd be more intrigued by us being together here—naked in bed!—than by the puzzles that will return in the morning."

"Morning, evening…"

Harley felt almost giddy and worried about herself all at once. It was too natural to be here with him. Too easy, too sweet.

She crawled on top of him, her breasts just teasing his chest. "Don't worry. I'm not at all distracted. Like I said, you're very, very good. Of course, feel free to reinforce such a notion at any time."

"Of course!"

He drew her to him. They were locked in a hot, wet kiss again, then disengaged to shower each other with featherlight touches, brushing with their lips and fingertips, delicate brushes that turned urgent and became fierce, passionate lovemaking that left them both breathless, hearts pounding once again.

It was incredible. Being together was incredible. She lay curled next to him as he held her. They were both silent for a few minutes.

"Okay, we know that while Yolanda Akeem might conceivably have had something to do with Henry's death, she couldn't have had anything to do with what happened to Vivian," Micah murmured.

Harley laughed softly. "So, *I'm* not that good, eh?"

He turned to her. "Good? Good? 'Good' is a total understatement. You are spectacular. And beyond."

They both went on to prove just how much they appreciated each other.

WHEN MORNING CAME, and they'd both showered and dressed, he sat on the bed next to her, adjusting his sleeves while she buttoned her blouse.

"Amazing, huh?" he said. "And that's not a word I use lightly."

"What is?" She grinned; she couldn't help herself. "'Very, very, *very* good'? Now, as to amazing…"

"Hey!"

"Okay…amazing."

"I meant that it was special to have a night like this, to be focused entirely on another person, without losing focus on the rest of your life."

"But remember, neither of us has a hold on the other.

How awkward! What I mean is…you didn't become for-ever committed."

He gently kissed her lips.

"No hold. I have to meet up with Craig at the office. I'll see you later, right?"

Harley nodded. "I'll be at Finnegan's this evening. I've gotten together with Kieran and Craig for Sunday roast the last few weeks. I imagine that if you're going to be with Craig, you'll end up there, as well."

"Excellent."

At the door, he lingered, kissing her goodbye.

He left and she leaned against the door.

Then she reminded herself that he'd been nothing but a forgotten voice until two nights ago. That she'd wanted to believe she'd be happy with just one night.

Except that now…

She wanted far more than a night.

MICAH SAT IN the New York office with Craig and one of the computer techs.

He stared at the security footage from the museum over and over again.

It didn't matter how long he studied the footage, it didn't change. He saw everyone involved with the ex-hibit as they arrived that day. Administrators and other key people got there early, heading straight over to the area that was about to be unveiled.

He saw the coming and going of visitors to the main part of the museum during the day.

The caterers arrived. Everything looked just as it should for the evening that would welcome a special group for the official opening of the Henry Tomlinson Collection.

"Whatever went on with Vivian, it was planned way before the event. There are security cameras just about everywhere except for the offices, and they reveal nothing and no one out of the ordinary. Of course, there are the subterranean so-called 'secret access' areas that Arlo showed Harley and me," Micah said. "There's no question in my mind that whoever did this planned it well ahead of time. The linens would've been on hand in the prep room. Even before the Amenmose exhibit, the museum offered Egyptology and they have classes for high school kids in which the religious and funerary rituals are demonstrated. As to the nicotine poisoning, it's easy enough to get hold of insecticide."

"We'll need warrants," Craig said, "if we want to check out credit card purchases. Although I sincerely doubt we'd find what we're looking for. And I'm not sure we can even get warrants unless we have information or evidence we can use to designate suspects."

"Whoever bought the poison didn't use a credit card. And he or she didn't buy it all at the same place," Micah said. "It's one of them," he added. "I know that one of them killed Henry. The same person apparently tried to kill Vivian. Either that or..."

"Or?"

"We've been chasing the wrong dog," Micah said thoughtfully. He looked at Craig. "Everyone involved in that exhibit and in the expedition knows that a lot of people didn't believe a verdict of death by accident—that Henry killed himself in a state of delirium—no matter what official reports said. I realize that most eventually gave up and accepted the verdict, or pretended to."

"What if someone was trying to kill Vivian, and trying to make it *appear* that it was Henry's killer coming after her?" Craig suggested.

"I don't know," Micah said with a long sigh. "Maybe that's far-fetched. I'm still suspicious about the entire thing that went on in the desert. The insurgency—the supposedly violent insurgency that killed no one and led to nothing but a few demonstrators being arrested. Also, there's another name that keeps coming up, that of Satima Mahmoud. The translator."

"She's in Egypt."

"I'd like to talk to her. If we can reach someone in our Cairo office, perhaps they can arrange a meeting."

"All right. I'll give tech a call. We'll see if they can get through to our people over there now. And if so, if the staff can bring Satima in and set up a satellite call."

"That's great. Either a video meeting or, if I have to, I'll fly back over."

"Alone?" Craig asked him.

"You're welcome to join me."

"I wasn't thinking about me. To be honest, I don't like the idea of Harley going back there—not now, and not in relation to this case."

"I wouldn't bring Harley," Micah said quickly.

"You're going to make damned sure you keep her out of danger, right? I know she'd say she can look after herself, and of course, that's true. But she's my cousin and I love her, so I can't help feeling this way. You understand?"

Micah nodded. He understood.

Craig was still looking at him. "Yeah, you do understand. Thank you," he said quietly.

And once again, Micah nodded.

CHAPTER SIX

EDWARD FILLMORE WAS an exceptional boss.

In many ways   although he was less on the slightly crazy academic side   he reminded her of Henry Tomlinson.

They were both decent men. Not on-a-pedestal wonderful; they had their moments. But they were both good people. Or, rather, Henry *had* been good until his unfair and untimely end.

Edward had founded his company years earlier. They handled private investigations, such as finding lost family members, searching for missing children and were certainly happy to participate in any "silver" alert, as well. He seldom took on divorce cases in which one spouse was trying to trap the other. In fact, he'd only take on such a case if he met with someone he saw as an injured party first, and then only if it meant getting suitable support for any children who might be affected.

When Harley had first gone to work for him, he'd told her to feel free to use her own time and whatever resources the company had to look into Henry's death. She'd never used work hours—say, when she was tracking down a credit card report or some lead on a missing person—to pursue her own investigation. But she'd accepted his offer, although she hadn't come up with anything yet. Henry was gone, had been cremated. And there was no lead to follow; it was all a stone wall. It was somewhat comforting to know that the FBI had encountered the same stone wall. No one had been able to crack the defenses established when the Amenmose expedition had ended, Henry had died and they'd all left the site.

Now, of course, she had a new crime to pursue—the poisoning of Vivian Richter.

She called Edward Fillmore and asked if she might have his blessing to head into the offices and search through info on various people.

Edward was quick to allow her access to his computers and databases.

So Harley spent her Sunday morning going through everything she could find on everyone she knew—including her colleagues on the expedition, the people she'd never suspected. Her search yielded little.

Ned Richter had been a CEO with a pharmaceutical company for nine years before joining Alchemy, where he'd been in charge of "Exploration" for over a decade.

His work record was spotless. He'd graduated from Harvard.

He'd married Vivian Clifford, a graduate of Cornell, a decade ago. When not working, the couple loved to vacation in historic places, including Peru, Mexico, Egypt and Greece. The couple had no children, but seemed devoted to each other.

Arlo Hampton had no criminal record, not even a parking ticket. He'd received his doctorate in Egyptology from Brown. He'd been with Alchemy for nearly eight years and had been hired by Ned Richter.

She looked up Jensen next. He'd gone to NYU. He was a New Yorker through and through.

He had a ton of parking tickets.

Nothing else on him.

Roger Eastman had been arrested once; he'd been protesting commercial testing on animals.

He'd received probation.

Belinda had no parking tickets—she didn't drive. She'd never been arrested. She'd been valedictorian of her high school class and had gone to Northwestern before arriving in New York for graduate work.

Joe —Joseph Rosello—had also been born in New York City, in the Bronx. He'd gone to Ithaca, in Syracuse, and then finished at Brown. However, she found something she hadn't known or even suspected. He'd paid his way through college by working as an extra in movies and doing a stand-up comedy gig at a place in Times Square.

According to his social media pages, he still enjoyed dressing up and playing parts.

She should have known this. And, of course, she would have—if she'd just spent more time on social media. So... he played roles.

Would that include the part of a mummy?

HARLEY WASN'T EVEN sure what she was doing at first when she reached for the phone; then she knew. She called Kieran and asked for Kevin's number, since Kevin was a working New York actor.

Naturally, Kieran wanted to know what was up. Harley told her.

"Kevin's performing at some kind of zombie walk today in Times Square. What's your guy's name? I can see if he's taking part," Kieran said.

But Harley didn't need Kieran to check it out for her;

she'd keyed in some more information and had come up with Joe's status for the day.

"Yes!" she exclaimed. "They're both taking part in the zombie walk. The walk's for charity, and Joe's one of the performers doing pictures with people. Hey, do you feel like heading down to be in a zombie walk?"

"Sure," Kieran said. "I'll be a good sister. What the heck, we can support a charity and investigate what's going on. Sounds like a plan to me."

They agreed to meet at a restaurant off Times Square—quieter and not as much of a tourist attraction— and get lunch before joining the zombie walk.

And watching the players.

A waste of time? Harley wondered.

A lot of investigative work was a waste of time; that was part of the process of elimination, as Micah had described it. But Kieran was right. If nothing else, their entry fees would go toward charity.

MICAH HAD NO intention of denying anything; he really cared about Harley—and Harley certainly behaved as if she cared about him. Was it forever and ever? How could they tell? Did he want to see her again?

Touch her again, breathe in her scent, be with her again and feel her, naked, against him?

Well, yes. That was a definite yes.

But he'd never been in precisely this situation before.

Was Craig supposed to ask him about his intentions? Or maybe he was supposed to give Micah a good left hook to the jaw.

"You're sleeping with her, right?" Craig asked.

"Define sleeping," Micah said. "I only knew her as your cousin and a voice on the phone until two days ago. Last night, yes. We were together." He hesitated and then admitted. "I actually tried to leave. Probably not hard enough."

Craig lowered his head, obviously amused.

"Just keep her safe," he said.

And then, before either one of them could say any more, the phone in the conference room rang.

Craig picked it up and frowned as he listened to what was being said. He hung up slowly, rising as he did. "Come on, Egan's office. He's got a video call up with one of our agents in Cairo."

"Already? They have Satima Mahmoud?" Micah asked.

"No, but they have some kind of information," Craig replied.

They strode rapidly down the hall. Egan's secretary waved them in and they entered his office. He was speaking with someone via his computer; they both walked around behind his desk.

Micah had met the agent on the screen. His name was Sanford Wiley, and Micah quickly greeted him. Egan introduced him to Craig.

"So, we got your inquiry just now and I happened to be in the office," Wiley said. "I don't know whether it means anything or not, but I wanted to get back to you right away with what I have. The local police are looking for Satima Mahmoud. Now, they're not always entirely forthright with us, but from what I've been able to gather, she's suspected of having something to do with agitating trouble—and insurrection. She was under suspicion by the Egyptian police, who are now helping our people with the investigation, we believe, as well. They've been searching for her for several days. We'll start our own line of investigation, since she's a witness or person of interest to you all. Fox, I know you had some interaction with her. Do you suspect her of being involved in Henry Tomlinson's death?"

"When I saw her, she informed me that the others had left. She had just gotten to Cairo herself when I was trying to head out to the expedition site," Micah told him. "I'm very interested in what she may know. Or more specifically, what she knows that she didn't share at the time. She was the one who first sounded the alarm about the uprising. Everything was pure chaos when I was there, which I'm sure you remember, Wiley. But, yes, if you find her, I'd very much like to speak with her."

"We're on it from this end—with the Egyptian police, of course."

"Of course."

"We get the impression that they're perplexed about the situation. She's disappeared."

"Thanks for letting us know," Micah told him.

There were a few more exchanges, and then they ended the video call.

Egan looked thoughtfully at Micah. "To be honest," he said, "I'm not sure what you can learn from this woman—or what you could prove—this late in the game. Crews are still going through whatever evidence they could find at the museum after Vivian was attacked, but…"

"I know, sir," Micah said. "But it's only been a matter of days. And I'm pretty convinced that Vivian Richter's attack relates back to Henry's death. And if not, well, we still need to know who the hell would attempt to murder a woman with nicotine-soaked linen wrappings."

"Yes, and we *will* find the truth," Egan said with conviction. "I'll inform you of anything we learn through our people here and in Egypt, and through any chatter they pick up." He hesitated. "If they can't find this woman…"

"There's always the possibility that she's dead," Craig finished.

"Why kill an interpreter?" Egan mused.

"There's also the possibility that she's alive—and more of a player than we'd imagined," Micah said. "Or that very fact could account for her death. If that's what happened."

"When you talked to her, did you get the feeling that she was involved in any way?" Craig asked.

"She seemed harried, frightened and glad to be back in Cairo. But I was still trying to catch up with the Americans involved. Now I realize I should have given her more attention then. The entire situation was terrifying, so of course it seemed reasonable that she'd be upset. And I still don't see her with a motive of any kind to strangle Henry."

"You never know," Egan told him.

"Except we do know that she's definitely not in the States," Craig said. He suddenly began to feel his pocket, which was apparently vibrating. "Phone," he muttered. "Excuse me, two seconds. This may be important." He answered the call, taking a step back from Micah and Egan.

"She's not in this country that we know of, anyway," Micah said to Egan. He hesitated, speaking carefully. "I still don't think she killed Henry."

"But you think she might know who did?"

"I think she knows *something*," Micah said. "She's Joe Rosello's alibi for the time Jensen Morrow and Harley Frasier were away from the camp. What if she lied because he either cajoled her or bribed her?"

Egan nodded. "That's a possibility."

"You're talking about Joe Rosello?" Craig asked, putting away his phone.

"Yes," Micah said.

"That was Kieran. She's going to Times Square with Harley. And it's about Joe Rosello. The man's an actor, and he's in a zombie walk today. Not sure I actually get it, but Kieran knew about it because of her twin, Kevin. He's one of the performers hired on as an improvisational actor and guide for the walk."

"Sounds like a good time for us to get to Times Square and see just what he's up to," Micah said.

"Zombie walk?" Egan asked, shaking his head.

"They're all over the country now," Micah told him. "The power of television and mass media today. The popularity of certain television programs can create some strange circumstances."

"There's a show on TV about mummies?"

"Mummies, zombies, walking dead. Close enough, I think. Let's head on out," Micah said to Craig. "With your blessing, sir, of course," he added, addressing Egan.

"Go, sir, with righteousness!" Egan said. "And get the whacked-out son of a bitch, will you? Speaking of media—they're having a heyday with this. Mummies! As if we didn't have enough of the plain old walking, living, flesh-and-blood kind of criminals!"

A MAJORITY OF the "zombies" there for the walk and to support the charity were dressed up.

They wore zombie makeup, tattered clothing and many looked as if they'd rolled in the dirt.

Luckily, not all the participants were dressed up, and since it was a charity walk, whatever one chose to wear was fine. Joining the walk cost ten dollars. The fee included a comedy "zombie" performance at the end, with the bleachers reserved for those who'd paid. Anyone could see the show, but since the entry fee went to charity—three of the major children's hospitals—virtually no one was going to mind paying.

"This would've been fun no matter what," Kieran told Harley, surveying the crowd. "A lot of the costumes on the walkers are really cool. Oh, there, at the sign-up tables. There's Kevin."

Kieran started walking ahead; Harley quickly followed.

Kevin Finnegan was an exceptionally good-looking man, tall, with great bone structure, a toned body and broad shoulders. He and Kieran were clearly related, but of course, they weren't just siblings—they were twins. Like Kieran, he had deep auburn hair and his eyes were a true blue.

Harley waited while Kieran greeted her brother with a hug and a kiss; she then greeted him, as well.

"I'm so glad you came out. I know how you feel about crowds in Times Square," Kevin told his sister.

"It's…well…" Kieran began.

"Ah. I'm being used," Kevin said, but his smile was affectionate. "What do you need? How can I help?"

"We signed up legitimately, don't you fear," Kieran said. "But do you know a Joe Rosello?"

"Not that I'm aware of."

"No? Oh, I guess you don't know everyone working here today," Harley said.

"Actually, I do."

"Oh! Well, supposedly, Joe's working."

"Maybe he works under a different name. SAG rules

mean you can't use a name if someone else has it already. Or even if he's not SAG, he might be using a stage name," Kevin said.

"That's him! That's him right there!" Harley exclaimed.

"Oh, so that's your guy. His name is Robbie. At least when he's here it is. Nice guy, or so it seems."

Joe—or Robbie Rosello, as he was calling himself for the day—was standing over by one of the tables. As Kevin had been doing, he was posing with people who wanted their pictures taken with a zombie.

He was dressed in tatters. Not like a mummy, just in tatters. His skin was painted white and he had very effective makeup that darkened his eyes and made his cheeks sink in.

As Joe so often did, he was flirting.

"Yep, that's him!" Harley said again.

The girls with whom he'd been posing moved on, and Harley ran over to him. He turned to look at her and his eyes widened with surprise, alarm—and wariness.

"Harley!" he said. "Um, what are you doing here? You're a zombie fan?" He sounded skeptical.

"It's a good cause, right? You know, I was shocked to find out that you're an actor."

"Oh, well…" He smiled at her awkwardly. "I'm not really an actor, more of an 'I love the movies' kind of guy who likes to get work as an extra. I don't hide it, but I guess I don't talk about it at work. There are people who don't think you can be a serious academic if you…if you do things like take part in a zombie walk."

"That's silly."

"Yeah? Well, we both know the world can be full of silliness, some of it malicious."

She nodded. "I guess, but if this is something you

love, you shouldn't have to be afraid that others won't approve."

He frowned. "I agree."

"I guess we have to work on convincing the rest of the world."

"The academic world, anyway. How did you even find out about this?"

"You remember Craig Frasier, my cousin? He's dating Kieran Finnegan. And her brother, Kevin, is an actor—"

"Kevin is a *serious* actor. He actually makes a living at it," Joe said. He grimaced. "I don't think I'd be able to do that, so I have to be a serious academic instead."

"By the way, you look great," she told him.

"Thank you."

"Is the costume yours? Do you have many…costumes?"

"Oh, no. No," he said firmly, apparently figuring out just where she was going with her question and why she was really there, "No! Emphatically no. I've never dressed up like a mummy." He hesitated. "I swear, I'd never have hurt Henry, and I did nothing to Vivian Richter. I swear!"

"Hey, Robbie! Zombie dance thing starting up," someone called.

"Excuse me, gotta go. Don't worry. I'll have thousands of witnesses for my every move today," he assured Harley.

"Have fun!" she said.

He gave her a thumbs-up and joined a number of other actors, Kevin Finnegan among them. Someone struck a chord on a guitar, and the group went into a shuffle dance, akin to the one in the music video for Michael Jackson's old "Thriller."

The song was very clever, and the words had to do with giving generously to fight disease.

And when it was over, Kevin—the head zombie, apparently—stepped out from the group and announced they'd be walking down Broadway. Volunteers with water were positioned along the route. The walk would end at the bleachers, where some of the entertainers would then be performing.

Harley turned and looked around until she finally saw Kieran. Kieran saw her at the same time and hurried toward her as a sea of people—some in zombie rags and makeup, some not—came between them. They were almost carried along by the crowd. Kieran shrugged and waved at her from a distance, then laughed as they were both pushed along.

Harley tried to thread her way through the would-be zombies.

Kieran did the same.

Now and then, they'd come across another kind of creature, something from Disney or perhaps one of Jim Henson's characters from his movies or television shows.

Harley ran into some comic characters she didn't recognize. A man in a very large banana suit struggled to maneuver to the side.

He fell over.

She tried to reach him, but he was helped up by a group of grapes. Police were everywhere on the street and they also tried to help the banana; the grapes were just faster.

It was Times Square, after all.

And Times Square on an especially crazy day. It reminded her why she usually avoided the area. But a lot of the theaters were down here, too, and she did love going with Craig and Kieran to see plays when Kevin was in them—and even when he wasn't!

But today…

"Hey there!" Kieran called. She was walking parallel with Harley, a few feet to the left.

"Hey!" Harley called back, grinning.

But then she saw the mummy.

On a day like this, it was difficult to discern the differences between costumes; many were tattered white, and appeared to have been made from linen strips.

But this…

This was a mummy.

It was a mummy that looked exactly the way Vivian Richter had looked when she'd staggered into the midst of the gala. It might've been created by the same costume artist! Or would-be costume artist…

The thing was behind her, lurching along. Harley scanned the crowd. The mummy seemed to be walking alone.

And walking in a casual manner that brought it closer and closer to Harley.

"Kieran!" she screamed.

At first, her friend turned to her with a broad smile. Then she saw the mummy. And she began to stride aggressively over to Harley—with the mummy between them.

The mummy sensed pursuit and headed toward Kieran. But then, it headed back in Harley's direction with a purpose and a vengeance, no longer staggering.

"Come on, come on, I'm ready for you!" Harley thought. "Police! Police!" she cried.

And then the thing was upon her, placing a hand on her chest. It looked right at her, but she couldn't see its eyes. They were covered in the same linen gauze that stretched over the body, dirtied and rendered old, as if— mummy or zombie—the creature had long been dead.

THE THRONG OF people was impressive, particularly for a charity event.

Micah assumed many people were out just for the entertainment value and, of course, the fun of dressing up as a zombie.

But it made for a massive crowd—tens of thousands at the very least, and maybe many more considering the size of New York City.

"I see Kevin Finnegan," Craig said.

"Where?"

"Leading the zombie charge."

"You're sure that's Kevin?"

"Yes, and if so, Kieran is near him, and if she is…"

"Then Harley's near Kieran. Let's go!"

Wending their way through the horde of people wasn't easy. Apparently, no one had thought to tell the regular performers who thronged Times Square daily in costume, charging for tourist pictures, that zombies would be ruling the day.

Maybe it didn't matter. As they hurried past the Times Square Marriott, Micah saw a zombie posing with a Disney figure and with one of the imitation "naked" cowboys who'd staked a claim on the street.

He kept up a brisk pace, saying "excuse me" almost every other second.

And then he saw Kevin Finnegan, laughing, talking, making announcements through a speaker and pointing to the bleachers ahead.

He also saw Joe Rosello dancing along with a group

as he moved forward in costume—ragged jeans, ripped rock band T-shirt and heavily made-up face and body.

And there...

A mummy!

A mummy, standing in the street, touching Harley, touching her with wrapped hands that appeared to be wet, soaked in something.

"Stop now!" he shouted.

He barely avoided knocking over a teenager playing zombie-on-a-crutch. In a circuitous route, he cleared a number of teens. As carefully as he could without losing speed, he continued to press forward through and around people.

The mummy saw him—and turned to run.

He heard Harley shout. She was starting to run after the thing.

"No!" He caught up with her.

"We have to catch that mummy!" she said.

"No, no—get your shirt off!"

"What?"

"Your shirt. Get your shirt off."

"Here? In Times Square?"

Craig, gasping for breath, had reached them. "Get your shirt off! The hands—the mummy's hands were covered in something. Get it off *now*. Harley, damn it, there could be poison on your shirt. Get it off before..."

She cried out, all but ripping the shirt from her body. It fell to the ground.

There were creatures of all kinds gathering around them.

"Way cool!" a passing zombie said.

"Yeah," said another. "It's legal, you know. Men can

go topless, and women can go topless! New York City, man. What a great place."

"Maybe she'll take off her bra!"

"Moron!" Harley breathed, swinging around.

"I've got the shirt," Craig said, slipping into gloves and reaching down.

"The mummy's probably shedding poison with every step," Micah said. "Cops. Get cops over here. Warn them there's a hazard…gloves, bags…"

He didn't need to talk; Craig knew what had to be done as well as he did. Micah had already begun moving, and as he did, he swore. The "mummy" was indeed shedding, leaving what was likely poisoned and hazardous material every few steps.

But the trail of wrappings at least gave him a direction to take, as clear as tracking any animal, human included, in a forested wilderness.

"Look!" a girl cried. "It was a mummy! A mummy!"

She'd picked up some of the shredded linen that had been cast on the ground. Micah swore again, using his gloved hands to snatch it from her.

"Hey!" she protested.

"Get to a cop. Get to a doctor. That might be poisoned material," Micah said. A man quickly appeared at the child's side, holding her, and taking Micah more seriously than she did, apparently.

"Cop! Doctor!" Micah ordered.

"Yes, sir!" the man said, clutching his daughter.

Micah hurried on.

Cops were filling the area. Craig had gotten to Kevin Finnegan, and Kevin was announcing the problem, warning people not to touch the linen, to get to a cop, hospital, or doctor if they had.

Micah kept running. He saw more of the linen along the road. Swearing, he knew he'd have to stop and add it to the growing cache he stuffed into a large evidence bag as he hurried along.

The "mummy" had planned well, knowing that the police and FBI were fully aware that poison—using poisoned linen—was his or her talent.

And that they'd definitely be delayed in their pursuit, trying to keep others from becoming victims of possible illness or even death.

The last piece of linen was in front of an alley that led from Times Square down one of the side streets.

Micah swung around the corner, racing down the street. And then he stopped.

The street was filled with massive office buildings; there was also a massage place, a Chinese restaurant and somebody's bar and grill.

And there was no one on the street.

It was New York! Where was everyone?

But it was Sunday. Offices were closed. Whoever was getting a massage was already inside; any diners at the Chinese restaurant were already seated.

Micah hurried along the street. The mummy couldn't possibly have changed so quickly.

Or maybe it had. Maybe the linens had been shed completely and the mummy was just a normal person now, enjoying a delicious bowl of lo mein.

Micah moved on down the street.

Yeah, by now, the mummy might be just a "normal" person.

But Micah was sure it was going to be a normal person he knew. And he was determined to find that person.

This time, he was chasing the damned mummy—person, whoever it was—to Jersey or Connecticut if he had to.

There! Up ahead.

The mummy was turning onto Fifth Avenue and heading north.

Micah started to run.

"Do you know who it was? Do you have any clue who it was?" Kieran asked Harley.

It had been a ridiculous, uncomfortable day. She was still half-naked, feeling embarrassed and exposed. Just because one *could* go topless according to NYC's equality laws, didn't mean she had any desire to do so! She was running through the crowd, Kieran keeping pace beside her, anxious to get to a car so she could go home and have a shower.

A taxi stopped for them when they made it over to Eighth Avenue. The driver grinned wolfishly at Harley, nodding when they gave him her address. A quick conversation with one of Craig's ME friends had assured them that Harley's going home for a shower would be fine; if the poison had touched only her clothing, there should be no problem, and of course, once the contaminated linen was analyzed, they'd know what they were looking at.

"We aren't even sure there *is* poison on the wrappings," Harley said.

"What do you want to bet?" Kieran asked her.

Harley didn't want to bet.

The mummy had taken her completely by surprise. She'd wanted to knock the thing in the head and rip the linen wrappings from it.

And instead...

It had touched her, and only Micah's arrival had kept her from contact with linen that was possibly doused in nicotine.

"How the hell is that damned mummy wearing poison and not dropping dead?" she demanded. The driver was staring back at her in his rearview mirror, even more interested than he'd been earlier. She leaned forward, ready to snap at him—and then didn't.

What the hell. She dropped back against the seat.

"Kieran, how is he or she doing it? All that poison?"

"Wearing something underneath the wrapping, I guess. We don't have anything analyzed yet, although I'm convinced that was actually an attempt on your life— or a warning for you to back off."

"Okay, so the mummy found me. But it looked as if the mummy was running through the crowd, touching anyone and everyone," Harley said.

"That was to stop the police or anyone in pursuit," Kieran told her.

"Hey!" Harley snapped. The taxi driver was grinning; he was about to take a roundabout route to her building. "No, go straight and then turn right!" she said.

"One-way street," the driver said in a singsong voice.

"And it's going the way we want it to!"

They reached their destination and Kieran paid the cabbie as they stepped out; Harley realized she was being rude.

"I'm sorry. Didn't mean to make you pay that!"

"Harley, that's the least of our concerns at the moment," Kieran said.

"They haven't called? Micah or Craig?"

"Harley, Micah was in hot pursuit and Craig was headed in to get those wrappings to the lab. It takes time.

We're here. Listen, just smile at the clerk or security guy on duty," Kieran advised. "He's staring at you just like the taxi driver was. Now let's get up to your place."

Harley did manage a nice smile for the security guard on duty. He was staring at her, as Kieran had said, but at the last minute sent her a confused smile in return.

Upstairs, Harley told Kieran to make herself comfortable, and Kieran said she would. Harley showered.

And showered, nearly scrubbing herself raw in the process.

She emerged from the shower, wrapped in a robe, and hurried downstairs.

Kieran was on the phone. She turned to look at Harley.

"Good call on Micah's part. Yes, those wrappings were soaked in nicotine."

There was something odd about the way she was speaking.

"What is it?"

"Micah followed the mummy on foot—all the way up to Central Park and the museum."

"The New Museum of Antiquity?" Harley said.

"Yes. And he found a mummy…half dead."

"Mummies *are* dead."

"No, I mean… I'm sorry, Harley. Arlo Hampton is probably going to die. He was found on the floor, stretched out in wrappings, right in front of the Temple of Ra."

CHAPTER SEVEN

THE SAME DAY Vivian Richter was released from the hospital, Arlo Hampton was rushed in, swiftly ripped out of torn swaths of mummy wrappings.

This whole thing was his fault, or so it appeared.

He was both the would-be killer—and his own victim, in the end.

At least, Harley thought, that was how it appeared. Or how it was *supposed* to appear.

It seemed evident that he'd dressed up as a mummy but carefully gloved his hands in plastic before soaking a number of loose and shredded strips of "decayed" linen in nicotine and then heading out to assault a "zombie" crowd. Afterward he'd returned to the museum, only to collapse there.

Perhaps he had started back in the Sahara. Perhaps his jealousy, his determination to rise in his field, had caused him to attack Henry Tomlinson back at the expedition prep tent. He must have attacked Vivian as a mummy. She'd blacked out and he had dressed her up and when she came to, he'd sent her, crazed, into the crowd, where she'd been saved.

Today…

No one really knew his intent. Had he just meant to poison a bunch of random "zombies"? Had he known, perhaps, that Joe Rosello was going to be among the actors? Had he thought Joe knew something and needed to be silenced?

He'd come up to Harley.

He had touched her with his poisoned linen rags.

But he couldn't have known Harley would be there; Harley hadn't even known that herself until the last minute. That seemed to make Joe the chosen target.

Unless, of course, Arlo Hampton had just wanted to indiscriminately poison people in the crowd. None of them could determine the truth as yet. And if Arlo died, they might never find out.

Arlo might be accused of killing Henry, or the attempted murder of Vivian—and intent to attack Joe Rosello and a number of innocent "zombies" in the crowd. But he'd calculated wrong; he hadn't taken the right care. He had not been immune to the poison he'd been trying to administer to others.

They knew this, because Craig gave them whatever information he could over the phone. He and Micah had managed to get to the museum quickly; in fact, Micah had reached it just minutes after everything happened. He'd pursued the mummy from Times Square!

Harley insisted that she and Kieran needed to get to the museum.

She didn't know why; she just knew the whole thing simply didn't feel right.

They got there fairly fast. Officers in uniform were maintaining crowd control—the entire museum had been closed down—but someone on duty recognized Kieran. Craig was summoned, and the two of them were let through with Craig leading the way past more officers, spectators, and a sea of media at the entry.

Arlo Hampton no longer there, of course; he'd been

rushed to the hospital. Photographers and crime scene technicians were still at work. Apparently, Arlo had been discovered by a pair of teenage girls who remained in a corner of the room, huddled together. They were still in shock. According to them, Arlo had grunted and tried to reach for them when they'd first found him, nearly giving them joint heart attacks. They'd now told their story a few times and were waiting for their parents.

Rydell and McGrady were there; it remained, after all, a joint investigation. They were with Craig and Micah, trying to create rational scenarios as to what might have happened.

Micah was looking at crime scene photos on his phone, photos snapped by the security guard first on the scene.

McGrady tried to stop Harley when she stepped forward to reach Micah.

"Ms. Frasier, I'm sorry, but you're in the way."

Micah immediately came to her defense. "She's got more degrees in criminology than the rest of us put together. She knew Arlo. She was stalked by him earlier and he tried to get to her at the zombie walk. Ms. Frasier may have something useful to say."

"What's there to say?" McGrady muttered. "He's probably going to die. We weren't there to get him to a hospital fast enough. Nicotine poisoning. Doc just said so—it's all over the wrappings. Jerk dressed up as a mummy for that damned zombie walk, and now he's dead by his own hand."

"It's not him," Harley said.

"What?" McGrady spun on her.

"That's not him—"

"Harley, it *is* Arlo Hampton," Craig interrupted, his tone firm as he frowned at her.

"Yes, Craig, I know Arlo's the one who was found here, but that's not the mummy who was at the zombie walk."

"Harley," Micah said slowly, "trust me. I've been running after him. Olympic-style running. I saw him when he turned north on Fifth. I followed this mummy from the zombie walk, and then I followed him down a bunch of streets, and I saw him go through the tunnel entrance to the museum. By the time I got through the maze down there and back up to the exhibit, those two teenagers were screaming." He was quiet for a minute. "Harley, it *had* to be him. We can't find any other mummies in the museum."

Harley blinked, looking at him.

"Yes, sorry, I know," Micah said, sounding aggravated and weary. "The museum's full of mummies. I mean living mummies. Living people dressed up as mummies. This place is crawling with security and we—"

"You're being an ass!"

He winced, and quickly apologized. "Yeah, sorry. I just don't see—"

"There are so many rooms and tunnels, and I'm telling you, this isn't the same mummy."

"What's different?" Micah asked her.

She didn't know! She couldn't tell. Judging by the photographs Craig and Micah had shown them, the wrappings appeared the same. True, the mummy walking through the crowd had been stripping off pieces of his wrapping, but that wasn't what bothered her, since Arlo's wrappings looked quite disheveled.

Somehow, this mummy—the mummy in the pictures, the Arlo Hampton mummy—was different. Not the wrappings so much, but...something.

"You think the cops are incompetent, Ms. Frasier?" McGrady turned his back on her.

Rydell shrugged apologetically.

"No, Detective, I think the cops are great. I've worked with lots of cops, including some of the ones here right now. Like I told you, I think they're great. You're not great. You've got a chip on your shoulder a mile wide."

"Harley," Micah said quietly.

"He's not just being patronizing and rude, he's jeopardizing an investigation!"

"Yes, that's true, but for the moment…"

"We're lead on this," Craig said.

"We need to start another search!" Micah announced, his voice booming.

"This is going to be reported," McGrady threatened.

"You bet," Micah promised him.

"Rydell, you saw it all."

"Yeah, I did," Rydell said.

Furious, McGrady stomped off. He seemed to be heading for the exit.

"Sorry," Harley murmured.

"No, you were in the right," Micah assured her. "Someone find me a blueprint of this place. Let's get on it. Every room, every display, every office. It's going to be a long day, folks. We're going to have to get down to the basement and below. Search everywhere."

A man in one of the crime scene jumpsuits approached Micah and Craig; they spoke for several minutes, and then a group of people in crime scene jumpsuits began to emerge from various corners of the exhibit. They were given instructions and dispersed, everyone going in a different direction.

"Micah?" Harley asked. "May I go to the museum

lab? I'd like to see what's been going on there. I swear to you, I'm not sure how I know, but I'm convinced that the mummy who confronted me in the street didn't look the same as those pictures of Arlo. Maybe I can find something in the lab."

"I'll keep her company," Kieran volunteered.

"All right. I'll inform the crime scene people," Micah told them. "I'm going down below. Arlo was the one who showed us all the basement tunnels and entrances and exits." He watched Harley as he spoke. She wondered if he believed her; he'd stood with her against McGrady, who was being such a jerk, but she had to wonder...

Just how many mummies could there be running around?

Living mummies, rather than the dead ones.

Micah turned away and spoke with the crime scene people again. She noticed that Detective Rydell hadn't gone with his partner; he was awaiting a discussion with Craig and Micah.

"Come on through. We're going to be searching the offices," one of the crime scene women told Harley and Kieran. "Just follow us."

As they left the exhibit space behind and came into an employee hallway, Harley saw that Gordon Vincent, director of the museum, was arguing with the crime scene people. He looked at Harley with annoyance and then pointed at her. "This whole exhibit has turned into a disaster."

Harley looked back at him, startled. "Mr. Vincent, I'm sorry you feel that way. I don't think the exhibit can be blamed for what this person's doing. The artifacts that were discovered are amazing, sir, and law enforcement will get to the bottom of this."

Kieran stepped forward, offering Vincent a hand, "How do you do, sir? We haven't actually met. I'm Kieran Finnegan, a psychologist with the offices of Fuller and Mira. They're psychiatrists who spend a great deal of time working with law enforcement. From my field of study, I'd guess that—sad though it is— these horrible events won't hurt your museum. On the contrary—this will cause an influx of membership and tourism. People love mummies…and mysteries. You're receiving unbelievable media attention, and while these days may be hard to weather, I believe that in the end you'll find that the museum itself is in an excellent position, no matter how discouraging a comment that might be on humanity."

Vincent turned to Kieran, blinking. "Fine. It's all closed for the day. Make sure the powers that be within the FBI and NYPD let me know if I can or cannot open my museum in all or part tomorrow!"

He strode on by them.

Harley looked at Kieran and laughed. "I'm not even sure what you said myself!"

"It worked, though. I guess that's what matters."

"You were excellent."

"You can be more excellent in this situation. You're so involved. You need to really think about the people who are connected to the exhibit, and how and why they might be acting a certain way. You know all the players, Harley, and you have to think about every one of them."

"Well," Harley said, "I guess we can let Joe Rosello off the hook. I'm almost positive that he was the intended victim today. But then I happened to be there. And who knows what was really planned, since—"

"Harley, are you absolutely sure that Arlo Hampton

wasn't the 'mummy' who came up to you at the zombie walk?"

"Kieran, I'm telling you, it wasn't him. And remember, Vivian Richter said a mummy came to her, and then, apparently, that mummy dressed her up as a mummy, too, in poisoned linen."

"I know," Kieran said. "But—"

"But that's the point, right? Vivian Richter was working in her office. A mummy came in and suddenly she's a mummy. Isn't it possible that the same thing happened today?"

"Of course," Kieran said. "But everyone's been searching...and they haven't found the stash of nicotine that's being used."

They reached the lab and walked through the outer entry; there were paper gowns and caps and booties to be worn inside the room.

"Really? Do we have to do all this?" Kieran muttered.

Harley laughed. "Yes! It helps prevent the spread of anything, any bacteria, that might be on antique, long-buried objects from getting out into the world. And it keeps us from bringing in anything that might be harmful to very old stuff."

"Okay, makes sense," Kieran said grudgingly.

"What I really want to do is get to Arlo's desk over there. The small one. See?"

Kieran nodded and followed Harley's actions as she suited up, donned gloves and booties, and then headed into the actual lab.

"What bothers me about this is the lack of clear motive," Kieran said. "It should be obvious, right in front of our faces. These people are dedicated to their work. It means as much to them as anything else in their lives.

Maybe more. Most of us live for our mate, spouse, and so on, first—or our children. The instinct to protect a child is strong, except when you're talking about a person who's truly mentally impaired. But in our type of science, in psychiatry and criminology, you come across people who are more devoted to their work than to family or friends."

"Yes, and we think someone was terribly jealous of Henry—which is why he was killed. Now it seems that someone is trying to kill Vivian and Arlo—who are also hardworking and respected members of the Egyptology community. But…"

"But what?"

"I know I keep saying this, but I don't believe that Arlo and the mummy on the street were the same person. I just don't believe it. And Arlo was the one to walk Micah and me all around this place the other day. Do you think…?"

"Think what?"

"There's another motive? There's something we're missing?"

"Of course. That's always possible."

"Love, hate, greed, jealousy. Vengeance," Harley murmured.

"Ah, vengeance. For what? And against whom?"

Harley made her way to the small aluminum desk in the far corner of the room. It was made so it could be constantly sterilized, but still allow for a notepad, pens, tablet, computer or whatever else the scientists and lab techs might need to accurately notate their work.

She opened the first drawer, which held a large plastic container of sanitary wipes.

She opened the second drawer. There was an unused notepad and a case of pencils.

There should've been a computer somewhere. A tablet. Even a voice recorder.

There was not.

Harley opened the third drawer. And there she saw, shoved against the back, a small, almost archaic, flip phone.

She pulled it out and studied it carefully. It had the look of a phone that might be bought at any convenience or drug store—pay as you go. She hit key after key; nothing on it denoted ownership. She went to contacts.

Her own number was there, along with the numbers of others who'd been on the expedition.

"Kieran," she said slowly.

"You found something?"

Harley looked up at her. "Maybe. I think I may just have found a way to reach our liaison, Yolanda, who hasn't been seen since the night of the party. And I think we might have a connection to our long-missing interpreter, Satima Mahmoud."

"In 1524, New York was called New Angoulême by the Italian explorer Giovanni da Verrazzano," Micah said to Craig as they traveled deep into the underbelly of the museum. "The first recorded exploration by the Dutch was in 1609. In 1664, English frigates arrived and demanded the surrender of the city. Peter Stuyvesant sent lawyers to arrange the capitulation—the Dutch and the English liked to go at it in those days. Well, come to think of it, over the years most European powers went after another. Anyway, it was in 1665 that the city became New York under English rule."

"A lecture on New York history while we're looking

for mummies—which happen to be a good bit older than the city," Craig said.

"True, but my point is that although it's not old in comparison with some cities in Africa, the Middle East, the Far East and Europe, New York *is* old. And while it all started downtown—Wall Street, Broad Street and so on—it's been many years since people came up to this area by subway. And down here in these tunnels, especially with so many routes now abandoned, it's just a jungle."

"Yep. And hey, love my city and all…but you just gave away the fact that you were some mean historian before you were a special agent."

"Actually, I'm complaining. This is like looking for a needle in a haystack," Micah said, and he sighed, leaning back against a wall to catch his breath.

He nearly fell backward.

"What the hell?"

"Hey!"

Craig made a grab for Micah's arm; Micah caught hold of him just in time to keep from plunging through a decayed section of wall.

They both half fell and half stumbled into the remains of an old subway tunnel.

The posters on the walls were peeling, but they were magnificent; they advertised Broadway shows opening in the 1930s. There were stairways to nowhere crafted of wrought iron and beautifully designed.

"There!" Micah said, gesturing with one hand at something extremely modern that marred the time-travel look of the place.

In a corner where plaster and paneling had decayed with time, there was a pile of insecticide containers.

At least fifty of them.

Enough poison to kill… God alone knew how many people.

"There has to be some evidence there, right? *Something?*" Harley asked anxiously.

She was seated at a corner table at Finnegan's, along with Micah, Craig and Kieran. Crime scene crews had gone into the offshoot of the abandoned subway station, and they were studying every piece of evidence—primarily the containers of insecticide—with every technique available to them to find out who had used them. Or at least where and when they'd been purchased.

No one had answered when they'd tried to reach Yolanda Akeem or Satima Mahmoud; Egan had people working the phones as well, trying to find a way to pin down the locations of the women's phones via the contact information.

Now it was a matter of waiting.

And it was still Sunday. Although it was late, they had friends in the kitchen, so they were able to enjoy Sunday's traditional roast.

"Here's the thing. We've known that Yolanda Akeem was here in New York. She was at the museum when everything happened with Vivian," Harley said. "And after they questioned her briefly, she left."

"She was visible on security footage," Micah reminded her.

"I think we definitely have a problem, and everyone's part of it—the museum and the Egyptian Department of Antiquities, as well as our government and their government," Craig said. "The truth was left to slide."

"Murder is ugly. No one wants a part of it," Micah murmured to Harley.

"Were any artifacts stolen?" Kieran asked.

"No. Not that I know of," Harley replied. "And what about the motives for any of this? Jealousy, as we already discussed? I keep thinking that a longing for glory seems obvious. Too obvious? The people who would've been jealous of Henry were Arlo and Vivian—and they were the ones who were attacked."

"And you don't think I was an intended victim?" Joe Rosello asked. "Rather than you?"

Harley looked up and smiled. Joe and Kevin had arrived together, all cleaned up and out of their zombie makeup.

Micah and Craig had risen; Kevin brought a couple of extra chairs to draw up to their table and then left, telling Joe he was going to arrange for two more meals.

"You *were* an intended victim," Micah told Joe flatly. "Had to be. The culprit couldn't have known that Harley was going to be there. Harley didn't know it herself until she talked to Kieran and found out about the zombie walk and that *you'd* be there."

"But...we should be safe, shouldn't we? I heard Arlo was the culprit and that he's in the hospital—and they don't know if they can save him or not."

"It's true that Arlo is in the hospital. And many people believe he was the mummy and that he was guilty of trying to kill Vivian. She did, after all, say that a mummy had come to her."

"Was there time for the mummy to have reached the museum and attacked someone else to create a new mummy?" Kieran asked.

"You did say that you were right behind him, getting to the museum," Harley said.

"I'm afraid that yes, there was time. I followed the mummy, but I was still some distance away when I saw him go down to the basement area of the museum. Then, of course, I stumbled around down there myself for a while. They need to wall all of that off, because if they don't, they're going to lose some curious fifth-grader down there one day."

"I'm taking a leave from my job," Joe said. "I'm getting out of here tomorrow morning. When this is all over, I'll come back. I called the museum I'm working at and they understood."

"That might be your best move," Micah told him.

Joe let out a long sigh. "Thank God! I thought you were going to tell me I wasn't allowed to leave town."

"We'll need your contact information. However, you were in full sight of thousands of people most of the day. It would be very hard to prove you had any involvement," Craig said.

"Thank God," he muttered again.

Kevin Finnegan returned to the table. The talk shifted back and forth between the zombie walk and the situation at the museum.

Suddenly they all seemed to realize it had grown very late.

"I'm going home so I can get out of here in the morning," Joe said. "You all take care."

"We need to know where you'll be and how to reach you," Craig said.

"You bet. Just no sharing anything that's gone on," Joe said.

"No sharing," they all swore at once.

"I take it you're getting Harley home?" Craig asked Micah.

Kieran looked at Harley—who refused to look back at her.

She didn't know. *Was* he seeing her home? She'd thrown herself at him last night; maybe he'd changed his mind about her during the very long day.

"Yes, I'll make sure she gets home safely," Micah said. He managed to keep a straight face. Harley was surprised that he could.

Actually, she was surprised that she didn't flush. She just smiled sweetly at Kieran, who was obviously amused, intrigued and, Harley hoped, glad that she and Micah seemed to be getting on very well, indeed.

As he drove her home, there was so much to say; so much speculation in which they could indulge.

But they didn't talk at all.

The minute they reached Harley's place and closed the door to her apartment, they were in each other's arms. Micah impatiently shed his Glock first; Harley shrugged out of her jacket, grabbing for his shirt as she tore at her own buttons.

Micah drew the shirt over her head before she could get to the last of the buttons. She had her hands on his waistband and his belt buckle, while their lips merged in a deep and fiery kiss that was also sweet and breathless and filled with laughter.

There was a fair amount of awkwardness that went along with stripping so quickly, with wanting nothing more than to touch, to feel, to kiss…

Clothing wound up strewn all over the floor.

Harley hoped there was no one on the street as she raced past the windows and headed for the stairway.

Micah caught up with her. He swept her into his arms.

"Oh, no! You can't…they're winding stairs. We'll end up—"

"I can do it this way!" he assured her, tossing her over his shoulder.

And he could. He made it up the winding stairway. Dropped her naked on the bed and fell beside her. Still panting, he raised himself on one elbow.

Harley pushed him back down.

She rained kisses over his naked body, reaching all around, taking him into her mouth.

He lifted her up, pulled her to him, rolled with her, kissed and teased and took his kisses everywhere until she cried out. They kissed and laughed in the tangled sheets, and then they were locked together again and the laughter was gone. They were too breathless, too desperate…

This was new. So new. It had been a long time since she'd chanced a relationship with anyone. It was wonderful because…

Because it was wonderful.

She knew with an indefinable certainty that it would always be good with him. They were so easy together. They could laugh, even do silly things, and those things somehow became erotic. She wanted to forget the world and curl up next to him forever, except that one could never really forget the world.

And, of course, that was it.

She could be with him—as if he were an oasis—and still talk about the burning sands and the desert around them. She could make love, hot and wickedly wet and exciting—and she could still tell him what she was thinking. They could share confidences and exchange opinions without any risk of betrayal.

She was in lust…and maybe falling in love.

"She knows something," Micah was saying. "I'm sure she does."

"She? Which she? Vivian, Belinda, Yolanda or Satima?" Harley asked. She propped herself up on an elbow to look down at him.

"Satima. I mean Satima," he said. "As for Yolanda, I think she just wants to keep her nose clean. She hates it that something connected to the Department of Antiquities has negative baggage attached to it. I'd swear she just doesn't want to get involved with the ugliness of it. Egan is working the diplomatic channel to get her to come and talk to us. As far as we can tell, she's still in the States. She may not have anything for us, but I'd still love to talk to her myself."

"McGrady could have turned her off American law enforcement forever and ever," Harley said.

"Sad thing is, he might have been a decent cop. You don't get to be a detective unless you come up through the ranks or know someone. He has no patience."

"And no ability with people," Harley put in.

Micah shrugged. "I want to talk to the missing girl, Satima, as well. And now we have a number for her that we didn't have before—thanks to you knowing where to dig. So to speak."

"Ah, yes…dig. The crime scene people would've found that phone. I don't know why Arlo had it where he did—or why he thought he needed a special phone."

"It's a chip phone, good around the world. Maybe that was the intent," Micah suggested. He sighed, bringing her closer. "I keep feeling we're looking at a giant puzzle and we should be able to see what it is, what the whole picture represents. Except there's one piece missing. If only we had that piece."

"We will have that piece," Harley said confidently. "You and Craig, the FBI, NYPD. You'll find that piece. It's like…"

Her voice trailed off.

"Like?"

"Well, you know my main role in the expedition was to find more clues as to what might have happened to Amenmose. He was murdered. He was buried hastily by someone who loved him. There are many suspects, of course. He was a threat to Ay, who was regent for Tut, and who did become pharaoh in his own right. He was also despised by Tut's sister and brother-in-law. But nothing I've found in any of the ancient stories or records suggests that one of those people killed him. He had a family, and servants, so I guess the suspects are endless. I feel the same way about that as you do—as we both do—about our current case. Suspects everywhere, but it seems impossible to get the real motive pinned down. Or to determine the whereabouts of each suspect at the crucial times."

"Process of elimination," Micah said. "Joe Rosello. People did see him all day long."

"Vivian Richter. She got out of the hospital late that morning."

"I'd still like to find out if she was home the rest of the day!"

"But…"

"Something might occur to her," Micah said.

"Everyone, including you, seems to believe that Arlo

Hampton is guilty. That he poisoned himself trying to poison others."

"Hey, I keep an open mind! You say the mummy who touched you on the street was someone different. I believe you."

"We don't know where Jensen Morrow was today. Or Belinda."

"Or—at this moment—Vivian or Ned Richter. Or Roger Eastman. But we'll know soon."

"We will?"

He smiled at her. "Of course. Craig and I are just cogs in a giant machine, a machine that doesn't stop. Anyway, I agree with you. Something still isn't right. First thing I want is a conversation with Satima Mahmoud. Then Ned and Vivian Richter. Then..."

"It's about motive," Harley said.

"Motive," he repeated.

He was done talking.

He pulled her back into his arms.

And she lost herself in the feel of him against her.

CHAPTER EIGHT

MICAH WOKE TO the sound of his phone ringing—some-where.

He remembered that he'd shed his clothing downstairs.

He leaped out of bed and hurried down the winding wrought iron staircase, glancing at the picture windows that looked out over the night, the city and Grace Church.

He sped across the room, thinking they had to re-member to buy drapes—major drapes—before night fell again. Of course, that was being presumptuous, but...

He couldn't force his thoughts in any other direction.

His phone. He dived for his jacket and caught it on the eighth ring.

"Fox."

"Fox!" It was Richard Egan. "We have Yolanda Akeem down here. She's going to be returning to Egypt later this morning. She's with a friend of mine from the State De-partment. I suggest you get in quickly. I'll inform Fra-sier, too."

"Yes, sir!"

Micah turned off the phone and ran around finding the rest of his clothing. He tore up the stairs.

Harley was sleepily beginning to rise.

"What is it?" she asked anxiously. "It's not even seven," she murmured. "I guess that's not so early."

"I have to go. Now. They've got Yolanda down at the

FBI office. She's leaving for Egypt, and she's with someone from the State Department."

"Go!"

He ran for the shower. She didn't follow him.

They both knew why that wouldn't be a good idea.

In a few minutes he was dressed and heading for the stairs. Harley had slipped into a robe to accompany him down. "We should've set coffee to brew last night," she murmured, opening the door so he could leave.

He paused to kiss her quickly on the lips.

"We weren't thinking about coffee. Personally, I'd forgo the coffee for what we did last night. I'll call you as soon as I know anything. You're not working today, are you?"

"No, nothing for Fillmore," Harley said. "Maybe I'll hang around and read for a while."

"Sounds good. Talk soon," he promised.

Then he was out the door. The office wasn't far, and once there, he could leave the car with a young agent in the street. No more than thirty minutes had passed since he'd answered his phone to Egan, but he couldn't help being a little afraid Yolanda might already have left.

She was returning home; this was his chance.

To his great relief, she was there. He learned from the receptionist that Egan was with her in the conference room. He hurried there—just in time to fall in step with Craig Frasier, who'd arrived, as well.

"Think she has anything?" Craig asked hopefully.

"Your guess is as good as mine." Micah shrugged. "But anything she does have might be worthwhile."

"Too true, when we keep stumbling in the dark. Literally. In the basement and below at the museum."

"Someone knows the museum—and knows it well."

They'd reached the conference room. When they entered, Egan and the handsomely dressed man who had accompanied Yolanda Akeem rose to meet them. Yolanda started to rise; they quickly urged her to remain seated.

"Gentlemen, Ms. Yolanda Akeem and Mr. Tom Duffy from the State Department," Egan said. "Special Agents Craig Frasier and Micah Fox."

Everyone sat then.

"Thank you for being here," Micah told Yolanda. "We know you don't have to speak with us. We're grateful that you're willing to do so."

Yolanda Akeem was an attractive woman, probably approaching fifty. Her eyes and skin were dark, a testament to a rich and diverse background. Her appearance was dignified, almost regal.

She nodded. "I would have spoken earlier, if I'd thought I had something of value to say," she said. She wrinkled her nose. "I spoke with that silly policeman when Vivian Richter was attacked. He wanted to know if I believed that mummies could come to life—if I thought that curses were real! They *are* real, of course, when we are cursed with foolish people!"

"We weren't in charge of the investigation then, Ms. Akeem," Egan said.

"Yes, I know. And I spoke with Special Agent Fox before, when we were both reeling from the loss of a dear friend." Yolanda Akeem looked over at Micah and smiled sadly. "So, so sad. So much trouble. Such a terrible time."

"Yes, a terrible time," Micah agreed.

Yolanda waved a hand in the air. "Everyone running and rushing—and Henry barely cold. And then, of course—the insurrection! Children mewling that they are not privileged enough. A mountain out of a molehill. But…safety first, always. Yes, it's a tough world and there are very real terrors and threats. But in this case…"

"Yes."

"My friend, Special Agent Fox, believes that something about this entire situation, and about the tentative conclusions we've managed to reach, isn't right," Craig said. "Frankly, we may be looking too hard at the wrong suspects."

Yolanda Akeem hesitated. "I wish I could say, 'No, you're wrong.' But, you see, there's a bad taste in my mouth, although I don't understand why. The expedition was going well, or at least I thought so. Henry had worked in my country many times before. We loved him. And his students…they were charming. I was happy to work with them, too. The people from Alchemy…well, I overheard them having arguments with each other over money now and then. How much was being spent, where they needed to save. Of course, it was funny because Mr. Richter was the on-site CEO for the company and he was watching pennies, while his wife… She's a true dreamer and scientist, I believe. Money meant nothing to her." She grinned. "Henry ignored them all. Arlo Hampton tried to remind everyone that *he* was the main Egyptologist for Alchemy. Still, despite the little spats, it all seemed to be going well enough. But then… Henry died."

"You were at the camp that night?"

"I was. Belinda was going to go into town with Harley and Jensen, but she's engaged, you know. They will marry soon, I hope. Video chatting with her fiancé was a highlight for both of them. Belinda used my equipment for her chats. I was doing paperwork, and she was with me."

Micah glanced at Craig. It seemed that they could

definitely scratch Belinda off any list that had to do with Henry's death.

"But you saw Henry."

"I saw Henry. Just for a few minutes early in the evening. I also saw our young interpreter, Satima Mahmoud, with Mr. Rosello. Joe, yes, Joe Rosello."

Micah nodded. Joe was already off their list. He'd been on the zombie walk—and he'd been costumed as a zombie, not a mummy.

He couldn't believe he was even thinking that way!

Yolanda suddenly frowned. "Perhaps trouble was in the air. I heard Satima arguing with Joe. They didn't usually argue. They were beautiful people, you know? Both of them. But that night Satima was tired. She just wanted to go home. Joe kept saying that he wanted to finish the work. She said the work wouldn't go away, and she had family she had to see. So it was…a hot, troubled evening. Yes, hot in the desert, of course. But the Richter husband and wife were arguing, and Satima and Joe were arguing. Henry was busy with his new treasures. Arlo wanted a bigger role, and I think he saw Henry as a means to that end, but he knew he had to leave him at some time. He was testy… That evening I wanted nothing more to do with any of them. Satima was…almost nasty to me! If I'd hired her, I would have fired her right then and there. I speak many languages. My father was Egyptian, but my mother was Mexican and French. I can interpret nicely. I wish I'd been the one doing that job."

She looked at them all and released a long breath.

"I will admit that I wasn't crazy about Vivian Richter, but I'm sorry she was hurt. Arlo… I'm sorry he was hurt, too. After Henry's death, he got his own way with Alchemy and the exhibit, but he did not seem like a bad person. Did he do all this? Why? For position? For glory? They say that he is going to die, most likely. He was not found as quickly as Vivian."

"We don't know if he was guilty," Egan said. "Or if he was a victim."

Yolanda shook her head. "I'm sorry. I know nothing more. And I did not mean to be...unhelpful. You may feel free to call me with more questions if you wish. I am returning to Cairo, but I will be accessible to you, if I can be of any more help."

Everyone rose, bidding one another goodbye.

Then the man from the State Department and the Egyptian liaison were gone. Egan, Craig and Micah were left to look at one another.

"This is the first I've heard of everyone fighting," Micah said. "Even when I was in Cairo, it didn't come up. Of course, everything was chaos then."

"That could explain," Craig began, "why Ned Richter wasn't sitting at his wife's side the entire time she was in the hospital. If they'd been fighting, I mean."

"And maybe he wasn't with her yesterday," Egan said. "Check into it. And also, we've got people hot on the trail of the interpreter, Satima Mahmoud. Let's hope they'll be able to find her. They work hard at keeping up good communications with the police, here and abroad."

"What about Arlo Hampton?" Micah asked. "Anything? He made it through the night?"

"He's alive, yes, hanging on. Unconscious," Egan said. "Doctors... Well, I'm used to speaking with medical examiners. Seems I understand them a lot better than the guys who treat the living. Anyway, Arlo Hampton's still alive but they're not sure about neurological impact."

"The guy could end up a vegetable," Craig said.

"He could pull through all the way. They had to put him in a medically induced coma. When they bring him out of that, we might learn something. Anyway, he's alive, but he's sure as hell not going to be working soon," Egan said.

"Let's trust that he makes it," Micah said quietly.

"I guess maybe we should try speaking with Ned Richter and Joe Rosello again," Craig said.

"Rosello came out squeaky clean," Egan reminded them.

"Yes, but I don't think our missing interpreter is so squeaky clean," Micah said.

"You really think this Egyptian woman—who isn't even in this country—is involved?" Egan asked, puzzled.

"Yes. But I haven't figured out how. She can't be found. I'm hoping that doesn't mean she's dead," Micah said.

"Joe wasn't playing a mummy yesterday. We know that. But I agree with Micah," Craig said. "It'll be interesting as hell to find out what was going on between him and Satima Mahmoud."

"I'M SO SORRY. You sound terribly depressed," Harley told Jensen.

He'd called early, right around eight. Of course, by eight, half of New York was already bustling, but with no real plans, Harley had actually thought she'd be able to sleep in.

And simply enjoy the fact that she lay in sheets where they'd been together, where Micah's scent still lingered.

But she was glad to hear from Jensen; he was still trying to function, despite all else.

"Well, of course, I'm depressed," Jensen Morrow said

over the phone. "Cops all over the place. It's necessary, I guess. Vivian came around fast—got better, survived!—but I understand Arlo's in bad shape. On the other hand, if Arlo did kill Henry and tried to kill Viv, he deserves whatever's happening to him."

"I don't think he did it, Jensen. He didn't commit any crimes yesterday, at any rate. I saw the mummy in the street, or *a* mummy in the street, and—"

She broke off. She suddenly knew what had been different about the mummy in the street and the pictures of Arlo Hampton as a mummy, passed out, almost dead, on the museum floor.

She wasn't sure it would be wise to share that information with anyone other than Micah, Craig and the police.

Jensen didn't seem to notice that she'd abruptly stopped speaking. "I'm here at work," he continued. "Let's see, Ned Richter is due in, and—you're not going to believe this!—Vivian Richter is coming with him. She's barely out of the hospital. She may be a bitch on wheels, but she's a trouper, I'll give her that. The woman loves her Egyptology! Needless to say, Arlo won't be here. And it's lonely without him. None of our buds are around. Belinda and Roger are busy with their own work. Talked to Joe—he left town this morning. He's scared. He thinks the mummy in the crowd was after him. And that might be true. Who knows? But if the mummy *was* Arlo, then none of us has anything to worry about. Right?"

The mummy in the street had not been Arlo Hampton. Arlo was tall. The mummy hadn't been very tall.

"Jensen, I don't think Arlo was guilty of anything."

"Some criminologist you are! You want to believe the best about everyone," Jensen muttered. "Are you going to come in and keep me company and help me ward off mummies?" he asked.

"I—I was going to spend some time with Craig's girl-friend."

"The lovely Kieran. So the two of you are going to dig deep into all our minds and figure out which one of us is the sicko? Whoever it is has to be crazy as a bat. I can see the defense in court. 'The bacteria made me do it!'"

Harley couldn't help smiling. "Defense attorneys. It's their job. But, yes, bacteria. It can affect the mind."

"Should I leave town?" Jensen asked her seriously. "Man, I love this place. I know I can come off as a jerk sometimes, but I love this city and this museum. I loved the expedition, too—until Henry was killed. But I can't let all our work fall apart, Harley. It meant too much to Henry. And it's too important for future generations."

"You're right," Harley agreed. "The cops—"

"Are idiots. Whoops, sorry. Maybe the Feds are better."

"Killers make mistakes—and they get caught," Harley said.

"And sometimes they don't."

"This time, they will."

"You haven't seen the half of it. The stuff here, Harley, it's ironic that it all started with a murder, isn't it? Amenmose, I mean. Maybe you can figure out who killed the guy. That was the major thing for you on our expedition, right?"

"Yep. I still find it incredibly interesting that he was killed, and yet he was rewarded with the kind of tomb that would allow him to move into the afterlife," Harley said.

"Come in today! I'll meet you at the doors. You'll be safe. Lots of cops around. I'll get you any piece of research material you want that I can find! I'll be like your apprentice!" Jensen said.

"Okay," Harley agreed. "I'll text you when I'm at the entrance."

She ended the call and glanced around the room, running her hands over the sheets. So much for luxuriating in memory.

She hurriedly showered and ran out, anxious to get to the subway and up to the museum.

Despite herself, she found that she kept scrutinizing the crowds of people who thronged around her. It was still morning rush hour. People were everywhere, on their way to work and school.

She was looking for a mummy, she realized.

That was ridiculous, she thought. And yesterday, it didn't seem bizarre at all that there'd be a mummy around; a mummy fit right in with the zombies.

Rush hour on Monday. Not likely that a mummy would be running around. Then again, it was New York, and people might see a mummy and merely shrug.

No mummies appeared—and she had to admit she was grateful.

As she neared the museum, she texted Jensen. He texted back that he'd meet her at the entrance.

Jensen and an NYPD officer were at the door; Jensen explained who she was and Harley showed the officer her ID.

She was allowed to come in.

It felt strange to walk through the entry with Jensen when everything was so empty. He told her there were at least ten police officers in the building, along with what he believed were "fledgling" FBI agents—probably bored to tears, but assigned to watch over the museum. Jensen talked about the museum itself with great enthusiasm; he just couldn't resist. She already knew that the facility was devoted to ancient civilizations, from Mesopotamia to Rome to Greece and ancient Egypt and other societies. He explained that he considered it a homage to humanity creating civilization; there was even a wonderful new section on the development of humans, back to the hominidae or great apes speciating from the ancestors of the lesser apes. "When this is…when this is solved, when things are back to normal, when life at least *feels* normal, you really have to come and spend a day here, just touring around, checking out the exhibits. It's a phenomenal museum. And I'm so happy to be here, except now the rest of the scientists, curators, historians—and even the café and gift shop employees!—hate us."

"Oh, I doubt that."

"Nope. It's true."

"When life does get back to normal, they won't hate you. And, as we've noted before, I'll bet all the insanity's going to make the museum more popular than ever. It has a really wicked mystery story now," Harley reminded him.

"Well, anyway, let's head back. In one of the prep clean rooms, there are some papers Henry'd been working on. Plus, there are a number of mummies in the room—still in their coffins, for the most part, except for our 'screaming' mummy, the one we saw with Henry before he…died. Anyway, I have a meeting with the museum director in a few minutes."

"Gordon Vincent," Harley murmured.

Jensen nodded. He glanced her way and sighed. "Yeah. They don't know if Arlo's going to make it or not. If he does, I heard he's probably going to be arrested."

"He didn't do it," Harley said again.

"But—"

"I'm telling you. He was a victim. Like Vivian."

"Well, from your lips to God's ears, right? Anyway—and honestly, I wouldn't want something to come about this way—I believe I'm going to be promoted to curator director for the Amenmose exhibit."

"Oh. Wow," Harley murmured. "Congratulations. Well, I guess… I mean, I understand, no one would want things to work this way, but wasn't Arlo employed by Alchemy?"

"Yes, but he was being offered the permanent position here," Jensen said.

They walked by the temple and the exhibits that were usually open to the public, then went to the employee section of the museum and one of the rooms next to Arlo's lab.

"It's mainly artifacts," Jensen said. "But that desk has boxes of Henry's notes. No one could read his scribbled handwriting as well as you could. Maybe you'll find something. I'll come back as soon as the meeting's over and we can go to lunch. Not in the museum, I'm afraid, since everything is closed down today. But I'm sure we can think of someplace you'll like."

"How about the sandwich shop over on Sixth?" Harley suggested. "It's a five-minute walk."

He gave her a thumbs-up and left. She listened as the door clicked shut.

This room didn't require "clean" suits, but it was climate-controlled. Harley assumed it would be taken for granted that anyone in the room would have complete respect for ancient sarcophagi, bodies and other artifacts.

For a moment, she just looked around.

Many things were still crated. There were just so many artifacts that they were switched in and out of the display. Some of the sarcophagi—the magnificent, beautifully designed and painted outer coffins—had been unpacked. They'd withstood time and climate well, since they were made of hardwood and precious metals.

Shelves on the wall held numerous canopic jars; others were heaped with jewelry. One shelf contained dozens of statuettes and, carefully set in a corner of the room, was a pile of chariot wheels, the body of a chariot and a set of harnesses.

Another shelf held several mummified cats.

Yet another held weapons, some of them simple, having belonged to rank-and-file soldiers. There were maces, shields, daggers, swords, knives and more. Some were inlaid with precious jewels and gold.

They were worth a small fortune.

But to the best of Harley's knowledge, nothing had ever disappeared from the museum.

The motive for murder wasn't for treasure. So it seemed, anyway. Then why...?

She shook her head. It was like a puzzle, as Micah had said—with one crucial missing piece. But if you could find all the pieces and put them together, a picture would emerge.

A picture from the past? Perhaps. And what might that have to do with the present? Probably nothing at all. But then again, sometimes just turning one's mind to a different puzzle helped solve the one that was more pressing.

Harley examined the many offerings in the room that would eventually be cataloged and join other treasures on the museum floor. Then she moved to the cheap aluminum desk—with the cheap aluminum chair in front of it—that was piled high with cardboard boxes of Henry Tomlinson's observations and recordings. They ranged from his calculations as to where they would find the tomb, to his reactions the day they discovered it. If she knew Henry, the boxes were also stuffed with research papers and anything else he'd found or received that complemented his own work.

Harley sat down and began to read.

Surely, museum staff had at least scanned them before this.

But maybe they hadn't read everything. Maybe they hadn't known Henry.

Maybe they hadn't been determined to catch a killer.

NED AND VIVIAN RICHTER had a house—a Victorian manor in Brooklyn, in the Williamsburg area, not far from the Pratt Institute.

"Swanky," Craig murmured, ringing the bell.

"It is nice," Micah agreed. "When I was around here several years ago on that special assignment I worked with you, this area was still kind of sketchy. Lots of drugs and crime—and 'swanky' places like this were usually turned into frat houses or apartment buildings with dozens of closet-size apartments."

"This area has come up in the world—and someone's put real money into this house. But Richter's been a CEO on expeditions with Alchemy. I guess he's earned plenty of bonuses and more through the years," Craig said.

"I guess so."

Craig rang the bell again.

"What do you want to bet a maid's going to answer?" Micah asked.

"I wouldn't bet against you!" Craig replied.

"Nothing wrong with being rich," Micah said. "I'd love to try it one day."

They were right; the door was opened by a pretty young woman in a maid's outfit that would've done any movie set proud.

"May I help you?" she asked. She had a strong accent, possibly Slavic.

They showed their badges.

"We need to see Mr. and Mrs. Richter, please," Micah told her.

The woman pursed her lips. "You are aware, sir, that Mrs. Richter is just out of the hospital," she said.

"Yes, we are aware. We plan to be brief," Craig assured her.

She led them into a parlor that looked like a furniture showroom. Micah wondered if anyone had ever been in the room before.

But they were only there a minute or two before Vivian Richter made an appearance. "Gentlemen. What can I do for you? I'm about to head into the museum. With everything that's been going on... Well, I keep thinking that maybe someone's out to sabotage the exhibit. I keep going over our books, our notes—and, of course, our artifacts. I'm saying 'our.' They aren't ours, as I'm sure you realize. Everything we discovered will be returned to Egypt. We're not thieves anymore. There was a time, though... Did you know that during the Victorian era, mummies were so plentiful they were often used as kindling? That's shocking, isn't it?"

"I think I've heard that somewhere," Micah said.

"Well, anyway...how can I help you? Would you like to come into the museum with me?"

"Actually, we'd like to know where you were yesterday, once you got out of the hospital, and if you were with your husband all day. We'd like to speak with him, too."

"Ned's already gone to the museum. But in answer to your question, he was with me all day. He's a devoted husband."

"When did he leave?" Micah asked. "This morning, I mean."

"A little while ago, I believe," Vivian said.

"You *believe*? You didn't actually see him?" Craig asked.

"I spent yesterday and this morning sleeping, resting. I know when my husband's with me. I can feel his presence. Are either of you married? No? You see, after years of marriage, you don't need to *see*, gentlemen—you *feel*. You're both still young. Wait until you've been married for years. You'll understand what I'm talking about."

Vivian Richter was dressed in an attractive, business-like pantsuit; she looked very thin and a little flushed, but otherwise well.

"Agents, why exactly are you questioning me?" she said to them. "I'm a victim. And you can't possibly suspect Ned of any wrongdoing! The whole expedition rested on his shoulders. He wouldn't want anything to go wrong."

"Our apologies, but questioning is necessary, under the circumstances," Micah said.

"Part of the job," Craig added ruefully.

"Oh, please!" Vivian said. "Agent Fox, I heard that you saved my life! And you, Agent Frasier, have been hard at work on the case. I'm grateful to you both, although—due to my recent bout with near death—I haven't had much chance to socialize with law enforcement."

"Mrs. Richter, I can't take credit for saving your life.

Anyone there would have dialed 911," Micah said. "We're just glad to see you looking so well."

"Yes! I thank God!" she said. "Great hospital staff, wonderful EMTs... I'm a very lucky woman. I understand I was poisoned with insecticide but apparently, according to the doctors, there's been an upsurge in problems of that kind because of the liquid nicotine used in electronic cigarettes. They hit me with activated charcoal, and they monitored me for seizures. I was lucky, so lucky. I hear Arlo may not fare as well, that he was exposed to a heavier dose of poison and that he was unconscious when he was found. But I also heard that the police believe Arlo was guilty. That he might've been the 'mummy' who attacked me. Who meant to kill me!" she ended in a whisper. "Arlo and I... We worked well together. I thought so, anyway. I wonder if he was worried because I'm married to Ned. Maybe he was worried that would put me in a better position for a raise at Alchemy. And I realize that some people are convinced that Henry was killed... I never knew what to think. I mean, we had to run! There was death coming at us from the desert!"

"Of course," Micah said sympathetically. "So, you believe we'll find Ned at the museum now?"

"Yes. He should be there working."

"But he didn't actually tell you he was going in. And you didn't actually see him," Craig said.

"No, as I was telling you..."

"Yes. You felt him. When's the last time you *saw* him?" Micah asked.

"I, uh... Yesterday's a bit of a blur for me. We left the hospital and then—"

"He came to the hospital to get you," Micah inserted.

"I told you! He's a loving and devoted husband," Vivian said. "Yes! He came to get me. I'm going to call your superiors, gentlemen, if you suggest once more that he's anything less than a wonderful man."

"You still didn't answer the question," Craig pointed out.

"All right! I don't know what time he left this morning. I know he was going to the museum. And he knew, of course—" She suddenly stopped speaking.

"Yes?" Micah prompted.

"I knew he was going into the museum, and he knew I was coming in later today. With everything that went on, and cops, technicians, crime scene people everywhere... I need to see to the integrity of our entire exhibit—especially in light of what happened to Arlo!"

"We'll see that you get there safely, Mrs. Richter," Craig offered. "We have a company car, so we can drop you off at the museum. However, considering what you've been through, I recommend you contact one of the policemen on duty there today. I think you should be under protection."

"I'll make a call," Micah said.

"It's not necessary to request protection," Vivian said. "Honestly, I'll be fine. Now I know to watch out for people coming near me."

"I'll make a call," Micah repeated firmly.

Vivian smiled. "Thank you. It's so lovely that you're watching out for me."

"We'll wait here until you're ready," Micah said.

"Well, then...thank you! Excuse me. I'll be right with you."

She left the room. "You'll take her in?" Micah asked Craig.

"You're going to speak with the housekeeper?"

"Yep."

"You think she's an illegal?"

"Yes. Okay, right now I'll call Egan and get him to talk to whoever's in charge of guarding the museum. They need to keep an eye on Vivian and get eyes on Ned Richter, too. Then I'll come back here and talk to the housekeeper. Find out the last time she saw Ned Richter."

"Okay. I'll get her to the museum," Craig said. He hesitated. "Richter. I just don't see him as a player in this game. He's in big with Alchemy, but he's not a fanatic Egyptologist."

"Maybe, this time around, jealousy isn't the motive," Micah said.

"Then what the hell is?" Craig murmured.

Vivian reappeared, a heavy bag over her shoulder. Craig politely took it for her, and they exited the house.

Micah opened the passenger door of the agency sedan for Vivian. She looked at him, obviously a little confused. "I don't mind riding in the back."

"Ah, but we'd rather have you ride up front with my partner. He'll enjoy your company," Micah said.

"You're not coming?"

"I have some things to do," Micah said vaguely. "Don't forget, Mrs. Richter—I'll get a cop assigned to you. Stay safe and take care of yourself."

When he started to close the car door, she stopped him. "Agent Fox, don't be suspicious of my husband. I know I'm repeating myself, but he's a very kind man. People love him and that's why he's good at his job. He'd never hurt me."

"Stay with an officer, Mrs. Richter," he said, and he managed to close the door.

He glanced back up at the house.

He thought he saw the drapes move and, as soon as the black agency sedan with Craig and Vivian Richter turned the corner, he went back up the walk to the door.

The housekeeper was afraid; he was certain of that. Her immigration status was probably not legal, as he and Craig had guessed.

She might try to hide.

But he wouldn't leave.

And he knew that—whether it was face-to-face or through the door—she would listen to him when he threatened her.

He hated threatening people, especially a young woman like this, working hard to get into the country.

But he had to know the truth.

Because someone else could die.

Standing there on the steps, waiting, Micah realized that he was afraid for more than just an elusive *someone*.

He was afraid for Harley. She'd been on that expedition, she'd been determined to voice her suspicions. Harley was poking her nose into everything.

And Harley Frasier was among those who might be targeted by a mummy. A living mummy armed with deadly poison.

CHAPTER NINE

HARLEY LOST TRACK of time.

She'd known for years, ever since she was a teenager and saw Craig join the FBI, that she wanted to solve crimes. She hadn't wanted to run around the streets with a gun, although she'd been more than willing to partake in classes at a shooting range. What she loved was the puzzle part of crime-solving. She also loved the concept of profiling, and was extremely glad of her friendship with Kieran Finnegan and, through her, Dr. Fuller and Dr. Mira. They were giving and generous with their time, and they'd talked to her upon occasion about criminal profiling. She'd considered going through still more school and entering the field of profiling.

She'd been part of the Amenmose expedition because of her fascination with figuring out motives, clues, possibilities. The puzzle aspects of a crime.

Not that solving the murder of a mummy could help with a present-day case.

Still, solving what might be considered an *extremely* cold case was certainly a useful exercise.

That afternoon, in the room with the mummies and the artifacts and Henry Tomlinson's notes, she found herself even more fascinated with the crime—committed thousands of years ago—because, despite time and place, people were people.

She was familiar with Tutankhamen, but read more about him, including some material that was new to her. She read about Ay. There were numerous references to Amenmose, as well. He knew the stars; he could navigate by them. He knew the heavens and the earth.

And he knew about Ra, about the dishonor Tutankhamen's father had done the ancient gods.

She reviewed the facts about Tut and Akhenaten in Henry's notes and translations, as well as those prepared by other scholars. The discovery of Tutankhamen's tomb by Howard Carter in 1922 had opened their ancient lives to investigation, leading to years of speculating. Some of that speculation had proved to be true; Akhenaten had tried to create a monotheistic society, his one god being Ra, the sun god. When Tutankhamen came to the throne, his father's efforts had been completely erased. In fact, his father's reign had been erased from records, and his mummy had disappeared.

Among Henry's papers, Harley found a research document dated 2010, of which he was a coauthor. It was about the discovery, in a cache of royal mummies, of one who'd proved through DNA testing to be Akhenaten.

But in Tut's time, there must've been many people who still believed what Tut's father had believed. Perhaps there were people prepared to kill a man like Amenmose, a man so ready to help Tut and Ay obliterate his father. Or not. Most experts concluded that Ay had ordered the murder.

Then Harley came across the translation of a letter mentioning a woman named Skrit; more digging showed that she was Amenmose's wife.

Harley rose and walked around the room for a moment. Was one of the mummies there Skrit?

She saw nothing that would indicate such a thing.

Why wasn't the woman buried with him? Of course, the tomb had been a secret. Had she, his loving wife, planned it, planned the burial? Amenmose had been murdered, but he'd been given all the correct funeral rites such a man would have required.

Frustrated, Harley sat back down. She began to read and research again, referring not just to the notes they had, but looking up entries online made by scholars through the ages.

She stopped looking for Amenmose. She started looking for Skrit.

And what she found was truly fascinating.

MICAH KNOCKED AGAIN.

He knew the housekeeper was in the house.

He'd been there for nearly ten minutes, and she had yet to answer the door.

But he knew she was in there. And that she was hovering close to the door.

"I just have a few questions," he said loudly. "If you don't care to answer them…well, I can have some people from Immigration come down here in a few minutes. I can call Homeland Security, too."

The door finally opened. The pretty housekeeper stepped back. Her eyes were huge and wet with tears she was trying not to shed.

Micah felt like a real jerk. "I'm sorry," he told her. "I don't want to hurt you in any way. I just have to ask you a few questions. And I need you to answer me honestly."

She nodded, looking anxiously out at the street, then pulled him quickly inside.

"I am Valeria. Valeria Andreev. I don't want to go

back, please. I want to be legal. Mr. Richter has said he will help me. He pays me well. He is a kind man."

"I don't want you to be sent back, either. You obviously want to be here, and you seem to know the language well."

"I want to be American."

"We can try to help you. But I need your help."

She nodded again, an earnest expression on her face.

"Did Mr. Richter go to the hospital to bring Mrs. Richter home yesterday?"

"Yes, that is true. It is not a lie."

"What time was that?"

"Close to noon."

"Okay, thank you. And then?"

"And then Mrs. Richter asked me for juice and some food, and told me that she would sleep, and she didn't want to be disturbed."

"And?"

"I did not see her again until this morning."

"Okay, thank you. And what about Mr. Richter? Did he stay with her? Talk to her, take care of her and make sure she was all right?"

Valeria looked stricken. She didn't want to tell the truth.

"I saw him… I saw him bring her home."

"He went into her room?"

"Yes."

"But he didn't stay there."

Valeria bit her lower lip and shook her head unhappily.

"I don't think so. I think…they argued. I think she was angry with him. I heard their voices, and then I heard nothing, and I thought…"

"Yes?"

"I thought I heard the door slam."

"Did you see when Mr. Richter left today?"

Valeria shook her head. "No… I… I saw him yesterday. I didn't see him at all today. But, of course, that means nothing. I do not sit here and stare at the door, you know. I don't mean to be a—what do you say?—wiseass. But I don't know."

Micah smiled. "It's okay. I don't think you're trying to be a wiseass. What you do know is this—Mr. and Mrs. Richter fought. They came home from the hospital yesterday at about noon. You saw them both go to her room. You haven't seen Mr. Richter since—and you saw Mrs. Richter for the first time today when you went to get her for my associate and me?"

Valeria nodded, wide-eyed.

Micah handed her one of his cards. "If you need help, call me."

Her eyes brightened and she held the card close to her chest.

Micah headed out to the street. He saw a taxi and grabbed it, pulling out his cell phone as he did.

They were nearing the bridge when he got through to Craig.

"The maid didn't actually see either of the Richters after about noon yesterday," he told Craig. "Until she brought her to the door this morning."

"Interesting," Craig said. "Because Ned Richter isn't at the museum. I talked to the officer in charge. No one's seen him since yesterday, sometime in the afternoon. In fact, right around the time Arlo Hampton was found."

HARLEY JUMPED UP, determined to find Jensen. She was almost certain that she'd discovered the truth about

Amenmose. She'd put well-known facts together with information from less well-known sources—and had come up with her theory.

She wondered if there was a way to prove what she believed she knew.

Not easy.

Because, of course, if the murderer was Ay or any other person with power, he or she wouldn't have performed the deed himself—or herself. He—or she—would have had lackeys.

But Harley was convinced her theory made sense. Perfect sense.

Amenmose had been killed. He'd been killed because he'd secretly been a far greater fan of Tutankhamen's father than he'd ever let on. Ay had probably known that Amenmose whispered in the boy king's ear. Amenmose had been skilled at playing the political game. He'd pretended to listen to every word that left Ay's mouth; he'd proclaimed himself a man of the future, not the past. But in his heart, he'd felt certain that Tut's father had been right. And because of that—because those closest to him had known and others might have suspected—anyone connected to him, related to him, or even just a friend or servant to him, might have been in danger.

She left the room and glanced quickly down the hall. There was no one to be seen; not a police officer, not an employee, no one.

"Jensen?"

No answer.

"Jensen, where the hell are you?" she wondered aloud.

She hurried down the hall, past the lab. No one there, either. Of course, Arlo was the person who usually worked in the lab. And Arlo...

She hadn't heard that he was dead. Maybe he was still clinging to life, even if his poisoning had been worse than Vivian's. She hoped so.

Because she just didn't believe that he was guilty.

"Jensen!"

Past the lab, she made for her friend's office and knocked. Once again, no answer. She tried the door and it opened easily, but Jensen wasn't inside.

"Damn you," she grumbled. "Bring me in—and then disappear!"

Harley closed the door and tried the offices of Vivian Richter, Ned Richter, Arlo—even the museum director, Gordon Vincent's. No one was in any of them.

As she stood there, she again heard the terrible screech of a cat.

Just as she had heard when she'd been looking at the cat mummy.

Nothing mysterious about that, she told herself. There was obviously a cat somewhere in the museum. She'd meant to ask someone. It had probably been a stray, and a museum employee, unable to stand the sight of the poor creature begging in the street, had brought it in. That person must have fed it and kept it hidden here somewhere.

Poor thing; it deserved better.

"Where are you?" she murmured aloud. "Little creature, where are you? Where's Jensen? Where's anyone?"

She went back into the hallway, listening for the cat.

She heard it meow. She thought the sound was coming from the walls—or from beneath her.

She guessed the cat was down in one of the old tunnels, maybe in a section of the abandoned subway.

Harley remembered the day she and Micah had been with Arlo, and she hurried to the stairway that led below.

It was dark, of course.

She had her flashlight—of course.

She turned it on and walked carefully down the steps, first to the basement, through rooms and rooms of storage, and then down another level.

To tunnels of nothing.

To darkness that led nowhere.

And then she heard it again. It wasn't a scream this time. It was a pathetic kind of mewling.

She hadn't even seen the cat yet, but she felt so bad for the little creature, which was obviously scared. It probably had no idea where it was, how to get out, how to find help or sustenance.

Maybe she could keep a cat. A cat would be a good companion.

She wondered if Micah liked cats.

She wondered if it mattered.

Harley knew she was definitely in lust and halfway in love, but she'd told herself it *was just temporary*, that she expected nothing. He was living and working in Washington, DC, and he'd go back there. He'd given her no hint, nothing to suggest Harley should go back with him.

And yet she couldn't accept the fact that he might walk away. They'd met and joined forces over Henry. They got along extremely well, but they were both determined and stubborn, and she didn't intend to forget that she wanted to pursue her career.

Everything had begun just a few days ago, and already she couldn't imagine her life without him in it.

She gave a little scream, startled when the cat let out another mew. The sound was very close.

"Kitty, kitty, where are you?" she called.

The pathetic squeaking began again.

"Where are you? Come on, kitty, kitty, kitty. I'll help you!"

She came around a corner and almost fell into a niche in the wall. She tried to steady herself and realized she was leaning on an old maintenance door.

It creaked open on very rusty hinges.

She heard the cat cry again, really loudly this time. She'd found it!

"Hey, there you are," she said. "Come on, little one. I'll take you somewhere safe and warm and get you something to eat."

What if Micah Fox was allergic to kittens? She'd never asked him about pets.

She'd never asked him about anything. She'd just fallen into something crazy, she'd wanted him so desperately.

She shone her light around again, seeking the cat.

"Hey, sweet thing, I'm going to find you," Harley said out loud.

And then she froze as her light fell on the crying kitten.

And on so much more...

"GET IN HERE. We've got Sanford Wiley, our man in Cairo, ready for a video chat in twenty minutes," Richard Egan told Micah. "He has some information."

"On Satima Mahmoud?" Micah asked.

"That's what I imagine," Egan replied.

Craig was doing the driving. He was a damned good driver, and as a New Yorker, he could maneuver the streets as few could.

Micah had a feeling that whatever Sanford Wiley had discovered, it was important to their case.

He put a call through to Harley, anxious to talk to her, to hear her voice.

She didn't answer.

Craig glanced over at him.

"She didn't say she was going out," Micah murmured. "Or, she might have said that she was going to be with Kieran."

"I wouldn't worry. Leave a message. If she's on the subway, she won't get it for a while."

"I'll bet she went to the museum. Jensen—that friend of hers—I think he keeps encouraging her to come in. I don't feel good about it, but I'm not sure why."

"At least Vivian Richter seemed fine. She seems to believe that Arlo tried to kill her and that he might've killed Henry Tomlinson."

"Yeah, well, I *don't* believe it, and I'm positive you don't, either. Also, I know damned well that Harley doesn't believe it. And, Craig, what I've said before is true—Harley's had more classes of all kinds than we have. Yes, in a classroom. She doesn't have much practical experience, not really. But she's smart as a whip. If she says something is off, it is."

"I'll call Kieran. She'll track her down. How's that?"

"Thanks. Tell her we'll join the tracking party as soon as we're done with the video chat," Micah said.

"Will do."

"She's at work, though, isn't she?"

"She won't have a problem. Tell them it's an active case and the good doctors will be more than happy to send Kieran off—or get into it themselves!" Craig assured him. He spoke to the car phone; it dialed Kieran.

"Anything new?" she asked. "What's going on?"

"Can you find Harley?" Craig asked her.

"Sure. I know where she is."

"You do?"

"At the museum. I talked to her briefly when she was on her way there. Jensen asked her to come in. They're good friends, you know, and I think he's feeling pretty lost and alone in all this."

"Yeah, lost and alone," Micah murmured. "Can you get over there? I tried to reach her by phone. She didn't answer."

"I'll go right over," Kieran promised. "I'll find her, don't worry. And when I do, we'll give you a call."

Kieran said goodbye and hung up; Craig looked at Micah. "Feel better?"

"I wish I did."

"You don't like Jensen."

Micah shook his head. "But he was with Harley when Henry was killed, so…"

"Yep." Craig was quiet for a minute, and Micah knew what he was thinking.

"Two people could've been involved," he said quietly. "It's a question of which two. Do you think maybe Ned Richter? Would Richter actually have done that to his own wife?"

"They fight quite a bit, or so we've heard," Craig said. "Yolanda told us she heard them arguing, and the maid told you that they were fighting yesterday."

"Yes, but…wrapping someone in nicotine-soaked linen?"

"She was found immediately. So she survived," Craig said.

They reached the office. Leaving the car, they hurried through the ground-floor security check and up to Egan's office.

Egan was already engaged in the call with Sanford Wiley.

On the video screen, they could see that Wiley looked glum.

"Did you find her? Did you find Satima Mahmoud?" Micah asked.

"Yeah, we found her," Wiley said.

"But you didn't bring her in."

"She's dead," Wiley told them.

Micah had been standing. He sank into one of the chairs in the conference room. "Dead? Not…as a mummy?"

"As a mummy? No. Right now, they have some of her friends in custody. She was likely killed by a member of her 'group'—although exactly who that is, I don't know—or by an enemy of this group. That's just what we're being told. The situation's complicated, but from what we've gleaned so far, there was no real insurrection planned for the night Henry Tomlinson died. We know this because the Egyptian police are questioning someone they pulled in. Some kid who didn't want to spend his life in prison. He says they were contacted by Satima Mahmoud. She had money, a lot of money. She was willing to pay them to get a fake insurrection going. That's why it was such a pitiable show. No one really wanted to bear arms, go against anything—or get caught," Wiley explained.

"So we've been thinking in the right direction," Micah said. "It was all a diversion to keep the police or any other authorities from discovering what really happened to Henry Tomlinson."

"Yes, that's what we believe on this end," Wiley said. "Satima Mahmoud was found with a bullet in her back.

We think it could've been fired by someone in a group with a different political view for the future—or, as I said, someone in her own group. Many people were arrested for taking part in the so-called uprising. Perhaps someone wanted revenge."

"Still hard to understand," Craig said. "The Amenmose find was worth a fortune."

"Yes, there were priceless objects. And, yes, they might have wanted them for their monetary value to support their cause, whatever that was. Thing is, the black market is hard to navigate these days. And if you're caught…not good. Cash—cold hard cash—is far better than even a priceless object. Someone gave Satima a lot of cold hard cash. At the moment, that's all I know. If we get anything else…"

"Thank you, Wiley," Micah said. "You've been a tremendous help. I'm sorry the woman is dead," he added.

Egan finished up with Wiley, and they cut off the chat.

"Cold hard cash? Someone with access to a lot of it?" Egan mused. "That's not your average grad student."

"There's Richter," Craig said. "Or…well, some grad students come from family money. That's how they manage to study forever and ever. We have background checks on everyone. I've skimmed all the files…"

"Morrow, Jensen Morrow. His father invented some kind of cleaning product. He's got money," Micah said. But it was true, too, that they'd just left the Richter house, which had to be worth millions.

Craig nodded. "Yeah. But to be fair, it *could* be Richter. He'd have the money. He was supposedly with his wife when everything was going on back in the Sahara. We know now that the two of them fight, although Vivian Richter swears that her husband is totally loving and good."

"But the maid said differently," Craig pointed out.

"The maid?" Egan asked.

Craig waved a hand in the air and said, "Sir, I think we may have to help that woman out when this is all over. She talked to Micah about Richter's whereabouts."

"Go and get Vivian Richter," Egan said. "Bring her in. I think it's time we had a conversation here in the office."

"On our way!" Micah said.

They hurried back to the street where the car was waiting.

As they drove, Micah tried Harley's number again.

"Still not answering," he muttered to Craig.

"We'll find her," Craig promised. "Don't forget," he said, "she's my cousin."

There was a grim set to Craig Frasier's mouth.

Micah was glad for it. That meant he wasn't alone; they were going to find Harley, and they'd damned well find her fast—and she'd be all right.

IT WAS RIDICULOUS, it was horrible, and it was like something out of a horror movie by a master of the genre.

Harley had found the cat.

And the cat was sitting on the head of a man.

The man was dead. It was Richter. Ned Richter.

She couldn't scream.

The last thing she *should* do was scream!

In fact, she was worried about having her flashlight on. But the whiff of gases or decay, some ghastly smell, that was coming to her made Harley think the man she was staring at had been dead for some time, probably at least twenty-four hours.

He hadn't been wrapped in linen. He probably hadn't died from any kind of poisoning.

Ned had been stabbed through the heart with an Egyptian dagger. He was shoved up against a wall; he'd probably died right there, she surmised, studying the pool of blood that surrounded him. Blood that had grown sticky.

He'd been killed yesterday. Either just before Arlo had succumbed to the linen wrappings and their nicotine, or just after.

If Arlo had tried to kill Ned Richter... Wait, that made no sense. Why stab Ned with an ancient Egyptian dagger, and then dress up in linen wrappings himself?

And who the hell had that been on the street, the person shorter than Arlo who'd approached her, touched her with the poison?

"Harley? Harley, where are you?"

Jensen?

Jensen was calling her now.

Sure, Jensen was taller than the figure who'd come up to her. But what if he was working with someone? What if he'd gone with her that night in the desert just to throw suspicion off himself? He hadn't killed Henry Tomlinson; that would've been impossible. But he might have been in on it.

She forced herself to stay silent.

But to her great distress, the kitten took that moment to mew desperately for help once again—apparently deciding that help wasn't going to come from Harley.

"Kitty! Aw, here, kitty, kitty!" Jensen said. "Who the hell would be keeping a cat down here?" he asked himself.

He was coming in her direction.

He didn't sound like a killer.

To make matters even worse, Harley's phone began to ring.

It was on vibrate, but even vibrate sounded shockingly loud to her!

She saw that it was Micah, and that he'd called several times. The calls hadn't gone through. Suddenly, now—now!—they were.

She backed as close as she could against the wall. She almost let out an involuntary scream; she'd backed into the corpse. She was stepping in the sticky blood.

"Micah!" she whispered.

He was talking as she answered. She didn't think he'd hear her, and she didn't think he had any idea that she wasn't in a good situation.

"Harley, you're at the museum, right? Kieran's coming there to get you. Leave. Leave with her. Wiley, the agent in Cairo told us Satima Mahmoud's body was found. She was killed either by a rival political group or by her own friends, they don't really know. But here's what's important—there was no insurrection. It was staged to cover up Henry's murder. The killer could be Ned Richter or possibly Jensen Morrow," Micah said. "You need to get out of there—"

"It's not Ned Richter," she said in a hoarse whisper.

"How do you know?"

"I'm looking at him. He's dead. Dagger to the heart," Harley said.

"Where are you?"

"Subbasement, I think. Near the old subway station."

"What are you doing down there, Harley? Never mind, never mind. We're on our way. You need to get out!"

"Yes, but—"

"Get the hell out of there now! It could be Jensen. Get out, Harley!"

"I can't!" she whispered.

"Why not?"

"Jensen is down here, coming right at me."

CHAPTER TEN

THERE WERE A number of hallways and tunnels, entrances and exits down here.

Harley knew that because Arlo had shown her and Micah around the basement and subbasement levels. She had to think; she had to remember everything they'd learned that day. She needed to...

Find a way out.

The kitten was continuing to cry. He had jumped off the body of Ned Richter and was coming to Harley at last, trying to wrap around her ankles.

Harley swept up the kitten.

Poor little thing was sticky with blood; so was she.

Ned Richter's blood. Ned hadn't done any of this. He was innocent —and he was dead. It was almost as if they'd all been victims of a pharaoh's curse.

"Hey, kitty, kitty! Where are you?" Jensen called. "Harley? Damn it. Where are you, girl? Why haven't the police gotten these damned tunnels closed yet?" he muttered to himself. "Harley? Hey, anybody down here?"

He was coming closer and closer.

A weapon. She needed a weapon!

There was a dead man right next to her. A dead man with a dagger protruding from his chest.

She carefully put down the kitten and crept toward Ned to get the dagger.

It wouldn't move! It was stuck deep in his chest, as if the man's body, his flesh and blood and bone, refused to give up what had brought about its demise!

She would've sworn out loud except that Jensen was coming closer and closer.

Micah and Craig were on their way. They'd be here soon. Kieran was up in the museum somewhere, and it was crawling with police. Kieran wouldn't wait long when she couldn't find Harley; she'd insist that the police start searching the place, tearing it apart.

"Harley?"

Jensen couldn't be more than twenty or twenty-five feet from her.

"Jensen Morrow! Stop right where you are!" a male voice thundered.

Harley knew the voice—it was McGrady. Detective McGrady. He'd followed Jensen down here. She hadn't even seen him, hadn't known he was at the museum.

Harley switched off her penlight.

The darkness seemed overwhelming, except...

She could see Jensen. He had his own light. "McGrady, what the hell is the matter with you? I'm trying to find Harley. You can help me. Harley, where are you and what the hell... Jeez! What's that smell? Is it cat poop? If so, it's the worst damn cat poop I've ever smelled."

He was talking about cat poop. He didn't know he was smelling a dead man. But if he'd killed Ned Richter, he would know.

"Stop, Morrow, or I'll shoot you, you murdering bastard!" McGrady called out.

"What?" Jensen demanded, obviously thrown. "I stopped! I'm right here."

Harley straightened in the dark, letting out a breath. McGrady was here. He was a cop. He had a gun.

But Jensen wasn't guilty. He was just looking for her. Looking for a cat. She believed it with her whole heart.

Harley held her breath for a minute, afraid to speak, to cry out—to warn Jensen and the cop—and afraid not to.

She had solved one mystery that afternoon. The mystery of Amenmose's death. His wife, Skrit, had ordered him killed. She had hired the assassins. She hadn't hated him—well, maybe she had. But despite wanting him dead, she hadn't wanted him deprived of an afterlife. She'd seen to it that he'd died; she had done so to protect herself and their children from the growing power of Ay. She'd been no threat to Ay's position, but her husband had. Still, she hadn't denied him their form of heaven.

And now...

"Harley!" Jensen called, sounding desperate.

She stepped into the darkness of the hall, ready to call his name.

But just as she did, she saw a dark figure streak out from behind Jensen, coming straight at him.

"Jensen! Watch out!"

Harley screamed the warning just in time. He spun around, avoiding a lethal blow from Vivian Richter, who was wielding a jewel-encrusted pike. But Vivian was quick to double back, hitting him hard on the head with the end of her weapon.

Jensen went down. And as he did, his light went out.

"What the hell?" McGrady roared. "Mrs. Richter, are you all right? Are you all right?"

Something flew through the tunnel—heading directly for the cop. Harley cried out his name. "McGrady! Get down!" she shrieked.

She couldn't see what happened next.

Jensen's light was gone; McGrady's was, too.

Harley and Vivian Richter were both suddenly left in absolute, subterranean darkness.

CRAIG AND MICAH arrived at the museum just in time to find Kieran telling a policeman that she was going down to the basement, with or without him, but if he valued his employment, he would be accompanying her.

The policeman was telling her that an officer had already gone down, following Jensen Morrow.

"Detective McGrady is down there. He said there's no good reason for any of those science people to be running around in the basement."

Micah didn't wait; he had to get down to the subterranean levels.

Craig went to explain to the officer that they were FBI and to get Kieran, from where she had been speaking with the cop.

Micah ran, ran hard. He reached the stairs Arlo Hampton had so recently shown him. He stumbled down them, afraid to use his penlight.

When he got to the bottom, he paused.

He began to move slowly, feeling his way.

Then he smelled death.

Yes, as Harley had told him, Ned Richter was down here. And he was dead.

Had Jensen Morrow killed him?

"Help! Oh, my God, help me!"

He heard the cry. It came from ahead, down the long hallway before him. It was coming, he thought, from the abandoned subway section where they'd found the stash of insecticide. The nicotine poison.

The voice belonged to Vivian Richter.

"I'm coming!" he called. "Are you okay? Are you in distress?"

"No…he's going to kill me. Agent Fox? It's Jensen. He's going to kill me. He and Arlo…they killed Henry. The two of them. They tried to kill me. Jensen tried to kill Arlo because he had to make it look like Arlo had worked alone… Oh, my God! He killed my husband. Jensen killed Ned, my poor Ned!"

"Where are you?" Micah asked.

He was moving very slowly and very carefully, determined not to give away his position. But as he spoke, he ran into something with his foot.

Something hard—and soft at the same time.

He stooped down, his heart in his throat. A body.

Harley?

It wasn't Harley. He quickly realized it was a man.

Ned Richter? Jensen Morrow?

It couldn't be Ned Richter; he wouldn't be warm.

He wouldn't be…breathing.

"So that's it!" he said loudly, checking for Jensen's pulse. It was weak, but it was there. The man would need help, though, and fast.

"Vivian, where are you? You poor woman, attacked… Thank God Arlo was still so new at it. He ended up killing himself, but you're all right, barely touched! And Ned—killed by Jensen! Where are you? Let me help."

They were both playing a game, pretending they believed what the other claimed as truth.

Harley. Where the hell was Harley? Was the woman holding her somewhere? Was she down on the ground, dying…bleeding?

He heard a scream of rage.

Light suddenly filled the dank, dark space.

And he saw Vivian. She was bursting out of the old subway tunnel, a lantern in one hand, a dagger held high in the other.

She was coming right at him.

He stepped out of the way; she would catapult into the wall.

But she didn't.

Because there was another cry of rage that tore through the darkness and death and decay of the tunnel.

It was Harley. And she'd found a weapon of her own—an old paving brick. She flew at Vivian, encountering her before Vivian could close in on Micah.

Both women went flying down to the floor. Vivian's lantern rolled away as they fell, casting light and shadow everywhere.

Micah reached down, catching Vivian's arm, grasping it hard.

Vivian screamed and released the antique dagger from the painful pressure he'd placed on her arm. He kicked it far from her.

Footsteps pounded down the length of the tunnel hall. Craig was there, Kieran right behind him.

Micah walked away from Vivian and drew Harley to her feet and into his arms. He held her; he wanted to hold her forever in the strange darkness and shadows, keep her from the horrors.

But of course, he couldn't.

Time meant everything just now.

"We need an ambulance for Jensen," he said. "And..."

"McGrady's here, too. I don't know how badly he's hurt. He's here somewhere!"

"Here! Here I am!"

They saw a form stumble toward them. And as it did, the tunnel blazed with light. Police officers, all carrying lights, came surging toward them.

"It was her!" McGrady said, swallowing hard, shaking his head. "Her! The woman poisoned herself to throw off any suspicion. She killed Henry, and she killed her husband. Yeah?"

Craig had Vivian Richter up by then. She was in handcuffs—and spitting mad. "I shouldn't have had to kill the bastard! Don't you get it? That mealymouthed little snake, Arlo Hampton—he was supposed to kill Ned. I did away with Henry Tomlinson, and Arlo was supposed to kill Ned. He said he couldn't do it! But I got him…oh, yeah, I got both of them!"

"Who the hell would have suspected this!" McGrady said.

Micah looked at Harley, and his eyes darkened with concern.

"There's blood on you!" he murmured.

"Not mine," Harley said.

"Thank God." Micah looked toward McGrady. "Then we're ready for the next step."

Harley smiled and nodded.

"McGrady, go ahead, do the honors. Bring Mrs. Richter in. We'll handle things down here. We'll get the medical examiner and the techs for Mr. Richter," Micah said.

"And an ambulance for Jensen. She got him pretty good," Harley said.

"Why don't you and Kieran go to the hospital with him?" Micah suggested.

"Yeah. Yeah."

They stared at each other for another long moment.

Then Harley turned away, bending down to Jensen.

The EMTs arrived, followed by the medical examiner and the crime scene people.

And the night went on.

LIGHT CONTINUED TO blaze through the tunnels and the abandoned subway station as day turned to night, as the medical examiner came, as the body of Ned Richter was taken at last to the morgue.

Micah and Craig worked the tie-up in the tunnels. Long hours, a lot of waiting, a lot of speculating and figuring.

Meanwhile, Vivian had been questioned at the station—and confessed to everything, despite her attorney's cautions.

"The whole thing sounds like Hitchcock," Micah told Craig. "In a sick and twisted way. *Strangers on a Train*, except they weren't strangers. Vivian Richter was working with Arlo Hampton. Arlo wanted Henry's place as lead of the expedition. And Vivian was willing to kill Henry. It was an easy trade, or so it seemed. She'd kill Henry and Arlo would kill Ned. And, of course, she was willing to pay so that Satima Mahmoud would get her political group of disenfranchised students to fake an insurgency to cover up the murder. But as I said, in return for Henry being killed, Arlo was supposed to kill Ned. He screwed up. Vivian was afraid that Joe Rosello might figure out that Satima Mahmoud had been paid, so she decided she should poison him, which was why she showed up at the parade. And it was how Harley knew it wasn't the same mummy. Vivian is nowhere near as tall as Arlo. But Arlo didn't follow through on his part of the bargain. And Vivian lost control. When she saw Harley, I guess she wanted to do her in. But she hated Arlo for leaving her in the lurch. She was ready to kill Ned without blinking—and poison Arlo."

"Yeah, so all that 'beloved husband' stuff was just an act. For our benefit," Craig muttered.

"In Vivian's mind, her husband never gave her the respect she deserved. She was bitter, says he constantly claimed that she only had a job because of him. I guess she grew to hate him. If Arlo had played his part properly, he would've been the big cheese and she would've held the second position. But Arlo failed her, so she poisoned him. Otherwise, what was he going to do? Blame her."

"So if Arlo does make it, he'll be under arrest. Conspiracy to commit murder —even if he chickened out on it," Craig said.

"Yeah," Micah agreed. "But…"

"But?"

"I'm glad that Jensen Morrow and the other grad students have been proven innocent. They're Harley's friends. For her, I'm happy."

"Yep. I'm going topside for a while. I'll try to find out about Jensen's condition," Craig told Micah. "I'll let you know."

Micah nodded. He hoped Jensen Morrow was going to be okay.

He was, Craig reported a short time later, upon returning to the tunnels. Jensen had a concussion, and they'd watch him at the hospital for a few days. After that, he'd be as good as new, according to the doctors.

Finally, just as dawn was breaking, they finished in the tunnels.

He and Craig left.

Craig didn't ask where he wanted to go. He dropped him off at Harley's.

"I should've called her, I guess," Micah said.

"She'll be waiting for you," Craig told him.

And she was.

The night security guard waved him in. He had no idea how Harley knew exactly when he'd reach her door, but somehow she did.

The door opened, and she hurried into his arms.

He held her tight. She was bathed and sweet and fresh, and the scent of her hair was intoxicating; he kissed her, a long and lovely kiss, then pulled away.

"The tunnels," he said with a shudder.

And the blood of a dead man and the rot of millennia, he might have said.

He didn't need to.

She drew him in and up the stairs, to the bedroom, where he tossed his gun and holster on the table, and undressed quickly with her help. In minutes, she got into the shower behind him, forgetting to shed whatever silky thing she was wearing.

The water was hot and wonderful. Sensual, erotic and yet comforting.

He wasn't sure when they left the shower; he wasn't sure when she shed the wet silky thing. He knew they were still damp when they fell onto her bed. The room was in shadows, dawn was breaking with a spectacular light, and nothing seemed to matter except that they were together, touching each other.

They licked, teased, breathed each other.

Made love.

And made love again.

And then they slept for hours and hours and finally awoke.

Just for good measure, they made love yet again.

Later, when another day was almost gone, Micah looked through the great windows at the beauty of the church beyond.

"We're going to get married there," he said.

And then, of course, he remembered that they'd really only known each other for less than a week.

"One day," he added. "Somewhere along the line."

"What a proposal," she said lightly. "So romantic!" But she smiled. "One day… Yes, I like it. I like it very much!"

As she replied, he suddenly heard a mewling sound. He looked at her with surprise.

"Oh!" she murmured.

She hurried away and returned with a little ball of gray fluff in her arms.

"Um, we have a kitten. I hope that's okay?"

He laughed. "How did you…?"

"I found him in the tunnel. With… Ned's body. I think he helped us, really. He…he needs a home."

"So where has the little guy been?"

"I guess he went into hiding while we were all down there."

"And then?"

"He followed me up to the ground floor, and one of the officers took him for me until I got back from seeing Jensen at the hospital," she said. "I was thinking of calling him Lucky."

"Lucky it is," he said, and he took her—and the ball of fluff—back into his arms.

Lucky.

Yes.

EPILOGUE

Two Weeks Later
Finnegan's on Broadway

"I WAS PART of it all—and I still don't get it," Jensen said, shaking his head. "Okay, back to the beginning. Vivian Richter and Arlo Hampton made some kind of devil's bargain. She'd kill Henry. He'd kill Ned. And no one would suspect either of them because it wouldn't make sense. They wouldn't be guilty of the same crime. But Micah wasn't going to give up and they both knew he was coming to the opening of the exhibit. So she poisoned herself to throw off any possible suspicion?"

"Something like that," Harley said. She'd just finished up the last of the work she'd told Jensen she would do. With Arlo and Vivian gone, he'd fallen behind with the exhibit. She'd also been eager to finish what she'd written about the murder of Amenmose. Everything would be on record at the museum, but it was a museum specializing in the ancient world—and her job here had been to explain what had happened to Amenmose and how it had all fit in with that world.

For Henry.

Arlo was still in the hospital. He'd regained consciousness, but the poison had swept away a great deal of his mind.

He had no idea he was guilty of conspiracy. Sadly, he wasn't even sure who he was anymore, or what he'd done.

Vivian's attorney was still telling her to shut up. She, too, however, had apparently had some kind of mental breakdown, because she wouldn't stop talking to the press. She was going to go for an affirmative defense and claim that she'd been horribly abused by her husband and that he'd made her say things that weren't true. She also insisted that Henry Tomlinson had killed himself and that she'd long been a victim of chauvinism and abuse at the hands of both men.

"It's crazy. All crazy, huh?" Jensen asked her. "And you know what's even crazier? That horrible woman killed Henry and her husband, she tried to kill you and me and that cop—and I still love being at the museum."

"It's a good museum. Henry was a very special man, and loving the museum just honors him," Harley said.

"Hmm. And what about that cop? He was a jerk, and... well, you know, he came by to apologize to me."

"McGrady," Harley said. "Yep. He apologized to me, too. And thanked me for saving his life. He told me he's going to be a good cop—and that it'll be because of me! I sure hope that's true."

"You can find out, I guess."

Harley smiled. "Not for a while," she said softly. "For right now—"

She stopped talking and got up; she saw that Micah and Craig had come into Finnegan's. She waved, so the two of them could see her.

"Still don't see why you have to go to Washington," Jensen said.

Harley flashed him a smile. "Because I'm in love," she told him.

"Yeah, yeah. And okay, he's decent. And I'm happy for you both."

"Funny, he says you're decent, too. And he's happy we're friends."

By then, Micah had come to the table. He greeted her with a kiss and Jensen with a handshake.

Craig reached the table next, and then Kieran arrived from her day job. Kevin came over, then Kieran's youngest brother, Danny, and her older brother, Declan, joined them. Micah and Harley were surrounded by friends and family, and they were toasted. It was something of a goodbye party.

They might come back to New York eventually; a transfer was always possible for Micah. But Harley wanted to train with the FBI academy and work toward joining a profiling team.

Washington was best for both of them right now. Harley wasn't giving up her uncle's apartment; they'd be up visiting often enough.

Everyone talked; everyone had a great time.

Joe, Roger and Belinda came later—with Belinda being the happiest of the bunch. Her fiancé was back from his deployment overseas and their wedding was coming up.

"Will there be any kind of Egyptian motif?" Joe asked Belinda, smiling.

"No!"

"What about you guys?" Jensen asked Harley.

"No! Grace Church, and you're all invited. We'll let you know when."

"No zombies, mummies, or any form of ancient lore?" Joe asked.

"No!" Harley and Micah said together, the word emphatic.

They celebrated awhile longer. Then it was time to split up, and they hugged and kissed each other on the cheek and promised to stay in touch.

The most difficult thing for Harley was to say good-bye to Kieran and Craig, but they wouldn't be far away and they'd all go back and forth often.

"I know you don't have a firm date for the wedding yet, but what are you thinking?" Kieran asked Harley.

"We have no solid plans yet. We just know where," she said. "What about you two?"

Kieran laughed. "We have no solid plans, either. Not yet. All we know is that we *will* have a wedding, and oh, yes! The reception will be here!"

Micah caught Harley's hand. "We have a lot of dating to do," he told Kieran and Craig. "And apparently my proposal was lacking. I'm going to work on a better one. I'll fill you in on how that goes. We might take a honeymoon before we actually do the marriage thing. I want to make sure Harley knows we have some great history down Virginia way, too. It's not ancient, but it's pretty cool. I've got a friend who's working a dig in Jamestown. We can visit him for a while. And meanwhile, we'll date…"

They left. They went to spend their last night in the apartment with the great windows and the beautiful loft that they'd have for a while.

"Yes, we need to date…" Micah said.

Harley whispered in his ear.

He smiled. "Oh, yeah. That, too. Lots and lots of that!"

The moon shone through the windows.

They hurried up the curving wrought iron stairway.

Tonight was an ending and a beginning.

And a beautiful night, made for love and for loving.

* * * * *

NEVER SLEEP
WITH STRANGERS

PROLOGUE

CASSANDRA STUART WAS BEAUTIFUL, and she knew it. She could manipulate others, and she knew that, too. If she could just make him turn around and look back at her...

"Jon! *Jon!*"

She knew that he'd heard her, but he didn't stop. He was really furious with her this time. As she watched, he continued down the gravel path that led to the loch. Maybe she had overplayed it this time, but she didn't want to be here in the back of beyond, in this godforsaken, remote patch of Scotland. Despite his famous guests, despite his famous charity game. They were *his* guests; it was *his* game. She hated the country; she wanted to be in London.

But she knew her husband, knew what he was thinking now. He'd known the day would go badly, that she would be rude and impatient and ruin it for them all. But damn him, he still wouldn't give it up! He'd hosted this event every year for the past decade. He'd made his plans; he had a life to live. The week was already under way. Besides, no matter how damned marvelous his wife might be, he'd told her—sounding awfully damned sarcastic—*he* would be damned if a woman was going to lead him around by the nose. *Any* woman.

"Jon!"

She knew that he didn't want to look back, didn't want to see her.

Because he knew what she was planning. And he had planned ahead himself. He wasn't going to let her play him, wasn't going to let her manipulate him the way she intended to.

She meant to leave. Today. It was the last disruption she had up her sleeve. She hoped her departure would get through to him the way her pouting and petulance had not.

But she wanted him to come back to her first; she wanted to make love, to be passionate and exciting, to remind him that he couldn't exist without her. She would tell him that she needed him, remind him why he had married her. She could make him happy, could make him laugh, and she was damned good in bed, even if she had just taken a lover because she couldn't bear the look in Jon's eyes sometimes, knowing that he might on occasion be thinking of someone else. *Come back!* she thought furiously. *Let me seduce you just one last time so you don't forget, so maybe...*

She would wait until he had slipped away, and then she would pack, leaving behind a letter addressed to "My Dearest Darling," explaining that she would be at the London Hilton, waiting for him when he could escape his dreary associates. And maybe, just maybe, he would come. He could be such a fool! She knew so much more about his guests and household than he did! Who was sleeping with whom. And why. Actually, she thought, and almost smiled, she knew a number of them very well. Intimately, one might say.

And still there was such a wretched hole of jealousy in her heart.

"Jon! Come back!" she called again. She experienced a strange new fear beyond the sense of powerlessness and loss she had been feeling so much lately. "Jon! Please come back! Or I'll make you pay!"

Her voice was both provocative and irritated. But he was still walking. So tall, hair so dark, shoulders broad and muscled. He was a beautiful man, and she was losing him.

Panic seized her. He had guessed she was having an affair with someone here. Did he know that she was trying to goad him, get even with him? Because she was certain he was having an affair, as well.

"Jon! Jon, damn you!"

Her tone was growing more petulant. She stood on the master bedroom's second-floor balcony, overlooking the rear courtyard. The rooms had been handsomely enough appointed, "remodeled" at the end of the seventeenth century and modernized by Jon himself just a few years ago. The balcony was a sweeping, curved affair that boasted views of three corners of the property. Here, in the rear, it looked over an elegant fountain with a priceless marble Poseidon, complete with trident, as its centerpiece. Despite the fact that winter was rapidly approaching, roses still bloomed around the tiled path that encircled the fountain. The path turned to gravel as it passed through the rose arbor and headed toward the loch. In the master chambers themselves, the walls were covered with antique tapestries, and there was a massive fireplace, as well as a state-of-the-art hot-water heating system with generator backup. A four-poster king-size bed sat on a dais, and one level down from the main section of the bedroom, just beyond a medieval archway, was a huge whirlpool bath and sauna. She had a huge dressing room and closet, as did he.

"What's not to like?" Jon had asked her impatiently, offended.

The decor was fine. She just hated the country. No excitement, no sense of life. It wasn't London, Paris, New York or even Edinburgh, for God's sake.

That was exactly why he liked it so much, he'd told her. He was walking away. Still walking away.

She was amazed to feel tears stinging her eyes. How could he care more about this pile of stones and his imbecilic friends than her? "Jon, Jon! Damn you, *Jon*!"

He'd talked about divorce; he'd said that things just weren't working out. But, he couldn't divorce her. He just *couldn't*! She'd already told him that she would make it impossible. She would drag him through the mud, give away a million filthy secrets about him and his associates.

"Jo—"

She started to say his name, then realized that someone was behind her.

She spun around to see who had slipped in. "You, damn you! Get out! Did he send you? Get the hell out of my room. *Our* room! I'm his wife. I'm the one who sleeps with him. Get out!"

She spun back to stare out from the balcony. "Jon!"

She heard a rush of movement, like a whisper of air, and she turned back.

For a moment she stared into the eyes of her killer, and she knew.

"Oh, God!" she breathed, and, desperate, she began to cry out again.

"Jon! Jon! *Jon!*"

She felt the pressure of the rail at her back. And she screamed.

Because she was falling.

And she could see her own death.

Jon Stuart had been angry, really angry. He'd intended to make good his escape. But something in Cassandra's voice gave him pause that time, and he swung around.

And there she was.

Falling…

It looked as if she were sailing. In this, as in all other things, she was elegant. She was wearing a white silk dressing gown, and it billowed out around her. Her ebony hair was caught by the golden glory of the sun and shone with blue-black lights. It struck him that she even fell with dramatic grace and beauty.

And only after a split second of the mindless realization that he could do nothing at all to stop it did he realize that she was already in the act of dying. Screaming, crying out, shrieking *his* name, plummeting to earth.

She died in Poseidon's arms. Cradled within them, like a wayward goddess. Eyes closed, ebony hair and snow-white gown caught by the breeze. She almost looked as if she were sleeping, except…

The trident had pierced through her.

And the snow-white gown was turning crimson.

His heart hammering, he began to shout, running desperately, as if he could reach her, help her, despite the fact that he knew…

He cried out.

Cried out her name.

Reached her, and held her.

As her blood spilled over him.

While her eyes stared into his with an ever silent reproach.

CHAPTER ONE

Three years later

THE SCENE WAS definitely a chilling one. A beautiful woman in medieval dress, her long blond hair waving over the workings of the mechanism, was tied to the implement of torture, with a dark-haired, bearded and mustachioed man standing over her.

The Earl of Exeter's Daughter, also known as the Rack, proclaimed the sign overhead. Named after the Man Most Proficient in the Art of Extracting Confessions from his Victims.

The artist who had created the wax figures had been proficient, as well. The blonde stretched out on the wicked wooden rack was exquisite, with fine, classically molded features and huge blue eyes widened by her fear of her tormentor. Any sane man would long to rescue her. While the fellow standing above her—his features were pure evil. His eyes gleamed in sadistic anticipation of the pain he was about to inflict.

Many of the exhibits in the hall were excellent, retelling ancient tales of man's inhumanity to man. This particular display outdid them all.

So Jon Stuart thought as he stood silently in the shadows, leaning casually against the stone wall, his presence obscured by the darkness of the dungeon. He stared watchfully, contemplatively, at the exhibit--and at the flesh-and-blood blonde now standing in front of it.

She was nearly—in face, coloring and form—a mirror image of the poor beauty stretched out on the rack itself. She was a young woman with a glorious mop of blond hair that cascaded freely over her shoulders and down her back. She was slender and beautifully shaped, doing incredible justice to the jeans and fitted sweater she wore. Her features were very feminine: fine, straight, slender nose; high, chiseled cheekbones; beautiful blue eyes; and full, lushly shaped lips. She was surveying the display with a certain amount of interest—and wariness. She looked as if she wanted to laugh ruefully, reminding herself that she was looking at wax figures, but the scene was scary, and she was alone in the shadows. Or so she thought.

Sabrina Holloway.

He hadn't seen her in more than three and a half years now, and though he was somewhat surprised by her presence; he was glad she had decided to come. She had politely declined his invitation to the last, fateful Mystery Week. The occasion when Cassandra had died.

Whether Sabrina realized it or not, she had most certainly been Joshua's model for the beauty on the rack; she was the victim's spitting image, and Joshua always enjoyed using people he knew in his art. He had mentioned to Jon that he had met Sabrina Holloway in Chicago, and he had sounded entirely infatuated, so Jon had refrained from telling Joshua that he, too, was acquainted with her. It was easy to understand Joshua's head-over-heels reaction; he'd experienced something quite similar when he'd met her himself. Before...

Well, there was a lot to admire—or covet—about Ms.

Holloway. Jon hadn't been the only one to fall victim to her charm; she had attracted the attention of Brett Mc-Graff, as well. Jon shook his head. She'd gone off and married McGraff. Whirlwind courtship, whirlwind marriage—scandalous divorce.

Jon watched her now, glad of the distance between them. He stared at her in simple assessment. She possessed a rare grace and beauty. Even though he'd been something of a recluse over the last few years, he'd kept up with her career, reading about her in the papers and tabloids. Reporters had leaped wholeheartedly on Brett McGraff's last, noisy divorce from such a beautiful young creature.

She had been stunning when Jon met her. So innocent, eager, fascinated. He was certain that the rose-colored blinders were gone from her eyes now. She had matured. And now she was...

Spectacular. More elegant than ever. She looked thoughtful, even wise.

And how would you know? Jon taunted himself.

She might well have matured into a hard, ambitious bitch, he reminded himself dryly. Life often did that to people. After all, she'd walked away from him with a will of steel. And she'd been able to stand her ground during the media blitz after her divorce, even in the midst of a shocking situation. Still, she now maintained a strange, compelling air that combined sophistication and innocence, although, God knew, he'd learned the hard way that the most delicate, fragile females could be the worst black widows.

She was a Midwestern farm girl, Jon remembered, and he had to smile. She possessed both warmth and reserve, and yet there had been moments when she'd let down her guard and he'd felt that he had known her forever. He had found her to be both captivating and as down-to-earth as her natural beauty. She'd been twenty-four, fresh from the country, when they met. She'd turned twenty-eight last month. Plenty of time to learn, to harden, to change. If only...

Well, it had been a different time, a different place, a different life. No one had ever been the wiser. He hadn't told tales.

She hadn't wanted any told.

Still...

Jon suddenly felt a deep irritation. His feelings were totally unjustified, he told himself. Brett McGraff was here, as well. She and McGraff had actually been married. Jon had no right himself. And yet...

Hell, it was his place, his party. And he intended to spend time with all his guests. McGraff's presence would only make it a more intriguing enterprise to attempt to get to know Sabrina again.

But was she in over her head? he wondered suddenly. Maybe he should have left her name off the guest list. But then, he hadn't really expected her to come. And they were all in over their heads. Still, he suddenly wished he hadn't taken the chance of making her, like the others, an unwitting pawn in this dark game.

But he'd set this board into motion; he'd had no choice. It was either this or give up his sanity. And there were others to whom he owed both the truth and justice, if not to himself. He wasn't exactly in this alone. He had promised to do things again, exactly this way.

Maybe he should just stay away from Ms. Sabrina Holloway. Of all the people here, she alone was clearly innocent.

He wondered if he could stay away from her. And he reminded himself that she was here by choice. They'd all come willingly enough, ready to play. Some for the fun of it, some for the publicity. Cassie, the inveterate journalist, had once told him, "Never miss a photo op, darling!" He'd noticed that very few writers, actors, musicians or artists ever tended to do so, and, in a manner of speaking, this week was a major photo op. Even the reclusive types who preferred to remain in the shadows wouldn't dare miss this. The world had gotten far too competitive, and name recognition could mean the difference between starvation and a healthy income.

Yet, he mused, Sabrina Holloway had inadvertently garnered enough publicity already. Marriage to and divorce from Brett McGraff had put her squarely in the public eye. But she had maintained a steady course, and though her notoriety had given her popular career a jump start, she'd managed to accrue a respectable amount of critical praise for the writing. He hadn't been in the States for a while now, so he wasn't sure who else was doing the talk-show circuit, but apparently she'd hit just the right chord with her Victorian thrillers. She was also young and lovely, and the media loved to hop on a personality with sex appeal and presence.

He was about to approach her when he realized that another woman was walking toward him. Susan Sharp. He groaned inwardly and considered a fast retreat up the secret staircase behind him. His ancestors had been Jacobites and had filled the castle with hidden doors and passages, a multitude of escape routes.

But Jon didn't escape; he didn't want his secrets known as yet, so he stood still while Susan sashayed closer, delighted with her good luck in discovering that he was literally cornered.

"Well, well," she said happily. "Darling! So here you are, in the darkness. How delightful. How wickedly delightful. Do give me a kiss, darling. We've all missed you so much."

SABRINA HOLLOWAY STARED at the disturbing display, marveling at its realism. The woman on the rack looked as if she were about to open her mouth and cry out. Her eyes were glazed, as if she were trying to deny the terror that was threatening her. Sabrina could almost hear the man demanding that his victim confess her terrible crimes and spare herself the agony of the rack.

A strange tremor snaked up Sabrina's spine.

Whoa. Excellently done. Totally unnerving. There were others ambling around the dungeon displays at Lochlyre Castle, many of them friends, but at the moment she felt thoroughly uneasy in the gloom. Just imagine. If the lights were suddenly to go out...

She would be alone. In the darkness. With him— the dark-haired torturer with the slim mustache and sadistic eyes who looked upon his victim with such pure evil in his heart. The figures were so realistically done that she could easily believe they might come to life in the dark. They would move, walk, stalk, wield their weapons of death and destruction...

Hands landed on her shoulders, and she almost screamed aloud. She jumped, but somehow she choked back the sound that had risen in her throat.

"Well, my love?"

Another little shiver snaked along her spine—she was again unnerved, but not so frightened this time. Brett

McGraff moved beside her then, settling an arm easily around her shoulders. She was ashamed to realize that his presence made her feel more secure in the shadowy dungeon, though still far from comfortable.

She was torn between clinging to him and shaking off his arm. As usual, she felt an amazing combination of emotions toward him. Sometimes he made her want to gag. Then again, she wasn't always immune to the purely sensual charm that had attracted her to him from the very beginning. Most of the time, however, she was only slightly impatient with him and fairly tolerant.

"It's very real," she murmured. "It actually scares me a little."

"Good."

"Why?"

"I think I want you scared."

"Oh?"

"Might make you a little clingy." He tightened his arm around her and lowered his mouth to whisper huskily against her ear. "We've each been assigned our own room in the castle—our host doesn't seem to remember that we were married—but I'd be happy to keep you company during the long, spooky nights."

"Were," she reminded him, "is the operative word here. We *were* married, once upon a time, more than three years ago—for all of two weeks."

"Oh, it took longer than two weeks to get a divorce," he said smoothly. "And don't forget how much we were together on our wonderful honeymoon."

"Brett, the marriage ended while we were still on that honeymoon," she reminded him.

He wasn't to be deterred. "And now we're getting to be such good friends again," he added with assurance.

Despite herself, Sabrina felt a rueful smile curving her lips. Brett was tall and good-looking, with unruly brown hair, dark bedroom eyes to match and a laconic charm that had made him a media idol. He wrote medical thrillers, with both commercial and critical success. He'd made a small fortune at his craft and still managed to be annoyingly arrogant only on occasion. Sabrina had met him soon after the sale of her second book before it had even been on the market—which had been soon after his divorce from his third wife. To say that she'd been naive was a terrible understatement. She'd also been healing from a far unhappier situation.

A whirlwind courtship had sent them on a honeymoon to Paris—at a time that happened to correspond with the French publication of Brett's latest thriller. She'd been amused, at first, by the number of women who gave him less-than-subtle hints regarding their carnal interest, then less amused when she realized how many of them he already knew. Carnally. Still, being an optimist who longed for a future, she'd decided she could live with Brett's past. It hadn't even been so bad that the women he'd known hadn't seemed to care that he had a new wife; she hadn't held other people's behavior against them. Ultimately, it had been Brett's indifference to the discomfort of her position that had disturbed her. He was a good lover; he could be amusing, charming. He'd made her laugh and love when she'd felt adrift and unsure.

But Brett could also be self-centered, selfish and downright mean. He'd disappeared with the voluptuous owner of a major bookstore for several hours and been totally impatient with his young bride when she'd demanded to know what was going on. Then he'd informed her that he was Brett McGraff, and opportunities were going to come his way. He'd told her she shouldn't mind; she should just be grateful he had actually married her, had made her his wife.

To Sabrina, his words had been devastating. She'd been stunned. Then furious—with herself. She'd been looking so desperately for someone to make her forget her past, to fill her life. And she'd been so wrong. She'd cared for Brett, believed things could work. But she'd been mistaken. So she was at fault, as well, for not seeing or believing that their visions of love and marriage were so wildly different.

Brett had seen the change, the new awareness, in her eyes, and he'd tried to placate her, to seduce her...

The rest had been hell.

She didn't want to remember. She'd learned some good lessons from that time, and maybe even taught him a few. To this day, he still couldn't believe that she'd left him and filed divorce papers, not asking for one red cent. In the months to come, when they'd met at various publishing events, he'd sought her out. He still referred to her as his wife, and she could actually smile sometimes now at the various lines he deployed to try to get her into bed. She should sleep with him because they had been married; because she'd already slept with him, and it wasn't good to sleep with strangers. Because she already knew him—and as a result there would be no ugly little surprises. Because he was good in bed; and she had to admit that he *was* good—naturally, because he was so practiced. Because surely *everybody* needed sex now and then, and since she was capable of being such a sweet, puritanical prude, coming from an apple-pie farm family and all, she was slow to form intimate relationships and therefore should simply indulge in a basic, necessary activity with him.

So far, she'd managed to resist.

She was certain that she wasn't alluring above all others; she was simply the one who had left him, and therefore she remained a challenge.

"Seriously, while we're here, wouldn't you like to share a room with me?" he asked now.

"No," she said simply.

"Admit it, I'm fun to sleep with."

"We have different ideas of fun."

"Look around you. This is a scary place," he urged.

"No, thanks, Brett."

"I can behave."

"That's doubtful. Besides, you remind me of a warning my mother used to give me Don't play with toys when you don't know where they've been."

He grinned. "Ouch! But if you'd stayed with me, you would know exactly where I'd been."

"Brett, I never knew where you were when we were married, and I really didn't have all that much time in which to misplace you. I realize that it never occurred to you that marriage meant monogamy—"

"Do you think it means that to everyone?" he demanded.

"Brett, I can't tell other people how to be married. I only know what I wanted myself."

He sniffed. "If only you knew how many people slept around—people you would never imagine."

"Brett, I don't want to imagine."

"Your own friends!" he persisted.

"Brett—"

"All right, fine. Later you'll be begging me for gossip, and I won't tell you a thing. When you need to know, you'll be in the dark. Unless, of course, you want to forget the marriage thing for a while and just have fun? My intentions are honorable, though. I will remarry you."

She groaned. "As I said, we have different ideas on fun—and marriage."

"Fine. Play hard to get. But if things start getting spooky around here, you're going to want to crawl into bed with me, and it may be too crowded by then."

"That I don't doubt."

"Hey, I'm asking you first. And surely you wouldn't want to sleep with a stranger."

"Brett, I've slept with *you*, and I really can't think of anyone much stranger."

"Very funny. You'll be sorry, my pet. You'll see." He shook his head sorrowfully, returning his gaze to the display before them. "Amazing, isn't it?" he murmured, staring at the characters, his arm still around her.

"Yes, very real," she agreed.

He shook his head. "So real that in this lighting, she could fool even me. And I was married to you."

"What are you talking about?"

"What do you mean, what am I talking about? You've been staring at this tableau." He sighed with impatience. "Sabrina! Take a good look. That's *you*."

"What?"

"Sweetheart, have you gone blind since you've been away from me? Take a look. That woman—she's you. To a T. The blue eyes, the blond hair, the gorgeous features. Nice body." He lowered his voice even further. "Great butt, too."

"You can't even see her butt, Brett."

"All right, all right, I'll concede that. But she's you. The spitting image."

"Don't be silly…" Sabrina protested, but her voice trailed away as she frowned.

Oh, Lord. Brett was right. The wax figure did bear an alarming resemblance to her. So much so that she felt chills begin to sweep up and down her spine again.

"Good!" Brett whispered huskily. "I can feel you trembling. You're getting uneasy, unnerved, good and scared. You're not going to want to be alone all night in this spooky old castle. You're going to want to come to me. Night will fall, you'll hear wolves howling, you'll run screaming from your bedroom and into mine, so you won't have to be afraid."

It was just a caricature in wax, nothing more, Sabrina told herself. Yet she still felt tremors racing through her limbs. It *was* her. The artist had executed the figure so well that the muscles and veins in the victim's arms fairly leaped into animation as she struggled to free herself from the ropes that tied her mercilessly to the rack.

The fear in the eyes was real.

The silent scream on the lips was far too eloquent. It could almost be heard in the air.

Brett whispered warningly in her ear, "You won't want to be alone."

From the darkness behind them, a deep, rich, masculine voice intervened. "Well, now, she'll hardly be alone, will she?"

Sabrina knew that husky voice.

She spun around to meet their host.

CHAPTER TWO

HIS EYES WERE on her, studying her. He smiled pleasantly as he continued, "Seriously, Brett, she'll hardly be alone, considering the fact that there are ten writers here—including ourselves, of course—along with an artist, my assistant and the castle staff, all in residence."

He sounded amused. Slipping from beneath Brett's arm, Sabrina stared at Jon Stuart. It had been a long time.

"Jon," Brett murmured, an unmistakable edge in his voice. The two were supposedly friends; still, it seemed that Brett was less than pleased with Stuart's timing.

"Brett, good to see you. Thank you for coming."

"It's always a pleasure. We were all damn glad you decided to do it again. Jon, you've met my wife, Sabrina Holloway, haven't you?"

Sabrina gazed at the mesmerizing owner of Lochlyre Castle, but Jon Stuart had already arched a dark brow Brett's way as he took Sabrina's hand. She resisted the odd temptation to wrench it away.

"Sabrina, good to see you again. I hadn't realized the two of you had remarried."

"We haven't," Sabrina said.

"Ah."

"Sorry. My ex-wife," Brett murmured innocently, smiling intimately at Sabrina as if there were still a great deal going on between them. "It's so easy to forget we ever divorced."

"Anyway, I'm glad you're both here. Thank you for coming," Stuart said politely.

"I wouldn't have missed it. You know that," Brett said.

"It was nice to be invited," Sabrina murmured.

"You've been invited before," Jon said pointedly.

"I... I was on a deadline last time." It was a lie, of course. An author's stock excuse for not being somewhere he or she didn't want to be.

"Well, it must have been worth it, then. Your last book was very good."

"You read it?" she inquired—too quickly. Instantly she wanted to kick herself. She was blushing, unaccountably pleased that he had been interested enough to read her work. Then she felt her flush darken, wondering what he must have thought of the book's graphic romantic encounters. And wondering how much her blush was giving away.

"I've loved all *your* recent work," she said quickly, trying to cover herself.

He smiled a slow, skeptical smile that clearly indicated he had heard the words before but somehow doubted them in this case.

"It's the truth," she murmured, wishing she could gracefully end her awkward monologue. Brett was staring at her now with real interest, having picked up on the tension between her and Jon Stuart.

"Really?" Jon murmured, either unaware of her discomfort or amused by it. It was disturbing to realize that he maintained such an edge over her both in maturity and in simple confidence. He had been a success since his first novel, a thriller based in World War II Italy, had been published soon after he'd graduated from college.

She forced a cool smile to her lips. She was not going

to be intimidated. "Okay, so I hated it when you killed the priest in your last book—he didn't deserve it."

Her words didn't offend him; he laughed, apparently pleased with her honesty. "Good for you, telling me the truth."

"The truth is always different through different eyes," Brett interjected somewhat irritably.

Jon shook his head. "No, there's only the truth, maybe just shaded a bit differently," he said somewhat solemnly, gazing at Sabrina. Then he seemed to collect himself and said more lightly, "And the truth is, of course, that I'm delighted you were able to tear yourself away from your busy schedule to be here, Ms. Holloway."

"She knew I was coming and that she'd be comfortable here," Brett said proprietarily.

"Great," Jon responded.

"I have a number of friends here," Sabrina murmured, wondering why she cared if Jon Stuart did or didn't think she was still sleeping with her ex-husband. But she kept talking. "You know how it goes. We authors tend to stick together. You have an impressive guest list. I'm flattered to be invited."

"I very much wanted you to be here," he said politely. "As you may recall, I wanted you last time, as well."

Right. He had wanted her. She'd first met him just months before his last Mystery Week party. And in that time, she'd married Brett—and they'd divorced.

And he'd married Cassandra Kelly.

"I had only one book out on the market at the time. I could hardly be ranked among the pros you had here then."

He arched a brow, cocking his head. "Dianne Dorsey was even more of a babe in the woods at the time, and she was here," Jon commented.

"But it did turn out to be a tragic occasion, so it's a good thing Sabrina didn't come," Brett said. "Glad to see you seem to be bucking up, old boy," he added, punching Jon lightly on the shoulder with his fist. "We haven't seen enough of you lately. By the way, wasn't Cassie actually the one who told us all what a great book Sabrina had written?"

"Yes," Jon said evenly, still studying Sabrina. "Cassandra thought you had created superb characters in a compelling setting, then concocted the perfect murder for just the right dramatic twist."

"That was quite nice of her," Sabrina murmured uncomfortably. Cassandra was dead—and she felt incredibly guilty, because she hadn't cared much for the woman when she was alive.

All right, so she'd jealously despised her. The one time they'd met face-to-face had been a horror worse than anything in this gallery.

It was only natural that she had hated Cassandra Stuart.

A hot tremor snaked through her again, having nothing to do with the tableau in front of them. The way Jon was staring at her was unnerving. Despite the ridiculously possessive way Brett was behaving at the moment, Sabrina was suddenly glad of his presence.

For Jon Stuart was imposing. Even intimidating, in a way. Perhaps by simple virtue of his height and hard-muscled build. He was very tall, about six foot three, and strikingly handsome in a rugged way. His hair wasn't just dark, it was jet-black, thick and luxurious, long past his collar though neatly combed back from his forehead. His eyes were a marbled hazel, truly unique, merging blue, green and brown into a compelling, moody mix that could appear golden at times, dark as night at others. His features were strong, arresting: firm, square chin; broad cheekbones; generous, sensual mouth; high, defined brow. At thirty-seven, he was a renowned master of adventure and suspense writing; in real life, too, he had been named by a prominent international magazine to be one of the world's ten most intriguing men. An American of Scottish heritage, he had never used fame or fortune to shirk duty; he'd served overseas in the National Guard during Desert Storm.

Though Stuart had recently lain very low, remaining in Scotland more often than not, he still appeared in news stories now and then, usually upon the once-a-year publication of his latest book or the reissue in paperback of the previous title. It didn't matter that he'd been something of a recluse for the past several years—that merely enhanced his reputation.

The mystery surrounding the death of his wife rendered him both fascinatingly dangerous and hauntingly sympathetic. Some journalists claimed he had gone into deep mourning for Cassandra, while others hinted he had retreated into guilt, that he had somehow killed her— even if he had been a hundred feet away from the balcony from which she'd fallen at the time. Some suggested she might have committed suicide, that her marriage had been failing and she had cast herself from the balcony in a moment of dramatic self-pity, putting the blame on her famous husband, creating a scandal that would torment him until the end of his days. Others thought that perhaps the cancer consuming her beautiful breasts had driven her to despair. Whatever had happened had certainly given rise to endless speculation. And Jon Stuart had endured legal hearings into the matter and been tried by the press, his peers and fans, as well. His annual Mystery Week, a famed writers' retreat orchestrated at his secluded castle in Scotland to raise publicity and funds for children's charities, had been halted.

Until now.

Three years after the death of his wife, he had opened the doors of Lochlyre Castle to the outside world once again.

"Come to think of it, Cassie's praise of Sabrina's work was noteworthy," Brett mused suddenly, "because she wasn't usually so generous. She supposedly liked my work, but she ripped *Scalpel* to shreds. Remember, Jon? She even blasted your work sometimes, and though I hate to admit it, that's hard to do."

"Thanks. That's quite a compliment," Jon said dryly.

Brett grinned. "I'm feeling chipper. Just got the word that *Surgery* is number two, the *New York Times* list, come a week from Sunday."

"Congratulations," Sabrina told him wholeheartedly. He always made the bestseller lists, but his position was rising steadily, much to his delight.

"Great," Jon said. "You can keep everybody's spirits up during the week. Remind them that, dire perennial rumors to the contrary, publishing is not yet dead. So...what do you two think of the chamber of horrors this year?"

"Ghoulishly wonderful," Brett said.

"Too real." Sabrina shuddered.

"Ah," Jon murmured, eyes pure gold with sudden devilish humor. "I wouldn't let your resemblance to the lady on the rack upset you," he said. "An artist named Joshua Valine created the figures for the exhibit. He's also done a lot of cover art—he met you at the booksellers' convention in Chicago and was duly impressed."

"Not very positively, if he has me on the rack," Sabrina commented.

Jon laughed, a deep, husky, compelling sound. "Trust me, his reaction was quite positive. He always uses real people, whether he's painting or working in wax. And if you'll look around, you'll see that there really wasn't a pleasant situation in which he could have put anyone. Look to the far corner," he said, that glimmer still in his eyes.

As hardened as she told herself she had become, Sabrina could still feel the force of his charisma. He had just the slightest hint of a Scotsman's burr in his deep voice, acquired from all the time he had spent here. His features and build—his entire presence—were exceedingly masculine. Even his subtle aftershave seemed intoxicating.

Indeed, Jon Stuart was a dangerous man, she reminded herself. And a stranger, really, though she had once known him well—in a way.

"In the far corner over there," he said now, "Louis XVI and Marie Antoinette are off to face the guillotine, and Joan of Arc is about to be burned at the stake. In the next display, Anne Boleyn is ready to meet her swordsman, and over there, Jack the Ripper is in the midst of slicing Mary Kelly's throat." He shook his head in mock sadness. "Joshua is not fond of Susan Sharp, I'm afraid. Go take a look at Mary Kelly."

"So I suppose I should be grateful to be on the rack? Tortured for endless hours before death?" Sabrina observed.

Jon cocked his head slightly, amused. "Actually, Ms. Holloway, the beautiful blonde on the rack is the only victim in this room to survive. She is Lady Ariana Stuart, and before she could be stretched and broken—accused of an attempt to turn young Charles over to Cromwell's forces when his father was about to be beheaded—her brother brought a plea regarding her innocence before the young Charles himself, who was by then returned to the throne as Charles II, king of England. Charles, being the lusty fellow he was, instantly saw the waste in destroying so fine a damsel, so he ordered her out of the torture chamber and into his bed. Naturally, being the charming man he was, he made her one of his mistresses. She bore him numerous illegitimate children and lived to a ripe old age."

"How comforting," Sabrina said.

"Very romantic," Brett sniffed. "I bet you made all that up to placate Sabrina."

"I swear it's God's own truth," Jon Stuart assured them.

"Well, Joshua certainly had a field day with Susan Sharp," Brett said, chuckling with malicious pleasure. "And what a perfect Ripper's victim. After all, she has been known to 'entertain' men for the rewards she might gain," he remarked.

"That's hearsay," Jon murmured, shrugging.

Sabrina gritted her teeth at Brett's boorish comment and silently applauded Jon's refusal to speak ill of others.

"Who did old Josh use for Joan of Arc?" Brett asked, unfazed.

"My assistant, Camy," Jon said. "She's actually quite religious herself, I believe, and a good, hard worker."

"How apropos," Brett said. "I approve."

Jon grinned. "So far you do."

Brett let out a groan. "So there's something I'm not going to like?"

"Most probably not."

"He used me?"

Jon nodded.

"As?"

Jon indicated the torturer about to twist the rack with the blonde beauty upon it.

"Take away all the facial hair..." Jon suggested with a touch of rueful apology.

Brett gasped. "I should sue!"

Sabrina couldn't help but laugh, which irritated Brett still further.

"Come on, Brett, be a sport. You were just a model—and with the beard and mustache, no one will guess. And remember, the weekend is all for charity. Have a sense of humor," she suggested.

"Oh, very funny. I get to torture my ex-wife. So are you in this rogues' gallery?" he demanded of Jon.

Jon arched a brow. "Yes. Yes, I am."

"Where?" Brett demanded.

"Come on."

Brett looked at Sabrina, shrugging. "He's probably set himself up as a king—or as Gandhi."

"Gandhi would hardly fit in here, and a number of kings weren't such great fellows," Jon reminded him. "But I didn't have anything to do with Joshua's choice of models. He doesn't tell me how to write, and I don't tell him how to sculpt."

They followed him down a corridor to another display. A tall man in European dress of perhaps the 1500s stood above the sprawled body of a woman. Her head was turned to the side, hiding her features from them. The man was staring down at the woman with a mixture of anger and confusion on his face. He had long, light brown hair, but he was still quite evidently Jon Stuart.

"Who are they?" Sabrina asked, confused.

"He's not well-known to Americans," Jon said, studying the display dispassionately. "His name was Matthew McNamara. Laird McNamara. He was a Scotsman who did away with three mistresses and two wives."

"How?" Brett asked. "I don't see a weapon."

"He strangled them," Jon said simply.

"How did he get away with so many murders before he was found out?" Sabrina asked.

"He was never brought to justice. He was considered so powerful among the clansmen that executing his own wayward women was considered his right," Jon said.

He turned away from the figures to look at her again, and she saw that his marbled eyes had gone very dark and cold. A strange trembling touched her as he slowly smiled. Was he mocking her? Or himself? She was afraid, she realized.

And worse.

She felt like a moth attracted to a flame. Time hadn't changed anything, nor had distance. That Jon Stuart was virtually a stranger to her meant nothing at all. She felt the same fierce and immediate fascination she had felt the first time she'd met him, a little more than three and a half years ago.

The first time…the last time.

"Who's the model for the wife?" Brett asked. Then, as if suddenly realizing that he might not want to hear the answer, he hurried on. "Joshua Valine is good. What an eye for detail."

"Relax, Brett. It isn't Cassie," Jon said, a dry smile curling his lip. "It's Dianne Dorsey. You can see her face if you look at the tableau from the other side."

"Dianne…well, yes, of course. I guess I thought of Cassie because of the black hair, but Dianne is dark, too…" Brett murmured, clearing his throat. He looked at Jon uneasily.

"Cassie's over there, Brett," Jon said, indicating a figure praying in front of mullioned windows. "Joshua used her for his Mary, Queen of Scots, contemplating the morning of the day of her execution."

"Yes, yes, that's definitely Cassandra," Brett said, staring for a long moment. His eyes jerked back to Jon's. "Doesn't that…bother you?"

"They all bother me—they're so real," Jon admitted. "But Josh is an artist, and that's how he works. Besides, I think Cassie makes a good Mary, Queen of Scots."

"They're all women, the victims," Sabrina commented.

Jon smiled. "Well, historically, it seems, lots of men were monsters. But I assure you, we have some lethal ladies here, as well." He pointed across the room. "There you have Countess Báthory, the Hungarian 'blood countess.' Allegedly she sacrificed hundreds of young women so she could bathe in their blood to retain her youth and beauty. V. J. Newfield is the model, as you might notice."

"Oh, you're in trouble there!" Brett warned.

Jon laughed. "V.J. will get a good laugh out of it. Besides, the countess was supposed to be quite beautiful as well as bloodthirsty." He pointed out another tableau. "There you have Lady Emily Watson, who poisoned no fewer than ten husbands to get their worldly goods. So you see, we do try to be an equal-opportunity chamber of horrors."

"Who's the model for Lady Emily?" Brett queried.

"Anna Lee Zane. And her victim is Thayer Newby."

Brett laughed. "Thayer, downed by a woman! He's going to love that."

Jon shrugged. "There's Reggie Hampton as Good Queen Bess, signing the death warrant for Mary, Queen of Scots."

"Who are the others?" Sabrina asked, indicating the rest of the tableaux receding into the shadowy depths of the castle's basement.

"Naturally Tom Heart and Joe Johnston are in here, but I'll let you find them. Joshua used a few of the household staff, as well, so don't be surprised if you find your breakfast being served by Catherine the Great."

"Sabrina," Brett puffed, "we really should remarry, and quickly! Jack the Ripper could arrive for your laundry!"

"Oh, I think I can manage my own hand laundry, and I'll make sure to have breakfast with a crowd," Sabrina told him. She wanted to kick him when she saw that Jon was studying her again.

Jon merely shrugged and seemed to ignore the exchange. "Joshua had lots of people working on this project for more than a year. We'll be donating the sculptures to a new museum in the north country when we're done here."

"You'll need releases from the models," Brett warned him.

Jon smiled. "I think I'll get them. The publicity will be phenomenal, you know."

"Great, I'll go down in history as a maniacal torturer!" Brett moaned, but the word *publicity* had won him over.

"Don't feel bad. One way or the other, I go down as a wife murderer. Well, if you'll excuse me, I have a few things to attend to. Enjoy yourselves. Brett, you know your way around. Ms. Holloway, please make yourself at home, as well. I'll see you at cocktails."

He turned and walked away with strong strides. In a moment the shadows swallowed him.

Yet somehow his presence seemed to linger, and Sabrina found herself turning to stare again at the wax tableau of Matthew, Laird McNamara.

Very tall, straight, broad-shouldered he was, with hands on his hips as he stood over the woman at his feet. Handsome, proud, merciless, powerful—laird indeed of his domain.

So powerful that he could kill and get away with it?

She forced herself to turn away, to look at the other figures as they engaged in their various dances with death.

The diffuse lighting made everything even more horrible. Shadows filled the room except where each scene stood, looming out of the darkness in eerie purple light, adding to the sensation of everything being *real*. Sabrina could imagine that the figures breathed. That they twitched, that they sweated. That they might move at any second…

Matthew McNamara stood over his wife, fists clenched.

Jack the Ripper wielded his knife.

And Lady Ariana Stuart continued to scream in terror and chilling silence.

A new wave of chills began a route through Sabrina's bloodstream, and she jumped again when Brett's hands fell on her shoulders.

"Let's get out of here, shall we?" he said.

And she realized that even he suddenly sounded afraid.

CHAPTER THREE

"Ms. Holloway!"

Cocktails were being served in the library of the castle, just down the grand staircase from the guest rooms on the second floor and opposite the great hall, where everyone would gather for dinner. Sabrina found herself arriving rather late. She'd lingered in the modern bath for a very long time, drawing together the courage to dress and go downstairs. Her brief meeting with Jon Stuart had left her far more unnerved than she'd imagined it would. For once she had to be grateful for Brett's presence. He kept her from feeling too lost and alone, even if he was annoying.

She'd barely reached the doorway to the library when she heard her name being called. A small woman with short-cropped, shiny brown hair was moving toward her, offering her a glass of champagne. She had powder blue eyes, a pretty, heart-shaped face and a tentative smile that immediately set Sabrina at ease.

"Welcome, welcome, we're so delighted that you could come. Well, I'm delighted especially, since I'm a true fan." She pressed the champagne flute forward into Sabrina's hand.

"Thank you so much," Sabrina said. "And you are...?"

"Oh!" The young woman said, and flushed, making

her appear even prettier and more delicate. "I'm Camy, Camy Clark. I'm Jon's secretary and assistant."

"Of course, Joan of Arc!"

Camy flushed more deeply. "Yes, that would be me. Joshua Valine is a good friend."

Sabrina laughed. "He must be. You look lovely, even being martyred."

"Well, Josh is a dear. He makes everyone look wonderful. You're definitely the finest looking victim I've ever seen on a rack."

Sabrina laughed again, lifting her champagne glass. "He's very talented, certainly."

"So are you. I love your work. The male writers can be so dry. You know, all action but no endearing characteristics to their people. I just love your Miss Miller. She's a delight. So real, so sympathetic, brave but not ridiculously so."

"Thank you again. Very much."

"Camy, Camy, Camy!"

A slim woman of about five-five, with short, artfully styled dark hair, was bearing down on them. Her off-the-shoulder cocktail dress was elegant designer wear; her shoes matched its soft mauve. Sabrina knew Susan Sharp, because Susan herself made a point of knowing everyone. Most writers both feared and appreciated the literary critic because she had so much clout, especially in the world of the wealthy, and thus, by word of mouth, could help make or break a book or an author. She had written two mysteries herself and done very well with them, since her characters were clearly based on her acquaintances among the rich and famous. But she could also be loud, opinionated and abrasive, drawing mixed reactions from friends and enemies alike. It was rumored that she had absolutely hated Cassandra Stuart, who had often been her competition in talk-show bookings.

"Camy, Camy, Camy!" Susan repeated, reaching out to curl her perfectly manicured fingers around Sabrina's arm. "You can't just pin Ms. Holloway down at the doorway—we're all waiting to see her. Authors get to be such good friends, you know."

"Yes, of course, Ms. Sharp," Camy murmured, flashing Sabrina an embarrassed look. Susan had put her in her place. She was just an assistant. The rest of them were *authors*.

"Camy, it was wonderful meeting you, and I look forward to getting to spend more time together," Sabrina told the young woman.

Camy lit up with a smile. "Thanks!"

Susan drew Sabrina on into the room. "How have you been? It's been ages since I've seen you."

"It was just last June, in Chicago," Sabrina reminded her.

"Yes, of course, you were doing so well. So many people adore that Miss Mailer of yours."

"Miller," Sabrina corrected smoothly.

"Yes, yes, Miss Miller. So tell me, what's up with you and Brett? Are you planning on remarrying?"

"What?" Sabrina demanded.

"Well, Brett does make it sound as if you two share so much passion, both of you being so talented and wild. I'll never forget how delicious it was when the tabloids ran those pictures of you running *naked* from your hotel room in Paris."

"Susan, maybe you'll never forget, but I'd like to. It was a very painful time in my life," Sabrina said firmly.

"Oh, look, there's V. J. Newfield. I haven't seen her in quite some time. Excuse me, will you?"

Sabrina escaped Susan and hurried toward V. J.—Victoria Jane—Newfield. V.J. was somewhere in her fifties or sixties and had been writing forever, or so it seemed. Her work was dark and scary but far more psychological than graphic, always striking a resonant note on the human condition. She was very slim, tall, with silver hair and a graceful carriage. She was a stunning woman and doubtless would be so until the day she died. Sabrina had met her early on in her career at a group autographing, where V.J. had assured her that the nicest thing about doing signings with other authors was that there was always someone interesting to talk to if no one stopped to buy a book.

"Trip the customers as they go by, dear," she had advised. "When they think you're sitting at a table piled high with books just so you can direct them to the nearest ladies' room, trip them! Then apologize to pieces, and you've snagged them!" V.J. had been great. Already popular, she had convinced most of her fans that they simply *had* to buy Sabrina's book, as well, and Sabrina remained grateful to this day.

"V.J.!" she now said with pleasure, approaching the woman at the buffet table, where she was studying caviar-covered crackers and trying to decide whether or not to indulge.

"Sabrina, dear!" V.J. said, turning with a smile and offering her a warm hug. "I wanted to call and make sure you were going to come. I was so sorry when I learned that you turned down the last invitation, though that did become quite a tragedy. I just got back from a cruise down the Nile—do you remember my telling you how much I wanted to take one of those?"

"Yes, and I'm glad you got to go. How was it?"

"Wonderful. Exhilarating. Awesome. The sense of history is so intense, so chilling. And I do just love a good mummy."

"I've got nothing against loving mommies," Brett said, slipping an arm around Sabrina's shoulder and smiling at V.J. "Mommies these days can be just as exciting as the innocent girls. It's great to see you, V.J. You look splendid. Sexy as ever. A great mommy."

"My children are all long grown up!" V.J. reminded him.

"Mummies, my boy, mummies. We're talking about dead women, though from what I hear of your indiscriminate womanizing, that might not make any difference to you. How are you, Brett? A kiss will be acceptable, but just on the cheek. And quit mauling Sabrina. The child has the good sense to be your *ex*-wife, and if the right man is out there, we don't want him being put off by your foolishness."

Brett laughed, freed Sabrina and good-naturedly planted a kiss on V.J.'s cheek.

"I am the right man, V.J.," Brett protested in a mock-pitiful voice. "One moment's bad behavior, and she won't forgive me."

"My boy, I'm no marriage counselor, but I sense that it might have been a bit deeper than that. Still…" She smiled, lifting her champagne flute to him. "Congratulations, I hear you're just below Crichton on the list."

Brett bowed his head in humble acceptance. "Thank you, thank you. Crichton just had to put out another book the same month, huh? I might have made number one."

"Well, there's always next year."

"So there is. And since we're all together here, a fine assembly of mystery, suspense and horror writers, surely we can come up with some new ways to bump off the competition. What do you say?"

"I say it's in bad taste, considering where we are," a masculine voice stated softly, and Joe Johnston stepped into their circle. Joe was an Ernest Hemingway look-alike, a handsome man with a bushy beard and a pleasant way about him. He wrote a series about a down-and-out private investigator, charming and laid-back, who still solved the crime every time.

Joe clinked glasses with Sabrina by way of hello and continued, "I mean, who really thinks that Cassandra Stuart threw herself from that balcony?"

"Joe, shush!" V.J. warned. "It was great of Jon to do this again after what happened last time."

"My point exactly," Joe said. "And that's why we can't talk about bumping off our competition."

Susan Sharp sidled into their group. "We can't talk about bumping people off?" she protested indignantly. "Joe, it's Mystery Week. One of us is *supposed* to be a murderer and bump off the others until the mystery is solved. That's the whole point."

"Right, but that's all pretend," Sabrina said.

Susan laughed dryly. "Well, let's hope that Cassandra's being dead isn't pretend. Can you imagine if she were suddenly to walk back into this room?"

"Susan, that's a horrible thing to say," V.J. admonished. "If Cassandra were to suddenly appear here, alive—"

"If Cassandra were suddenly to appear here, alive, more than half the people here would be thinking of ways to kill her again," Susan said flatly. "Cassandra was vicious and horrible."

"And smart, talented and very beautiful," V.J. reminded her smoothly.

"Oh, I suppose. And just think—everyone who was here when she died is back again. The guest list is exactly the same," Susan said.

"I wasn't here," Sabrina reminded her.

Susan shrugged, as if her presence were of little importance. "Well, you were invited, and the point is that those of us who were here then are here again. All of us. Ready to defend ourselves if we're accused."

"Accused of murder?" V.J. asked.

"Accused of anything," Susan said blithely. "We all have our little secrets, don't we?" she demanded, staring hard at V.J.

V.J. stared right back at her.

"Susan, if you're going to start implying things about the rest of us —" Joe began.

"Oh, come now, Joe, we're all grown-ups. Everyone knew that no matter how polite and controlled he seemed, Jon was furious with Cassandra. He thought she was having an affair—and she implied to me on several occasions that she was!"

"Susan, 'Pass me the butter' has made you think people were having an affair on at least one occasion," V.J. said impatiently.

"V.J., it's all in *how* someone says it. The point is, Jon thought she was having an affair, and *she* thought *Jon* was. If they were both right, then you have two other people involved. And God knows, Cassandra nearly destroyed some careers. Any number of us despised her at various points for what she said about our work."

"*You* might well have despised her," a soft voice said. It was shy, retiring Camy, who smiled apologetically at Susan. "After all, Ms. Sharp, you two were often in direct competition, weren't you?"

Susan arched a brow, staring at the girl imperiously. She didn't mind the accusation; she minded Camy's interrupting her. "My dear child, I have no real competition. But just for the record, I did despise Cassandra Stuart. She was an opportunist who used and manipulated people, and you should be grateful that she's dead, because she would have had you fired by now otherwise. Now please excuse me." She turned her back on the girl and spoke to the others. "You mark my words. Everyone here has a secret, not to mention a reason to hate Cassandra Stuart."

"Except Sabrina," Joe commented quietly.

Susan stared sharply at Sabrina. "Who knows? Maybe she had as much reason as the rest of us. But you couldn't have tossed her over the balcony, could you, Sabrina? You turned down the invitation to come here last time. Why? Most writers would kill—if you'll pardon the expression—for such an invitation."

"Fear of flying," Sabrina said sweetly.

Susan kept staring at her. "I'll just bet," she said. Then, whirling around, she left the group.

"I think *she* did it," Brett said with such simple conviction that they all laughed.

"According to the police, no one did it," Joe said.

"Cassandra didn't commit suicide," V.J. commented. "She loved herself far too much for that."

"But I thought she had cancer," Sabrina said.

"She did, but *maybe* it *was* treatable," Brett said.

"Maybe she simply tripped," Sabrina suggested.

"That's probably just what happened," another masculine voice interrupted. It was Tom Heart. Tall, lean, white-haired, handsome and dignified, he was the unlikely author of some of the most chilling horror novels on the market. He smiled, lifting a champagne flute to them all. "Cheers, friends, gentlemen and ladies, Brett, Joe, Sabrina… V.J. Good to see you all. And, Sabrina, you may be right on the money. From what I understand, Cassandra was shouting at Jon, who had simply had it with her mood of the moment and was walking away. Perhaps she leaned over to shout louder and leaned just a little too far. Ah, there's our host now, with the lovely Dianne Dorsey on one arm and the exquisite Anna Lee Zane on the other."

Sabrina looked toward the library door. Their host was indeed just arriving—in style.

He was in a tux, and achingly handsome. His height and dark good looks were enhanced by the elegance of his attire. His hair was slicked back, his crystalline eyes enigmatic as he talked and laughed with the two attractive women.

Anna Lee was a writer whose novels were based on true crimes. She was somewhere in her late thirties, very petite and feminine, and rumor had it that she happily chose her sexual partners from either gender.

Dianne Dorsey was considered the up-and-coming voice of horror. She was fond of creating alien beings with a bizarre hunger for human flesh. She was very young, having just turned twenty-two, and had published her first novel as a junior in high school, her second as a senior, and now, just out of Harvard, she was a veteran, with four books on the market. She was considered a genius and already had a huge following. Older writers had a tendency to be jealous of her amazing success at so tender an age, success acquired with what appeared to be so little effort. Sabrina was only envious because Dianne seemed to have acquired such self-assurance at so young an age. She would still give her eyeteeth for that kind of assurance. She had a feeling, though, that Dianne had had a tough childhood, that something had happened to make her a fighter even early on.

As she contemplated Dianne, Sabrina realized that Anna Lee was waving at her, smiling. She smiled and waved back.

Then Dianne spotted her, and she, too, grinned and waved. Sabrina lifted a hand in return. Dianne was into the gothic look. She always wore black; her hair was jet-black; her lipstick was black; her skin was flawlessly white. She favored huge medallions, medieval-style jewelry and slinky clothing and yet managed her look with a sexy femininity that made her unique and appealing.

Still smiling, Sabrina suddenly became aware that Jon was watching her.

Once again, she was right next to Brett. Brett was, in fact, brushing up against her.

She quickly lowered her eyes. She told herself that she didn't want to get involved with anyone. She hadn't come here hoping to find something she had lost. She was a mature woman now, with a good career, lots of friends and a great family. She was here as a guest, participating in an important charity event, and it was icing on the cake that it might be a boon to her career, as well.

Liar! an inner voice taunted.

"Ladies, gentlemen, dinner is being served in the great hall," Jon announced. He excused himself from his two companions, and Sabrina bit her lip to keep from taking a step back as he walked purposefully toward her. "Ms. Holloway, you're the only one here who might not have had a chance to meet everyone. Excuse me, Brett, may I claim your ex-wife for a moment?" he asked lightly.

"Sure—for a moment," Brett replied in kind.

Sabrina was dismayed by the warmth that filled her when Jon took her by the arm, flashing his smile, and led her across the room to where a tall, slim man with curly blond hair and clean, handsome features was standing. He looked like an artist, impeccable in his dress clothing except for a tiny drop of paint on his tie. "Ms. Holloway, I'm sure you remember Joshua Valine, our sculptor extraordinaire."

"Oh, yes," Sabrina said, instantly remembering the man as his warm brown eyes touched hers. They'd met briefly in Chicago, at the booksellers' convention. She'd been signing books, and one of the sales reps had introduced him. "We've met," she told Jon, shaking Valine's hand. "How nice to see you again. Your wax work is incredible. But so real and scary! I'm going to have nightmares about being tortured by my ex-husband," she told him.

Joshua flushed and flashed a smile. "Thank you. Forgive me for putting you on the rack. You do live, though, you know."

She laughed softly. "So I've been told."

"You're rescued from the rack on the command of the king."

She nodded, adding, "I'm glad I didn't have to be one of Jack the Ripper's victims."

Joshua wrinkled his nose, lowering his voice. "Susan Sharp does it well, though, don't you think?"

"Shh. Susan has exceptional hearing," Jon teased.

"Let's see, Joshua, is there anyone here that Sabrina might not know yet?"

"Have you met Camy Clark?" Joshua asked.

"Yes, she's charming. You're very lucky to have her, Jon."

"She's organized and incredibly competent, and I *am* very lucky," Jon agreed. "How about…?"

As he turned to look around the room, they were joined by a solid-looking man with his bright red hair in an old-fashioned crew cut. He flashed a smile at Jon and Joshua and extended his hand to Sabrina. "We've met, but only briefly, at a conference in Tahoe. I don't know if you remember me or not, but I'm—"

"Of course I remember you," Sabrina told him. "You're Thayer Newby. I went to every one of your lectures. You probably didn't see me, because the rooms were so full every time you were speaking."

Thayer Newby flushed to the roots of what there was of his hair. He'd been a cop for twenty years before becoming a writer, and his talks on police procedure were excellent.

"Thanks!" he said, staring at her and still holding her hand. He shook his head slightly. "How did McGraff ever let you get away?" he inquired. Then he suddenly blushed again. "Sorry, none of my business. I did see that picture, of course."

Sabrina gritted her teeth, trying not to blush herself. But she could feel Jon at her side, looking at her, and she knew that of course anyone who had ever seen that tabloid photo would wonder just what had caused her to go running naked from her honeymoon suite.

"Brett and I have different ideas about marriage," she said as smoothly as she could manage.

"But you've remained friends, huh?" Thayer said, trying to be casual.

Somehow the words didn't sound right. And Sabrina realized that he'd probably seen her with Brett most of the night and, like others, had jumped to the conclusion that they had remained more than just friends.

"Yes, we've managed that," she said flatly.

"Ah, there's Reggie," Jon said, lifting a hand. "Do you know Reggie Hampton?" he asked Sabrina.

Old yet somehow ageless, Regina Hampton might have been seventy or a hundred and ten. She had written scores of books about an amateur sleuth who was a grandmother and solved local mysteries with the help of her cat. Reggie was blunt, intelligent and a great deal of fun, and she had walked straight across to them as she came into the room. "Reggie," Jon began. "Do you know—"

"Of course I know the dear child!" Reggie exclaimed. She was tiny and thin and looked as if a breeze would blow her over, but she hugged Sabrina with an amazing strength that gave proof to the rumor that she was a tough old bird. "How lovely to see you here, Sabrina! Jon, however did you convince this lovely young thing to come visit a morbid, reclusive old man in his decaying castle?"

"The same way I convinced you, you old battle-ax," he teased her affectionately in turn. "I sent her an invitation."

"Well, it's just wonderful that you're here. We need new blood in on these affairs!" Reggie said.

"Ah," teased Susan, striding over to the group, "let's just hope we don't *shed* new blood, eh?" She smiled wickedly.

"Let's eat—I'm famished!" V.J. called from across the room. "Jon, you did announce dinner, didn't you? If we don't eat soon, we'll all expire, and not so mysteriously."

"Perish the thought!" Joe Johnston quipped.

"Perish! That *is* the thought," Reggie retorted.

"Right, Jon, let's eat," Brett said. "And by the way, think we could break out some brewskies? This champagne just doesn't cut it for me. How about you, Thayer?"

"There's a full bar in the great hall, with beer on tap and all kinds, domestic and imported, in the bottle. Go on in and help yourselves," Jon said.

He glanced down at Sabrina, his eyes strangely dark. She felt as if he were studying her, assessing her. And he looked as if he suddenly wanted to push her away from him.

"Excuse me, will you, please?" he said quietly. And then he was gone.

CHAPTER FOUR

REGGIE HAMPTON LINKED arms with Sabrina. "My dear, you are a breath of fresh air. Tell me, what's been happening with you since July?"

Sabrina tried not to watch Jon Stuart as he strode away from her. She forced herself to focus on Reggie, and replied with enthusiasm, "I've been home visiting my family."

"At the farm?"

"Yes. I have an apartment in New York now, but I've been staying at my folks' and my sister's for a while. She just had a baby, her first, a little boy. Naturally, we're all just delighted. I spent a few months out there to help when the baby was born."

"You should be having your own babies soon."

"Reggie, not every woman has babies these days."

"But you want children, don't you?"

"Yes, I do, when the time is right."

"Are you going to remarry Br—"

"No. Enough about me, Reggie. How is your family?"

Reggie told her briefly about her sons, grandsons and new great-granddaughter as they crossed the entry to the great hall, where dinner would be served. They all milled around the bar first, making drinks.

Brett popped up again to supply Sabrina with a gin and tonic, heavy on the lime, then whispered happily that he'd moved the place cards around at the dinner table and put her next to him. They sat down to a magnificent meal of pheasant and fish. As they ate, they all talked and laughed; it might have been a high school reunion. Then Jon, at the head of the table, thanked them again for coming and reminded them that they were there not only for fun but also for the benefit of children's charities. Each writer had submitted a favorite cause, and the one who solved the mystery claimed the lion's share of the donations.

"When do we start?" Thayer called out.

"Tomorrow morning," Jon replied. "Those with the energy are welcome to catch up on each other's lives tonight. Those who are too exhausted from jet lag can get some sleep. Things will be pretty much the same as they were previous years. Camy and Joshua have worked out the particulars. I won't know who the murderer is any more than any of you will. In the morning, you'll all receive your character roles and a description of the situation. The murderer will discover who he—or she—is, and then he or she will have to get busy before being discovered. The murderer will have been assigned the order in which the victims are to be dispatched. The victims will be 'murdered' with a washable red paint, and naturally we'll take care of any cleaning expenses. Any questions?"

"Sure," Joe Johnston said, speaking up. "Even if I'm not the murderer, can I shoot Susan anyway?"

Laughter rose, then faded, as Susan stared them all down. "You're right at the top of my list, too, Joe," she told him sweetly. She pointed a finger at him and made a popping sound, as if she were pulling a trigger. "And you'll be covered in something a lot worse than red paint!"

"Come, come, children, behave," Anna Lee Zane drawled.

"Well, shit, I'm sorry!" Joe said.

Anna Lee shook her head, as if it were as impossible to deal with writers as with unruly children.

Jon rose. "If you all will excuse me, I have a few things to attend to," he said. "Please, make yourselves at home. We'll meet here at nine tomorrow morning. For the early birds, coffee will be on the buffet by six."

He exited the great hall, closing the double doors behind him. Sabrina stared after him, biting her lower lip, wishing suddenly that she hadn't come.

Brett's hand landed on hers where it rested on the table. "Want to see my room?" he inquired hopefully.

She withdrew her hand, smiling because he could be so much like a child, so eager, so unwilling to admit defeat.

"No. I'm going to bed."

"That will work with me."

"To sleep. I'm one of those guests with jet lag. I got to London late last night and came here this afternoon. I'm tired."

"All right. I'm right next door to you, if you change your mind. If things go bump in the night."

"Thanks. I'll keep that in mind," she told him.

She waved a good-night to the others as she escaped the great hall.

The castle foyer and magnificent staircase were empty. With the doors to the library and great hall closed, she suddenly felt very alone in the ancient edifice.

She hurried up the stairs and down the second-floor hallway with its Norman arches toward her own room.

It was huge, retaining a historical feel yet updated to offer incredible warmth and comfort. The bed sat on a richly carpeted dais, and heavy draperies hung at the balcony doors to ward off cold drafts. The closet and bath were large, and an antique desk sat to the side of a massive hearth. A fire had been built and stoked, and it burned brightly as she entered her room, hesitated, then carefully shot the bolt.

She kicked off her shoes and stripped away her stockings, then found herself wandering to the glass-paned balcony doors that closed out the night beyond. She opened them and stepped outside. From this vantage point she could see rolling fields, the shimmering waters of a small loch and the purple crests of mountains in the distance. The scenery, even by moonlight, was breathtaking. This trip was the opportunity of a lifetime.

She never should have come.

Sabrina drew a long, shaky breath. "So," she asked herself aloud, "did you come to try to convince yourself that your brief, shining moment in his company is completely over and forgotten? Or were you hoping to sleep with him just once more, whatever the consequences?"

She felt her cheeks redden. How humiliating. Would he sleep with her again? She undoubtedly had a reputation for being rather...casual. Just think of the way she had left Brett, running away naked...

Funny. Brett was okay. She liked being friends. It was even flattering that he still pursued her. What he had done *was* terribly wrong, but what she had done was wrong, as well. She had married him without truly loving him.

Because, of course, she had been in love with Jon Stuart.

A cool breeze suddenly wrapped around her, and she remembered being in New York City for the very first time and winding up at a party for one of her publicist's other clients, who had just had a Broadway opening. Sabrina had had no idea who the handsome party guest was when she met him, other than that his name was

Jon. He'd had her laughing, telling her about the terrors of the big city and how it might well be a death-defying feat simply to survive her first experience with a New York cabdriver.

Admittedly, she'd drunk too much. She'd been exhilarated with the success of selling her book and excited at being in his company. He had a car, and he offered to drive her back to her hotel.

She'd fallen asleep on his shoulder in the car, and when they'd reached her hotel, she was still drowsy, intoxicated and giddy. She remembered opening her eyes and seeing his face above hers, his eyes dark, marbled, fascinating. "We're here," he'd told her.

And she'd nodded, though she hadn't moved, and then he'd said, "I can carry you up to your room. Which is what I should do. Because if I bring you home with me, I'll take advantage of you. I won't be able to help myself."

Even with the breeze caressing her now on the balcony, she could still remember her reply.

"Please do."

No amount of alcohol could forgive that, she told herself now. She hugged her arms around her chest. Yet it had been wonderful. The best time of her life. They'd driven to his apartment in the city, and he'd carried her upstairs. He had undressed her in his bedroom, and, still dressed himself, he had demanded to know if she was sure…

Then he had kissed her, and for the rest of her life she would remember his touch on her body, his lips, burning, intimate, demanding, everywhere. She would remember him, the feel of his flesh, the touch of his hands, the mole at the small of his back…

The night had been pure magic. The next day they'd

cooked breakfast together, wandered through the Metropolitan Museum of Art and gone out for Chinese before returning to spend the evening making love again. Absurdly, after all that, it wasn't until the next morning that she'd asked his last name and learned that he was "the" Jon Stuart, the well-known author.

Jon had been in the shower when his "fiancée," Cassandra, showed up. Sabrina herself had been wearing a terry robe, her hair wet and plastered around her face. She'd been stunned when the door opened. Cassandra had stared at Sabrina, looking her up and down, not appearing angry—just amused. Then she'd made a comment about Sabrina being an annoying little whore, thrown some money at her and told her to get out.

One of the biggest regrets of Sabrina's life was that she had done so—after throwing the money back, of course. She'd come from the farmlands of the Midwest, and even with a college education, a little work experience behind her and a four-year relationship with the captain of her college debate team, she was incredibly naive. Every time she replayed the scene in her head, she was newly humiliated and newly furious with herself. Where had her backbone been? Why hadn't she challenged the woman? She should have—but she hadn't. Maybe she had just been too stunned, or too insecure. She'd grabbed her own clothing and left.

Jon hadn't made any promises to her. He'd been honest, asking about her life, admitting his involvement with Cassandra, saying that they were on and off more often than a water spigot. When Sabrina looked back at the situation, she realized that she had simply been too afraid she might lose if Jon had had to make a choice between the two of them. Life, she'd since learned, meant taking chances. She'd just learned it a little too late.

Jon had tracked her down, all the way to Huntsville. But she'd told her mother to tell him that she'd gone to Europe. He'd written to her, telling her that he wasn't engaged, and that he'd had no commitments whatsoever the night they met. He'd asked her to contact him, since he hadn't been able to convince her mother to quit lying for her.

Sabrina had just reached the point of deciding she was being a worse fool not to respond when she heard that he and Cassie had suddenly done the deed, marrying after a late night in Las Vegas.

Not much later, she'd married Brett.

End of story.

Until she'd run naked from her honeymoon suite. And Cassandra Stuart had plummeted from her balcony into the waiting arms of death.

The wind was growing sharp. Sabrina shivered and looked out into the darkness.

The moon was high, struggling to shine through the clouds. Outdoor lights slightly illuminated the courtyard below. The castle was built in a horseshoe shape, surrounding the courtyard. The maid who had brought her to her room earlier had told her that the far end of the left wing comprised the master suite, with balconies opening to the central courtyard and to the rear.

Glancing in that direction, Sabrina saw the shape of a man standing on the far balcony in the moonlight. His shirt ruffled in the wind; his hair flowed back. He stood tall and still, staring at the moon.

Then he turned, and she knew he was watching her, and she was watching him.

It was Jon. And standing there, watching him, she wondered if he was in pain, if he was missing his wife, if he was reflecting on her death.

He lifted a hand, as if saluting her.

Sabrina backed away, right into the door, and for a moment a scream lodged in her throat as she thought that someone was behind her.

She felt a moment's strange fear. She was standing on a balcony. And whatever the situation, Cassandra had fallen to her death from a balcony not far away. She had plummeted into the arms of a statue of Poseidon below. His trident had torn into her, and she had died instantly, even before her husband had come running back to her. Poseidon still stood below that balcony, though the rosebushes surrounding his fountain were no longer in bloom.

It was so easy to feel that someone was standing behind her now, ready to push...

But when she spun around, no one was there. She went into her room and discovered that the bolt was still thrown.

The rooms were all supplied with brandy.

Sabrina hated brandy, but she poured herself a snifter, wrinkled her nose and swallowed a fairly large portion. "If you're going to survive this week, you're going to have to cool your imagination," she told herself.

She'd claimed downstairs that she was tired. And she was. Shaky, exhausted from the time change and lack of sleep.

But she couldn't seem to get drowsy.

She stayed awake for hours. She sipped brandy, making faces at the taste, and read some magazine she'd brought for the flight.

She had V.J.'s latest book, and after she finished the

magazines she began to read, until she realized that she just couldn't concentrate. She finally lay down, determined that she had to get some rest.

But even when she finally slept, she tossed and turned and began to dream disturbing dreams.

IN THE DARKNESS of the night, he moved down the steps, silent, a wraith. He tried to tell himself that it would all go well, that he didn't need to be afraid.

But he was afraid. Because he loved her.

They had prearranged their meeting, yet even so, he was suddenly, perhaps ridiculously, uneasy. In the ancient dungeon, he suddenly felt as if long-dead murderers had come to life, as if they were mocking him, telling him that he was no better, even if he hadn't actually performed the deed. The lighting was pale, purplish, seeming to cast a ghoulish fog over the faces of torturers, swordsmen and more. Executioners in their dark masks seemed to move, taunting him, warning him.

He came to the tableau of Lady Ariana Stuart upon the rack, and for a moment he paused, forgetting both fear and reason. She was the finest of all the pieces. Something in her eyes was real, a touch of the innocence and sincerity that belonged to Sabrina Holloway. Startled anew by the resemblance to the living woman so nearby, he was tempted to reach out and touch her, to rescue the beauty from the beast who threatened her.

"My love!"

The whisper drew him back to the present, and he spun around. She had come. She rushed to him, and he wrapped her in his arms. "Why are you so afraid? Why did we have to meet in secret?" he queried gently.

She shook her head against his chest. "This is all so

dangerous. I know that they know. I know that we're in danger. I just wish..."

"Don't be so afraid. Don't create trouble before trouble appears."

She shook her head and stepped back. "You don't know how vicious, how dangerous, they can be!"

"Our game is dangerous, my pet. We mustn't overreact. We must just wait, listen, watch...and see what comes."

She leaned against him. "I'm so afraid. Hold me."

He did, feeling the movement of her body against his, her touch. He felt her tugging at his clothing. Felt her hands...finding bare flesh. To his amazement, he hardened instantly, a streak of desire flashing through him. He looked around at the ghoulish setting, amazed, somewhat aghast, and all the more excited because of it.

"Someone could come. Look where we are..."

They seemed to be staring at him. Headsmen in their black hoods, murderers, executioners, rogues. Joan of Arc, so saintly on her cross.

She laughed softly, and the sound washed over his senses. He groaned and slipped down with her, and within seconds they were sprawled out on the cold floor. She was as naked as a jaybird as purple light bathed them. She was insatiable, rising above him, crying out. He tried to hush her, but she laughed, and when they were both spent, she lay at his side and looked up at the faces surrounding them. "It was fun, like an orgy," she teased.

"You worry me."

"Come on. It was as if they were all watching. It was an incredible turn-on."

He hesitated. "You liked to watch...her," he said, suddenly realizing the truth of his own words.

She shrugged. "So? That was a turn-on, too."

"But this is dangerous, meeting here, like this," he told her. "Everything we do now is dangerous. The days to come are dangerous. We don't know what people know, what they saw, what they might have suspected..."

"We'll be careful," she whispered. "We'll be okay. But I have to be with you..."

He nodded slightly.

She knew how to move him, how to make him need her. Because he loved her, of course.

He closed his eyes and opened them, then started.

She was looking at him. Lady Ariana Stuart was turned his way, and she was looking at him with her huge, wide, beautiful blue eyes.

She was watching.

He could feel her eyes. Looking at him, seeing him. Watching...

It was a turn-on.

And yet dangerous.

He was both aroused and afraid.

It was as if she knew...

SHE DIDN'T WANT Jon Stuart; she'd told herself that time and time again. She wasn't absurdly, naively young anymore; she was older now, wiser. But in her dreams, she was lying in her bed, naked, waiting, wanting...

Because he was there. Tall, towering, dressed in black. Standing over her...

It was Jon.

It wasn't. The tall figure was surrounded by fog and changed with each slight flutter of a purple-gray breeze.

It was a torturer, intent upon her agony and destruction, and she was caught, tied, unable to move, to escape, because ropes bound her tightly, and all she could do was look up into the eyes of death with a silent, wax-cast scream…

She awoke with a start, shaking, drenched in sweat. She sat up wildly, looking around.

Her room was empty. The fire burned low; moonlight filtered in.

She could see plainly that she was alone, entirely alone.

And yet it seemed…

There was a presence, a scent, a feeling, something in the air. A feeling she couldn't shake that someone had been there. Jon? Or Brett? Or an artist's rendering of a medieval torturer in wax?

"Too much time in the dungeon," she told herself softly. But her unease persisted.

She leaped up. The bolt was still secure. She'd been dreaming, and she was alone.

Shaking, she curled back into bed and tried to sleep again. But the moon began to set, and soon daylight was filtering in.

She sat up again. "Oh, the hell with this!" she groaned aloud.

So she rose and showered and was the first one downstairs for the six o'clock coffee.

But not even coffee and sunlight could dispel the strange feeling that she *hadn't* been alone…

Someone had been with her in her locked and bolted room.

CHAPTER FIVE

SABRINA HAD A pounding headache and felt so tired and wretched that she could barely sit up.

So naturally the first person into the great hall for breakfast was Susan Sharp.

"Good morning! Nice to see you up!" Susan said with a cheerfulness that was doubly irritating. "Don't you just love this place? I slept like a baby."

"The castle is beautiful," Sabrina replied.

Susan drew up the chair beside Sabrina's at the polished oak table. "Can you believe that Cassandra absolutely hated this place?"

Sabrina told herself that she didn't want to gossip, but with Susan there was little choice. And despite herself, she wanted to know everything she could about Cassandra Stuart.

"Did she really?"

Susan nodded grimly, stirring sugar substitute into her coffee. "Hated it. I never understood why Jon put up with her." She shrugged. "Frankly, I never understood why he married her."

"Well, she really was beautiful. And smart," Sabrina heard herself comment.

Susan wrinkled her nose. "Yes, but...well, Jon is gorgeous himself. He could have dozens of women. *Has* had dozens of women. Why marry that one?"

"He must have loved her."

"Well, maybe he did. But I can tell you this—he was ready to divorce her when she died."

"How do you know?"

Susan added milk to her coffee. "Because I was here, remember? They were fighting like crazy. Jon has always loved it here. He didn't grow up with money, you know. The family inherited this place, but it was a disaster, an albatross hanging around his neck when he first came into possession of the property. Cassandra's family was swimming with cash—she never wanted or needed for anything. Jon's dedicated to his children's charities, and these little Mystery Weeks of his make some really big money. Cassandra didn't like games, hated half of Jon's friends. She couldn't bear V.J., because V.J. would never suck up to her. She said whatever she damned well felt like saying—you know her. Cassie tortured Jon every time he held one of these. He'd be in the middle of something, and she'd supposedly be his hostess—and then she'd suddenly decide she simply couldn't bear it and throw a tantrum or be off. I know Jon had decided that he was done with her when she died."

"Susan, maybe they had problems," Sabrina said, "but how can you possibly know their marriage was over?"

"Because I know Jon," Susan purred. She leaned back, lifting her long-nailed fingers in a casual gesture. "But then again, Jon wasn't the only one fighting with Cassandra. She and Anna Lee Zane had barely been civil to one another all week. For one thing, Cassandra had given a scathing review of Anna's last book on national television in the States. And, of course, Anna is stunning, and she and Jon have been good friends for a very long time. Cassandra never understood the concept of friendship, especially not between a man and a woman, even a woman who goes both ways. Then again, I admit, I don't quite get friendships, either. I mean, it's hard to like a man and *not* want to sleep with him."

Susan shrugged. "But that's beside the point. Cassie also completely dished Tom Heart in a review that might have cost him a spot in a really important anthology that came out last year. And of course she was also afraid that Jon was sleeping with someone who was a guest here, and she herself was supposedly sleeping with someone else, as well. I don't know if she really was or wasn't, since she adored Jon. She really did. She just didn't know how to be a wife to him. She was always jealous but always taunting him. It was as if she thought she had to let him know at all times that other men found her desirable, that she was a special prize he needed to cherish. Jon never did take well to threats. But then, she threatened everyone all the time—she seemed to need to hold something over the head of every single human being she ever met."

"And you fought with her, too, of course."

"Of course," Susan said, smiling. "I've admitted I hated her. She was the worst bitch known to man."

"Oh, come now!" Brett exclaimed, entering the great hall. He poured himself coffee and sat down at Sabrina's other side. "Was Cassie really such a bitch? Or was she misunderstood? Maybe it was hard being married to Jon Stuart and giving in to his every whim. She loved cities, glamour, excitement, and he liked to tuck himself away here in the country and watch the wind blow."

"That's not true," Susan said, staunchly defending Jon. "He has homes in London, New York and LA, as well."

"Poor fellow," Brett murmured lightly.

"Poor fellow, indeed!" V.J. announced, sweeping into

the room with an audible sniff. She ruffled Brett's hair. "As if *you're* going to be suffering financially after your next contract!"

Brett smiled sheepishly. "Okay, so I'm not a poor fellow, either. I'm a happy one right now. And I'm going to be really, really rich, as well. You truly should remarry me, Sabrina."

"Not a chance, I'm afraid."

"Sleep with me, then. Men always buy their mistresses better presents. And we were good together, right?"

Susan and V.J. were both staring at her.

"Brett!" she said, nearly strangling.

He ignored her protest, his eyes suddenly on Susan again. "Here you are, Sue, defending Jon now, but you seemed to be absolutely convinced he killed Cassandra when it happened."

"Don't be silly. He was outside when she fell."

"He could have paid someone to do the deed," Brett said, waggling his eyebrows.

"Isn't it rather rude, the way we're sitting around discussing our host as a potential murderer," V.J. queried.

"But it *is* a Mystery Week," Brett said.

As if on cue, Camy Clark came into the room bearing a stack of envelopes. "Good morning, everyone."

"Everyone isn't here," Susan said snidely.

Sabrina frowned, wondering why the woman was continually so rude to Jon's assistant. Camy didn't intrude; she was quiet and tended to stay out of the way.

"Well, it's still early," Camy said. "But if you'd like—"

"Ah, you have our character descriptions and our instructions!" Brett said, flashing her one of his devastating smiles.

Camy flushed, smiling. "Yes, I do. Now remember,

everyone is to know one another's character but nothing else. You'll receive more instructions as we go along. The murderer will, of course, know who he or she is and where to get the murder weapons. And remember, the murderer may have an accomplice. If you're killed, you're dead, but you're a ghost, and you can still warn others of impending danger and help solve the crime."

"I'm dying for my envelope, darling," Susan told her, drawling the word *dying*.

The others laughed. As Camy began handing out the envelopes, more of their number began to arrive: Anna Lee, looking fetching and slim in stirrup pants and a halter top; Reggie in her inevitable flowered dress; Tom Heart, tall and dignified in a smoking jacket and flannel trousers; Thayer Newby in a Jets T-shirt and slacks; Joe Johnston, casual in a golf shirt and chinos; Joshua Valine looking very artistic, with a paint-smudged denim shirt over a plain white T and baggy pants; Dianne Dorsey in a calf-length skirt and sleeveless knit top. And Jon.

Jon, too, was casual, in a navy denim shirt, the sleeves rolled up, and form-hugging jeans. His dark hair was damp, as if he'd just showered, and Sabrina couldn't help but wonder if he'd slept late…because he'd been up late, wandering restlessly around his castle at night. She reminded herself that her door had been bolted. And that just because she hadn't forgotten a reckless sexual encounter in her youth, there was no reason to assume Jon might have any remaining interest in her whatsoever. Her reputation wasn't exactly a sparkling one.

She rose for more coffee. V.J. came up beside her, offering her cup to Sabrina to fill, as well.

"Ah, you're watching our host," V.J. whispered to her

as Jon greeted Camy and Joshua, listening to some of their last-minute instructions.

"He's an intriguing man," Sabrina said noncommittally.

"And, of course, the question remains—is he a murderer? Does Susan really think so? Except I'm sure Susan wouldn't think of Cassie's death as murder. To Susan, if Jon did kill his wife, it was justifiable homicide."

V.J. shrugged, sipping her coffee. "Honey, to half the people here, killing Cassandra Stuart would have constituted a public service."

"Ladies!" Reggie admonished from behind them. "We're not supposed to speak ill of the dead."

"Even if the dead caused tremendous ills?" Joe Johnston whispered from behind her.

"Sabrina," Camy said, walking across the room to her. She stopped, flushed and corrected herself. "Ms. Holloway."

"Sabrina, please."

Camy flushed again. "Your envelope. You only get to know your character now. You'll get instructions later regarding what you're supposed to do and where you're supposed to go."

"Great, thanks."

"Do you have mine, dear?" V.J. asked.

Camy gave V.J. hers, then handed Reggie her envelope, as well.

"Ouch!" Reggie exclaimed, looking up. She smiled. "I'm the Crimson Lady, a stripper, trying—or pretending—to reform."

"Great," Thayer Newby groaned, flexing his muscles. "I'm the effeminate male dancer, JoJo Scuchi."

"JoJo Scuchi?" Brett said with a laugh.

"Check yours out," Thayer warned him.

Brett read the letter in the envelope and made a face. "I'm Mr. Buttle, the butler. Number two on the *New York Times* list, and they make me the butler!" he groaned.

Sabrina, reading her sheet, began to laugh.

"And who are you, my dear?" Brett demanded.

"The Duchess. I run the church choir," she told him.

"Oh, now that is apropos. The lady who ran naked from her honeymoon suite," Susan said, staring at Brett. "Neither of you has ever explained that situation," she reminded him smugly.

Sabrina had lived with what had happened for a long time now, but she still felt her temper rising and her cheeks reddening, especially since she realized that Jon had been watching the exchange. Waiting for a reply?

Or perhaps not, because he was the one who responded to Susan. "And I imagine they don't feel they owe you an explanation, Sue," he said.

Susan opened her mouth, then quickly shut it, lifting her chin.

"Ah, but, Susan," Joe Johnston said, reading over Sabrina's shoulder, "the Duchess runs the choir by day—and a high-class call-girl outfit by night!"

"Hey, it's a dirty job, but someone's got to do it," Brett declared. "Does the butler get to be in on it?" he asked.

"The butler always did it, you know," Reggie teased.

"I mean in on the sex," Brett said.

"You would," V.J. said with a sigh.

"You know I've always wanted to make it with an older woman," Brett stated.

"Older than what?" V.J. demanded tartly.

He smiled innocently. "Older than God, darling. That's you, isn't it?"

"Cute, boy, cute!" V.J. sniffed.

Dianne Dorsey suddenly started laughing. Sabrina leaned past V.J. to look at her. As usual, Dianne was in black. Black denim shorts, a ruffled black blouse, black socks and black hiking boots. "You'll never guess who I am."

"Who?" V.J. obligingly inquired.

"Mary, the Hare Krishna!"

They all started to laugh.

"Susan, who are you?" V.J. asked.

Susan shuddered and looked up at Camy accusingly. "I'm Carla, the call girl with the clap."

Another round of laughter followed, but Susan was not amused. She glared at Camy. "You did that on purpose!"

"Sue, chill!" Brett said.

"Camy didn't make these up, you know that. We hire writers from the game company," Jon said impatiently. He sighed. "Trust me, mine is worse."

"Why, who are you?" Susan demanded.

"Demented Dick," Jon said dryly. "Serial killer, supposedly cured by his cousin, Sally Sadist, the psychologist."

"That's me!" Anna Lee called out.

"And I'm Nancy, the naughty nurse, hired by Sally Sadist to look after you. Nancy the naughty nurse!" V.J. repeated with a shudder.

"You think that's bad?" Joe Johnston said, laughing. "I'm Tilly the transvestite, Demented Dick's mother!"

"Hey, Mom!" Jon said, and they all laughed.

"Oh, no!" Tom Heart groaned, looking at Joe.

"What?" Joe demanded.

"I'm Demented Dick's dad—which means you're my wife. Ugh!"

"Well, baby, you're sleeping on the couch," Joe told him.

As they teased, Jennie Albright, the housekeeper, with the help of two younger maids, brought in the food platters, setting them up on the buffet. Jon thanked them and announced, "Breakfast is served. While we eat, Joshua will show you the weapons with which you might be 'killed.' We'll wait until everyone is seated."

With a lot of talking and good-natured joking, they fixed plates of food and took their places at the table. Sabrina was glad to find herself next to V.J. rather than Susan, but Brett managed to remain on her other side. He was definitely trying to create the impression that they were a twosome.

Jon took a seat toward the end of the table between Anna Lee Zane and Thayer Newby. Anna spoke to him, and he lowered his head, smiling. Sabrina couldn't help but wonder if something *had* gone on between the two of them, since it was rumored that Jon and Cassandra had both been having extramarital affairs at his last Mystery Week. Still, so much about the past was speculation. What wasn't speculation, however, was the fact that Cassandra Stuart had died.

Joshua cleared his throat, smiling. "Ladies and gentlemen, here is the situation. Demented Dick is newly home to take over as heir apparent to the family fortunes, due to the untimely—and unnatural—demise of his older brother, Demented Darryl. Naturally, since he had the most to gain, Demented Dick is a likely suspect in his brother's murder, but since this is a whodunit, it's for you to discover who did in Demented Darryl and why. Everyone in the house has a past and is hiding a secret, and it will turn out in the end that everyone had a reason for wanting to do Darryl in. The killer—or killers—are naturally afraid of what everyone else may know, and therefore, one by one, they will begin picking off the others. Now, there are a number of murder weapons, since the killer is to continue his or her spree until he or she is caught or until the entire household has expired."

"So shoot," Joe said. "What are our weapons?"

"Fine, we'll start with the pistol," Joshua said, showing them the gun in question. "Shoots red paint." He proceeded to lift the other toy weapons as he described them. "Rifle, shoots red paint. Bowie knife, complete with 'blood' sack. Jackknife, bow and arrow, heavy vase, rope with noose, poison—actually, it's a grape drink guaranteed to turn your mouth purple for twenty-four hours—and last but not least, a candlestick. So that's it, ladies and gentlemen. There will be clues left around the castle, and instructions for your characters will be slipped to you at various times as the week moves on. I'll warn you all, the first murder is planned for sometime today, so everyone take care. Oh, and anyone who chooses—living or dead—can meet at seven each evening for cocktails, to be followed by dinner at eight, and at that time discuss the case. More coffee, anyone?" he asked blandly.

"Only if you drink it first," Anna Lee replied dryly.

"Sure," Joshua said. He procured the coffee carafe from the buffet, poured himself a cup, sipped it, then walked around to Anna Lee's place, pouring her more. Smoothing back his blond hair, he leaned close to her, a teasing light in his eyes. "One can't be too cautious around here."

"I'll take more coffee, too," Jon said, pushing his cup forward. "Late night," he explained.

"Death by poison!" V.J. said with a shudder. "Well, I'd

been intending to go on a diet anyway. I can live without food, but never without coffee."

"Never without a good gin and tonic," Reggie argued.

"No, never without beer," Brett corrected.

"Well, as far as coffee and food—or even cocktails and beer— go, you can indulge now," Jon said dryly. "The game doesn't begin until we've all exited the dining room. Everyone is then to go to his or her room for the next hour, while Camy and our master sculptor make sure that the weapons you've just seen have been properly hidden. If someone finds the weapon with which he or she was to be murdered, it can be used against the killer. But for now, feel free. Indulge."

"Well, then, let me have just a wee bit more toast," V.J. said, adding a touch of a Scot's accent to her voice.

"I'll go for the bacon," Joe said.

"Toast for me, too, V.J.," Sabrina called to her.

And suddenly everyone at the table was hungry again. They ate like a group of loggers about to head out for hours of hard labor. But, finally, one by one, they began to leave. Sabrina, seeing Brett ahead of her, purposely lagged behind, lowering her eyes as she sipped her coffee. When she lifted her gaze again, she was startled to realize that only she and Jon remained in the room. He was seated across the table, studying her.

"It really is good to see you again," he told her, voice husky, eyes firmly on her.

To her dismay, she felt a fluttering in her heart. "Thank you."

He sat back, still watching her. She felt as if his eyes were penetrating her skin, and she groped about quickly for something casual to say.

"So, are you the killer?" she inquired.

He arched a brow. "Are you talking about the game—or real life?"

She flushed. "The game."

"If I were," he answered slowly, "I couldn't tell you. Just as you couldn't tell me. It wouldn't be fair." He leaned forward then, a dry smile curling his lips. "But don't you want to know about real life?"

She stared back at him, feeling as if her breakfast had suddenly sunk from her stomach to her feet. "Jon, I didn't come here to question you or to bring back unhappy memories."

"Why not? It's why most of the others did, both my friends and my enemies. Don't you want to know the truth? Or did you really run away from me simply because you didn't give a damn?"

She wasn't going to answer that, so she stared at him and demanded, "So did you kill Cassandra? What a question! If you had killed her, you couldn't tell me, could you? There's no real difference between the game and real life."

"Oh, there's a difference, all right. As far as the game goes, I can't tell you if I'm the killer or not. As for real life...no, definitely, decidedly, on pain of every torture God or the devil could inflict, no. I did not kill my wife. Do you believe me?"

"Yes."

He arched a brow, sitting back cautiously. "Why? Why should you believe me?"

"Well, I..."

"You what? You know me?" he queried, taunting slightly. He shrugged. "You know me," he repeated mockingly.

"I don't pretend to really know you," she snapped back angrily. "But you were nowhere near her when she fell—"

"She was pushed," he stated flatly.

She lifted her hands. "How do you know?"

"Because I knew Cassandra. Very well. She was far too fond of herself for suicide."

Seated at the huge table, his eyes dark and sharp, he looked like a medieval lord, powerful ruler of all his domain. But there was a touch of bitterness in his voice, and despite his harsh demeanor, she reflected that the years since Cassandra's death must have hurt him very badly. Had he really loved her, despite their fights? Or had there been another woman involved, an affair gone tragically wrong? Had there been another man, and did Jon Stuart still harbor anger deep in his soul?

He was still staring at her, his dark marbled gaze seeming to pierce through her, seeking something, giving nothing. The lines around his eyes had deepened since she'd seen him last; he had aged, and yet he was even more attractive than he had been, and she felt as if she could feel his power reaching out across the table to mesmerize her.

Was she a fool? Even if he hadn't pushed Cassandra himself, he could have been her killer. Plenty of people seemed to think it would have been a miracle if he wasn't the one to murder her...

He was still watching, waiting.

She shrugged. "From what I understand, nothing is certain. You can't be certain of anything, just because you think you knew her. She might have simply slipped and fallen. She might have been reckless. We none of us really ever know one another, do—"

"Cassandra didn't kill herself."

"Maybe that's what you want to believe."

"Maybe it's the truth."

"Jon, she had cancer. She might have felt that—"

"She was already undergoing treatments."

"But she was a woman, and women can be vain. Maybe she was afraid of losing her hair, her looks—or even losing you because of it."

He shook his head impatiently. "She knew about the cancer when we were married. She told me about it, so she knew I was aware of everything we might be going through. She didn't kill herself. And she was very coordinated. She didn't trip."

"Well, then, in your mind, you definitely believe that *someone* murdered her."

"Yes," he said.

"But who—"

He leaned forward. She could see leashed tension in the pounding of a vein in his throat.

"Someone killed her," he said harshly, "but I didn't. And the matter of who did is not your concern. I don't want you involved in any way."

"But—"

"Why did you run away from me?" he asked abruptly.

"What? I—I—"

"Don't stutter. And don't tell me that it was a long time ago, or that you don't know what I'm talking about."

She lifted her hands. "Cassandra came. I left."

"Why?"

Sabrina stared at him blankly. "It really was a long time ago—"

"Why?" he interrupted more heatedly.

"She said she was your fiancée. Apparently, she was."

He shook his head angrily. "We were broken up. I had no commitments. I told you that."

She shrugged. "But you married her."

"Later. Yes, I did marry her. She was beautiful and tempting and all the rest, and we did have a history between us. And she was afraid of facing her illness alone, and she wanted me to be with her, and yes, she was a bitch as well, and yes again, it wasn't working at all and I was planning on getting a divorce."

There was a strange anger in his voice, as if he were revealing intimacies under duress, as if the words were spilling from him against his will. Then his tone changed abruptly and he queried wryly, "And what about you? Running naked from your honeymoon suite in Paris?"

"That was a long time ago as well, and it's really- -"

"None of my business? You're absolutely right. It isn't. But that doesn't mean I don't want to know." He smiled a little. "Whenever you're ready to tell me."

She stared at him, surprised to find that she was not offended. His words might have been blunt, even arrogant, but from the way he smiled, she suddenly realized that he understood a great deal.

"Hey!"

Camy Clark came back into the great hall and put her hands on her hips. "You guys are supposed to return to your rooms for the next hour—and that means you, too, boss!" she said firmly.

"Okay, okay, we're leaving," Jon assured her.

He got to his feet with a lithe, easy movement and managed to be at Sabrina's seat before she could rise. He stood behind her, graciously pulling out her chair. His scent was masculine and subtle—of soap and a hint of aftershave. He remained one of the most attractive and sensual men she had ever met, and even without touching, she could feel him at her back with every fiber of her being. She was tempted to turn around and throw herself at him.

Naturally, she didn't.

She rose, thanked him and smiled at Camy. And, leaving the great hall, she fairly flew up the stairs.

Yet as she reached her door on the second floor, she felt him behind her again. Knew he was there before he spoke.

"Good luck, Duchess."

She spun around.

As always, his dark gaze was unreadable.

"Good luck?"

"Catching the killer."

"Oh, the game."

"Of course, what else? Ah, but then, there is real life, right?" he queried. His voice was very deep, and he suddenly seemed very close.

"Are you angry with me?" she asked nervously.

"What do you think?" he said.

Then he pushed open her door, urging her into her room. His hand on her elbow, he led her outside. "Look around you," he said. "Feel the wind. Soon it will be cold and brutal. This is a harsh place, especially to those who despise it. Do you suppose the castle itself might have turned on Cassandra? The place was rumored to be haunted, you know. Well, naturally, now Cassandra haunts the castle, as well. Imagine how she must have felt, out here on a balcony, feeling a breeze...this same breeze. Seeing this land she so disdained. This same land. It must have been a terrible shock when she realized that someone had the audacity to be murdering her."

His grip on her arm was very tense, and Sabrina felt the heat and anger and frustration that emanated from him. He stared out on the day; he seemed to have forgotten how tightly he held her, how he had wedged her against the balcony rail.

She felt her heart pounding. And for a moment, she was afraid. She didn't know this man. Sleeping with a man didn't keep him from being a stranger.

Yet along with the fear rippling through her veins was a strange warmth, a static excitement. She liked the feel of his hand upon her, liked his being so close. She wanted him to stay; she was tempted again to throw her arms around him. She felt so strange with him. She had never known another man who could create such a sensual, aching hunger within her. She tried to tell herself that she was a fool, that women who fell for dangerous men were, quite simply, stupid.

But Jon hadn't killed his wife.

Still, he might have wanted her dead.

Yet lots of people had wanted her head.

"Imagine," he repeated now, drawing Sabrina closer to him, farther over the balcony rail. "Imagine looking, leaning, and then—"

"Jon!"

He jerked back at the sound of his name being called. Sabrina let out a long breath, then swung around with him to face her open doorway.

Camy stood there, smiling but shaking her head impatiently. "We're never going to be able to get this game started!"

"Oh, I am sorry," Jon said smoothly. Then he smiled at Sabrina. "Good luck finding the killer. It can be a matter of—"

"Life and death," she said softly.

To her surprise, he took her by the shoulders and kissed her forehead. Then he strode from the balcony and the room.

For a moment, Sabrina stood very still. Then she turned to look after him and saw that Camy was still there.

"We've got to get on with the game!" the young woman said somewhat impatiently.

And Sabrina's door was finally closed with a sharp little click.

CHAPTER SIX

JON STRODE THE length of the hallway to his room, aware
that Camy was watching him, anxious for him to reach
his room and shut himself in. He smiled to himself. She
and Joshua took this all very seriously, which was why,
of course, he had asked them to help host the affair rather
than participate as players. For, along with the fun and
publicity the writers would enjoy, the project was for
charity, and he didn't want any more scandal. And who
better to see that things ran smoothly than hardworking
Camy Clark and meticulous, painstaking Joshua Valine?

Jon reached his room, waved at Camy and locked the
door behind him. Alone, he stared at the bed. Why in
hell had he ever married Cassandra?

He walked into the bathroom and doused his face with
cold water. He stared at himself, noting the lines around
his eyes. He'd been younger but still no kid when he'd
married Cassie. She'd been a manipulator of the highest
degree, capable of appearing pleasant, reasonable and
loving when it suited her purpose. But what had truly
snared him then, and haunted him now, was the feeling
that she had really loved him. True, she had never given
up the battle; she had wanted things her way. But as best
as Cassandra could, she had loved him.

He walked out to the balcony and stared down at the

fountain, remembering. Despite the time that had passed, he felt real pain. Poor Cassie. She had loved life so much.

She hadn't killed herself; he really did know that about her. Her death had been ruled accidental. Perhaps she *had* fallen?

No. He remembered the way she had called his name... remembered the change in her tone of voice. And he remembered that, at the end, he had failed her completely in a way he never should have.

Jon felt a sudden, terrible dread of this Mystery Week. He had thought about it, of course, weighed the grim idea over and over again—for nearly three years now. And it had seemed a sane, sensible, if chilling thing to do. Until...

The irrational unease had seized him when he was with Sabrina. In her room. On her balcony.

He stared down at the Poseidon statue that had cradled Cassie as she died. He'd thought to catch a killer this week. He'd never thought that, in one day's time, he might be wishing for a future rather than trying to resolve the past.

And it made him afraid.

Fear made a man weak.

He couldn't afford to be weak.

He heard a sound and turned. An envelope had been thrust beneath his door.

He reached for, opened it—and felt a chill sweep through him.

The note he'd received was a warning...and not part of the game...

THE WOMAN BURST in on him while he was in his own room, at his desk, head in his hands.

He straightened, staring at her.

Her eyes were downright vicious.

And she pointed at him.

"I know what happened. I know exactly what was going on. Oh, maybe I haven't complete proof, but I've got the story pieced together nicely, and once I give out the truth, well, honey, you can kiss your wonderful little lifestyle goodbye!"

He stared back at her, filled with dismay, totally speechless at first. Then he got a grip on himself and sat straight and impassive. "Whatever you think you know doesn't matter."

"Doesn't it? Oh, come now, I can see that you've got a new passion in your life. Maybe an old passion. So hard to tell. But aren't you looking forward to the future?"

"I don't understand this. Why are you here? If you knew the truth—or suspected you knew the truth, why haven't you already shared it?"

Her smile deepened. "Because everything in life is negotiable."

"You mean you're blackmailing me?"

"Oh, dear, what an ugly word! No, no, no, not blackmail. I don't mean to torture you forever or anything like that. But I will admit to having a slight cash-flow problem at the moment, so you see..."

"And what happens if you have another 'cash-flow problem' in the future?"

"Well, I do try to be reasonable. I seldom find myself strapped as I am now."

"And there are no morals involved here, I take it? You really don't give a damn that Cassandra Stuart was murdered?"

"Of course not. Many people would have been tempted

to push her over. They didn't all get the opportunity to do so. A mean, nasty woman died. Who cared?"

"There were those who cared," he told her angrily.

She shrugged with a total lack of interest. "I wasn't one of them. This is a business negotiation, nothing more. I'll not be troubled by my conscience later or anything like that, so you needn't fear."

"But there is the cash-flow thing."

"So unlikely to occur again!"

"Name your figure."

She did.

He nodded.

She smiled and left. After all, everyone was supposed to be in his or her own room.

He stared at the closed door long after she had gone, a wave of desperate depression washing over him. She would have a "cash-flow problem" at least once a year—that was simply the way she was. And what if he ran out of hush money?

But what choice did he have?

Of course, there was one other choice...

ALONE, SABRINA TRIED to shake the unease that had settled over her. A feeling of intimacy had sprung up so quickly between her and Jon, yet it seemed he was trying to warn her away from him at the same time.

She phoned home, checking in with her parents, asking about her sister, brother-in-law and the baby, and telling them that Scotland was wonderful. She assured them that the rumors they had heard about Jon Stuart were just tabloid garbage and that she was in no danger at Lochlyre Castle. Finally she bid them a cheerful goodbye, apologizing for having called so early, and hung up. She tried to lie on her bed and close her eyes and rest. She was too restless.

She wandered back out to the balcony. For a moment, she couldn't go near the edge. How odd it had been to stand there with Jon! To feel a hint of fear. But he wouldn't have thrown her over the edge; he would have no reason to do so.

Had there been a reason to kill Cassandra? Silly question—everyone seemed to think there was a reason to kill Cassandra.

Sabrina gazed down the length of the castle toward Jon's suite. She wondered if things would have been different if she hadn't been so young when she'd met him, been with him. Not just young, but so naive. She felt her pulse quickening and bit her lower lip, admitting at last why she had come here. She was still in love with him.

But surely, that was absurd. She hadn't seen him in far too long.

And there were some who still hinted that he *had* been involved in the death of his wife, no matter what the findings at the inquest.

But logic was proving worthless at the moment. She didn't believe for a minute that Jon had killed Cassandra. Still, was she being hopelessly naive again?

She heard a noise and hurried back inside. A note, her first set of instructions, had been slipped under her door. She ripped open the envelope and studied the words.

Duchess, head to the chapel for choir practice at dusk. Meet with wayward girl. Show her the light. Directions to chapel included.

Studying the little map beneath the printed sheet, Sabrina shuddered and muttered to herself, "Great! The chapel is in the dungeon beyond the chamber of horrors!"

There was a tapping on her door. She answered it, to find Brett waiting with a smile. He didn't exactly push his way in; he brushed by her before she could stop him.

"So what were your instructions? What are you to do, Madame Pimp?" he asked. "Are you the murderer?"

"I can't tell you that. It will spoil the game, and you know it!"

"You should tell me," he said determinedly, hopping up on her bed, stretching out and lacing his fingers comfortably behind his head. "You should confide in me, and I should confide in you. We could catch the killer that way and become a real husband and wife sleuthing team. Then we could write stories together and get fabulously rich and famous."

"We're not married, Brett."

"Oh, that can be easily rectified. You're just being stubborn."

"Because I'd like a husband who'd like to be monogamous?"

"I can do that."

"Brett, I don't think you can, but that's beside the point. Now get off my bed."

"Come help me up."

She sighed with irritation as he stretched out a hand entreatingly. She took it, intending to pull him up.

He pulled her down instead. "Gotcha!"

He said the word with such childish delight as she landed on his chest that she didn't have the heart to either yell or slug him in the jaw. "Brett McGraff, you—" she began in laughing protest, trying to push away.

But she never finished. At that moment, they heard the explosive sound of shots being fired.

Brett clutched her, his eyes wide.

"Sabrina! What happened?" V.J. cried, swinging around the doorway. "Oh!" she gasped, seeing the two of them together on the bed. "Oh, I am so sorry, but the door was open, and—"

"How absolutely delicious!" Susan Sharp exclaimed.

There suddenly seemed to be a meeting occurring in Sabrina's doorway.

"Everyone in there alive?"

Sabrina felt her cheeks flood with color at the sound of the deep, slightly burred, masculine voice. Jon Stuart was now standing between V.J. and Susan in her doorway.

"Hey, who got shot?" demanded a second male voice. It was Tom Heart, peeking in over V.J.'s shoulder.

"No one in here. We're fine," Sabrina said irritably, trying to push free of Brett's grasp.

Brett held on. Tightly. He grinned at her wickedly. "I haven't been so fine in a very long time."

Sabrina gritted her teeth, tugged herself free at last and stood. As she straightened her clothing, she checked it and Brett's for red paint. "No, we've not been shot," she said with a false cheerfulness. Her cheeks, however, were as red as tomatoes.

"Well, I wonder who has been?" V.J. demanded.

"Let's go see," Tom suggested.

"What's happened?" Standing in the hallway, red-haired, muscular Thayer Newby had his hands on his hips, looking every inch the cop he had once been in Houston, Texas. His tone was sharp, and he was ready to question them all.

Dianne Dorsey stepped from her room into the hallway. Two doors down, Anna Lee Zane did the same.

Joe Johnston stepped out from behind Anna Lee.

"Oh, now, this is all just too rich!" Susan exclaimed.

"We were just talking," Joe said indignantly.

"Ah, then perhaps it's those two who are conspirators!" Susan said, pointing into Sabrina's room.

"Conspirators at what?" Sabrina asked. "A gun went off, but we're all alive, and none of us is wearing red paint."

"Now there's a fabulous investigative deduction!" Brett exclaimed, applauding. "We're all still alive."

"What happened?" Joshua asked, striding down the hallway. Apparently his room was at the end of the wing, near Jon's suite. He looked around with a frown. "Where's Camy?"

As he asked the question, Camy came up the stairs from below. She looked at her watch, then at the guests gathered in the ancient arched hallway. "I can see that we're going to have to keep a strict eye on all of you!" she declared. "The time is barely up, and every single one of you is out of your room!"

"Shots were fired. We were trying to figure out who had been killed first," Tom Heart explained.

Camy shook her head. "I think that you're all mistaken. It wasn't time for shots to have been fired."

"We heard shots," V.J. insisted.

"A car backfiring, perhaps?" Camy suggested.

"Whose car? What car? We're all here."

Camy smiled, shaking her head. "We do receive mail and deliveries here, you know. It's not the end of the earth."

They all looked at one another.

"Could it have been something other than gunshots?" Dianne asked.

"Well, it must have been," Tom Heart replied. "None of us was shot. Unless the murderer has horrible aim. Anybody's doors or walls covered in red paint?"

They all shook their heads.

"It had to have been something else," Camy insisted.

"Sounded like shots to me," Thayer Newby said.

He should know! Sabrina thought. He'd been a cop for over twenty years. Surely he recognized the sound of gunshots.

But the bottom line was none of them had been shot.

Sabrina saw Jon staring at Camy, neither agreeing nor disagreeing with her. His arms were crossed over his chest.

"I was actually working," Dianne said.

"So was I," Anna Lee said.

"Working on what, dear?" Susan queried, arching a brow toward Joe, who had exited Anna Lee's room with her.

"Joe recently did some extensive forensic research with a bone expert. He was giving me some really great ideas."

"Ah," Susan said archly, the one syllable dripping with doubt.

"Don't forget, we've actually got a bowling alley and a heated pool in the dungeon, just down from the chamber of horrors," Camy reminded them. "For those not working," she added innocently.

"I haven't gone bowling in years," Sabrina said, looking at V.J., who was usually up for almost anything. That way she could return to the dungeon area and find out exactly where the chapel was—without being alone—before it was time for her to go down and play the mystery game at dusk.

"Great! It always takes one person to get things started!" Camy said.

"If you and Brett aren't *working*," Susan purred.

"We're not," Sabrina assured her, trying to keep her voice level.

Jon arched a dark brow her way, murmured that he had some phone calls to make, and walked away without further comment.

"I wouldn't mind a dip in the pool, either," V.J. said. "Why don't we put on suits so we can throw some heavy balls, complain about our aching arms, then relax in the water."

"Sounds fine," Sabrina said. She turned away to get ready. And glared.

Brett hadn't left yet.

"I think I'll join you two," he said cheerfully.

"The amenities of the castle are open to all of us," she said, adding dryly, "but you'll need your swimsuit, which I'm sure must be in *your* room."

He reached over and pinched her cheek.

"Brett—"

"You really do love me," he assured her.

But at last he walked away. And she closed and locked her door.

CAMY'S ROOM WAS near the grand stone stairway that led to the foyer and the library and great hall below. The hallway had emptied of writers when Jon exited his room to reach his assistant's, but Joshua stopped him on his way, calling to him from his own doorway.

"Jon, come in here, I think you should see this."

As Jon entered Joshua's room, the sculptor gestured at the large television set. A weatherwoman from a Stirling station stood before a large map of northern England and Scotland. Jon stood silently beside Joshua, watching as the meteorologist smiled her way through an explanation of the storm moving in from the North Atlantic. It was already hitting the islands, covering John o' Groat's with a blanket of snow and ice, and moving southward.

"What do you think?" Joshua said.

As if on cue, the weatherwoman smiled more broadly. "Due to atmospheric conditions, it's difficult to forecast the exact movement or speed of the storm, but it's possible that within the next twenty-four to thirty-six hours we could have snow and blizzard conditions across the midsection of Scotland, all the way down to Yorkshire, England."

"I think it's going to snow," Jon said. "The staff here are extraordinary—I don't think we've ever run out of anything. But I'll speak with my housekeeper and make sure we're doubly provisioned, just in case we wind up snowbound."

"Good idea. I thought you might want to know," Joshua said.

"Yeah, thanks," Jon told him. He hesitated. "Josh, you and Camy are working together on all the clues and instructions for the game, right?"

"Yeah, why?"

"Did you slip the envelope under my door?"

Joshua shook his head, looking a little uneasy. "No, Camy was distributing the instructions today," he said with a shrug. "Why, is something wrong?"

Jon showed Joshua the message he had received.

The sculptor went pale, shaking his head. "Someone is playing a dirty game," he said angrily.

"So it seems."

"Do you think you're in any real danger?"

Jon shook his head. "No."

"But—"

"Never mind. I'm sorry I even bothered you with this."

"Sorry!" Joshua said indignantly. "Someone did this! We have to know who—"

"Josh, I can handle it. Hey, you're an artist, my friend, filling in as game master for the good of my charities. This isn't your concern. Excuse me, and thanks for the weather report. I'll check with Camy."

He left Josh and walked down the hallway to tap on Camy's door.

"Come in!"

He opened the door, strode to where she sat at her desk and tossed down his note. "Not funny, Camy. What in God's name would induce you to do something like that?"

"Something like what?" she demanded indignantly. She stared at him, then frowned and lifted the note and began to read.

He watched her face go parchment white. "Joshua said you did the notes and slipped them under the doors."

"I did, but I didn't do this, Jon. Honestly. Honest to God, I swear! How could you think I would write something like that to you?"

"Is this what the other instructions look like?" he demanded harshly.

She nodded. "Yes, but—"

"Who had access to your office? This is castle stationery."

"Well, I guess anyone might have slipped in here. And there's more of this stationery in the desk in the library. I think it's even in the guest rooms. Jon, I can't prove anything, but, honestly, I've seen how you've suffered over all this, and surely you can't believe that I…" She trailed off helplessly.

Jon felt the tension in his shoulders ease as he watched Camy. She was so distressed. "No, I don't believe that you would be so cruel, Camy. I'm sorry. But it did arrive under my door."

She shook her head. "That's not what I sent you. Your note read, 'You're demented but cunning. Watch the proceedings, and listen well. Naturally, you're Demented Dick, which makes you a suspicious character.' That's all that I said. And that's what I put under your door."

"Did you see anyone else in the hallway at the time?" he asked her.

She shook her head strenuously, and he began to feel guilty; huge tears were brimming in her eyes.

"I didn't see anyone at all," she said. "I went downstairs to check on arrangements for dinner, and I turned on all the lights in the cellar—dungeon, sorry. I keep forgetting it's a dungeon, no matter how long your family has owned this place! And then I came back upstairs, and everyone was in the hallway."

"Well," he murmured, "apparently, someone doesn't think I've suffered enough for Cassie's death. I would like to know who wrote this," he said, pocketing the note again.

"Some of your friends are a bit eccentric," she suggested meekly.

"Some of them are simply bizarre," he agreed, grinning. "Well, keep your eyes open," he said, and he turned to leave.

"Jon," she said, calling him back hesitantly.

He paused, turning to look at her.

She cleared her throat. "I think… I think Cassie really was having an affair. I mean, she loved you, the best Cassie could love, but I think she was convinced that you had lost interest in her, that you were seeing someone else. And I think that she was seeing someone else. God knows, with Cassie, maybe she was seeing more than one person."

He arched a brow. "And...?"

"Well, if Cassie had a lover, maybe he blames you for what happened."

He nodded. "Was there something else?" he asked as she continued to look at him imploringly.

She flushed. "Well, if *you* were having an affair, maybe *she's* angry that you haven't pursued things, with Cassie now out of the way. Were you...having an affair with someone?" she ventured.

He crossed his arms over his chest, hiking up one eyebrow, a slight curl to his lips. "Camy, I'm not the type to kiss and tell. Never have been. So if I had been having an affair, I guarantee you, very few people would have known about it."

"Maybe that narrows down the question of who might have written that note," she suggested hopefully.

"Maybe. Except that I didn't say I'd had an affair."

"You didn't say you didn't, either."

He started to laugh. "Never mind, Camy. Some of my friends are bizarre—let's leave it at that."

He left her combination bedroom-and-office suite and started down the hall. Then he paused, noticing an irregularity in the smooth stone wall. He reached out and touched it, amazed. He ran his fingers over the grouting.

"Sweet Jesus..."

CHAPTER SEVEN

THE DUNGEON WAS a remarkable place.

Actually, the entire castle was remarkable, Sabrina reflected. A flawless combination of the new and the ancient. From the main foyer, a sweeping stone stairway curved down to a central hall; to the left were doors that led to the horror chamber, the chapel and the crypt, while to the right were doors that led to the recreation areas.

Sabrina stood next to V.J. staring at the sparkling water in the heated pool. Lounge chairs graced its deck, and at the far end was a complete bar taken from a turn-of-the-century Glascow pub. The bar had been modernized to offer a sink, a refrigerator, a coffee urn and a microwave. The ultramodern entertainment center at the rear of the bar, complete with big-screen TV, somehow blended artistically with the antique stained glass.

"This is living," V.J. commented with a soft sigh. "I do love Jon's invitations to come here. It was such a shame that something so terrible had to happen last time. I'm so glad he's decided to rejoin the world of the living. Imagine, a swimming pool in a dungeon!"

Sabrina had to admit that she was amazed, as well. The castle had so many sides, so many faces. It was so incredibly historical that it was possible at times to walk along its hallways and imagine that hundreds of years had faded away. Yet she had yet to smell any mustiness or even feel a draft.

"It must cost an arm and a leg to keep this place up," V.J. said, whispering suddenly as if someone might overhear.

"I'm sure. But Jon must make really good money with his books, don't you think?" Sabrina queried.

"Well, yes, he is really at the top of the commercial heap. And I understand he's also a smart businessman. He played the stock market extremely well, getting in very early on a number of computer and internet companies among other things. How on earth Cassie managed not to be happy with him is hard to imagine."

Sabrina looked around, certain that others—Brett, for one—would be coming down to enjoy the amenities soon. But at the moment they were all alone in the big rec room. Two billiard tables and a Ping-Pong table separated the pool area from the two-lane bowling alley and some comfortable chairs and love seats cozily set up around a woodburning stove. It all looked so innocent, so fun. Yet Sabrina wondered if, despite the contemporary atmosphere in this part of the dungeon, she'd feel so comfortable in the castle depths if V.J. weren't with her.

"I thought that Cassandra actually did love Jon," she finally replied. "I got the impression they had one of those passionate artistic marriages, that they were very much in love despite their quarrels."

V.J. shrugged. "There's only so many mysteries one can solve in a week," she said gaily. "Let's forget bowling; shall we? This pool looks just too delicious. I'm going in."

She slipped out of her terry cover-up and headed for the deep end. Still elegant with her long legs and trim, toned figure, she executed a beautiful dive and emerged at the far end. "It's wonderful in here!" she called to Sabrina.

"Look at that!" Sabrina called back. The television in the entertainment center was on, and though the volume was low, she could see that much of the country was being blanketed in snow.

V.J. swam to the edge of the pool and rested her chin on her arms on the tiled rim to watch. "Imagine! All that cold weather out there, and here I am, swimming in eighty-degree luxury. Indeed, our boy does know how to live!"

She pushed away from the ledge and continued swimming laps. Sabrina shed her own cover-up and dived in after her. She, too, swam laps for a while, then finally stopped to rest.

V.J. joined her, picking up the thread of their earlier conversation. "Cassie couldn't have been happy with Jon. All he had to do was say hello to someone, and she was instantly jealous and suspicious. She hated this place, hated it, and always came up with some excuse to try to make him leave it. Before she died…"

V.J.'s voice trailed off, and Sabrina wanted to scream in frustration. "Before she died?" she prodded.

V.J. shrugged her shoulders, smoothing back her wet hair. "They had an awful fight at breakfast. We were into the third or fourth day of the week, I believe. My character had already been killed off—a few of the others as well—and everyone was having a wonderful time. Susan was being a pain, naturally, but she was having fun, too. I think she actually enjoyed sparring with Cassie. And they did spar. Fur flew!" V.J. laughed in reminiscence.

"But what about Cassie and Jon?" Sabrina prompted.

"Well," V.J. continued, "Cassie seemed to be going

out of her way to upset Jon. Dressing in outrageously revealing clothing, being provocative with every male in the place. But I think part of the problem was that she wasn't making Jon angry anymore." She reflected for a moment. "When they were first married, I think Cassie put on a good act. She could pretend to be gentle and sweet, an ideal wife. But she had a mean streak in her, and the more it came out, the more Jon lost interest. I remember her trying to sock his jaw once when they fought, and he just caught her hand, stared at her, then waltzed away. He wasn't fighting anymore. I suspect he'd long since fallen out of love with her."

"Maybe," Sabrina said. "But, V.J., how can anyone know what someone else is feeling?"

The older woman looked at her, arching a brow. "Sabrina, love is something you can see in someone's eyes. And believe me, it was no longer in Jon's."

"V.J.! I never imagined you to be a closet romantic," Sabrina teased.

V.J. shrugged. "You just never can tell about people, can you?"

"Ah, correction, you can about me!" Brett called, striding into the pool area, wearing sandals, bathing trunks and a robe. He discarded the robe and struck a playful beefcake pose. "The entire world knows that *I'm* an incurable romantic," he announced. "Right, V.J.? Tell my wife that, would you? And remind her that I'm in supreme shape, too, please."

V.J. glanced at Sabrina, then back at Brett. "Sorry. But I imagine your ex-wife knows all about your glorious shape, Brett. Why don't you behave, dear? I'd love a mild vodka and soda, lots of lime. Why don't you go fix me a drink before you plunge in? I might find a few nice things to say about you."

"Make it two," called Thayer Newby, walking into the pool area.

He hadn't bothered with a cover-up; he had come down in cutoff jeans. Sabrina noticed that the ex-cop was wall-to-wall muscle. Thick-necked, broad-shouldered, and imposing, he looked a bit like the Incredible Hulk with red hair.

He plunked down into a deck chair, smiling. "Now all we need is a little sunshine."

"No sunshine in the dungeon," Brett said, "but there is a sauna back there beyond the bar, next to the restrooms."

"A sauna sounds good. If I ever decide to move," Thayer said. He looked up at the entry to the rec area as Anna Lee Zane came in. She didn't need any sunshine, her tan was already perfect. She wore a white gossamer caftan over a white bikini, and she looked stunning.

She was followed by Dianne Dorsey, who was wearing a black openwork cover-up over a stunning black suit.

"We could just lie on these lounges all day and imagine ourselves in a very strange paradise," Dianne said, taking the chair next to Thayer. "Brett, you brilliant novelist you, will you make me a drink as well, while you're at it?"

"Mine is vodka and tonic," Anna Lee advised him.

"Hey," Brett protested, "what do I look like here, the—"

"The butler, Mr. Buttle," Jon Stuart reminded him, joining them.

He was smiling, but in the strange light of the dungeon reflected by the pool, Sabrina thought that he looked tense and unhappy.

"But," he added, "since I'm Demented Dick, what do I know? Right, Sabrina?" he inquired.

She hadn't realized he had even noticed her there in the water. But he was staring at her, and the expression in his eyes made her uneasy. Then she started as a loud, crashing sound suddenly filled the rec room. Jon didn't flinch; he kept looking at her.

"Strike!" Reggie called out happily. And Sabrina realized that Tom Heart and Joe Johnston had arrived, as well, opting to bowl rather than swim.

"So, Sabrina," Jon said, "will you trust me to fix you a drink?"

Now, here was a man in extremely good shape. His shoulders were handsomely broad, his waist tight and lean, his legs long and nicely shaped. And Sabrina couldn't stop staring at him, remembering...

She forced her eyes to his, about to refuse a drink. It was so early.

"Gin and tonic," she said weakly.

But he already knew her choice, and he'd already started for the bar.

She swam the length of the pool to step out at the shallow end. White-haired Tom Heart had left the bowlers and now offered her a towel as she walked up the steps. V.J. came out behind her, and Tom, in a courtly fashion, draped another towel over V.J.'s slim shoulders. Sabrina wrapped hers around herself and approached the bar. Dianne, Thayer and Anna Lee had already taken seats there and were laughing as Brett and Jon argued over the proper way to make a martini.

"Stirred, not shaken," Jon said.

"Oh, come now, that's a bunch of British rot," Brett protested. "This is the way!" he said, shaking a canister.

"The ice just ever so slightly melts, giving the alcohol a perfect frost!"

"Speaking of frost," Jon said, addressing all of them, "I'm afraid we've acquired a rather grim weather forecast. It has occurred to me to suggest that we nix this Mystery Week and that I move you all into Stirling so that—"

"What?" Tom interrupted. "Nix the party now?"

"Some bad weather is moving in pretty fast," Jon said. "I'd like—"

"I'm not leaving," V.J. insisted. "Jon, dear, I've come all the way from California for this! A little bad weather isn't going to drive me away."

"I'm not going, either, old buddy," Thayer said firmly. "Hell, I don't make your kind of money yet, Jon. Maybe not ever. This is my vacation with the rich and famous."

"So what if we're snowbound?" Anna Lee demanded.

Jon hesitated. "I just have a bad feeling that—"

"Oh, Jon," Reggie said, joining them, her elderly voice full of grandmotherly empathy. "Jon, I thought when you planned this that you'd gotten over what happened the last time. We're all here for some fun and for a good cause, and we're not going anywhere."

"Cassie fell," Dianne Dorsey said firmly. "It was simply an accident, and that's what the coroner said."

"Exactly, Jon," Anna Lee added, an edge to her voice.

They both defended him so passionately, Sabrina noted, and she couldn't help thinking that either of them might have had an affair with him. Either of them might have really hated Cassandra, too.

Jon shook his head. "Thanks, but I'm afraid there's more to my concern than unhappy memories. Or even the snow. Remember the gunshots we heard this morning?"

Nods and a chorus of yeses met his words.

"I found a bullet in the grout in the stone in the hallway."

"What?" Thayer demanded.

"Well, Jon, this place is ancient, much older than even I am!" Reggie exclaimed. "Perhaps—"

"It wasn't an old bullet, Reggie. It was a new bullet," Jon told her.

Tom Heart shook his head in puzzlement. "Then it's part of the game."

"It wasn't part of the game. It's a real bullet," Jon said somewhat impatiently.

"Adding a little spice to the mystery, Jon?" Joe queried with a knowing smile, stroking his bushy beard.

"He's good at this," V.J. said in agreement. "Jon, did you ever consider acting?"

"Ladies and gentlemen, we're talking a real bullet, really fired in the hall, and someone might have gotten hurt. Or even killed," Jon said grimly.

"Okay," Joe protested, "so maybe one of us is an asshole who made it through the airport with a gun for protection in a strange country. God knows, we're all off the wall a bit. But I can't see ruining this whole Mystery Week because some moron mistakenly fired a gun in the hall." Joe sounded for all the world like the world-weary, no-nonsense PI in his books.

"All right, then, who fired the gun?" Jon demanded, looking from one of them to the next.

There was no confession.

"Well?" he said softly.

"Someone is trying to add to the mystery. No one was hurt," Joe mentioned.

"There's a bullet in the wall," Jon repeated flatly.

"Can you be absolutely certain it wasn't there from sometime before?" Thayer Newby asked, sounding, as he often did, as if he were grilling a suspect at headquarters.

"I'm familiar with firearms and bullets," Jon said.

"I'll take a look at it," Thayer said. "But I, too, say it's one of us adding a little spice to the Mystery Week."

"Please, Jon," Dianne said quietly. "We all just love doing this. Don't let what happened last time make you paranoid. Cassie didn't kill herself. She was very beautiful but maybe not particularly coordinated. She fell, Jon. She fell, you've gone through hell and that's that. It was a long time ago, we're all having a wonderful time now and we'll all be extremely angry with you if you make us leave!"

"And that's a fact," Anna Lee said determinedly.

"I'm just very concerned about you all, and—" Jon began.

"Jon Stuart, you are not going to throw an old lady out on the streets!" Reggie said indignantly.

And he was defeated. Sabrina could see his expression change as he looked at the elderly author. He took her hand and kissed it. "Never, Regina, in a thousand years would I think of putting you out on the streets."

"Damn straight, dear boy!" she declared, and she leaned across the bar to kiss his cheek.

Jon set down the drink he had been making. "All right, ladies and gentlemen, let's leave it at this. If there are any more incidents, or if it looks as if the weather could present real danger, it's over." He poured himself a straight shot of bourbon and hoisted it.

Anna Lee smiled. "Hear! Hear!" she cried, and she too leaned over the bar, planting a kiss not on his cheek but on his lips.

"Whoa, hot one!" Brett declared. "Well, I'm awfully damned glad we're going to keep this party going, but I'm sorry, I'll be damned if I'll kiss you, Jon."

"You'll be decked if you kiss me!" Jon warned in turn, and the whole group laughed.

"You won't deck *me*, will you?" Dianne Dorsey asked sweetly. "My turn," she said, leaning over the bar and kissing him on the lips, as well.

"Hey, ladies, I'm bartending here, too," Brett commented. "Don't all fight to kiss me at once!"

"Silly boy, those are surely the most used lips in history," V.J. drawled.

"Oh, let's be nice," Anna Lee said, and she kissed him, lingering just a bit.

"Much better. Share the wealth," Brett told Jon.

Jon shrugged. "Well, it is my house."

"House!" Susan exclaimed. "He calls this a house."

Sabrina wasn't sure why—she didn't mean to be a killjoy in the least—but she suddenly wanted to be away from the crowd, away from the joking.

And away from all the well-used lips.

She felt strangely like an outsider. They had all known each other much longer—and much better. They had all been here when Cassandra died. They seemed to form an enclave, and she felt oddly excluded, yet at the same time a little relieved to be so. She needed to get away for a bit, to feel a touch of reality.

Jon had mixed her drink; she saw it on the bar. But she took her towel and silently slipped away, making her way upstairs to her room.

She showered, washed her hair, wrapped herself in a towel and curled up on the bed to call her sister. Tammy was two years her junior, an archaeology major who had married one of her professors. Nothing in the world made either of them happier than digging in the dirt for ancient relics, unless it was their newborn son, Tyler Delaney. Though she was happy as a lark, Tammy was also feeling the confinement of new motherhood, and she was eager to hear all about Scotland.

"Aren't you having fun?" she inquired now.

"Sure. Why do you ask?" Sabrina replied.

"Well, you've already called Mom. Now me. Surely you have better things to do with your time. So tell me, what's going on? Are you having problems with the master sleuth himself?"

"Who?"

"Oh, don't play innocent with me. You know I'm talking about Jon Stuart. Tall, dark and handsome. Man of mystery with the great accent. The faster-than-a-speeding-bullet affair of your life. So, did he or didn't he do in his beautiful, bitchy wife? Have you learned anything new over there?"

Sabrina stared at the phone. "He was cleared of all charges, you know."

"Lots of people have been acquitted on all kinds of charges. That doesn't make them innocent."

"No, I don't believe he did it," Sabrina said firmly.

"Oooh, listen to you. So the flame is still burning brightly. He remains tall, dark, handsome and totally enchanting! So where is he, and why are you on the phone with me?"

"Everyone's down by the pool—in the castle dungeon, if you can believe it. Jon was threatening to call the whole week off because he found a bullet in the wall."

"Well, it is Mystery Week," Tammy commented. "Isn't

that the kind of thing that happens? Mysterious clues and all?"

"He says it's not part of the mystery."

"Is he telling the truth?"

"I imagine. He was trying to make us all go home. Reggie Hampton—she's a tough old bird who writes adorable mysteries featuring a cat—refused to go."

"Good for her," Tammy said. "Then again, maybe you should come home. That way you could quit calling us long distance."

"Very funny. See if I call you for a friendly chat again."

"How's your ex, by the way? Brett is there, right? Honestly, I have to admit to being totally jealous. I'm sitting here with baby oatmeal, poo-poo diapers, and my boobs are swollen enough to burst. And you're off jet-setting in Scotland with the rich and famous. Not fair. Besides, Mom always liked you better."

Sabrina started to laugh at the old joke, glad that she had called. "Mom never liked me better, and you're being totally irrelevant." She and Tammy had fought like the dickens growing up, but now her sister was her best friend, and the only person other than herself and Jon who knew she'd had a faster-than-a-speeding-bullet affair with him.

"So how is old Brett?"

"Brett's fine. He's at the pool, too, whining because he isn't getting as many kisses as Jon."

"Ah," Tammy murmured, "so that's it. Those other writers—those hussies—are down in the dungeon kissing tall, dark and handsome. And you're jealous, so you ran to your room and phoned home."

"Don't be silly. I called to ask about Tyler," Sabrina protested.

"Our beautiful baby is fine. He's an angel, too—sleeps all the time. I'm waiting for him to wake up."

"Think you deserved such a good baby?" Sabrina teased.

"If you want me to suffer, I'm suffering. I'm going to have to poke the kid awake soon. I'm not kidding—this nursing thing is killing me. I think I could do lethal damage with a jet spray of milk at the moment. But back to you and Mr. Mystery. Now seriously, pay attention to me here. Why not take the bull by the horns? Sleep with good old tall, dark and handsome again, and find out if you've been carrying a torch all these years for something imagined or something real. Just remember that it's Mystery Week, and make sure you know who you're sleeping with. Don't go sleeping with any strangers!"

Sabrina was startled to feel an uneasy sensation sweep over her as her sister jokingly, unknowingly, echoed what Brett had said in the chamber of horrors.

"I'm here as a professional fiction writer involved in a charity event, nothing more," Sabrina said. Yet to her own ears, even as she spoke the lie, she froze, certain she had heard a soft clicking sound on the line.

Had someone been listening in on her conversation?

"Sabrina?"

"Yes, I'm still here," she said softly. She didn't know why, but she felt the same deep sensation of unease again. It was unnervingly akin to fear.

It was a big house—castle—and she was certain it had several phone lines, but not necessarily one for each guest room. Someone had simply accidentally picked up in the middle of her conversation and then hung up again.

So why did she feel someone had been listening in?

"Give my nephew a kiss for me," Sabrina said quickly. "Love you. I'll call again in a few days."

"Great, bye, have a good time!" Tammy said.

Sabrina stared at the phone for a moment, then hung up. And suddenly she had the uneasy feeling that someone was behind her. She whirled around on the bed.

She was alone in her room, but the doors to the balcony were open.

She held tightly to her towel and rushed over to step outside.

There was no one there.

But she could see Jon Stuart, out on his balcony. For a moment, she was relieved to see him. He, too, had left the crowd and come upstairs. Okay, so maybe she had been jealous. And maybe she had felt out of his league down by the pool, realizing that he'd had many lovers in his life, and she had just been one of them. After all, it was rumored that he'd been having an affair at the time Cassandra died, and if so, that affair would have been with someone who was here now...

The thought hurt. Like a knife in the pit of her stomach. She gazed at him, wondering what was going on in *his* mind...

Then she realized that she was standing on the balcony with only a towel around her.

Maybe he hadn't seen her.

He raised a hand in a silent salute.

She waved back and retreated in a flash, anxious to get dressed.

At least, she told herself, if Jon had been on his balcony, he couldn't have been in her room. No one had been in her room. True, the balcony doors had been open, but no one had been out there, and, despite the celebrated guest list, she doubted there were any superheros among them who could have *flown* away.

Of course, Jon might have been on the phone in his room, listening in on her conversation, she thought.

No, he would have apologized, and he would have hung up right away.

Surely he would have done so. But how did she really know? Had she made of him what she wanted him to be? In fact, if she thought about it, maybe she didn't know him at all. And so much time had passed.

Maybe he truly was a stranger.

And some very strange things were happening here...

Stop! she told herself. Get dressed, and get ready to take part in Mystery Week.

It got dark so early, and now it was almost dusk. Time to head down to the chapel.

She loved the chamber of horrors.

It was just so good.

The people were so real. The fear and the terror were so real. And deep in the dungeon, with the recessed lighting, it was like a secret world where famous killers could come to life. Their victims could almost be heard in their silent yet eloquent screams.

Walking softly through the fantastic exhibits, she felt a pleasant sense of power.

No one knew.

"Here!"

She spun around at the whisper, trembling with a pleasant fear.

For a second, just a split second, she thought that one of the wax figures had come to life, that Jack the

Ripper prowled the dungeon or that a headsman was stalking her.

The pale, purple-gray light was so eerie.

The figures were so real.

She could hear her heart slamming against the walls of her chest. Someone was moving, furtive in the darkness...stalking?

Then she heard her name whispered, and delicious chills cascaded down her spine. It was him. He had come.

Then she saw him, and she started to hurry to him, wondering at the stricken expression on his face.

"She knows!" he gasped. "She knows, and she intends to blackmail us. Oh, God, I don't know what to do. I don't—"

She threw her arms around him, hushing him, calming him. "Now tell me who you're talking about and what exactly happened."

He did, and as he spoke, he shook. He was afraid. Afraid for the future, afraid for her. She had never been loved so in her life.

"My God, I couldn't bear it if—" he began.

"Hush, hush, my love! Nothing bad will happen."

"But I don't know what to do!"

She smiled, shaking her head. "I do," she said softly. "Don't you worry." She held him close and looked around at the tableaux. Hooded headsmen, masked murderers. She smiled and soothed him. "Don't you worry. I know exactly what to do."

CHAPTER EIGHT

THE CASTLE WAS most definitely large, Sabrina thought, descending the main stairs to the foyer. It was full of people, guests and staff, and yet now, at dusk, as she hurried to her appointment, she didn't see a soul. Eerie.

She headed around the stone expanse of the main stairway to where the second set of winding steps led down to the dungeon beneath. She hadn't felt unnerved just glad that they were going swimming. Now, however...

Turning away from the cheerful recreation area, she came to a pair of heavy, brass-accented wooden doors and paused. They were open to the exhibits, of course, Joshua Valine's fabulous tableaux of lives—and deaths—gone by. The track lighting within allowed an eerie mauve glow to whisper out of the room like fog on a dark night. She shivered, then thought that she had heard someone inside.

"Hello in there!" she called. Her voice seemed very loud. She stepped in, following the path to where Jack the Ripper stood over his last victim, Mary Kelly. Sabrina found herself pausing again, biting her lower lip. Mary Kelly really did resemble Susan Sharp. The sculptor obviously had an odd sense of humor—or aesthetics. After all, he supposedly liked Sabrina and he had made her the victim on the rack. Then again, none of the women in the exhibit had fared any too well.

She heard a noise behind her, like a whisper of air, and she spun around. "Hello? Who—"

She broke off, looking around. She could see no one moving about at all. Camy Clark as Joan of Arc gazed heavenward from her stake. She herself was stretched out on the rack. Joe Johnston, shaved and wearing a white wig as Louis XVI, faced the guillotine with Anna Lee Zane, appearing again, as Marie Antoinette at his side. They all looked incredibly real, as if they had just been in action but suddenly stopped dead when Sabrina turned around.

Goose bumps broke out over her arms, and she took a step backward. She nearly screamed as she backed into someone. Then she saw that it was only the straw setup for the Joan of Arc display.

Face it, this place is scary as all hell, she told herself. No one had been in here, watching her, even if she had felt a presence, felt someone's eyes on her. It was just the eerily realistic wax figures "watching" her. All the figures, with their penetrating glass eyes.

Sabrina hadn't meant to run, but she did.

And as she did so, she thought she heard the sound of laughter. Soft, whispering laughter, like an airy breeze.

Okay, so you're losing your mind here, she told herself as she hurried toward the second set of wooden doors. She assumed they led to the chapel, and she pushed them open, entering the room.

It wasn't the castle's chapel, but the crypt.

Stone shelves and flooring housed ornate tombs, with angels hewn of marble, crosses, death's-heads and more funerary art decorating individual graves. Sabrina felt as if she had entered the catacombs of a great cathedral, there seemed to be so many dead from so long ago, stretching out at least the length of one wing of the castle. Only here, in the entry, was there dim lighting to show the unwary guest what he or she had stumbled upon. There was nothing awful about the crypt— —no visible bodies decaying in shrouds, no skulls or bare bones upon the shelving. If she weren't alone, she'd be fascinated, eager to study the crypt's dates and art. And Tammy would be in heaven here.

But, admittedly, Sabrina was spooked. Goose bumps were popping out on her arms again. She turned about, then paused, turning back. A stone sarcophagus lay dead ahead of her, a shiny new cross and fresh flowers atop it. Sabrina saw that a banner was tied to the flowers, and she approached the casket to read the words. *Rest in peace and God's love, dear Cassie.*

Sabrina backed away, startled and uneasy. She'd had no idea that Cassandra Stuart had been buried here, in this castle, where she had died.

Feeling suddenly as if the crypt were closing in on her, Sabrina turned and hurried out. She closed the massive doors behind her, and as she did so, she was suddenly certain that she heard the laughter again.

"Get a grip!" she whispered angrily to herself. If the creatures in the tableaux were coming alive to taunt her, they weren't magically making their way into the crypt, as well. This place was simply spooky as all hell.

"Great setting for a Halloween party," she murmured irritably, realizing that, of course, it was also a great place for a Mystery Week. They had taken place here before Cassie died, and they should continue to do so. She, Sabrina Holloway, was a mystery writer. She was supposed to come alive with excitement over this type of affair, the way the others did. This was supposed to be fun.

She leaned against the crypt doors. "Right. I'm having so damn much fun, I can barely stand it," she whispered softly to herself.

She straightened her shoulders and headed for the third pair of doors, which had to belong to the chapel.

They did.

She breathed a sigh of relief, looking in. The chapel was beautiful, with its stone arches, altar and ancient pews. The stations of the cross had been etched in stained glass along the walls, with special lighting set behind to show them off even in the gloom of the dungeon. Evidently a few Stuarts had their tombs in here instead of the crypt and these were between the stations, their occupants elaborately carved in stone atop their final resting places. Like the crypt, the chapel seemed to be immaculate, with nary a cobweb or spider. Tapers burned on the altar and from beautiful candlesticks at the end of each pew.

Sabrina started toward the altar. As she reached it, she heard footsteps behind her, and she spun around, thinking she'd scream and tear out her hair if no one was there this time.

But Dianne Dorsey, clad in a black cocktail gown, her neatly cut ebony hair swinging, was coming toward her, a smile on her face.

"Am I glad to see you!" the young writer exclaimed.

Sabrina smiled. "I'm glad to see you, too."

"Are you the murderer?" Dianne asked anxiously.

Sabrina laughed. "I'm not supposed to tell you if I am."

"Well, if you are, I'll be the first to go."

"And vice versa, of course."

"Your note sent you here?" Dianne asked.

Sabrina nodded. "I'm supposed to meet with one of my wayward girls. Choir practice."

Dianne laughed. "Well, despite the fact that I'm Mary, the Hare Krishna, by day, evidently I moonlight for your call-girl outfit at night."

"Oh, no, you mean you're not an angelic but misguided chorister?"

"Well, I'm sure I sing just as angelically as anyone, but my note said that I'm to be reprimanded for missing the last 'appointment' you arranged for me."

"With whom?"

"Demented Dick—who else?" Dianne laughed.

"Oh, well, consider yourself duly reprimanded."

"Not that I would have missed a date with Jon as Demented Dick had I had one!"

Her airy comment had Sabrina turning with curiosity about the nature of Dianne's relationship with their host, but Dianne had begun walking through the chapel, looking at the stained glass stations of the cross.

"These are really beautiful, aren't they?" the young woman observed.

"Gorgeous," Sabrina agreed.

"It's Tiffany glass," Dianne explained. "Jon's grandfather put them in, turn of the century. Jon told me the last time we were here."

Curious, Sabrina followed her. "That week must have been so awful. So tragic."

Dianne shrugged. "I hate to sound like Susan, but Cassie was so…hated." She flashed a small smile at Sabrina. "Mostly by women, of course."

"Apparently Jon was happy with her," Sabrina ventured, just a little embarrassed by her not so subtle fishing expedition.

"Jon was planning on getting a divorce."

"How do you know that?"

"He told me."

"He…"

Dianne smiled. "You're assuming I was sleeping with Jon?" she demanded.

"I wasn't assuming anything. I—"

"Actually, I adore Jon. He's a good friend, one of the best guys out there. Tough and rugged, willing to go to bat for a friend."

"So are you saying that you weren't having an affair with him?"

"I'm saying that I would, wouldn't you?" Dianne said pleasantly.

"I wasn't here," Sabrina reminded her without answering the question.

"Oh, I see. This is the mystery that everyone *really* wants to solve this week. So you're looking for the criminal, too. You're asking if I was having a mad, passionate affair with Jon, flew off the handle and threw his nasty wife over the balcony? No, Sabrina. Jon was a big boy, he could handle himself. He wouldn't have thanked anyone for interference on his behalf. Besides, he did care about Cassie. She could be dazzling when she chose to be. I think she was becoming rancid because she realized she was losing him, and she was trying desperately—and pathetically, perhaps—to win him back."

"You think so? Then you hated her but felt sorry for her, as well?"

Dianne shook her head. "Nope. Don't go giving me any gentler emotions where Cassie was involved. I simply hated her. I had good reason. But don't think that *only* women despised the little darling, no matter how dazzling she could be. She did a few terrible things to men, as well. Then again, I must admit, there were those who absolutely adored her. Like your ex."

"Brett?" Sabrina said, surprised.

Dianne looked at her, arching a brow. "Oh, dear, I'm sorry—are you two getting back together? Brett does keep implying that you're a twosome, but V.J. told me it wasn't so."

"V.J. is right—it isn't so. I had just never realized that Cassie was among Brett's...women."

"Really?" Dianne said, sounding startled. "Well, maybe he didn't want his feelings known...especially by you. You may not be back together, but Brett seems to wish it were so."

"Dianne, are you saying that Brett was having an affair with Cassie? Here, in Jon's house?"

"His castle, darling. You mustn't call it a house," Dianne said, amused. "But yes, they were having an affair, in Jon's castle. They were discreet. Brett was in the midst of a wild infatuation—but you know Brett well, so you know how his infatuations come and go. Cassie probably wanted to irritate her hubby, but Brett really does value his friendship with Jon."

"But not enough to avoid sleeping with his wife."

"Now, that's a dangerous tone. Moralistic, even. How intriguing. But then, our host does have an impact on most women, doesn't he? We all instantly spring to his defense. Like Lucy defended Count Dracula even as he sucked her blood dry!"

"I'm not trying to be moralistic, and I hardly see Jon Stuart as Count Dracula."

"Tall, dark, handsome...devastating," Dianne said. "I

admit, I adore the man. He'd be welcome to my blood anytime."

"But, Dianne, I can't see where, with any man, sleeping with his wife would encourage a friendship."

"I told you, Brett was infatuated. Madly in love."

"Dianne, you bitch!"

Dianne and Sabrina both swung around at the sound of the voice coming from the doors to the chapel.

"Brett, this is a house of worship!" Dianne said. "He can't say that in a chapel, can he?" she asked, glancing at Sabrina.

Sabrina shrugged. "He said it, didn't he?"

"You could go to hell for that, Brett," Dianne taunted.

But Brett wasn't amused. He was striding down the aisle between the pews. "It's not true!" he stated furiously, glaring at Dianne, then looking more petulantly at Sabrina. "You know me, it's not true!"

Sabrina looked at him, slowly arching a brow. "What isn't true, Brett? Are you trying to tell me that you weren't having an affair with Cassandra Stuart?"

He didn't exactly deny it. He spun on Dianne again. "Where did you get your information? It's all a pack of lies!" He was clearly agitated, hands on his hips, handsome face contorted.

Dianne lifted her chin. "From someone who knew."

"Oh, come on."

"Someone Cassie confided in."

"She was delusional! Don't you dare go around spreading the story that I was sleeping with Cassandra."

"Is it a story, Brett?" Dianne challenged.

"Damn you, Di—" he began.

But Dianne interrupted him, black hair tossed back

defiantly, hands—with long, black polished nails—on her hips. "Maybe *you* pushed her over the balcony, Brett."

"Me? Oh, this is rich, Dianne! Come on, I wasn't married to her. I didn't need to get rid of anyone. You were crazy about Jon. Always have been, always will be. And now you're pointing a finger at me, trying to make my wife think—"

"Ex-wife, Brett," Sabrina interjected.

He ignored her and kept talking. "You're trying to make Sabrina think that I was involved with a married woman—and then in the next breath you're accusing me of killing her!"

"Maybe you were afraid that she was about to tell your buddy, Jon, the truth of the situation. She was just using you, Brett. Oh, I know you're the great lover, but she was in love with Jon in her warped, sick way. And—"

"If anyone had a reason to kill her, it was Jon. So why are you trying to make me look guilty?"

"Jon wasn't in the room! He was outside."

"So someone else was in on it. One of the guests, his staff—a bloody stranger!"

"And maybe she teased you just a little bit too much, a little bit too long, and—"

"I should give you a black eye!" Brett exclaimed. "Not that anyone would notice, with your damn black makeup. What is it with you, Dianne? Are you trying to scare your readers into buying your books?"

"Oh, Brett, is that all you can come up with? Is everything in your life about book sales, about securing a place on a list? We're talking about a woman's life here."

"Yes! Life—not death. I mean it, Dianne. How dare you make such accusations? You want the truth, the real truth? I did care about her. I didn't want her dead or—"

The sound of a gunshot suddenly exploded in the quiet chapel.

Startled, Sabrina ducked, and Dianne, too, dropped to the floor.

Brett didn't move as quickly. And the back of his tailored blue silk shirt was suddenly soaked in red.

Bloodred.

THE NOTE HAD sent him to the crypt.

Not his Mystery Week instruction note, but the first note he had found thrust beneath his door—the note Camy had denied writing.

It had read:

"You are a demented dick, thinking that you're slick. You're only sick, you maggot tick. You must go below, lie with your wife, minus all life. If a night's sweet passion you still crave, you must go sleep down in her grave."

And so he had come here, to the crypt, where his ancestors rested. Along with Cassie. Despite her alleged hatred of Scotland, her will had actually requested that she be laid to rest in Jon's castle. To avoid morbid scandal-and-celebrity seekers, he had allowed reporters to believe she was being buried back in the States. Her family, happy to comply with his wishes and to avoid prurient interest, had been vague about her burial.

So there lay his wife, in the center of Lochlyre Castle's crypt.

Apparently his guests knew where she rested. For on her tomb lay flowers in her honor.

He swore softly, staring at them. Were they truly in

her memory, or a taunt to him? Did someone here really think he had killed her?

Or was someone suffering a brutally guilty conscience and trying to cast blame his way.

If he'd been with her, she wouldn't have fallen. She wouldn't have been alone. Alone for a killer to come upon in a precarious position...

The sound of a gunshot galvanized Jon into action. He raced from the crypt, certain the blast had come from nearby.

He ran straight into Thayer Newby. Tom Heart and Joe Johnston were close behind.

"Anyone else down here?" Joe demanded.

"The chapel!" Thayer shouted.

They ran the short distance to the chapel doors, bursting in together.

Dianne and Sabrina were there, hunched down by the altar.

Brett was on the ground. Between the two rows of pews.

Swearing, despite the fact that it was the chapel.

Brett looked up as the men entered. Jon realized that they were followed closely by Reggie and Anna Lee.

"Can you believe it?" Brett said, disgusted. "Me! I'm the first to go. Damnation! I didn't see a thing, didn't hear a thing. I was a damned sitting duck, an idiot, a fuc—"

"Brett! It is a chapel," Sabrina reminded him.

She was by Dianne's side, and obviously the two of them had been trying to make McGraff feel better about becoming a ghost. Sabrina's blue eyes were huge, her hair shimmering as it fell around her shoulders. Jon felt a strange pulse ticking against his throat and forced his attention back to the situation at hand.

His heart, he realized, was still pounding. The bullet he had found in the wall earlier had unnerved him. It had been real. And it hadn't been there before. He would have seen it. He walked that hallway every day of his life when he was in residence. He'd been afraid that someone was toting real fire power with real purpose.

Now he was so relieved to find that this gunshot was part of the game that he needed to sit.

Brett was flushing, staring at him. "Sorry, Jon. I suppose this place is sacred or something, huh? But the game instructions did tell us to come here."

"Well, it is a chapel, yes," Jon said. "But I think you can get away with 'damn,' especially if you've just been shot with red paint. So who did it?" He looked questioningly at Dianne and Sabrina.

Dianne smiled like a cat. Sabrina shrugged. "We didn't see. We were in the midst of an argument."

Jon frowned. "About what?"

"Oh, some silly thing. I don't even remember, do you, Dianne?"

The young woman arched a brow, then lifted her shoulders. "No... I can't quite remember. At the moment."

"Five minutes ago you were all arguing so passionately that you didn't pay any attention to what was going on, and now you can't remember what you were talking about?" Jon asked skeptically.

Sabrina shook her head. The color in her cheeks heightened, and her lashes fluttered before her eyes met his again.

She was lying, Jon knew.

"You are all acting like a bunch of lunatics!" Thayer accused.

"Well, what do you want?" Brett said irritably. "I'm shot all over with red paint. Damn! Damn! Shit! Ah, hell, sorry, Jon."

"I say it's cocktail hour," Reggie announced.

"Hear, hear," Tom agreed.

"Well, now, wait!" Joe protested, rubbing his bearded chin and looking at them all. "Let's check out the situation first. We're here to solve a mystery, Sabrina, what happened here?" he asked.

Sabrina looked at him, started to speak, then stopped. She glanced at Jon, looked away.

What the hell? he wondered.

Then she shook her head sheepishly at Joe. "Honest, you know how opinionated we all are, Joe. It was dumb, but we got so involved talking, none of us was paying any attention."

"Well, this is a total loss!" Joe said, disgruntled.

"No, it's not," Tom argued. "We know that the butler didn't do it, since Mr. Buttle, the butler, is now dead."

"The butler is dead?" a new voice suddenly inquired. Susan Sharp, in a deep blue cocktail dress that emphasized her darkly attractive looks, swept into the chapel. She spotted Brett and burst into laughter.

"Well, you didn't last very long, did you, dear?"

"Susan, trust me, you won't last very long, either," Brett promised her direly.

"Oh, don't be a spoilsport. They killed you, and I'm alive and well."

"No, Susan," Brett informed her firmly. "Carla—the call girl with the clap—is alive and more or less well. For the moment."

"As Sherlock Holmes would say, 'The game is afoot!'" Reggie informed them. "And the week has just begun.

We are beginning to learn a few things. The butler is out of the picture. We now know that Sabrina isn't the killer, or Dianne."

"That's not true. We don't know anything, except that none of them will talk!" Tom protested. "Remember, the killer may have an accomplice. Someone to lure the victims to their dooms. That means that Dianne or Sabrina could easily be guilty of complicity in murder."

"But who pulled the trigger?" Joe demanded. "Let's see, everyone is here except... V.J."

"Excuse me—right here, at the chapel door," V.J. called, and they all turned to look at her.

Entirely elegant in a floor-length, sequined gown, V.J. was casually leaning against the doorjamb and watching them all with amusement as they argued.

"Ah, but where were you?" Tom demanded, smiling as he sauntered over to her.

For the first time it occurred to Jon that his two friends made a very nice looking couple. Tom Heart, too, looked elegant, in a dinner jacket, tie and vest, his silver-white hair gleaming. Interesting. Maybe something was brewing there. The two had always seemed so compatible. The last time they'd all been together here, V.J.'s husband had been living. No more. And rumor had it that though Tom was still married, he'd been separated from his wife of thirty years for several months.

V.J. lifted a champagne flute to them all. "Where was I? Where I was supposed to be. I was at cocktail hour— all by myself. I had no idea that the party was in the chapel." She looked around. "So the butler bit the dust. That kind of ruins the fun—we know we won't get to say that the butler did it! Well, the chapel is lovely. Much better than the crypt. If we're all going to spend time down here, at least it's with this beautiful stained glass and not with coffins and dead people." She winced. "Oh, sorry, Jon. I forget they're your relatives."

"I understand, V.J.," he told her. "I prefer cocktails with the living myself."

"I told you it was cocktail hour," Reggie said. "V.J. is the only one of us with any sense."

"Hell, I agree with that."

"Brett McGraff!" Reggie reprimanded him indignantly. "We're in a chapel!"

"Sorry," Brett muttered in resignation.

"Oh, Brett," Dianne warned, "that stuff is dripping onto your pants now."

"Hell, you're right, it is. Damn! Oh, shit. There I go again, swearing in the chapel. I wish I could stop that!" Brett said. He leaped to his feet, glanced at the crucifix on the altar and crossed himself quickly. The others were staring at him. "All right, all right, I was brought up in the Catholic Church. Do you mind?"

With that he spun around. "I'll be changing my shirt so that I can come to cocktails in ghostly white apparel." He stomped out of the chapel. "Shit!" he swore one last time.

The tension was broken as the others burst into laughter. Reggie started out after him. "Ladies, gentlemen, I'm going up for cocktails. Anyone joining me?"

"Definitely," Jon agreed.

"Joe Johnston, get up here and escort an old lady," Reggie commanded.

"Yes, ma'am!" Joe said, hurrying to her side.

The others began filing out. Jon paused by the door, waiting.

Tom escorted V.J. Dianne, Thayer and Anna Lee exited together, Dianne still insisting to Thayer that she hadn't seen anything. Susan brushed by Jon.

Sabrina remained by the altar. She looked at him as if she was trying to figure out how to escape him when he stood blocking the only exit.

He walked toward her. "Were you intending to stay behind for some reason?" he inquired.

"No," she said quickly.

"Are you trying to avoid me?" he inquired.

"No," she repeated.

But she was lying again. And he thought he knew why. The argument between Brett and Dianne had been over him. Or Cassie. Or what had happened three years ago.

And Sabrina didn't want him questioning her.

Well, maybe it wasn't the time.

She stood very still, trying to keep her beautiful blue eyes level with his. Her hair was falling around her shoulders like silk, and he suddenly ached to reach out and touch it.

No, he admitted to himself, he wanted more than that.

There was so much in life that went by so swiftly. So much that a man barely remembered. But he remembered Sabrina. Her tentative smile. Her gentle touch. Her passion. The way she'd been so trusting way back when.

She was still tentative at times.

But not so trusting.

She was very wary, watching him.

He felt a renewed bitterness that she could suspect he would cold-bloodedly kill his wife. He wished he could reach out, shake her and tell her he was innocent. No, he didn't want to shake her. He wanted to touch her. Hold her. Again. Hell, Brett McGraff was worrying about the things he'd been saying in the chapel. The things Jon wanted to *do* in the chapel were surely far less forgivable.

God, he could remember the way she looked naked, covered with a sheen of sweat, crystal blue eyes half shielded by the fall of her lashes, every curve of her body inviting.

"The others are way ahead. I guess we should hurry," she said, and she stepped past him, striding quickly toward the doors.

He followed her, and, unable to stop himself, caught her arm, swinging her back around to face him.

"We have to talk," he said.

The words came out sounding far more harsh than he had intended.

She gazed at his hand where it rested on her upper arm. Her long blond hair brushed over his fingers, soft as silk. To his dismay, that slight sensation was arousing.

"Not here, not now," she said nervously.

"We have to talk," he insisted.

"Later," she said, pulling free.

"I'm taking that as a promise," he told her.

He ushered her out. Aware that, though she had shaken off his touching, she was sticking very close to him.

And he realized that she didn't want to be left alone in the dungeon of Lochlyre Castle.

With him.

But then again…who did?

CHAPTER NINE

AMAZINGLY, SABRINA DIDN'T dream that night; she slept like a log. The evening had ultimately gone pleasantly, with everyone trying to figure out why the butler had died first. Dinner had been delicious, rack of lamb, and she'd been starving. She had opted for regular coffee rather than decaf with their late dessert, and despite even that, she had come upstairs, changed into a nightgown— and slept.

Only the persistent tapping on her door forced her to wake up. And by then it was morning.

"Sabrina, hey, wake up! Hurry!"

At her ex-husband's urgency, she catapulted out of bed and into her robe and hurried to her door.

Brett was in jeans and a heavy sweater. "Hey, sleepy-head, you've got less than a week now to find the killer. If you sleep the whole thing away, you'll never be the master sleuth."

"I'm awake. What's the rush?"

"Riding!"

"Riding?"

He nodded. "A riding party is going out. Come on, hurry, we're probably late already. The others might have headed out. Come on, you want to see the countryside before bad weather moves in, right? Get dressed. I'll wait for you."

"I need coffee, Brett."

"I'll get it for you." He waved his hands at her. "Go on, get moving. I'll bring you coffee."

He closed her door and disappeared. She shrugged and decided that if the rest of the household was headed out riding, she didn't want to be left behind. She loved horses, and the countryside did look beautiful.

She hopped in and out of the shower, careful to bring her clothing into the bathroom with her. She emerged in jeans, shirt, jacket and boots to find that Brett had returned and was comfortably curled on her bed—offering her coffee.

She took the cup.

"Get up," she commanded him.

"Why?" he demanded.

"You make it look as if you've been sleeping here."

He frowned, studying her. "What are you so afraid of?"

"What do you mean?"

"What do you care what something looks like?"

"Brett, you're my friend, I care about you, but you are my ex-husband, and though I'll surely make lots of new mistakes in my life, I'm not going to repeat old ones. I'm not marrying you again, and I'm not sleeping with you again, and I don't want people thinking that we're a twosome."

He was still studying her as he stood up. "So."

"So what?"

"So there is something between you two."

"Who two?"

"You and our host. I was right."

"You were right about what?"

"You slept with him."

"Oh, Brett, please."

"I still love you, Sabrina."

"Brett, you never loved me."

"I did. I do. But don't worry, I'm going to prove to you that I can be good for you. Drink your coffee, and let's get going."

There was no one in the hallway, on the stairs or even in the great hall as they walked out of the castle into the front courtyard. The stables were ahead to the right. Two horses were saddled and bridled and ready for them.

"I guess the others have gone on ahead," Brett murmured.

"Are you sure?" Sabrina demanded, suddenly suspicious.

He laughed. "Well, since I'm already a ghost, you know that I'm not the murderer, so I'm not luring the Duchess to her doom."

"You've got a point there," she said. She walked up to one of the horses, a sleek bay that stood about sixteen hands high. She stroked the horse's velvety nose. "What a beauty. This is a great idea, Brett. Thanks for coming to get me."

"Yeah, sure, let's get started."

He gave her a hand before leaping up on the roan that had been tethered next to the bay. He started from the castle at an easy lope, looking back a little uneasily. Sabrina thought he was worried about her.

"Go on, you know that I can ride!" she told him delightedly.

Riding had been one of the benefits of growing up in the Midwest. But this was some of the most spectacular scenery she had ever seen. The ground was rolling here in the valley, while majestic hills rose up around them.

Leaving the castle behind, they came up on a little promontory. She could see the hills rising higher and higher toward the mountainous country to the northwest, the loch shimmering in the sun below them and a sea of grass and flowers seeming to flow all around them. The air was crisp and cold with the promise of strong weather to come, yet it felt delicious, and she was delighted to be out.

"Which way did they head? Do you know where we're going?" she asked Brett.

"Of course."

"How?"

"I was here before, remember?"

"Where are we heading?"

"That way." He pointed to the northeast.

"Oh. Race you to that copse!" Sabrina called out, and she nudged her mount. Her horse smoothly began to run. The animal was graceful, the air was invigorating, the world around her was beautiful. Sabrina felt a pure rush of exhilaration.

She heard Brett pounding up behind her, and at the copse she reined in, waiting for him.

"Remember when we went riding outside Paris?" he asked her. "There were flowers everywhere."

"There were women everywhere," she corrected him.

He shrugged that off, looking at her, his brown eyes sincere. "I've learned my lesson, Sabrina."

"Brett, you make sexual innuendos every time you're around anyone who's even remotely female."

"Even remotely female? I resent that!"

"Brett, you—"

"Sabrina!" He reached over, placing his hand on her thigh. "I only do that because I want you so badly and I can't allow other people to see just how much."

She stared at him. "Oh?" she said softly. "Brett, were you having an affair with Cassandra Stuart when she died?"

"Me?" he demanded, startled. Then he huffed, "This place is getting to you, Sabrina. You can't let it. Cassie is dead and gone. We need to let her rest in peace, forget the past and get on with our lives. Come on, I'll race you to that next little hill there!"

He took off; she followed. As they rode, the wind whipped around her, colder than it had been only minutes before.

She looked up. The sky had been a deep, striking shade of blue. Now it was darkening to mauve. She reined in next to Brett on the hill. "Looks like that bad weather is coming in. We should find the others."

"Maybe they're up ahead in that hunting lodge."

"I don't see any horses."

"Maybe the horses are in back. Let's get there and see."

He nudged his horse into a lope. With little other choice, Sabrina followed.

JON'S NOTE THAT morning had read simply: "Attend the séance in the crypt at eleven o'clock."

Joe Johnston and Tom Heart were in the great hall when he went down for coffee, and like the good game players they were, they were trying to figure out why the butler should be the first to die.

"He knew something. People who know things are dangerous," Joe said.

"He was blackmailing someone," Tom suggested.

"Obviously," Joe agreed.

"I say there's an accomplice in this. Not a single person acting alone," Tom continued to theorize.

"I say that there isn't enough information in as yet, but I agree with you—I think we have two people acting on this."

"Now the danger involved in having an accomplice to murder is that, even if you commit the perfect crime yourself, you have to worry about the other person. Leaving a clue. Panicking. Giving something away."

"Being an idiot and doing the wrong thing."

"Exactly!" Tom said, pleased that Joe seemed to agree with his thinking. "Especially when the murderer is a clever enough person but emotionally involved with the accomplice."

"And the accomplice is an idiot. Happens often enough."

"And naturally, a man can prove to be a real fool himself when he commits murder because of a woman—"

"Meaning," V.J. interrupted from the doorway, "that the woman, who is, naturally, the accomplice, is an idiot?"

"Now, Victoria—" Tom began.

"Oh, now, Tom, don't you 'Now, Victoria' me!" V.J. said sternly. "You were implying that the murderer must be a clever man with a female accomplice who must be an idiot."

"Both could be incredibly clever," Joe suggested diplomatically, but it was too late.

V.J. gave him a withering stare. "Perhaps a woman is the killer, and her bumbling assistant is a male," she said.

"Perhaps a woman is the killer," Tom said, looking at V.J., "and her male accomplice is a bumbling idiot madly in love with her, trying to keep them both from spending the rest of their lives behind bars."

"Either that," Jon interjected smoothly, "or both of our killers are women. V.J., my love, we know that women can be deadly. We grant you that!"

V.J. sniffed, shaking her head sadly at him. "I can see that I'm outnumbered. Excuse me, gentlemen. I have a date with destiny." She exited the room.

Joe glanced at his watch. "Well, excuse me, too."

"Crypt?" Jon asked.

"Séance?" Tom queried.

"The séance is in the crypt. We might as well head down together," Jon said.

"Sir, it's your castle," Tom said gallantly. "Lead the way."

Jon was surprised to feel an uneasy sensation prickling the back of his neck as his colleagues followed him down the back stairs to the dungeon. He was surprised to realize that having anyone behind him had become an unnerving experience.

They reached the crypt, however, without incident. V.J., Dianne, Reggie and Anna Lee Zane were already there. Candles had been lit, and a crystal ball sat on a low wooden table. Pillows strewn around it served as seats. The women were at their places around the table, which had been set as far from the tombs as possible, about ten feet away. Still, there was an eerie feel to the setup. Candlelight paled to shadows. Flames reflected in the crystal ball. Wisps of smoke vanished into the air. Cassie's tomb, one of the closest, gleamed dully.

"Join us, gentlemen," Dianne invited. Seated at the crystal ball, she was reading the game instructions propped in front of it. In black stretch pants and sweater, with her fashionable short black hair, pale skin and bloodred nails, she looked the part of a prophetess.

Her brooding eyes met Jon's, belying her light tone. "We're to contact Mr. Buttle, the butler," she said dryly. "Join hands and chant and ask the spirits of the castle to bring him to us." She made a face. "I assume that our boy Brett, the poor, deceased Mr. Buttle, is hidden behind a tomb somewhere, about to make a 'spirit' appearance. Shall we start?" she inquired.

"We're not all here," Jon said. Sabrina was among the missing.

"Well, here's Thayer coming now," V.J. said, curled comfortably on a cushion. "We'll wait a minute for Susan and Sabrina —"

"Well, we can't wait forever," Anna Lee said impatiently. "Maybe they weren't instructed to come to the séance."

"And maybe one of them is the murderer," Joe suggested.

"Conspiracy theory—they're both the murderers," Tom said.

"Well, maybe Sabrina can't be here," Anna Lee said with exasperation, "since she rode out of here with her ex-husband not too long ago."

"Rode out with *Brett*?" V.J. said incredulously.

"Rode out where?" Dianne asked.

"Rode out on what?" Thayer demanded.

Anna Lee looked at Thayer incredulously. "A horse, obviously. It doesn't take Sherlock Holmes to figure that one out!"

Jon strode to where Anna Lee was sitting, drawing her to her feet to question her. "When? When did they ride out?"

She seemed startled, almost unnerved, by the pressure he was putting on her. "I guess about an hour ago. I saw them leaving the stables at—"

"Alone?" Reggie asked.

Anna Lee nodded.

"How delicious! Rumors about those two must be true," Dianne said.

"Which way did they go?" Jon demanded.

"They were headed northwest."

"Oh, Jon, don't look so concerned. They'll be all right. They were married, and they're obviously getting back together—" Dianne began.

"And there's a major storm system moving in! The fools could be stranded in it. Even killed," Jon said angrily. "Excuse me." He turned abruptly on his heel to leave.

Jon didn't understand his sudden sense of fear. Sabrina could ride; she wasn't an idiot. And whether he liked it or not, she had been married to Brett and had evidently gone off with him willingly.

Still, he knew he had to find them. The weather coming in could be treacherous, and neither of them was familiar with what an early storm could be like in this wild countryside.

As he strode from the crypt, he heard the others commenting on his hasty exit.

"Well, he's in a bit of a mood, wouldn't you say?" Dianne murmured.

"He's concerned," V.J. said in his defense.

"Think he would have raced after the butler that way?" Dianne again, sounding resentful. He could just imagine her face tilted up, eyes staring at him, challenging, angry. "Out to rescue the lovely Ms. Holloway, right in front of her beloved ex. Cassie must be spinning in that grave."

"I think that Jon is a responsible man worried about his guests," Reggie announced impatiently. "Now, I'm an old woman contorted into a ridiculous position on this silly cushion. Can we get on with this thing?"

Bless you, Reggie, Jon thought.

Moments later, he was up the stairs and out of the castle, looking up at the sky. Gray clouds billowed in an angry pattern, rapidly darkening the day. The wind picked up even as he stood there. He hurried on to the stables.

THE FIRST DROP of precipitation seemed mild enough—a little wet kiss on the face as Sabrina dismounted from her horse. "Snow!" she called to Brett.

"No, just a little rain!" he called back. "But that's okay, we'll hole up in the lodge!"

He came to her, slipped an arm around her, and they ran together to the door. Brett pushed it open, and Sabrina stepped inside, looking around for the others.

No one was there. The lodge was empty except for the furnishings and the cozy little fire that burned in the hearth.

It was an inviting if masculine place, a true hunting lodge, with rough wood paneling, a boar's head over the mantel, and a quilt-covered bed. The small kitchen area had a pump in the sink and an old-fashioned icebox. The entire look was rustic—except for the ice bucket and champagne that sat surrounded by finger sandwiches and chocolate-covered strawberries on a table by the bed.

Sabrina spun around to look at Brett. "Where is everyone?" she asked him.

He shrugged. "They didn't get here? Maybe they're lost."

She stared at him sternly. "Brett, where are they?"

He shrugged again, but then looked contrite. "Sabrin—"

"You deliberately lured me out here alone, didn't you?"

"I know that if we just had some time together—"

"Brett!"

He stayed across the room from her, staring at her. "I love you, Sabrina, you know that."

She shook her head impatiently. "Brett, you may think you love me, but trust me, you love anything female."

"Give me a chance. We'll take things slowly. Dear God, Sabrina, surely you must have needs, as well."

"Brett, you're my friend. Let's just stay friends."

"It's him, isn't it?" Brett said angrily.

"What?" she queried carefully, because it seemed as if something about him had changed. His devil-may-care bedroom eyes had a sharp, hostile glint to them.

He moved toward her. "It's him, our great, wondrous host. You've got some kind of an obsession going there. It's him, all right. You *would* sleep with me, except that you want to sleep with him."

"Brett, you've got to understand—"

"Well, there it is. It's true. You want to sleep with him—again. It is again, isn't it? Exactly when did you sleep with him, may I ask?"

"No, you may not ask! When you and I were married, I was faithful. You were not. So no, you can't ask questions. Brett, I want to stay friends with you. Don't make that impossible. Let's get out of here. Now."

She started past him, walking toward the door.

His arm snaked out; his fingers closed like a vise around her wrist. Startled, she saw the deep-seated anger glinting in his eyes.

"Oh, no," he told her. "We're not leaving. Not yet."

"Brett, let me go."

"Never, Sabrina," he said passionately. "It's you, it's all you. Everything—even Cassie—everything. I can't let you leave. Haven't you guessed?"

V.J. WAS ANXIOUS. Too anxious to sit silently at a table in the crypt. "Well?" she said.

"Well, I say Jon has been our basic killjoy. And it's his party," Dianne complained.

"He's worried, dear," V.J. said, studying Dianne. The girl was so restless. What had caused her strange mood? She suddenly looked very young and very upset. V.J. sighed, surprised to feel sympathy for a young woman who had stormed her profession at a ridiculously tender age. "Dianne, there's some fierce weather coming in, and neither Brett nor Sabrina knows this country at all."

"Snow is snow," Thayer Newby said. "Can't be much worse in one place than another. Why, I remember one year when I was in basic training up in New England, it was so cold and there was so much snow that people froze right in their cars. Can't be much worse here."

"How reassuring that a storm can't be much worse than one that killed people," V.J. murmured.

Tom placed a hand over hers, seeming to feel an empathy with her controlled impatience. "They may be in trouble," Joe agreed, rubbing his bearded chin.

"Think Jon needs help finding them?" Thayer asked.

"Think any of us knows this countryside well enough?" Reggie queried.

"Reggie, no offense," Tom interjected, "but you can't possibly mean to help Jon—"

"Hey," Reggie protested, "you're no spring chicken

yourself, Tom. V.J., tell the boy he's an old man, will you?"

A moment's laughter rose among the group, then faded.

After an uneasy silence Dianne said, "I've been here to Scotland many times. I actually do know the countryside."

"You don't know it as well as Jon, dear," Reggie said. "He'll find Sabrina and Brett."

"Hey, where's Susan?" Thayer asked, as if suddenly noticing her absence and considering it highly suspicious.

Anna Lee, snickered. "Maybe she followed Brett and Sabrina to spy on them. She's forever nosing into everyone else's business, and the more potential for dirt the better."

"Okay, so should we leave Jon to the rescue and just get on with this séance?" Joe said. "Then we can get up from this stupid table."

"You're right, let's play the game," Anna Lee intoned.

V.J. looked around the circle. Dianne was definitely behaving strangely. Anna Lee was in a nasty mood. Reggie was in her Queen Victoria mode, and right now, scratching his bearded chin, Joe looked something like a cranky homicidal maniac. Thayer was staring at Anna Lee as if he knew something he shouldn't. Susan was missing, and it was true, she was probably nosing into somebody's dirty laundry. My friends, she thought. What a group! Then she felt Tom's eyes on her, and she calmed down a bit. "Yes, let's play the game," she said.

"You know," Joe said, "if Brett and Sabrina *are* out shacking up somewhere, at least they've found shelter and they're safe from the snow."

"If Brett is out shacking up with his ex-wife, he won't be playing the game as the dead butler. 'Mr. Buttle' will not be appearing here out of the tombs to make ghostly noises," Dianne said flatly. "So, you all still want a séance?" she inquired. She lowered her head and began swaying back and forth. "Spirits of the dead, give us a sign. Knock on wood, cry out!"

As if on cue, they suddenly heard a succession of eerie, muffled screams.

"What the hell is that?" Thayer demanded, leaping up.

They all rose, looking around. The sound seemed to fill the crypt, and yet wasn't coming from the crypt itself.

"Help! Help! Jesus, sweet Jesus, for the love of God!"

"Oh, Lord!" Dianne cried, pale as death herself.

"It's coming from—" V.J. breathed.

"The chamber of horrors!" Reggie finished.

They all stared at one another.

And raced from the crypt toward Joshua's excellent exhibition.

BRETT LET GO of Sabrina's arm, and he was suddenly on his knees, clutching her. And she was unbalanced and startled.

"Sabrina, give me a chance! I can change. I've been wrong. I've been reckless ever since we parted. I've done things I'm not proud of. But I think I really love you, and—"

"Brett…"

"Sabrina, I had to see you alone. Please forgive me for—"

"Brett, what were you saying about Cassie?"

"Cassie?" he said blankly.

She was alone with this man. Alone and far from the castle. In a snowstorm. She told herself that she couldn't believe Brett would ever kill anyone, but he had said that everything was her. Everything. Even Cassie.

"Brett, did you kill Cassandra Stuart?" she demanded.

"No!"

"You said that—"

"My arguments with her," he mumbled. "Sabrina, okay, I lured you here dishonestly, but you have to listen to me."

"Brett," she protested again, trying to step backward. He was still down on the ground, his arms wrapped around her knees. The situation was ludicrous. A good percentage of the female reading populace would gladly have changed places with her; Brett McGraff was famous, charming, and rich—a number two bestseller, right behind Michael Crichton. But then, those women hadn't been married to him. And then again, how flattered could she be when he'd said, "I *think* I really love you."

Still, Sabrina couldn't really believe that Brett was a killer. He could be so childlike and endearing, and he seemed to be in earnest now. She didn't want to hurt him.

"Give it a chance, a real chance. I'm on my knees to you, Sabrina!"

"Don't Brett, please." Again she tried to back away. Again he clung.

"It is him, isn't it? I knew. I just knew that there was something between the two of you."

"Brett, you're tripping me."

"Sabrina, I can get past it. I can forgive you."

"You can forgive *me*? Brett—"

"Sabrina, I can't tell you how passionately I want—"

"Brett, you only want me because I'm saying no, and you're not familiar with the word where women are concerned. Please, Brett—"

She'd backed up until she struck something behind her. The bed. She lost her balance completely and fell backward.

And Brett was quick to take advantage. Up in an instant, he threw himself atop her. As she tried to crawl out from beneath him, she began to slide, the bed coverings coming with her. In seconds she was on the floor, entangled with Brett, a pillow and the quilt. Another pillow fell on her head.

"Brett—" she began breathlessly.

But as more of the bedding tumbled down on her, she heard a crack like thunder as the door burst open.

"THEY'RE STUCK! THE DOORS are stuck!" Tom told Joe, leaning his weight against them.

More shrieking came from the other side.

"Do something!" V.J. commanded.

Dianne Dorsey stood back in the corridor, arms folded over her chest. "It's just Susan, being a melodramatic pain," she said.

"Oh, come on, she's frightened. Get her out," Anna Lee said.

"Help!" Susan pleaded. "Please, please, he's coming after me! He's going to kill me with his knife! Please—"

"Who's coming after you with a knife?" Reggie called to her.

"It's—it's Jack the Ripper!" Susan shrieked.

"Susan, Jack the Ripper is made of wax—he can't move. Just open the doors. I think you've got them locked," V.J. called.

Susan started screaming again.

"Step aside," Thayer Newby said firmly, all-cop. They cleared the doors.

Thayer stepped back and hunched his formidable shoulders. Tom and Joe joined him. Thayer nodded, and they all started forcefully for the doors.

Susan screeched hysterically, an ear-shattering sound. Then she was silent.

TANGLED IN THE BEDCLOTHES, Sabrina went still, listening as long strides brought someone close.

"What the hell—" Brett began.

The quilt was pulled off Sabrina's head. She found herself staring at Jon, who was hunched down before her. At her side, Brett struggled out of the tangle. "Excuse me for interrupting," Jon said smoothly, "but the storm is worsening. The snow—"

"Is just snow!" Brett interrupted. He sounded petulant, making Sabrina feel even more embarrassed.

"It's a big storm, Brett, and we're likely to be cut off from civilization, even at the castle. But at least there we've got real heat and supplies. You'd perish out here," he said politely.

Sabrina started to rise; Brett caught her hand. She gritted her teeth. "Let me go." At her glare, he reluctantly released her, and she struggled to her feet. Both men also rose, exchanging suspicious stares.

"What the hell is going on here?" Jon demanded curtly of Brett.

"A reconciliation!" Brett snapped.

"Is that true?" Jon asked, looking at Sabrina.

"We're not recon—" she began.

"Damn you, Stuart, who the hell do you think you are?" Brett fumed. "The great lord of the castle? Just because you host this damn thing doesn't mean you—"

"I certainly don't host it for you to abduct women into the wilds and put their lives in jeopardy."

"You self-righteous bastard!" Brett countered, and he suddenly took a swing at Jon.

Jon's reflexes were excellent, and he ducked. But when he came up, Brett swung again, catching his chin. Jon swung back in a fury. He caught Brett on the jaw. Brett fell back on the bed, stunned, then shook his head and surged back into the fray like a maddened bull.

"Stop it, stop it!" Sabrina cried, trying to step between the two men.

Though testosterone was at work, and it didn't seem that either of them paid her the least attention, they took no more swings, settling, instead, for soothing words.

"So you think you're the great man to the rescue," Brett snarled, "telling me how to treat my women! Why don't you tell the truth about how you've treated yours?" he challenged.

"The truth? My past is none of your business, Mc-Graff. But maybe you'd like to tell *me* the truth about the past," Jon growled in return. "After all, I was the one with a wife. You're the one who simply can't get over something that happened that had nothing to do with you!"

Both strong, fit, tense and all but flaring at the nostrils, the two stared at one another with clenched teeth, and Sabrina realized that something far deeper than the current circumstances was ripping through them both.

She heard a sound and was surprised to see that Joshua Valine was standing at the door.

He smiled crookedly, sympathetically, at her as the argument raged behind them.

"We must get back to the castle," he told her. "This storm is only going to get worse and worse."

Sabrina nodded. Leaving the warriors to Joshua, she walked outside to her horse and mounted.

Soon after she did so, the two combatants came out of the cottage, neither of them speaking. Jon's features remained tense, his eyes hard and crystalline. Brett, too, oozed tightly leashed anger. Joshua emerged a few moments later, having evidently seen to closing up the lodge.

In silence, the men went for their horses. As they mounted, Sabrina started moving. The day that had seemed so crisp and beautiful when she rode out earlier had undergone a startling transformation. The landscape didn't seem the same at all; she might have been riding into an endless world of nothingness. She couldn't see trees, foliage or even a distinction between sky and ground. In the short time they had been indoors, the snow had become blinding, and she was surrounded by a sea of white.

Jon apparently knew she was lost and had every intention of leading the way. He kneed his mount past hers without looking at or speaking to her. But she knew enough to stay behind him, followed by Joshua and then Brett.

The snow pelted harder and harder, icy crystals that hurt her face.

Jon turned back, shouting to them, "We've got to move as quickly as possible!"

They nodded, and Jon began to ride hard, taking advantage of an open field and level land. They followed closely.

Suddenly Sabrina heard a cracking sound and an abrupt cry. Turning back, she saw that Brett had fallen. His horse raced pell-mell past her.

"Brett!" she cried, reining in, turning back. She raced

to his side, hastily dismounting. The snow was falling with a vengeance. "Brett!"

He lay facedown in the snow, seemingly stretched atop a red ribbon.

As she reached for him, she realized that it wasn't a red ribbon at all.

It was a splatter of blood, brilliantly crimson against the white purity of the snow.

CHAPTER TEN

SUSAN SHARP WAS lying just inside the doorway as the men burst through to the chamber of horrors.

She was sprawled on her side, her hair covering her face. Staring at her, V.J. felt as if her heart stopped, then slammed back into a frenzied beat.

"My God!" she breathed, hurrying to Susan, her mind racing with flights of horrible fancy. Had Jack the Ripper truly come to life to kill her?

She knelt by the woman's side, as did Thayer. The ex-cop, evidently accustomed to emergencies—and even to dead bodies—was calmly lifting Susan's wrist and checking for a pulse. He slowly smiled across Susan's body at V.J.

"She's not dead. She has a strong, steady pulse and easy respirations. She's just passed out. It seems she scared herself half to death."

"She's not hurt?"

"She doesn't appear to be," he said as he quickly and expertly guided his hands over her, checking for injuries.

"Well, how'd she get locked in here?" Tom Heart asked, studying the doors.

Thayer rose, looking over the doors with Tom and Joe. "She didn't. We couldn't get in because the bolt wasn't completely free of the catch. As to why she couldn't get out, I don't know. Maybe she didn't realize that the bolt wasn't quite open. The doors themselves might be swollen, too. Damp weather causes stuff like that, you know. I don't think there's any great mystery here. Just swollen wood, a loose bolt and panic."

Dianne stared at Thayer. "She scared herself into thinking she was locked in?"

Thayer shrugged. "That's what it looks like. What else could it be? It's obvious, swollen wood can stick. It took the three of us slamming ourselves against these doors to get in. And we didn't break the bolt free. Look yourself. The wood is barely damaged."

"Strong wood, though," Tom Heart said dryly. "If someone was bolted in here…"

"But the bolt was only a hair over, right?" Dianne persisted.

"This really can be an incredibly creepy old castle!" Anna Lee said with a shudder.

"People are creepy, dear," Reggie said dryly. "And, at my age, at least, creepy and creaky and cranky. I'm old, I've had it, I'm going up for a drink and some lunch." She turned and walked out.

"Maybe one of us should go with her," Joe mused aloud.

"Reggie will be fine. Woe to the spirits who mess with her. But shouldn't we do something about Susan?" V.J. said. "She is lying on a cold stone floor."

They all looked at one another, slow, guilty smiles on their faces. It occurred to V.J. that there probably wasn't a human being here Susan hadn't hurt in some way at one time or another. If they had found her dead, would any of them have felt deep sorrow?

"Well, she is quiet this way," Dianne commented. A

chorus of grunts and chuckles from the others seemed to back the truth of her observations.

"Oh, come now!" V.J. said. "What are we, a bunch of monsters? If someone would just please—"

"I'll get her, I'll get her!" Thayer grumbled. "I can consider her my weight-lifting exercise for the day. Anyone know which one is Susan's room up there? She should be coming to soon."

Just as he began to lift Susan, her eyes flew open. "Put me down, you ox!" she fumed.

Obligingly, Thayer let go, and Susan's rear bounced back onto the cold stone floor. V.J. turned away, suppressing a laugh.

"You bastards!" Susan charged them all. "Who did this to me? What kind of sick joke is this? I swear, you should all be hanged. So, you think this is funny, Victoria Jane Newfield? You'll be sorry, I swear you'll be sorry."

"Quit threatening V.J., Susan," Tom Heart said angrily. "She was the one among us most concerned about you."

"She probably locked me in, or pretended to be Jack the Ripper coming after me!"

"Susan," Anna Lee said impatiently, "no one was pretending to be Jack the Ripper. Your imagination just got the best of you because you thought you were locked in."

"I didn't *think* I was locked in. I *was* locked in," Susan said stubbornly. "And somebody must have taken the Jack the Ripper costume and come after me."

"Susan, Jack the Ripper is wearing his costume," Joe said, stroking his beard absently as he looked around the horror chamber. "If you take a good look," he said gently, "you'll notice that nothing has changed in here at all. You were a victim of your own imagination."

"Or your guilty conscience," Anna Lee suggested pleasantly.

Susan rewarded her with a look that could kill. "I'm telling you something sick happened here!" she snapped furiously, tossing her head. "I was locked in here and deliberately terrorized. I came because my note said to attend a séance here, and—"

"The séance was in the crypt," Dianne stated, slinging her hair back and kneeling down by Susan. "Didn't your note send you to the crypt?"

"No, to the chamber of horrors," Susan said. "So one of you bastards switched it and locked me in here. When I find out who did this—"

"Where's your note?" V.J. demanded. She looked around the room. All wore masks of complete innocence.

"I had it. It was right here," Susan insisted. She stood, looking around the area where she had fallen. There was no note. "Whoever tricked me stole the note!"

"Maybe you were sent here as part of the game," Joe suggested, still trying to ease troubled waters.

V.J. glared at him with a bit of contempt. There would be no placating Susan Sharp, and she would be damned if she'd suck up to her or tolerate her nonsense, no matter what the woman might write in a column. She'd come too far to play the sycophant to the likes of Susan.

"Look," Thayer said with an air of practicality, "the other ladies were in the crypt when we came down, and we men all came down together, so no one of us could have done anything evil to you without someone else knowing it, Susan. I think you accidentally scared yourself silly and in your panic inadvertently locked yourself in."

"Oh, bullshit!" Susan snapped furiously. She dramatically paced around the room. "This old place is full of false doors and secret panels. Any one of you could have slipped in to torture me."

"Susan, frankly, if I were going to torture you, I'd do a more thorough job of it," Thayer barked.

"Maybe it was the master of the castle himself, Jon Stuart, who locked you in," Dianne suggested suddenly. "Jon was here earlier, you know. And he would certainly know the castle's secret passages, wouldn't he?"

"Jon would never do such a thing to me," Susan said affectedly, smoothing back her hair. "Where is he now? We're going to get to the bottom of this!"

Once again, everyone in the room looked away from her, evidently reluctant to give Susan any bit of information she might use against someone else.

Then V.J. shrugged, because it was no great secret that Jon had gone after Sabrina and Brett. "There's a storm coming in. Some of the others had gone riding, and he went out to make sure they made it back in," she said.

"Some of the others?" Susan repeated. Then she smiled like the Cheshire cat. "Could it be that Brett and Sabrina took off—to be alone? How positively darling. Perhaps they're the ones hiding guilty consciences!"

"Oh, right," Anna Lee murmured dryly. "After one of them locked you in here while the other pretended to be Jack the Ripper. An incredible feat, when you consider that both of them would have had to be in two places at the same time."

"Well, one of *you* bastards did this, and I will find out which one," Susan assured them bitterly. "Where's Reggie?" she demanded.

"Probably sipping a martini in comfort by now," Tom said.

Susan's eyes narrowed. "And that wretched Joshua, who made these horrid creatures—"

"He was never even down here this morning," Joe said.

"And that despicable little worm of a woman who works for Jon?" Susan asked.

"Upstairs somewhere," Joe said with a shrug.

"I wouldn't put it past that horrid little mouse to have been in on something like this!" Susan said. "In fact, I'm sure she planned this, the sniveling wretch. I will demand the truth from her, and—"

"Susan, I'm telling you, it looks as if you accidentally locked yourself in," Thayer reminded her firmly.

"Oh, and dressed myself up like Jack the Ripper?"

"Jack the Ripper is wearing his own clothes," Joe Johnston said, walking impatiently to the tableau. "Look, Susan. He's dressed, he's in place, okay? But fear is a terrible thing. It plays upon the imagination. We all know that—we make a living out of the concept. It's dark down here, scary, shadowy—easy to imagine things."

Susan's eyes narrowed. "Joe Johnston, you are an ass. I'm going upstairs, and I'm going to gouge Camy Clark's little eyes out!" she announced, turning on her heel and stomping off rather dramatically for someone who had just been unconscious.

Joe groaned.

"We'd all better go with her and protect Camy," Tom advised.

"Actually, maybe questioning Camy isn't such a bad idea," Dianne said. "We can ask her about the game note sent to Susan and find out if someone was maybe playing a trick with different notes."

"Good idea," V.J. exclaimed.

Dianne smiled, pleased. To V.J., she suddenly looked

very young again. Despite her outlandish determination to be different, she was really just a little girl cast into an intimidating adult world, V.J. mused. She determined to be a better friend to the young writer, even if she did happen to be stealing places on the all-important best-seller lists!

Well, that was life, V.J. reasoned. No one said life—or death—had to be fair.

"All right, then let's all go up—" Thayer began.

But at that moment, the room was plunged into darkness. And the only thing to cut through the wall of black was a hysterical scream.

DOWN BY BRETT'S side in the snow, Sabrina suffered a wealth of fear and agony. Okay, so he could be a jerk. Their marriage had been over before it had begun. But she did love him in a way. And he was a friend. And she was suddenly so scared.

"Oh, God!" she breathed, looking at the splatter of blood, tenderly touching his cold face. So cold. "Brett!" she cried.

Jon rode back and reined in, snow whirling in the air around him. He came down by her side, Sabrina found the courage to feel for a pulse at Brett's throat.

A beat. Another beat. Another. He was alive!

Jon looked at her, and she nodded, tears brimming in her eyes. She saw the relief flood his handsome face, and she knew that whatever differences there were between the two, Jon cared deeply for his friend, as well.

With long, supple fingers, he carefully searched for the wound emitting the blood. "It looks as if he struck his head when he fell. We have to get him back to the castle and get him warm before we lose him to shock.

I've had some emergency medical training, but not much. I hope to God he's not hurt too badly, since we're likely to be snowed in."

"What about broken bones, or his neck?"

"No, I'm pretty sure his neck isn't broken," Jon murmured, carefully fingering muscle and bone. He began gently skimming his fingers over Brett's limbs.

"Wait, I've taken lots of anatomy," Joshua said, dismounting and joining them. He knelt down in the snow, studying Brett and touching him carefully with the gentle hands of an artist. After a moment he looked up at them both. "The only injury seems to be the crack to his head from that rock there. I can't find any breaks."

Sabrina looked at him and Jon gratefully. Then Jon began lifting Brett. Staggering a bit, he rose to his feet. He must have seen the fear in Sabrina's eyes because he paused for a moment and gently teased her. "We'll get him back, and he'll be fine. But he sure is a heavy sucker. Must be the weight of a swelled head from his successes lately, huh?"

She was able to smile weakly in return. Then Jon turned to Joshua for help. They didn't sling Brett's unconscious body over his horse as they did in the old Western movies. Instead, with Josh's aid, Jon arranged to hold Brett before him in his own saddle, almost as he might carry a child, sheltering him from the snow with a blanket from his saddlebag. Sabrina quickly mounted her horse and followed closely behind him at a walk.

When she realized Joshua wasn't with them, she glanced back.

He was kneeling by the rock where Brett had fallen, staring at it in a puzzled manner, then looking all around him, though what he sought in the snow-white landscape, she couldn't begin to fathom. There was no one, nothing. Then again, there might have been an entire army of Highland soldiers advancing over the next rise, and they wouldn't know it, the snow was swirling in such a heavy, windswept barrage.

"Joshua!" she called out. But he didn't seem to hear or see or heed her. Should she go back for him? But they couldn't turn back; they couldn't lose any time with Brett unconscious, facing shock and a long ride through the snow.

Biting her lip, she looked toward Jon, who was moving ahead quickly. Should she call out to him? She turned to glance back at Joshua Valine once again, and she was relieved to see that he had finally risen and was mounting his horse to follow them. She turned quickly away, for some instinctive reason not wanting him to know that she had been watching him.

They all rode on in silence until, finally, like a giant boulder cast down upon the snowy land, the castle rose out of the sea of white before them. They were almost home.

"OH! IT JUST fucking figures, doesn't it?" Susan swore from a few feet away, her voice sharp in the sudden total darkness. She hadn't gotten very far before the lights went out.

Then V.J. thought she heard something else. A whirring or whooshing sound, as if a cape swept by her, nearly touching her.

A cape.

Jack the Ripper?

Jack the Ripper, real and running amok in the chamber of horrors? They'd all been so determined that Susan was dramatizing, that her imagination had been running away with her. But mightn't someone dressed up like the figure have been hiding nearby, gloating, laughing, thinking that he—or she—had only to wait for the power to fail, then they'd all be like lambs at a slaughter, helpless, perfect victims?

A second scream pierced the darkness, and V.J. thought she might perish of a heart attack.

But it was just Susan, and the sharp cry was followed by swearing. "You burned me, damn it!" she yelped.

"Well, damn it, you're standing right on top of me!" Thayer said as his lighter flicked to life, giving them a small spot of illumination.

V.J. strained her eyes in the darkness. The figure of Jack the Ripper was standing right where he'd been. Silly woman! she taunted herself.

"Here—a lantern," Tom said, lifting an old-fashioned candle lamp from a hook by the door. "They probably lose electricity in most of these storms. This thing looks as if it was in use not too long ago."

"There's another here," Joe stated.

With the lanterns flaring, the chamber of horrors was alight again, actually brighter than it had ever been before.

"I'm telling you, someone is—" Susan began.

"Oh, Susan!" Joe protested, pulling on his beard in total aggravation. "Storms are acts of God, and power outages are failures of mechanics, and neither is a conspiracy against Susan Sharp."

"The hell with this storm. You haven't seen anything yet!" Susan assured them. She strode to Thayer, snatching a lantern from him. "There's going to be one big hurricane around little Miss Camy Clark."

She started once more out of the chamber of horrors, still determined that she'd been the victim of an evil trick. The others followed her.

V.J. found herself last in the chamber, with the blackness swiftly creeping in around her. She gazed at the wax figures as the light began to fade. It seemed that they were beginning to move, just waiting for the light to dim entirely before leaping fully to life.

"Wait!" she tried to cry. But her throat was dry, the sound barely a whisper. They were all going to leave her, and she'd be standing here, stupidly paralyzed, as the figures came alive and started menacingly after her, seeking her blood in the black void settling around her.

"V.J.?" boomed a masculine voice.

"Tom!"

Bless him. He'd come back for her, lifting a lamp high. Light flooded around her, and the wax figures stood obediently still.

"Victoria, you're not staying down here, are you?" Tom asked softly.

V.J. felt life and movement return. She flashed Tom a smile and hurried after the group with him. Susan was leading the way, striding ahead of them all. It was amazing to V.J. that a woman like her, who sometimes made an art out of the act of walking itself, could swing her shoulders and stride with the tough-guy gait of a trucker.

On the ground floor, candles gleamed all around them. The household staff had been at work.

And there, three of their number deserted the gang. As Susan started up the stairs to the second floor, barging along like the Wicked Witch of the West in search of Camy Clark, Thayer Newby followed her, but Tom Heart halted.

"You do your best with this one, Victoria. I'm not watching a lamb at her slaughter," he announced, shaking his head.

V.J. bit her lower lip lightly, knowing how he hated Susan.

"I'll be joining Reggie for a drink," Anna Lee interjected, walking toward the library. Over her shoulder she added, "Maybe Thayer can keep Susan from extreme violence. The rest of us should just huddle around the fire like the true chickens we are."

"I'm with Tom," Joe Johnston agreed.

V.J. looked at them both. They stood side by side: Tom tall, handsome, so dignified with his beautiful crop of silver-white hair, and Joe, bearded, heavier, coarser and a bit gruff. One dressed Versace, one Salvation Army. One was a second Sean Connery, the other a Grizzly Adams. They seemed strangely united now.

"Susan's going to do her best to humiliate young Camy," Tom explained. "And Camy might not want an audience," he added softly.

V.J. nodded, but stood her ground. "We don't all need to barge in on her, but I'll go and back up Thayer."

"I'm with you," Dianne said, her eyes curiously wide with excitement. They all looked at her. She tossed back her perfectly cut black hair. "Susan can be a real monster—we all know it. I'll be there to back up V.J. as Susan tries to draw blood, so V.J. won't have to take the heat alone."

"Just remember, after this weekend we may *all* be paying for the fact that Susan's a monster," Joe said dourly.

Tom was watching V.J., his thoughts held in check. She turned away and hurried up the stairs, Dianne right behind her.

Susan had already burst in when they reached Camy's room. As usual, Jon's diminutive assistant was sitting at her desk. Evidently power failures didn't daunt her. She was working by the light of a large battery-powered lamp.

"You stupid, miserable, little bitch, I will have you fired for this!" Susan raged at her.

Camy jumped up, shaking, staring at Susan. Her mouth worked, but no words came. Tears stung her eyes, and she looked helplessly past Susan to Thayer, V.J. and Dianne.

"I—I..." she began, stunned. She looked as vulnerable as a baby chick fallen out of its nest.

"Susan, do you at least want to tell her what you're accusing her of doing?" V.J. snapped firmly.

Susan swung around to glare at her.

Well, even if her next book were the Bible, V.J. thought wearily, Susan was still going to trash it in the media.

Susan swung back to Camy, her face contorted in fury. "She knows what she did. She wrote me a note, sending me into the chamber of horrors, then she snuck down one of the secret staircases and did her best to scare me to death. She shouldn't just be fired, she should be arrested, and I intend to see that it happens!"

"Susan," Camy cried in self-defense, "I didn't... I don't know... I swear to you—"

"Lying little maggot!" Susan said through gritted teeth, starting forward.

"Now, wait a minute there," Thayer interrupted angrily, taking a step to stop Susan.

"Oh, let her bitch," Dianne said casually.

"Oh, Susan, why don't you just quit being such a royal, self-righteous bitch!" V.J. blurted.

Oh, great. Mystery Week, and she'd turned suicidal. She was mincemeat in the press.

"I—I—I didn't give you instructions to go to the chamber of horrors," Camy said to Susan. "Everyone was ordered to the séance in the crypt. Joshua was supposed to make a tapping sound from behind the tombs, but he followed Jon in case there was any trouble—I mean—uh, in case someone was stranded or the snow got too bad." She stuttered and paused, realizing she was admitting that her boss was in a high temper when he rode out after Brett McGraff and Sabrina Holloway. "He—he thought Jon might need help in the snow, and that you would all amuse yourselves just fine in the crypt."

"Oh, yeah, nothing like an amusing morning among the dead," Dianne said dryly.

Camy shot her a pathetic look. Dianne instantly looked contrite. "Well, it was definitely more important for Josh to make sure no one got lost in the snow," she added quickly.

The truth hung in the air. Or to make sure Brett and Jon didn't come to blows over Sabrina?

"Susan, I swear, if you had a note sending you somewhere else, I didn't write it," Camy said.

"Then just where did the note come from?" Susan demanded.

Camy was still shaking and in distress. "I don't know, I don't know. I don't know where the other one came from either—"

She broke off, staring at them all, white as a sheet.

"Someone else got a note you didn't write?" Thayer demanded.

"I—I—"

"God in heaven, quit stuttering like a complete ninny!" Susan cried.

"Who else got a misleading note?" V.J. asked quietly.

"Yes, please, who?" Dianne asked softly.

"I'm not at liberty to—" Camy began defensively.

"Jon! It was Jon Stuart!" Dianne guessed. She appeared strangely excited again.

Camy remained white. She looked like a little lost doe, standing there shaking.

"You know what I think?" Susan demanded. "I think this is all a pile of B.S. I think you're a troublemaker. Who else could be giving people different notes and stealing the ones you had *really* written? You're doing it all, Miss Clark. The only question is why."

"No, oh, no, please, Ms. Sharp. I couldn't. I wouldn't. Honestly," Camy said, desperately trying to state her innocence. "I'm so sorry you were frightened, but—"

V.J. felt as if she were watching a puppy being slaughtered. She had to risk stepping in again. "Oh, Susan, get off your high horse! None of us is in chains. We're all free to sneak around the castle! It could be anybody playing tricks!" she said angrily.

Susan stared at her with pure venom in her eyes. "You weren't locked in with some awful monster breathing down your neck. He could have killed me. I know he would have killed me if you all hadn't gotten to me first!"

"He who? You're accusing Camy of sending the notes," Thayer said.

"He, she, little precious Camy here pretending to be Jack the Ripper—what difference does it make? Someone meant to kill me, and I'm certain it was this little bitch right here!" Susan accused.

"Oh, Susan, stop it. You really don't know anything at all," Dianne told her quietly.

The young woman seemed oddly disappointed, and V.J. belatedly wondered if Dianne had looked forward to this confrontation, hoping it would help her discover something that was eluding her. She was so young, V.J. mused again, watching her, and she suspected that life had given her a few hard kicks, not just early successes, along the way.

Susan looked from one of them to another. She remained furious, her face pinched and ugly. V.J. thought that, at that moment, any one of them would happily lock her away with Jack the Ripper.

"Well, fuck you all!" Susan said softly. And once again she looked around the room at them. "And trust me, you *are* fucked!"

She stomped out the door, slamming it behind her.

Once again, V.J. had an image of the Wicked Witch of the West.

Camy started to cry softly, Thayer looked grim, and V.J. realized that she was trembling herself from all the dramatic emotions swirling about.

"I think we all need a drink," Dianne announced. "Come on, Camy, come on down and have a drink with us."

"I—I—was working," Camy said, a ragged sniff following her words as she tried to control her sobs.

"That's all right, you can work later, dear," V.J. said gently.

"But I'm not one of you. This is Mystery Week, and you're supposed to be solving a whodunit."

"Oh, we've enough mystery going on without having to work at it too much," Dianne said. "Either that or we're capable of making a mystery out of anything. Come on. Jon wouldn't mind. He'd want you to take a breather after an encounter with old Medusa there."

Camy nodded. "Jon would never mind," she said softly. "I do know that."

"Then come on," V.J. said. "I need to sit down before I fall down, and right now, I want a martini when I sit."

She started from the room, and the others followed.

And just as they did so, a high-pitched, bloodcurdling scream sounded from the first floor.

CHAPTER ELEVEN

NEVER, IN FACT or fiction, had Sabrina ever heard such a shriek. Following Jon into the house, she nearly jumped a mile at the sound.

It was Anna Lee, standing in the entry, her beautiful eyes huge as she stared at Brett, unconscious in Jon's arms. Clearly she thought Brett was dead.

"He's alive!" Jon announced quickly. "He's alive."

And at that, Brett stirred slightly. His eyes opened. He groaned. Then he looked up at Jon, the friend who was carrying him, and tried to smile. "Jon, we've got to stop meeting like this. Rumors will begin to fly."

"I think he's going to be all right," Jon said dryly, striding toward the library.

By then Reggie, Tom and Joe had rushed into the foyer from the library, and V.J., Dianne, Thayer, Susan and Camy had made an appearance, running down the stairs. Sabrina felt Joshua crash into her from behind.

"What happened?" Camy demanded.

"A riding accident," Sabrina explained quickly.

"Stupid horse threw me," Brett said, grimacing. "Right onto a rock! I'm in pain, ladies. Be kind to me!"

Jon groaned wryly, seeing that his patient was coming to in good form. He called over his shoulder, "Someone get a cloth and cold water, please."

Camy rushed to do his bidding. Brett was soon ensconced on a sofa in the library, and among them all they determined that his only injury was the blow to his head that had knocked him out. Brett was lording it over them all nicely, wincing, playing on their sympathies, insisting that Sabrina be the one to bathe his wound and press cold cloths to his head. Dianne Dorsey produced some pain-killers to relieve the pain and swelling, and Brett gave a dramatic rendition of how his wild steed had suddenly reared, sending him flying into the snow. Listening to him, Sabrina found herself newly curious about what Joshua had been looking for out there, and she turned to glance at him. He stood in the shadows by the fire, alone and watching.

"Electricity is gone?" Jon asked, looking up at Thayer.

"We lost power a while ago. Actually, while—"

"Right after I was viciously assaulted!" Susan declared.

Jon, accepting a drink from Anna Lee, arched a brow at Susan. "Assaulted?"

"I was sent to the chamber of horrors, while everyone else was involved in that silly séance in the crypt. I was locked in, and Jack the Ripper attacked me!" Susan cried.

Joshua made a strange, choking sound.

"Jack the Ripper came to life?" Brett said politely, laughter just behind the words.

"Susan wasn't locked in," Thayer said firmly.

"The door had jammed," Joe explained.

"So they say," Susan stormed. "But I think *she* did it!" Very dramatically, she pointed at Camy.

Brett let loose with a snort of derision. Camy softly started to cry. Joshua pushed away from the fireplace, as if to come to Camy's defense.

"Camy?" Jon said very softly.

"I don't know what she's talking about, I swear to you!" Camy cried.

"Since it seems that no one really knows anything, I suggest we not point fingers at one another—unless it's in the fun of the game," Jon said firmly.

"Jon Stuart, you're not going to ignore me!" Susan declared. "I'm not crazy, and I assure you that—"

"That what?" Jon demanded grimly.

"Your guests are a pack of liars with plenty of secrets to hide," she said, staring at them, one by one. As she did so, she added furiously, "And I warn you all, I will not be ignored. Someone will pay."

"Susan, if you know something—" Jon began.

"Oh, I know everything!" she snapped. "But I'm not out to tell tales about anyone—yet."

"Susan, if you're afraid you're in danger," Dianne said, twirling a strand of black hair, "maybe you should stop threatening people."

"Yeah," Thayer added.

Sabrina thought that they all sounded and were acting like a group of children, finally ganging up against the neighborhood bully.

"Maybe you all—every one of you—should take a look at your nice little lives and think about the pathetic, hypocritical lies you're living!" Susan retorted.

Jon sighed deeply. "Susan, for the love of God, if you'd quit playing games—"

"Oh, but we came here to play a game, didn't we?" she demanded.

Jon shook his head, clearly leashing his anger and aggravation. "If you're really scared, then the stakes have gotten too high. Maybe we should call a halt to the whole blasted week."

"Oh, no. The game is going to be played, all right—or we're going to expose whoever it is who wants to play outside the rules," she said. "And, Jon, I expect you to—"

"I'll take a look at the doors in the chamber of horrors, Susan," Jon said. "But I imagine it is possible that you only thought you were locked in."

"The mind can play very mysterious tricks," Anna Lee said in a soft, sultry voice.

"My mind doesn't play tricks," Susan said flatly. "And again, I promise, someone will pay."

"Susan, I'll do my best to find out what happened," Jon repeated. "But I'm afraid we're in a rather sorry situation. I warned you that a storm was coming, and God knows how long we'll be snowbound. Now we've lost the electricity as well, and though we've got generators and batteries, I'm afraid we can't keep this place as well lit as I would like. There's only so much we're going to be able to see, and only so much we're going to be able to do."

"But we do have a nice buffet set up in the great hall," Reggie said. "I think we should all get something to eat, and we'll feel better, and we won't be so prone to wild hysterics."

"I wasn't hysterical!" Susan snapped.

"Oh, Susan, you're always hysterical," Brett complained. "And you're stealing my thunder here. I need all the attention I can get, people flocking around me with wonderful concern. So get a grip. *I* am supposed to be the patient here," he reminded her petulantly.

"I hit my head falling, too," Susan said.

"Yes, but rock against rock…" Dianne murmured.

"I heard that!" Susan snapped at her.

"So you did," Dianne said smoothly, her eyes venomous as they met Susan's.

"Susan, we've generators for hot water," Jon said. "We

need to use the water a little sparingly, but right now I think that a drink and a long hot bath might make you feel better."

Susan looked mollified at Jon's words. "Yes, a hot bath, a drink. A strong one. Make me something, darling, will you? And will you stay with me while I bathe? Stand guard? I'm so very nervous now."

"Susan, I'm going to take a look around below, search the chamber of horrors, the chapel, the crypt," Jon said. "You'll be all right. Someone else can——"

"I'll stand guard at Susan's door," Thayer volunteered.

"No," Jon told the ex-cop, "I'd like you to come downstairs with me."

"I'll watch over her," Sabrina heard herself say.

"No!" Brett protested, capturing her hand where it lay on the cold towel pressed to his head. "You can't desert me now. Please, Sabrina." He winced as if in great pain. Looking down at him, she had to admit that he did have a nasty gash, and she was glad that he was alive.

"I'll stand sentinel at Susan's door," Tom Heart offered.

Sabrina looked up and saw that Jon was staring at her. She felt as if his eyes were piercing through her. There she sat on the arm of the sofa, her hand on Brett's head, his hand now upon hers, as well. It must make a cozy, intimate picture.

"Help me up to my room, sweetheart, will you?" Brett asked then. "Please, I don't think I could manage alone. You could bring me a small lunch, make sure I don't have convulsions or anything."

By then, Jon had turned away. And, followed by Thayer, he was soon gone.

"Well, let's eat. I'm famished," Reggie said.

"Two people hurt, and you're famished?" Susan protested.

"Two silly, careless people, and yes, I'm famished. Susan, you're a mess. Go take your bath. Sabrina, go ahead and get that randy little rooster upstairs and come back and have some late lunch with us. It's going to be a long day!"

It would be a long day. Sabrina knew that right after she helped Brett upstairs.

His clothing was soaked, and naturally, he insisted that she help him out of it, thanking her as she dispatched his boots, his jacket and his shirt. She drew the line at his pants, however.

"Oh, come on, Sabrina, it's not as if it isn't familiar territory," he told her. He looked at her pathetically. "Sabrina, I swear, I haven't an ounce of strength. Help me."

"All right," she conceded. "Lie down, and I'll drag off your pants. And you'd better be wearing underwear."

He laughed.

"Just because you were hurt doesn't mean that you didn't behave like a slimy bastard, you know," she reminded him as she wrestled with the sodden trousers, which now seemed plastered to his legs.

Naturally, just as she fell against the bedpost, his pants in her hands, Jon came striding into the room, while Joshua and Thayer lingered in the hall.

"I decided I should come by to see if you needed any help, McGraff," Jon said dryly. "But you seem to be doing all right."

"Of course. Sabrina does know how to take my clothes off," Brett said.

Jon stared at her, arching a brow, then strode from the room.

Sabrina threw Brett's pants to the floor.

Brett caught her hand. "I wish I could figure out when you slept with him," he grumbled.

"Brett, stop, now."

Amazingly, he did. He looked up at her and smiled. "You're a great nurse, Sabrina. Now how would you like to help me out of my underwear?"

"Your only saving grace at the moment, Brett McGraff, is that you're *wearing* underwear!" Sabrina scolded him.

"Please, show some mercy, will you? Would you put that cold towel on my head again?"

She was angry, feeling that Jon condemned her, convinced she was sleeping with Brett because of her ex-husband's seemingly endless ploy to seduce her or, at the very least, to land her in compromising positions. But what could she do about it now? Nothing. She sighed. "Get under the covers and behave."

He did so. He closed his eyes and winced, and she realized that he really must have one pounding headache.

Angry with Jon, too, for leaping so easily to the wrong conclusions, she fussed over Brett a bit. But she refused to be drawn into another of his traps. "Don't you ever give up?" she asked him, plumping up a pillow and refusing his outrageous request for a drink. "Not with that knot on your head," she told him. "Don't drink, and don't go to sleep. Just rest, and if you get blurry vision—"

"We'll call the doctor, Nurse Sabrina?" he said, amused.

"I think you're going to be all right," she told him.

"Nothing a good whiskey wouldn't cure," he said wistfully.

"No alcohol today. You could have died, you know."

"Stupid horse! I wonder why it reared like that?" he complained. Then he sighed. "Stupid me, for not being a better rider."

"Hey, things happen," Sabrina said gently.

"Too many things happen around here," Brett said dully. He paused. "So what do you think happened with Susan?"

"How would I know? I wasn't here."

"Everyone hates her," Brett mused. "Any one of us might want her dead."

"But she's not dead, is she? And normally, just because people hate someone, they don't become homicidal."

"Ah, but think about murder. You have your psychopaths, and then you have your people who commit the crime in the heat of passion, your opportunists engaged in other felonies—the list goes on and on."

"Well," she mused, "I don't think Susan is the type to scare *herself* to death."

"Those wax figures are awfully scary, though, don't you think?"

Sabrina agreed wholeheartedly.

"God, I'm suddenly famished," Brett said. "Want to go down and see if there are some grapes you can feed me?"

"I'm not going to feed you grapes, but I'll bring you up some lunch," Sabrina said. "Rest now, and I'll be right back." Slipping from Brett's room, she started down the hallway toward the stairs.

Behind her, she heard a door close quietly. She looked around. She didn't know which door had closed, or indeed, if she had only imagined the sound.

The hallway was as quiet as a tomb, she thought. She shivered and hurried down the stairs.

JON LOOKED AROUND the chamber of horrors. Absolutely nothing seemed amiss.

Thayer gave him his theory, showing him how the old

bolt had been turned just a hair. "And with the weather swelling the doors..." Thayer shrugged. "Let's face it, Susan is a powerful bitch, but something seems to be unnerving her. Do you think she just scared herself into a tizzy?"

Jon, too, shrugged, staring at the wax figures. Joshua had done such a good job. The figures were haunting and scary and all the things they should be. But they *were* wax and wire and fabric and mesh. They weren't inherently evil, and they weren't capable of coming to life.

And Susan was a bitch.

But he, too, had been the recipient of a nasty note unrelated to the real play of the game. And he was feeling especially tense because they were now likely to be snowbound and dependent on generators for power. For how long, he didn't know. And he was responsible for his guests' welfare.

"The thing is, most of us were at the séance," Thayer said. "You, Brett, Sabrina and Joshua were gone. Camy was working. Maybe someone on the staff had something to do with it?"

"My household staff? They're all hardworking and far too busy and responsible to play pranks on my guests. Besides, I'm sure none of them could care less about scaring Susan Sharp."

"So she had to be imagining things," Thayer said. Hands on his hips, he sighed. "Well, if we had the equipment, we could dust this place for prints, but, hell, we'd find everyone's. Everyone has been down here."

Jon went to stand before Jack the Ripper. He reached out to touch the figure. Still wax, he told himself dryly.

But Susan likely had received a different summons from the others; he didn't doubt it, since he had, too.

He did have to wonder if someone was just playing cruel tricks, however…or if they were all to be snowbound with a maniac. Hell, now *his* imagination was running away with him.

"I guess there's nothing more to be done down here," he told Thayer.

"I agree. There's nothing here to prove or disprove anything Susan said. It was something, though. I wish you'd been here. The power suddenly went while we were here, with Susan screaming that I was trying to burn her when I lit my lighter!"

"The storm must be surely an act of God," Jon said dryly. "I hardly think there's someone up there shooting down lightning bolts and saying, Oh, good, let's get Susan!"

Jon smiled wryly. "I guess there's only one way left to solve any of this."

"Oh?" Thayer inquired.

"Play the game," Jon said grimly. "Play out the game, just the way we intended."

THE CASTLE IN darkness was utterly eerie.

It wasn't that Sabrina hadn't been places where the electricity had gone off before. She had. Storms downed electrical wires across the globe.

But the castle was different. Haunting shadows filled corners and crevices. Candles and kerosene lamps shot flickering patterns against the stone walls. Each nook and cranny seemed to hold a mystery, a dark, fluttering menace.

She all but ran down the stairs and hurried into the great hall.

It was empty. The others had eaten and gone.

The food was still out; chafing dishes were aligned on the buffet, though many of the Sterno heating fires were out. Someone had begun clearing the table, but a few plates remained.

She began to inspect the contents of the chafing dishes. Suddenly, a stark chill of unease raced down her spine. She spun around, certain that someone was watching her from the shadows.

Then she felt like a fool. No one was behind her. Like Susan, she had simply begun to imagine a cloaked figure ready to bludgeon her to death when she wasn't looking.

But she did hear footsteps from the foyer, heading toward the great stairway. She started out of the great hall and paused in the shadows of the doorway.

Jon was coming up from below. Anna Lee met him on the stairs to the second floor. She set a hand upon his arm. Her wavy hair fell forward, brushing her face. She smiled. A beautiful smile. But then she said something, looking worried. Sabrina couldn't make out her words. Jon took her hand in both of his. She looked frail next to his tall, muscular form, and as he took a step up and whispered down to her, he looked like her protector. Something tender seemed to pass between them. Anna Lee turned around, accompanying him as he continued up the steps.

Sabrina slipped back into the great hall, leaning against the wall, feeling weak.

"It wasn't Anna Lee," a voice said out of the shadows. Sabrina nearly jumped; she was amazed she didn't scream.

Reggie Hampton suddenly appeared, rising from a huge antique chair set into the recess of the kitchen doorway. She looked old and tired but very straight and dignified.

"What?" Sabrina whispered.

Reggie shrugged, smiling slightly. "I watched you watching Jon and Anna Lee just now. Watching people— that's what keeps me going. And keeps me good, too, by the way. You're wearing your heart on your sleeve, and—"

"I don't know what you're talking about, Reggie," Sabrina interrupted.

"Our host, dear," Reggie said kindly, her keen old eyes assessing still. "You just watched Anna Lee and Jon. And somewhere in your mind you were remembering the rumor that Jon was having an affair when his wife was killed."

Sabrina arched a brow. "Reggie, I really have no right—"

"They're friends, Anna Lee and Jon. But don't worry, dear. He doesn't care about her now. Sexually, that is."

"He's free to care about her in any way he wishes. Including sexually," Sabrina said.

Reggie smiled. "Certainly, dear. Whatever you say. I can see that you don't care in the least. Ah, well, then my lips shall remain sealed about what I know. So why don't I help you make something for your patient up there? The food is so wonderful here, isn't it? Let's fix Brett a plate of the lamb. He'll love it."

"Reggie…"

"Nope. My lips are sealed."

"Reggie, if you know something imp—"

"I know lots of things. Or I think I do. But some of them would hurt innocent people, so I don't talk. Truth will tell itself when the time is right."

"Reggie…"

"If you're going to be tiresome, dear, then you can fix your own plates." And, shoulders squared, back straight,

Reggie walked out of the great hall, leaving Sabrina alone for real.

Or was she?

Again she turned around and peered into the shadows. No one.

She fixed two plates of food. And she tried to walk calmly, rather than run, back to Brett's room.

THE STORM WAS bad enough. Being snowbound was worse. But now they were snowbound without electricity, and though Jon could keep the castle functioning, not even he liked the shadows.

He felt that he could kick himself a thousand times over.

Why hadn't he insisted that they end the game? He should have forced them all out before the weather came—even old Reggie, whether she wanted to go or not.

But he hadn't.

And so now they were all trapped together for the duration. And like rats in a cage, they were starting to scurry around, ready to cannibalize one another.

Yet they were coming to him. One by one.

Anna Lee.

And as he approached the door to his room, she followed. He sighed softly. "Now, what in God's name—" he began.

"Shh! Please, Jon!" she insisted, urging him into the room. She was clearly excited. "It's happening! Don't you see? Everything is unraveling. The truth is out there and—"

He caught her by the shoulders, trying to steady her. "The truth is out there—but meaning what? Anna Lee, are you behind any of these threats against Susan?"

"No!" she cried, trying to wrench away angrily. He wouldn't let her go.

"Susan is a bitch, and she can certainly make up nasty

tales. But this time I think she knows she is in trouble, is being pursued. I think she knows what happened three years ago, and I think you should force it out of her."

"Force it out of her? Beat her up, you mean? Straddle her and choke her and force a confession?" he demanded dryly.

"Don't you see? I think that she's threatened the killer—blackmail, maybe. And now she's scared and unnerved, and she's stirring up a commotion among the game players, keeping herself visible and safe, rather than admitting that she's blackmailing someone."

"What makes you so certain Susan knows the truth?"

Anna Lee shook her head. "I don't know. I don't know. Maybe I'm just grasping at straws."

"We still don't even *know* that there was a killer. And lots of people here were keeping secrets when Cassie died. Hell, probably everyone here was keeping a secret." He hesitated. "Cassie was sleeping with—"

"Speaking of sleeping with," she interrupted quickly, "you could easily seduce Susan and get the truth out of her that way."

"What?"

"You know she has the hots for you," Anna Lee stated.

"Out!" Jon said explosively.

"Jon…"

"Out! And you be careful, do you hear me?"

"Yes," she said sullenly.

"No tricks on your part to stir up the kettle," he warned.

She turned to leave, then turned back. "I do love you," she said very softly.

He nodded. "I love you, too."

V.J. OPENED THE door to her room and looked carefully down the hallway. No one was about.

With no electricity, the hall seemed a frightening place. Shadows danced on the walls. Outside, the sound of the wind had become a low keening. It seemed as if the whole place had come alive, that the very walls breathed.

She gave herself a shake.

She left her room, a heavy flashlight clutched tightly in her hands. She didn't need to turn it on; kerosene lamps hung from ancient fixtures along the way, casting their eerie, flickering glow.

She moved quietly, step by step down the cavernous corridor.

She came to Susan's room and opened the door.

She heard the sound of the shower.

And before the closed bathroom door, Tom, tall and handsome, paced.

He didn't hear V.J. at first. When he did, he looked up at her.

She saw that he was carrying a pocketknife, flicking the blade open, then closed.

Open, then closed. Open…

It was a wicked blade. Surprisingly long. It looked as if it were sharply honed.

V.J. stared at Tom. He went still and stared at her.

He took a step toward her.

Reached for her.

"What are you trying to do?" she whispered desperately. "No!"

The water in the shower continued to run.

SABRINA RETURNED TO Brett's room, bringing his food, finding that she was ravenous herself. It was a very late lunch; it was almost three o'clock. Brett ate with a hearty appetite, and she was glad to realize that his bump on the head seemed not too serious. He was in good spirits, happy to have her waiting on him.

She was curious, though, about Susan, and about whatever Jon might have discovered in the chamber of horrors. She had thought he might come back to Brett's room with a report.

He didn't. Telling Brett that she'd be right back, Sabrina went to Susan's room and knocked on the door.

No answer.

As she stood there, she thought she saw a figure in the shadows near the bend of the hallway.

The bend toward the master chambers, Jon's private domain.

She hesitated, then began moving along the corridor, close to the wall, watching.

As she did so, a figure moved toward Jon's door, hesitated, then rapped. His door opened; the woman slipped in.

Sabrina held her breath, staying flattened against the wall. A few minutes later, the woman came out.

The figure was slim, graceful, wraithlike in the shadows. She moved in a supple flow of black, coming along the hallway, her head down. If she had looked up, she would have seen Sabrina, despite the shadows.

But she didn't look up. She passed within three feet of her.

It was Dianne Dorsey. Dressed in a long, black, flowing caftan, she seemed a haunt in the eerie light and shadows of the hallway.

A haunt very deep in thought.

"I do love you!" she whispered softly, and, suddenly stopping, she looked back at Jon's door. "I do love you."

A sheen of tears made diamonds of her eyes.

"So I have to do what I have to do!" she added in an anguished whisper.

Then she moved on along the hallway.

Never seeing Sabrina.

Staring after her, Sabrina waited. Dianne followed the hallway to the stairs and descended to the floor below. For long moments, Sabrina just stood where she was.

Then she walked on to Jon's room and tapped on the door.

He threw it open irritably. "What?" he demanded sharply, then stepped back, eyes narrowed as he saw Sabrina.

"You were expecting me?" she said in response to his obvious displeasure.

"I wasn't expecting anyone," he told her.

"Not even Dianne Dorsey?" she inquired.

He crossed his arms over his chest. "Are you spying on me?"

She shook her head, yet felt absurdly guilty. "No. No, I just came to hear what you found in the dungeon. I happened to see Dianne leave your room."

"Nothing. I found nothing at all."

He didn't invite her into his inner sanctum. He stood at the door, jaw set, staring at her.

"She loves you," Sabrina blurted.

"What?" he demanded sharply.

"Dianne. She left your room muttering that she loved you but that she had to do what she had to do," Sabrina told him, studying him for his reaction.

He swore softly. "Excuse me," he told her, starting by her.

"Is she the one with whom you were having an affair?" she called after him.

He paused, turning around, scowling. "No."

"Anna Lee?" She wanted to kick herself.

"No, and you will have to excuse me."

"Sure. I have to get back to Brett anyway."

His jaw tightened, but he said nothing more. Turning, he walked away from her down the hallway.

She started violently as she felt a tap on her shoulder. She spun around to see Anna Lee. Had she, too, just slipped from Jon's room?

"You've got it all wrong," she said, her beautiful green eyes assessing Sabrina with amusement. She looked exceptionally pretty and feminine in a pink sweater and jeans that hugged her slim, shapely figure. Her sandy blond hair curled around her classical features.

"I have it all wrong?" Sabrina said.

"Mmm."

"You weren't having an affair with Jon when Cassandra died, but you are now?" Sabrina inquired politely.

Anna Lee laughed. "No, actually, you still have it all wrong."

"Oh?"

"Yes. You see, I *was* having an affair when Cassie died."

"Were you?" Sabrina hated the fact that she sounded so stiff and jealous when she meant to be nothing more than competently curious and composed.

Anna Lee smiled, running her fingers through her hair. "But I wasn't sleeping with Jon."

"No?"

Anna Lee laughed, and Sabrina realized just how uptight she must sound.

Anna Lee reached out and briefly stroked Sabrina's cheek. "I was sleeping with *Cassie*, Sabrina." She shrugged, serious and sincere, yet still amused. "Ah, but don't go getting any wrong ideas. Cassandra hadn't given up men. I wasn't the only one sleeping with her. But I was one among many. Just like she was one among many with me. Variety can be the spice of life."

"Was Jon upset?" Sabrina asked softly.

Anna Lee shook her head. "He'd known," she said simply. "Cassie always played people against each other. She used to ask him if he wanted to do us both together. He wasn't interested. Not very flattering, eh? I always did have a crush on him. And Cassie…well, Cassie had her way of making people love her, too. With Jon, I think she just misjudged her man. Poor Cass. It was all awfully sad, really. She was a bitch, hell on wheels. But she *was* beautiful."

Smiling, her hips swaying, she started down the hall.

Sabrina's knees felt strangely weak. She was ready to slink back to Brett's room.

Maybe Anna Lee had explained herself—to a degree. But Sabrina didn't pretend to comprehend what was going on with Dianne Dorsey.

Or with Jon.

CHAPTER TWELVE

SABRINA STAYED WITH Brett throughout the afternoon, suddenly glad of a friend she knew and understood and anxious lest he suddenly go into convulsions from his concussion.

She felt numb yet wired. She wanted to see Jon, yet she was furious with herself for wanting to.

For waiting.

And hoping.

That he would come to her.

Brett had brought a tape player with him, and they listened to the latest book by Dean Koontz—which might have been a mistake, since it was about a young woman being stalked by a maniacal killer. But the time passed quickly enough, and as cocktail hour neared, a note was slipped beneath Brett's door.

"What does it say?" Brett asked Sabrina. "Are we playing more games now? Another séance? It's a wretched enough night for one."

She shook her head. "No, no games tonight."

"What does it say?"

She read it aloud to him.

"Dear Guests:
Due to the storm, the lack of electricity and the accidents that have already befallen us, dinner trays

will be delivered to all rooms. Please lock yourselves in for the evening, and we'll meet for brunch
tomorrow in the great hall. Characters dropped,
we'll confess all our sins.

> Your host, Jon Stuart."

"Good. You're locking yourself in with me, right?"

She kissed him on the top of his head. "Wrong. In
fact, I'm leaving you now. You're cozy and warm in bed,
and I—"

"You can be cozy and warm in bed with me."

"Do you have another book you want to listen to? I'll
set up the first tape for you."

Brett sighed, looking at her like a deserted blood-
hound. "Michael Crichton," he said dourly.

"Great. That will keep you entertained."

"He's ahead of me on the list," Brett said sulkily.

"Better yet. You can study your competition," Sabrina
said. Before leaving him, she slid the first tape of the
audio book into the player. "Holler if you need anything.
I'll check in on you before I go to bed."

He wrinkled his nose at her. "If you really love me,
you'd crawl in here and keep me company until morning."

"Brett, I've been with you for hours. I want a nice long
bath while the hot-water heaters are still going strong."

"You can take a bath here. We can save hot water—
bathe together."

"Good night, Brett."

She let herself out of his room. As she did so, she ran
into the housekeeper, Jennie Albright, with two fresh-
faced young maids, delivering trays.

"Ah, there, Ms. Holloway, would ye mind, dearie,
takin' this on in to Mr. McGraff?" Brett's name burred

warmly on Jennie's tongue, and Sabrina took the tray from her.

"Certainly."

"Thanks so much, my dear."

"My pleasure. You'll be at this all night, Jennie. Can I help you downstairs?"

"Ah, lass, what a sweeting ye be! But no, my thanks, these were the last. Mr. McGraff, Ms. Sharp and yerself."

Sabrina pushed open Brett's door with her rear and brought Brett his tray.

He smiled happily. "You're back. I knew you couldn't bear being parted."

"Your dinner, Brett," she said, setting the tray by his bed. "See you tomorrow."

"Hey, room service stays longer than that!" he called after her.

She shut the door behind her just as Rose, the younger of the two maids, gave up knocking at Susan's door. "Jennie, there's no answer here," the girl said.

"Then just leave the tray outside the door, there's a good lass. There's your tray now, Ms. Holloway," Jennie said. "Cooked up fresh fish, come in just before the storm. Eat it while it's hot."

"Thank you. If you need help picking up—" Sabrina began.

"No, now, what a love, being so helpful!" Jennie said gratefully. "But Mr. Stuart said that the lasses and I are to take our suppers and lock in for the night. We'll pick up with the dawn, hoping we've got some natural light by then. This snow must stop sometime and the sun shine again. Take care, dear."

Sabrina accepted her tray from Tara, the second of the maids, with a soft thank-you. The housekeeping trio bid her good-night, and as she watched them go, she suddenly felt uneasy alone in the hallway.

She took her tray with her into her room and closed and bolted her door, wondering why she felt so edgy. The fish smelled delicious; it was flaky and perfectly cooked over an open fire. She ate it hastily, appreciating the excellent chablis served with it. When she was done, she found that she was strangely loath to open her door; she had begun to feel safe within her room. She chastised herself, unsure why she should suddenly be so afraid.

The remains of a fish dinner, however, could smell. Determined, she set her tray outside her door, looked hastily up and down the hall and locked herself in.

With her door bolted, she gave herself a shake, went into the bathroom and liberally added soothing salts as she filled the bathtub, delighted to see that the hot water was holding out.

But neither the chablis nor the tub seemed to ease the restlessness in her spirit.

Anna Lee Zane had admitted to an affair with Cassandra Stuart. Dianne Dorsey had come from Jon's room, whispering of her love for him. Susan Sharp had claimed she was attacked. And now they were all snowbound. They might all be in danger. And all she wanted to do was touch Jon Stuart, make love with him…

Impatient with herself, she rose from the tub, dried briskly and slipped into a soft silk negligee. She should have been chilly. She felt hot. She opened the doors and stepped out onto the balcony to cool her heated thoughts and flesh.

The snow had stopped. The air was crisp. The stars were unbelievably beautiful.

It was then, as she stood there, that she suddenly felt him behind her.

She should have been afraid. It had been a very disturbing day. And once, not so long ago, a woman had plunged from a balcony of this castle to her death.

His wife.

Sabrina wasn't afraid. Because she knew, intuitively, that it was he. Yet she held her breath. If he wanted to kill her, it would be easy. Come up behind her. Push. No real effort. She was fairly light. As Cassandra Stuart had been.

And there had been other women in his life. She wasn't a fool; she knew that.

But the facts no longer seemed to matter. She sensed that she knew this man, and that there was something right about her wanting him, no matter what the past. His or hers.

No matter, even, what she might fear about the present.

She didn't know how she knew that it was he, she just did, assuring her that people were indeed in possession of a sixth sense, hidden somewhere deep within the psyche. She wasn't afraid. He hadn't come to hurt her.

She didn't turn around. She waited. She tried to remind herself that what had been between them had been a long time ago, that he had had relationships with others, that she should show some restraint, some dignity.

She didn't hear him move, nor did she start when he touched her. He took her by the shoulders and turned her around. His marbled eyes held a strange frustration and a simmering, potent anger. She held her breath and waited for him to speak, to ask the questions so obviously on his lips. She needed to speak herself, to tell him that there were many things they needed to talk about. She needed to ask him about his other relationships.

But he didn't question her, and she couldn't find words at all. He swore softly and dragged her into his arms.

The hard, forceful passion in his kiss sent a wave of electricity shimmering throughout her body. She'd never thought a simple kiss could be so bluntly intimate, but the feel of his tongue lashing hungrily within her mouth seemed so sensually hot that her limbs began to quiver, her body to quicken. She felt the hardness of his erection through the velour of his robe and the silk of her night-gown. The intensity of his body heat seemed to fuse his length to hers, settling in her center as if she were stark naked and touched in the most personal, intimate way.

Then he abruptly drew his lips away a fraction, and his eyes found hers. "Are you still sleeping with McGraff?" he inquired huskily.

Anger, intense as her desire had been, flooded through her. She tried to draw back, but he held her too tightly. She didn't answer because he continued in what sounded like a mocking tone.

"Forgive me, but nearly every time I see you two, you're in somewhat suggestive situations."

"God knows who *you're* sleeping with," she responded angrily. "Today your room reminded me of Grand Central Station. Are you sleeping with all those women? And does that mean you killed Cassandra so you could continue to do so?" she countered.

She was instantly sorry. His body tightened like a bowstring.

"All right, then, be a bitch. And I won't give a damn if you're still sleeping with Brett."

His eyes were sharp and damning as he stared at her.

Then, abruptly, he spun her around again, and she felt his fingers and thumbs at the base of her neck. He began massaging her nape, her shoulders. She wanted to say something in response, to snap back at him, by God, to move away like a sensible person with at least a modicum of pride. She stood motionless instead, furious, but lulled by the sensual, powerful feel of his hands on her. He was so close behind her. Still aroused. Tense, hot. And seductive.

"If you're angry with me, suspicious, you could leave, you know," she finally managed to say.

"I could."

"You might have knocked."

"I might have."

"I could throw you out."

"No, you couldn't."

"I can tell you to leave."

"I wouldn't go."

"Then you're extremely rude."

"What a shame."

"And just how did you get in here?" she inquired belatedly.

"Secret passage. It's my castle, remember?"

"Right. That would make you king of the castle, master of all you survey," she murmured sardonically.

"One would think."

"Where's the entry?"

"Castle secret. My castle, my secret."

"My room."

"In my castle."

"You've come before," she murmured accusingly. "No fair. You don't play by the rules."

His fingers stopped moving. She couldn't see his face,

but she could sense his frown. "No," he told her. "No, I've never come before. Why do you think that I have?"

She shook her head, aware that he had grown even more taut, wired, tense. "It was just a feeling. Waking from dreams. A sensation."

"You felt it was me."

"I felt..." She hesitated. What had she felt? "I don't know. I just awakened thinking I wasn't alone."

"I didn't come to this room before."

"Really?"

"Did you think that I was uncontrollably lusting after you?" he inquired with a touch of amusement.

She started to pull away.

His hands clasped her shoulders more tightly, and he continued, "I was. But I didn't come here before—other than in lusting spirit, of course."

She smiled slightly, glad that he couldn't see her face. "Maybe someone else knows about your secret passage," she suggested.

"No one else should know. The passage I came by connects straight from my room to yours."

"Interesting. Did you plan it that way when you put me in this room?"

"Yes," he said bluntly.

"But you didn't come before?"

"No."

"Why now?"

"I gave up waiting for an invitation. And I quit giving a damn about your ex-husband." He sounded irritated again. And tense. She still couldn't see his face, only feel his robe against her. "And," he added softly, "the uncontrollable lust finally got the best of me."

"Oh, really?"

"I came for sex," he said very softly.

"Me, too," she replied coolly.

"With which one of us?" he inquired.

"You are a royal bastard, and you should crawl back into your secret passageway and—"

"Not on your life, my love," he whispered with a quiet intensity that left her shivering, wanting, all over again, despite herself.

He was still, as if he waited for a response. She refused to give him one. Then she felt his hands moving again, along her nape, along her shoulders, beneath the silky straps of her nightgown.

The negligee began to fall. She instinctively caught the fabric over her breasts, yet inclined her neck and thrilled to the hot touch of his lips against her shoulder, the side of her throat. She felt the muscled form of him behind her, the movement of his fingers on the silk over her hip and thigh, his hard palm gliding low over her abdomen, between her legs. Her limbs seemed molten; her knees nearly gave. His heat seemed to radiate into her, enwrap and engulf her, and she thought that she would melt into the floor, with no will to halt the flow of sweet, wicked warmth that filled her.

Jon suddenly seemed to realize that they were still outside on the balcony, possibly within view of others, and he slipped his arms around her waist, drawing her back into the room. Once there, he turned her to face him and, gazing into her eyes, caught her hands, releasing her hold on her nightgown. Silk shimmied down the length of her, like a cool breath against her fevered skin. She seemed to ache, to long, to desire from every pore. He said nothing, surveying her, and it was as if she felt the very touch of his marbled gaze, and it felt like fire.

CASSANDRA'S KILLER WATCHED. From a distance, with binoculars.

They weren't paying enough attention to what was happening around them. Not that the killer was playing infantile tricks. No, the killer was serious.

The killer saw the balcony. Saw the woman beneath the stars, saw the man behind her. Watched the scene, riveted.

Saw both their faces.

Felt the eroticism.

The woman, tall, willowy, her nightgown flowing in the night air, her hair caught upon the breeze.

Jon Stuart. Enraptured. Touching. Tall, handsome, so masculine in his robe. His fingers, long, bronzed, moving seductively over the woman's flesh. Her breasts, nearly bared, him touching, touching, touching, and you knew there was a stroke of fingers between her legs, and you could almost feel the manly bulge against the cleft at her bottom.

Then...

He drew her inside. As if he were aware that there might be eyes on them. Watching. Torn. Wanting. Angry.

Still angry. Why the anger?

Why the longing?

The strange longing.

Wanting.

And wanting to...

Kill.

And kill again.

And actually...

It was nearly time to do so.

SHE FELT HERSELF trembling under his gaze. She was naked, cold, yet burning with infuriating, arousing anticipation. Oh, God.

Jon went down upon one knee, his muscled arms encircling Sabrina's buttocks, drawing her forward to him. His kisses glided over her abdomen, then slid to the very center of her sex.

His bold, aggressive intimacy was staggering. Electric currents seemed to rip through her, rendering her aware of nothing but sheer sensation. She cried out in protest and desire. Her fingers tore into his dark hair; her body shook, raced alarmingly toward a shattering climax and convulsed in a startling, swift pinnacle of saturating pleasure.

She was swiftly in his arms, tasting the sexy muskiness of his lips, feeling his nakedness beneath his loosened robe as he bore her down onto the bed. She was dazed, stunned, even embarrassed, yet ever more eager for his kiss, his touch.

Memory came to join the fever of passion he quickly awakened again. He had made love to her before, and she remembered every nuance of him—his touch, his lips, his scent. She had held them sacred in her heart, and the sheer joy of feeling him again was overwhelming. She should have been skeptical, aloof, angry, indignant. He'd had no right, master of the castle or no, to slip into her room unasked, to touch unasked. Yet logic and emotions didn't matter. Nothing mattered. He had come because he was done with waiting. He wanted her, and he had come for her, and he knew that she had no will to deny him. Perhaps he even knew that she had been dying for his touch, and dying to touch him in turn. Perhaps he had seen the hunger in her eyes.

She returned his kiss with equal passion, arms enveloping him, fingertips eager to reach his flesh. His mouth was hard, his cheeks slightly rough as his face moved against her flesh, tongue and mouth teasing her throat, the globes of her breasts, closing around her nipples, teasing, tasting, grazing, making them pebble under his assault. She dug her fingers into his hair, cradling his head to her, her body arching, small, desperate sounds escaping her lips. His weight was between her thighs; she felt the tip of his erection against her, slick, insistent, arousing, and then he was sheathed within her, and the shock of sensation was dizzying again.

He angled his hips, thrust and withdrew, slowly at first, filling her as deeply as she could be filled. Her fingers dug into him, holding him, clutching his back, his muscled buttocks. His hands were beneath her, lifting, guiding, bringing her ever closer with a heady, impossible intensity.

She buried her cries in his shoulder when climax seized her again. She shook, convulsed, held him, damp, seeking breath, feeling the thunderous pounding of her heart as if it were a kettle drum. His hands still cradling her hips, he arched his body hard against hers, into hers, and she felt his heat spill into her, permeate her depths. He didn't release her right away, nor did he withdraw from her, and their ragged breaths mingled, as did the drumming of their hearts.

PEOPLE WERE OUT and about. Jon had instructed Camy to deliver the notes asking his guests to be careful and stay put. But the trickster had been at it again, writing new notes, and a number of guests had fallen for the second set of notes sent around, risking life and limb running around the darkened castle rather than remaining smart and safe.

Finding one of the notes that summoned guests to the

"dungeon below," Camy was perplexed. Was everyone writing his or her own directions, playing new games?

The upstairs hallway was quiet. Jon wasn't in his room. She hadn't been able to find Jon; he wasn't in his room. She wanted to tell him that something was up, but she didn't know just exactly where he was right now. And so, despite the fact that she was shivering and frightened, she knew that she had to go below herself.

Descending the first set of stairs, she was certain that she saw shadows moving ahead of her. Wraiths in the night. She told herself that she wasn't afraid of the castle, of the crypt. She lived here. There were no ghosts, no goblins. Joshua Valine was a talented artist who had sculpted figures from wax and wire, nothing more. There was nothing to be afraid of.

She knew the castle.

Still...

She started silently down the next flight of stairs, to the dungeon. She was convinced that she heard furtive sounds. People guarding their secrets and their fears.

Secrets and fears that could make them want to kill?

There was a sound, like the scurrying of rats running about, afraid of the light, glad of the darkness and the shadows of the castle. Strange, she could almost see all Jon's guests as rats in her mind's eye. Big rats, little rats, frightened, dangerous rats. Reggie Hampton, for instance, would be a plump rodent with a flowered dress. Susan Sharp would be a scrawny creature with big rat teeth. Thayer Newby would wear a cop badge on rat patrol, while Joe Johnston would be a scruffy gutter rat. And good old Tom Heart would wear a top hat and cane, a Fred Astaire scurrying gracefully among the rest of them.

Camy felt a strange chill. What was going on? It was

so weird. She could feel the secretive movements in the castle. She didn't like it. She was uneasy.

Furtive and careful herself, she entered the chapel. A single lamp was burning there to protect visitors from stumbling in the dark. She saw no one. Yet it seemed even there that the dim light set menacing shadows to flickering in every corner.

Where was Jon? Was he down here somewhere, silently trying, as she was, to find out what his guests were up to?

She left the chapel, carefully looking out the doors before she did so, and slipped into the chamber of horrors. She wondered if Joshua himself could have known just how frightening this place could be even without his purplish lighting, with the eerie flicker of lanterns against the stones of the castle. She blinked, half expecting Jack the Ripper to lift his face to her and offer her an evil, taunting grin. She was convinced, for a moment, that Marie Antoinette turned to look at her. On the rack, Lady Ariana Stuart screamed in silent anguish, her eyes upon Camy, desperate, accusing...

She waited, barely breathing, thinking again that she heard the scurrying of rats. Was someone there, hiding among the wax figures? Or were the figures alive, moving each time she blinked, coming closer, closer, ready to strike?

Idiot! she accused herself. Chicken! How silly. She was a sensible adult. She knew better.

She eased back out of the chamber of horrors, leaning against the wall, breathing deeply. To her other side, barely illuminated, were the recreation areas. The pool, the bowling alley. Might she hear a splash? As her imagination soared, she pictured a murderer casting a victim into the pool, blood fanning out in rich waves. Or, rolling toward the ten pins, a phantom bowling ball that would prove to be a human head.

Ugh! She'd been hanging around those who dealt in death and the macabre for far too long, she told herself. There were no sounds coming from the pool or the bowling alley.

One more place...

She glided toward the crypt and tried to open the double doors there in silence.

Naturally, the doors creaked.

It probably wasn't that noisy, but it sounded loud enough to wake the dead.

She stepped into the crypt.

The light was so muted that she could see almost nothing in the shadows. She blinked, adjusting to the hazy glow cast by the single lantern hanging from an ancient wall fixture.

Then she froze, staring in absolute terror, chilled to the bone...

For there she was.

Cassandra Stuart.

Oh, Jesus Christ, Cassandra!

Beautiful in purple silk and gauze, the very gown in which she'd been buried, her pitch-black hair flowing around her shoulders. She lay atop her own tomb, hands folded over her breasts.

And then she began to move, sitting up, smoothing back her hair, staring at Camy with her haunting eyes...

THEY LAY FOR a very long time, entwined, and at first Sabrina could do nothing but savor the delicious feel of him. His body still a part of her, his scent, heat, strength cloaking her nakedness.

Then, with a sudden, renewed burst of anger, she shoved him from her, rolling to pin him down on the bed. He stared at her with surprise.

"You're a complete ass. Jon Stuart! Giving me a hard time about Brett. Yes, I was married to him. And you know what? I still care about him. Oh, he's capable of being an ass, too—it seems to be something men, especially egotistical writers, are quite good at. In a way, I suppose you could even say that I love him. But our marriage is honestly over, and if you want to keep believing otherwise, then you can just crawl back under whatever rock in this big pile of stone you came out from!"

His left brow arched, and a smile tugged at his lips. "Does that mean you came for sex specifically with me?"

She started to swear, swiftly pummeling his chest. He grunted with surprise and suddenly, easily, seized her wrists. Then he rolled and, straddling her, pinned her beneath him.

"Fine," he declared. "Let's be open as hell. You know what? Yeah, Cassandra was a royal pain in the ass, an incomparable bitch when she chose to be. But there was a time when she really loved me, when I loved her, and yes, in my way, I cared about her until the day she died, even if our marriage was over, and even if she was sleeping with half the castle, male and female. That's why I—" He broke off abruptly, his lips thinning.

Sabrina inhaled sharply, staring at him. "Oh, my God! That's it, isn't it? The entire reason you had this party. You did love her, and you're trying to catch her killer."

He pushed away from her, sitting up on the side of the bed. He ran his fingers through his hair, shaking his head. "I don't know that she was murdered. I saw her fall, that's all. I was there, and all I saw was Cassie pitching over the balcony rail. It was as if she were flying, and that damn Poseidon is so close to the damned balcony that she landed right on his trident," he finished wearily. "I was grilled by the courts, but I also hired every expert I could myself, trying to find out if she possibly could have fallen onto the trident or if she would have needed the impetus of a push."

"And?"

He grimaced. "One scientist showed me mathematical angles that indicated she had to have been pushed. Another showed me a set of diagrams that showed why it was impossible to tell." He shook his head again. "I wish I could have let it go, accepted it as an accident. I wish we all could have gotten on with our lives. But actually, it wasn't my choice alone, and in the end, the wondering, the not knowing, has been worse than anything in the world. Every day of my life since she died, the tragedy has haunted me. I just keep wondering…"

"But, Jon—"

She broke off, frozen, as a sound that seemed to shake the castle itself slashed through the night. It was a scream of terror so deep and unearthly, that it was almost like a banshee wail. It seemed not so much muffled by the thick castle walls as amplified by them.

Jon was instantly up and tying his robe.

"My God!" she breathed. "What—"

The sound came again, a howl of horror and fear.

"The dungeon!" Jon exclaimed.

Even as Sabrina scrambled for her nightgown and robe, he was hurrying swiftly out the door.

"Wait!" she cried, racing after him into the hallway.

He'd taken a kerosene lamp from a fixture beneath an arch and was already moving down the stairs. She followed, trying to close the distance between them. The stone floors felt icy under her bare feet, but she knew she hadn't time to go back for shoes.

They were halfway down the stairs when a third bloodcurdling scream shrilled through the night.

And then...

There was the horrible sound of silence.

CHAPTER THIRTEEN

THAYER WAS JUST ahead of them, running into the crypt as they arrived below.

They followed.

Racing, Sabrina blinked in the dim light. Then she nearly screamed herself.

Cassandra Stuart was not inside her tomb. She was atop it, in all her beauty and glory. She was feminine and elegant and even as a ghost, in death, looked amazingly well, sitting up on the stone sarcophagus that bore her name.

Someone crashed into Sabrina's back and screamed with instinctive, primal fear. Anna Lee, Sabrina noted vaguely, still too stunned to move or begin to comprehend what was happening in the depths of the ancient crypt.

Camy Clark, she now realized, lay in a crumpled heap on the floor.

"Sweet Jesus!" Sabrina heard someone gasp, and she saw that Reggie had come in now as well, clasping her heart.

"Dear God!" Joe Johnston had come running in as well, only to stop short at Reggie's side. He was followed by Joshua Valine, still tying the belt of his terry robe.

Joshua's jaw dropped, and a strange sound escaped him.

Joe Johnston spoke again, repeating, "Dear God, dear God!"

Then Cassandra muttered a terse "Shit!" as she saw Jon, furious rather than frightened, striding across the crypt to reach for her, grabbing her forcefully by the arm.

"What the bloody hell do you think you're doing?" he demanded with an anger that caused his voice to shake.

"Let go, please!" she cried out. "I'm sorry. Don't be angry. I didn't intend—"

"You must have intended for someone to have a heart attack!" Jon declared, lashing out.

Sabrina just stared, certain that the world had gone insane. Jon had just been telling her remorsefully how he had nearly gone mad wondering about his wife's death. And now here she was, flesh and blood, and he was yelling at her.

It nonsensically occurred to Sabrina that she had just committed adultery, which bothered her greatly, even if she was in a castle where it seemed that a group of rabid, insane people played musical beds.

"Look what you've done to Camy!" Jon thundered.

By that time, Thayer was down beside Jon's fallen secretary, checking for a pulse. Joshua hunched down on his knees in concern, as well.

"She's all right," Thayer said. "Better than I am. I—I saw Cassandra dead, bleeding, three years ago," he said in agitated confusion.

"Cassandra *is* dead!" Jon said irritably, and as he did so, he reached out to the ghost who had risen from Cassandra's coffin, wrenching at the woman's hair.

The long, flowing tresses came away. It was a wig. And then, even in the darkness, it became evident that the woman on the tomb was neither Cassandra nor Cassandra's ghost. It was Dianne Dorsey. Despite the eerie light and chilling surroundings, something that should

have been evident for years but hadn't been became star-
tlingly obvious. Dianne Dorsey bore a stunning resemblance to Cassandra Stuart.

"My God!" Anna Lee breathed.

"This is the cruelest, most vicious trick I've ever seen
played," Jon snarled angrily at the girl.

"I'm sorry, Jon, I'm sorry!" she cried. She looked at
the group that had formed around her. Most of the household was there—Joe, Thayer, Joshua, Anna Lee, Reggie,
Jon and Sabrina. The housekeeper and the two maids,
with rooms in the attic, evidently hadn't heard Camy's
screams, and V.J., Tom, Susan and Brett had apparently
slept through them.

Camy, coming to, suddenly started screaming again.
Sabrina knelt before her and the two men supporting her.
"Camy, Camy!" she said, touching the woman's face. "It's
all right. It's not a ghost. It's just Dianne, playing a trick."

"It's not a trick!" Dianne protested. "All right, I suppose it was a trick, but I didn't mean to be vicious or
cruel, I was just trying to find out which of you hated
my mother enough to kill her!"

"Mother!" Joe grunted, sounding as if he was strangling.

Jon walked across the room to Camy and touched her
hair. "You all right?" he asked gently.

Camy nodded. Sabrina stared up at him accusingly
before rising and helping Camy to her feet. Jon stared
back at her, but offered no apology.

"Mother?" Joe croaked again.

Anna Lee started to laugh. "Oh, this is really rich.
Is it true?"

"Yes," Jon said, striding back toward Dianne. His
anger hadn't abated, but it seemed to be in check. "Cassie

had Dianne when she was very young. And to Cassie, no matter how young she'd been, having a grown daughter was something she didn't want to admit publicly."

"You knew—all along?" Joshua said, looking at Jon.

He nodded. "I thought you knew, too. I mean, I thought it would be obvious to you when you were doing their wax figures." He shrugged. "Cassie and Dianne had both asked me not to say anything, for their own reasons, and I respected their desires. But Dianne, evidently, has changed her mind."

He stood in front of Dianne, glaring at her.

"But... I thought you hated her!" Joe said to Dianne.

"I did," Dianne said. Then she started to laugh. But as she laughed, tears began streaming down her face. "I hated her because her looks and youth and image were everything to her, far more important than I was. I wanted you all to think that I hated her because that was the only way you'd talk openly in front of me, say what you were really feeling or thinking. But she was my mother, and when she was with Jon, he made her realize that I was her child, and she took an interest in me, and in my work, and we were like conspirators, both of us preserving her image of youth and beauty. And she could be so horrible and mean, but she had times when she could be loving... and...and...it didn't matter, she was my mother, and one of you killed her!"

Jon slipped an arm around her. His anger gone, he held her tenderly. "You don't know that anyone killed her, Dianne. And dressing up like Cassie wasn't going to help you, honey. It just scared Camy half to death and could have put you into serious danger."

She clung to him, suddenly looking extremely young,

her makeup running, her eyes lustrous, the tough-girl image completely gone.

"If no one killed her, why would I be in danger?" Dianne whispered.

Jon was silent for a split second too long. "Because it's a dark and stormy night in a creaky old castle," he told her lightly.

"And we have a full moon now, too," Reggie said.

"Are you implying that we have werewolves about?" Joe murmured teasingly, also trying to lighten the mood.

It was a strange gathering. They'd gone through shock, terror, disbelief and anger. Now they were banding together in sympathy because it was all too painfully obvious that Dianne had been deeply hurt by her mother, and just when she had finally begun to receive the love she had craved, her mother had been snatched away. She looked like a lost child; she *was* a lost child.

"I think vampires like full moons, as well," Sabrina offered.

"Especially when cats are leaping out of the bag," Anna Lee murmured.

"I think there are probably a few more cats ready to do some leaping out," Jon said sternly, staring from one to the other of them. "We'll meet tomorrow in the great hall and try to get to the bottom of all our little secrets, shall we?"

Anna Lee shrugged. "I've admitted mine."

"You have?" Joe said.

"Never mind, for the moment," Jon told him. "We'll get to all this in the morning, when everyone is present. We should get some sleep for what's left of the night."

"I'm sorry, Jon," Dianne said again, looking up at him. She still rested against his chest. His arm was supportively around her. "I suppose it wasn't a very smart trick. I just thought that someone might panic and shriek out the truth— that I couldn't be there, alive, because they'd killed me. It didn't happen. Maybe the right person isn't here. I'm sorry. I guess it really was dumb. Please don't be angry with me."

"It was stupid and dangerous, and I am angry. I'm angry with myself, because I shouldn't have had you here this week," he said.

"Are we all here to confess our secrets and find out the truth about Cassie?" Anna Lee asked.

"We're all here for charity—and to find out the truth about Cassie, if there is a truth to be discovered," Jon said honestly. "I'm sure you all came for exactly the same reasons I arranged the Mystery Week."

"Amen to that," Joe muttered.

"I can't believe that V.J. is missing this!" Reggie said.

"V.J." Anna Lee snorted. "It's Susan who's missing her big chance—thank God!"

"Well, she'll know the truth about everything soon enough."

"Yes, the sins we know now and the sins we'll share tomorrow," Thayer said dryly.

"There's really no help for it, is there?" Jon asked. "There's apparently a lot we need to get out in the open— if we don't want any more startling performances."

"Susan will still be deadly," Reggie warned.

Anna Lee smiled. "We'll see, won't we? Maybe we can all tie her up and gag her—or wall her into the castle. What do you say?"

"I say it's better when the truth is out," Dianne said suddenly, passionately.

"Definitely," Jon said.

"So why didn't you tell us all the truth about Dianne?" Thayer demanded of Jon.

"I asked him not—" Dianne began.

But Jon, apparently, wasn't about to have anyone fight his battles for him. "I already told you, it wasn't my truth to tell," he said flatly. "Other than the obvious emotional reasons, Dianne wasn't certain that the truth wouldn't hurt her career now. She's worked very hard at her writing, and one of the reasons she hesitated about letting the truth be known after Cassie died was that she didn't want people thinking, belatedly and erroneously, that Cassie helped her write or helped her get a publisher or special considerations. Dianne has earned every accolade that has come her way. So I respect her decision."

Dianne smiled up at him. "I know why she loved you so much," she whispered softly.

He cleared his throat, obviously uncomfortable. "Let's let Cassie rest in peace now, shall we?" he murmured. With his arm still around Dianne, he helped her stand and led her from the crypt. The others stared at one another for several seconds, then followed him out.

They mounted the first step of stairs as a group, and they were still together as they reached the second floor. There they said their exhausted good-nights and departed for their own rooms.

Sabrina stood in the hallway briefly, looking after Jon. He was still talking to Dianne, walking her to her room. He glanced back at her.

She turned and entered her own room, closing the door firmly behind her.

She wondered if he would come back to her, and she paced.

After half an hour, restless, she stepped into the hall

and tried Brett's door. It opened, and as she looked in on him, she worried that she hadn't a way to lock it from the outside. Nothing really bad had happened; still, she wished she could make sure that he was locked in. He was sleeping, and she checked his breathing and his pulse. With his bedroom eyes closed for the night, he had a strange innocence. He looked absolutely cherubic.

She kissed his cheek and left him.

She walked back into her own room, still unhappy about leaving her ex-husband so defenseless. She closed her door, locked it, hesitated.

As she did so, a hand descended on her shoulder.

She spun around, almost screaming, but it was Jon. Once again, his marbled eyes were dark and dangerous— and very suspicious.

"Going back to the ex?" he inquired softly.

"You! You have your nerve lecturing me when—"

"I'm not lecturing. I'm asking. You were just with him, right?"

She gritted her teeth, hating his cool nonchalance and the piercing feel of his eyes.

Which still left her wanting him. Against her will.

"He's sound asleep. I was just worried about him."

"Why?"

"I don't know exactly. You said we should all lock ourselves in. I can't lock his door."

"Oh." He looked at her for a moment, the released her, opened her door and stepped into the hall. She followed him and watched as he drew a key from his pocket and attended to Brett's door.

She stared at him, then tried the door. It was locked. With narrowed eyes, she stared at him again.

"It's a master key," he told her.

"Because you're the master?"

"Of course."

"Your castle, right? How could I forget."

"I don't know. How could you?"

She turned and stepped back to her room. She entered it and started to close the door. He followed, closing and locking the door behind him.

"So this is all to catch a killer," she said. "You know, there are those who believe *you* to be the killer."

"No one with good sense."

"You do have the ability to sneak up on any of us— whether we want company or not."

"Do you really want me to leave?" he inquired.

She stared at him, but then lowered her eyes. "Why didn't you tell me about Dianne? You knew that I was…" Her voice trailed off.

His hands fell on her shoulders. She felt their strength and warmth, and for the life of her, she couldn't help but remember how they felt when they were more intimately upon her.

"Why didn't I explain that she was my stepdaughter and that I wasn't sleeping with her?"

"You—you could have," she stuttered.

He shook his head. "No, I couldn't have. I had promised her that I wouldn't, though, of course, I would have forbidden her to come to Mystery Week or thrashed her hindquarters if I'd had any idea she meant to pull such a dangerous stunt."

"You care about her," Sabrina said softly.

"Of course. She was just a young kid, scared, unsure, who'd never known her father and wasn't allowed to have a mother. I liked her from the start. She's searched for an identity, done all sorts of ridiculous things, but she's worked hard, and, despite all appearances, she's become a decent young woman."

Sabrina nodded, her head down. "Dianne is your stepdaughter. And Anna Lee…"

"Anna Lee seduced Cassie. And Cassie was happy to be seduced. She wanted to be shocking, and titillating. She thought that I was interested in Anna Lee as more than a friend and colleague."

"But you weren't?" Sabrina said, looking up at him.

He shook his head, smiling slowly.

"The rumor is that you were having an affair, as well, with one of the guests at the party. Perhaps V.J.?" she inquired, thinking of her beautiful older friend —married at the time, but then, stranger things had surely happened.

"V.J.?" Jon exclaimed. "I do love her, but as a dear and cherished friend."

"Susan?" she whispered.

He made a face.

"Reggie?" she inquired incredulously.

"Oh, please!" he groaned.

"Well, that's the group, other than—"

"Has it never occurred to you that it might have been rumor and nothing more?" he asked softly.

"But—but you knew that your wife was having affairs—"

"Yes, and I had a life other than the week in which I had friends out here for a charity function," he said.

"Then you were seeing someone else?"

"I was seeing someone, yes. But neither one of us was deeply involved. She knew that I was married, and she knew that there were difficulties. We weren't in love—it was a brief relationship, that's all. I wasn't seeing anyone who was here at the Mystery Week. From what I knew and suspected, most of them were already pretty busy, and that's all there is for me to tell," he said.

And she knew that the matter was closed. "But, Jon," she ventured, trying very hard to sound determined, sure and matter-of-fact, "So much has happened, there's so much that we don't know, and—"

But he interrupted her. "Yes, so much has happened, and there's a million things between us to discuss. We could fight over a dozen things for a dozen weeks, but—"

"You came for the sex," she interrupted bitterly.

He went still, watching her. "I came to make love. Because I'm not sure that I've actually *made love* since you walked out on me years ago."

It might not have been true. It might have just been the right thing to say. But it didn't matter. He was tense, and passionate, as if he'd rediscovered a hunger that couldn't be simply sated. His energy was electric, and she wanted to feel him again.

Still, she hesitated.

"But, Jon, I don't know what I feel. Anger, fear…"

That last word did it. He backed away from her and started across the room toward the balcony. He touched a brick in the wall, and a slim doorway slid open with the silence of well-oiled if ancient mechanisms.

"You can slide the top lock on your hall door to keep me out," he said curtly. "And you can wedge this door shut by shoving the fire poker into the crack," he told her.

Then he was gone.

She was stunned. Then she suddenly, belatedly found realization. And regret. She had told him she was *afraid*. She ran after him, hurrying to the secret door. But she couldn't even see it anymore. The bricks hid it completely. "Jon!" she whispered, and she banged against the wall. "Jon!"

He didn't reply. She pressed brick after brick. No passageway opened to her.

She sank down on the foot of her bed. A minute later, she curled up on it.

She closed her eyes, feeling ill, wishing she hadn't thrown him away when she'd had him. If he came back, she would tell him...

Tell him what? That she'd never gotten him out of her mind? Her heart? That she was *willing* to be afraid, to risk anything, to forgive anything, to believe anything, to be with him?

She closed her eyes.

Uncertain how long she might have lain there, her mind numb, she suddenly became aware of him again. She jerked herself upright. And he was there, standing at the foot of the bed.

"You didn't put the poker in the door," he told her.

"No," she whispered, and she jumped up, throwing herself into his arms. "Jon, I—"

"I don't think that we should talk," he said roughly.

And for the moment, she agreed with him.

She didn't want to talk. Not now. She wanted to make love.

She opened her mouth, but said nothing, for he kissed her hard, forcefully, demandingly, leaving her no room for speech or argument. She returned his force, eager just to have him, touch him, feel him touch her.

His hands brushed over her clothing, and it was gone. And then he was naked with her, touching her, and in a few frenzied moments he was within her, and the taste, touch, scent and feel of their lovemaking was all she needed.

What remained of the night became a blur. She was sated, dazed, floating on clouds, and then he was within her again. And then, exhausted, she slept, secure in the arms that held her so tightly.

Yet later she awoke feeling cold, her teeth chattering. She was alone in the darkness. He had left her.

Sabrina rose, seeking her nightgown and robe. She hurried to her door, and it was locked. He hadn't left that way. Why should he have? He had come by the secret passageway; he had surely left that way.

Yet she suddenly felt uneasy. She unlocked her door and looked out into the hall.

It was empty.

Strange what night, darkness and being alone could do. It seemed as if there were sounds, movements, coming from every dim corner, from the stairway, from below. The wind outside gave a low moan as it swept around the castle. She thought that she heard cries and whispers within that sound.

She stood in the hallway shivering, trying to tell herself that she was sensible, that the wind didn't mask the cries of ghosts, nor was death shooting across the night sky in a banshee carriage to take any of them away.

Yet he had left her. Jon had left her. And to her deep dismay, she was afraid.

Worried, she moved to Brett's door. She hesitated, then tapped on it.

She was startled when the door drifted slightly open at her knock.

"Brett?"

She pushed the door open.

In the very pale lantern light from the hall, she could see nothing but a mound upon his bed. She hesitated in the doorway, suddenly terrified to walk into the room, afraid of what she might find.

"Brett!" she whispered more urgently.

Still no answer.

She didn't want to walk into the room. It was dark; it was filled with shadows. She was tempted to run back to her own room, bolt her door, curl into a ball on her bed and start praying for morning.

Even if she bolted the door, however, she could have visitors, of course. Jon.

Jon had said that he hadn't come before. She hadn't pressed the point; she hadn't actually seen anyone. But she'd had that feeling, at times, that she hadn't been alone. So either she was highly imaginative, or Jon had been lying...

Or someone else was aware of a passage into her room?

It didn't matter, she told herself. She wasn't being threatened. But Brett *had* been hurt. And though he had seemed okay, she should make sure.

Still she clung to the doorframe.

Then she became angry. Silly fool, she charged herself. If Brett was hurt...

She gathered her courage.

"Brett!"

No answer still. She walked into the room.

And discovered why he hadn't spoken.

SUSAN SHARP WAS dimly aware of movement.

She was annoyed at first, and nothing more. She couldn't remember anything. She must have fallen asleep…somewhere. And now she was groggy. And angry. Though a little hazy, she knew she had a right to be furious. She'd been played for a fool, and now they were going to pay. Oh, definitely, they were going to pay.

Except that she didn't know where she was. Or why she was feeling…movement.

It seeped into her clouded mind that she'd been drugged. She should have known, should have been wary. She'd been so busy being furious, demanding that she be paid and that the tricks stop. Yes, definitely, drugged. The merlot?

It had made her eyelids heavy. She couldn't move them. She wanted to open her eyes, rip into someone.

But she couldn't quite force herself to move anything. Not her limbs, her mouth, her eyelids…

Yet she felt…movement.

Then, in the midst of her haze and anger, it began to occur to her that she really should have been more careful. Even dealing with sniveling cowards, she should have been careful.

Where on God's earth was she?

She became aware of being cold. Stone. She could feel stone against her flesh, and the icy cold that could settle into stone like nothing else. It seeped into her side, where she lay.

Then she heard laughter—nervous, desperate, edgy laughter. Voices so low she could barely hear them.

"There, right there, yes, perfect."

"This is madness. It will never work."

"It will for a while. What else is there now?"

"There's time to change—"

"No, there's no time."

"But…"

The voices trailed away. Susan had heard nothing but whispers, low, sexless whispers, yet she knew who her attackers were. And when she got the strength to get up, she'd kill them.

She finally managed to open her eyes, slowly, so slowly. And she was staring up into the face of a killer...

No! No, it was an image. Yet am image of evil.

Not a killer.

Not real.

Was she losing her mind? She couldn't move, could barely breathe. If she could just see a bit more...

Tremendous strain. She twisted. Half an inch. It was enough. Just enough...

For her to look into her own face. And, looking, she saw her own death.

Sheer terror seized her. Yet still she couldn't move, scream, make a single noise.

Glass eyes returned her stare. Painted blood covered a knife. Her own face, contorted in the agony of death, lay just inches away. She looked at it. It looked at her...

Inside, she felt the welling of a scream. But she couldn't scream, couldn't move, couldn't make a single sound.

She should have told the truth, told what she knew! She had thought that she could deal with this. She had thought that her fury, her power, would be forceful enough to get her what she wanted. She had thought that...

"She's awake!" a voice whispered.

"She can't be awake."

"I tell you, she is! Look at her eyes!"

"Don't look at her eyes! Don't look at her eyes, you fool!"

Her eyes. She could see her own eyes. She could see her own scream. See her own death...

She had to scream. Plead, maybe, cry out, give promises. They'd never believe her; they'd know that she'd skewer them the moment she had the chance. Oh, God, no...

"Her eyes are open!" She heard the fervent cry once again. "We can't do this! There's got to be another way!"

"We have to do this. There is no other way. And, frankly, it's only what she deserves."

"You said she'd be unconscious."

"She is. She isn't moving."

"But her eyes..."

"Do it! Or do I have to do everything myself?"

A cry of impatience.

She tried to scream. Couldn't.

And so she stared into her own eyes, her own face. She saw the horror and the anguish.

She saw her own blood.

Watched her own death.

Powerless.

Couldn't move, couldn't scream, couldn't cry.

But then, at last, she made a noise. It was a terrible, gasping, choking sound...

CHAPTER FOURTEEN

SABRINA WAS FURIOUS.

Brett wasn't there. She was prowling around in the darkness, scaring herself half to death, and the little shit wasn't there. The mound on his bed was just a pile of sheets and blankets. Brett's door was open because he'd left his room.

In the middle of the night.

"Where the hell did you go?" she whispered, ripping back the sheets angrily, even though she knew he couldn't be hiding in some little ball at the bottom of the bed.

"Last time I worry about you," she muttered aloud. She ducked down, looking under the bed. Foolish. She rose and looked around the room, the bath, making absolutely certain that he wasn't there.

There were no closets in the room, but there was a huge wardrobe in the corner. She stared at it for a long moment. Almost floor to ceiling, it was enormous.

It could easily hold a few bodies, she found herself thinking.

She forced herself to walk to the wardrobe, telling herself how silly she was being all the while. When she reached it, she suddenly wanted to turn around. But she was standing right in front of it. Again she told herself that she was being an absolute idiot. Every time she watched a horror movie, she grew irritated because the foolish would-be victim was walking around some dark and shadowed and lonely place alone. When help could have been summoned so easily.

That was the way it was done, of course. It was a dark and stormy night…

She was being ridiculous. It hadn't been dark or stormy when Cassandra Stuart had died. It had been broad daylight. And probably she had simply fallen. In light of what they all did for a living, they had *made* a mystery out of it.

But Jon had been haunted all these years by what had happened. And he wasn't prone to exaggeration or hysteria. He still wanted to know what had happened.

Unless, of course, he'd been involved?

There was no one in the wardrobe, she told herself. No living person ready to leap out at her. No cold, mutilated bodies.

So open it, she commanded herself. She had no logical reason to assume that anything was amiss at all, she told herself.

She reached for the wardrobe door.

But before she could open it, a hand descended firmly upon her shoulder.

She started to scream in sheer terror, but a second hand fell over her mouth.

"Hey, Sabrina! Shh! What's the matter with you? Want to wake the dead? Or the whole household, at the very least? It's me! You're in my room, remember? I'm the one who should be screaming. Maybe with pure delight. Because you finally realized that you can't live without me. My God, what irony! You finally come to my bed—and I'm not in it! But I'm here now. Ready, willing and able. You did come to sleep with me, I hope?"

His hair was mussed; his eyes had never seemed more lazily sensual.

Her heart was still thundering faster than the speed of light.

She wrenched his hand from her mouth. "You scared me half to death!"

"How?" he inquired innocently. "You were in my room."

"I was worried about you!"

"That's so nice."

"I'm serious!"

"So am I. It's great that you care and I do appreciate it. But as you can see, I'm fine."

"What are you doing, skulking around the castle in the middle of the night?" she asked him.

"I went down to the great hall to see if there was any food around." His eyes narrowed. "What are *you* doing, skulking around the castle in the middle of the night?"

"I was looking for you."

He smiled again. "Honey, I'm here now." He reached for her, drawing her into his arms.

"Brett, let go."

"Sabrina!" he protested, hurt. "You just said you were worried about me. And you came to me in the middle of the night."

"Yes, and you seem to be just fine!" she told him.

He grinned. "So do you. You feel great."

"Quit feeling me. Let me be, Brett, please."

He finally did so, though a bit sulkily. "What were you doing up?" he asked her.

"I—I'm not sure. I just woke up...cold."

Brett turned away from her. "You were sleeping with him, I bet," he said gruffly. "And he left you in the middle of the night."

"Brett, don't. I want to be friends, I think we can be friends, but don't meddle in my personal life. I came just now because I was honestly worried about you and—"

He spun around. "*I* wouldn't have left you in the middle of the night."

"You don't know that anyone did."

Brett shook his head. "He's moving around the castle, too, you know." He shook his head. "Strange night. You can tell that everyone is skulking around, and yet no one sees anyone else. Bizarre."

"How do you know?" she demanded.

"I have my ways," he said, jiggling an eyebrow.

She sighed with impatience. "Brett, what's going on? Who else is up? And how do you know they are if you didn't see anyone?"

He shrugged. "I was lonely, looking for company for a midnight snack. I tried Tom's door—no answer. I tried Joe's door—no answer. Thayer—no answer. I even went so far as to tap on Susan's door. No answer there, either."

"You tried Susan's door?" she inquired wryly.

He made an apologetic grimace. "I was desperate for companionship." He shrugged again, casual and handsome in a long velvet robe.

"So you ran around in the middle of the night, tapping on doors seeking company to raid the great hall for food?" she asked skeptically. "Why didn't you tap on my door?"

He looked at her, his face suddenly taut. "I did."

"I didn't hear you."

"Of course not. It was a while ago. And you were making too much noise to hear me. I almost burst in on you, afraid you were being hurt. Then, of course, I felt like an idiot, because I, of all people, should surely know the difference between pain and your little cries of pleasure."

Sabrina was glad it was dark; she was blushing furiously. "Brett..."

"Sabrina, it's late. If you're not going to sleep with me, just go away."

"Brett..." she began again.

"Please. I'm fine. I appreciate your concern. I'm glad to be your friend. But I do love you and it's hard to—"

"Oh, Brett, we've been through all this. You love every woman!"

He shrugged. "Maybe I discovered how much I wanted you too late. But you don't want me, so go back to bed now, huh?"

She turned around, feeling strangely sad, wishing she could make him feel better.

"Sabrina?" he said suddenly.

She looked back. He was seated on the edge of his bed, examining a fingertip, then sucking on it.

"What?" she asked.

"You did know him before, right? Before we were married. I was always convinced of it."

"Brett—"

"Come on, Sabrina, just answer me. You met Jon somewhere and had an affair with him. I never really had a chance. I felt it all along. I resented him for it, you know."

"Brett, I married you, remember?"

"But you didn't love me."

"I did. I still do."

He shook his head slowly. "Not the way you loved him. Not the way you love him now. Even when you barely know him. When you've barely seen him for years. When you can't even be certain that he didn't kill his own wife."

"He didn't kill his wife," she said automatically.

He shrugged. "It's okay. I just wanted the truth from you. I always knew it, somehow."

"Good night, Brett," she told him softly. He nodded and returned to sucking on his finger.

She walked to her own room, locked and bolted the door and started to take off her robe. She realized there was a small dark stain on one sleeve. Frowning, she stared at it, remembering how Brett had gripped her arms.

She threw the robe back on and rushed back to his room, entering without even knocking.

He was still sitting on the bed.

"Brett, you're hurt. You're bleeding," she told him.

He arched a brow at her and smiled. "Bad night," he told her. He lifted the finger he'd been sucking. "Cut myself on a knife while coring an apple."

"Let me see it," she said worriedly.

"Oh, don't go turning into Florence Nightingale on me," he said impatiently. "You're far too tempting when you play nurse. It's just a little cut. I'm sorry if I got blood on your robe."

"Brett, let me see it."

"Out!" he commanded. "Seriously, you either hop into this bed instantly, or you get out of my room!"

He rose, came to her and ushered her out his door and into the hallway. Accompanying her to her room, he said, "Look around, quick! No ghosts. No people. Empty. Kind of like one big tomb, eh? Too bad the great and mighty master of the castle isn't around right now. Maybe he'd think I got in a shot when he was done."

"Brett, I swear—" Sabrina began furiously.

"Sorry! Just teasing you. Now get into your room and lock your door."

"Why are you suddenly so worried about my locking my door?"

"Maybe I'm afraid of creatures who prowl in the night."

"You're prowling around in the night," she reminded him.

His eyes were suddenly hard on hers. "And maybe you should be afraid of me!" he said softly.

He pressed her back into her room and pulled her door shut.

"Good night, my love!" he said firmly. "Lock your bolt."

She did so, and she heard him walk away, enter his room, close and bolt his own door.

"Great. I was only gone an hour, and you go running off to him!"

Stunned by the sound of Jon's voice, Sabrina spun around. He was in his robe, arms crossed over his chest, standing in the rear of the room by the secret passage.

"Damn you!" she told him vehemently.

"Me?" he demanded, brow arching, clearly angry to have seen her with Brett.

She strode across the room to him, pointing a finger. "You walked out on me in the middle of the night."

"So you went running next door to be with your ex-husband?" he asked furiously.

"You must have heard what he said."

"No, I didn't. And I can't imagine what he could have said that would make this look any better."

"I wouldn't sleep with him, so he threw me out. He wasn't even in there when I went—"

"But you did go to him," Jon stated angrily.

"Stop it! Yes, I went over to make sure he was all right. Because I was suddenly scared—"

"Why?"

"I don't know. Why not?" she demanded.

"But he wasn't there?"

"No," she said quietly, suddenly disturbed by the tension in his voice. "Why?"

"Oh, I don't know. Maybe because I sent my guests warnings that, just to be on the safe side, they should all lock themselves in. And instead, the castle is suddenly busier than a beehive. So Brett—injured, poor baby— wasn't in his room when you went to check on him?"

She shook her head.

"Where had he been?"

"Just down to find something to eat."

"So he says."

"Where do you think he went?"

"I don't know."

"And why do you say the castle is so busy?" she asked.

He shrugged. "I saw shadows on the stairs."

"Did you look?"

"Of course."

"Well?"

"I walked around. I didn't see anyone."

"Maybe you imagined the shadows."

The gaze he cast down upon her was withering. "I don't imagine things," he told her.

"No, of course not," she murmured. "So where else did you go?"

"Just back to my room. For clothes. For tomorrow morning."

He was telling the truth about that, at least. A neat pile of his clothing lay on the chair by the bed. "I wasn't gone that long. It never occurred to me that you'd go out prowling around in my absence."

"I didn't prowl around."

"No, you didn't. You went straight to Brett's room."

"He was injured today."

"Yes, the poor fellow. And you're such an angel, despite the divorce, letting bygones be bygones. You're such a wonderful, gentle nurse."

"You're jealous!"

"Naturally, don't you think?"

"But I told you that I care about him."

"It's how much you care about him that concerns me."

"I've been with you," she said softly.

He cocked his head slightly. "Nice to think that tonight has solidified our relationship."

She crossed her arms over her chest. "I suppose I could be jealous of lots of people."

"If you weren't somewhat jealous, I would be entirely insulted."

"So I should be flattered that you think so little of me that you assume I could jump from bed to bed?" she inquired.

He smiled slightly, his eyes dark and marbled. She felt a strange tremor streak through her. He was still a stranger, no matter how well she thought she knew him.

"I didn't say that," he told her.

"You suggested something very close."

He caught her arms and pulled her up against him. "Sorry. I am just…jealous."

She held herself stiffly, but she didn't want to resist him. She felt his warmth, his scent, the pounding of his heart. She didn't want to say more, but she heard herself ask, "You left my room and returned by way of the secret passage?"

"Yes." He held her close, his voice drifting over her hair.

She pulled back, looking up at him. "But you said you had been out in the hallway, chasing shadows."

He smiled, looking down at her. He rubbed his chin, saying, "I went back to my room to shave."

"You decided to shave in the middle of the night?" she asked him.

He smiled again and touched her cheek. "I noticed I'd given you razor burn. Sorry. But I've paid for my sin. Knicked myself incredibly."

He touched his own cheek, and when he drew his hand away there was a smudge of blood on his fingers.

"That's from a knick?" she inquired.

"Took out a fair hunk of skin," he admitted.

"I'll say."

"Sorry, looks as if I got it on your robe."

"No, no, you didn't—" she began, then broke off.

"Then who did?" he inquired, eyes narrowed.

"Uh... Brett."

"Brett bled on you? This is pretty wild. Don't tell me, he'd been shaving, too, before wandering into the night?" he said suspiciously.

"No, he didn't decide to shave in the middle of the night."

"He's just running around bleeding, then."

"He cut himself coring an apple."

"How'd he get the blood on you?"

"Oh, please."

"Sabrina, how?" Jon demanded tensely, taking her arms again.

She sighed. "He caught my arms while he was talking to me, just as you're doing now."

"Oh?" he said, his voice grating.

"Jon, he knows that I'm—that I was—that we were together."

"How?"

She felt the color flooding her cheeks. "He heard us."

"Through the walls?"

"Through the door."

"What was he doing at your door?"

"Seeing if I wanted to raid the great hall for food with him."

Jon was silent for a moment. "This is a busy place," he said very softly. "You running around, Brett out and about. Susan won't answer her door—"

"So I heard."

"From whom?"

"From Brett," Sabrina said sharply. She offered him a hard smile. "And since we're busy casting stones here, why were you knocking on Susan's door?"

"To make sure she was all right. She was really angry today, and someone—Dianne included—has been playing some pretty mean jokes. Actually, Dianne and Thayer didn't answer their doors, either."

"Nor Tom," Sabrina murmured, "nor Joe."

"You were knocking on Tom Heart's door?" Jon demanded. "And Joe's?"

"No!"

"Then—"

"Brett. Brett was out knocking on doors. He was looking for company."

"In the middle of the night?"

"You were knocking on doors in the middle of the night," she reminded him.

"But it's my castle."

"Still, it's the middle of the night..." Sabrina sighed, relenting. "Brett was simply hungry and trying to find someone else who might be awake and about."

"We should have had a midnight buffet, like a cruise ship," Jon murmured.

"I think it's well past midnight."

"Hmm. And you sound as if you don't trust me."

"Why wouldn't I trust you?"

"Oh, a little thing like half the world thinks I killed my wife."

She shook her head. "I belong to the half of the world that doesn't think you did."

He smiled, smoothing back her hair. "Do you think that's smart?" he queried huskily. "You know how it goes in horror tales. The sweet, innocent, noble young heroine is sucked dry by the bloodthirsty vampire."

"I don't think you've been accused of being a vampire."

"Just Bluebeard."

"You've only had one wife."

"But, alas, they say, she is dead. Do you think I should leave?"

"Should you leave? Well, what good would that do? You left before—you simply return."

"That's true, isn't it?" he mused, and she realized that he was just slightly bitter, and just slightly mocking her, and himself.

"You could bunk in with Brett, your good buddy."

"He would protect me with his life," she agreed blithely, watching his marbled eyes.

"Ah, would he? But if I'm not a dangerous man, perhaps your ex-husband is."

"Maybe I would be best off bunking in with V.J.," she murmured.

"Well, you probably would be. But V.J. isn't answering her door, either," he said dryly.

She felt a strange shiver. He was taunting her, almost as if he had pulled her too close and now wanted her to step back and find fault with him.

To be afraid?

"It's your castle, isn't it? Couldn't you actually follow me almost anywhere I went?"

"If I chose."

"Would you choose?" she asked softly.

"Yes."

She lifted her chin, studying his eyes. "I take my chances then, with what's left of the night."

"Not much, I'm afraid," he murmured softly. "Want to try to get some sleep? No more wandering? We both stay put?"

"Sleep?" she murmured.

"Sure."

Sabrina slipped out of her robe and into her bed. The sheets felt very cold, but then Jon doffed his robe and slid in beside her, curling an arm around her, pulling her close. His hands slid beneath the hem of her gown, over her calf, her knee, her thigh.

"I thought we would be sleeping," she murmured.

"Just trying to get comfortable. I hate these things," he told her, tugging at her nightgown. "I mean, they have their place, just not in bed."

"Nightgowns don't belong in bed?"

He shook his head. "Most certainly not," he said. Then

his marbled eyes grew very dark in the shadows. "I can't seem to leave you alone," he admitted.

She didn't want to be left alone. She didn't know if he got rid of her gown or if she did. But soon her arms were around him, and she wanted him. "Then don't," she told him.

"I let you go once," he told her, voice soft, lips muffled against hers. "I can't do it again."

She didn't reply.

It was a dark and stormy night...

He was a stranger.

But she felt such a keen sense of intimacy, and whether or not she should be afraid, she had no intention of allowing him to let her go.

LATER, SHE SLEPT. She roused slightly when Jon rolled out of bed and stood staring toward the balcony. She felt a stirring in the region of her heart. Warmth. Possessiveness. Her lashes slightly parted to allow her an unobserved surveillance, she studied him. Tall, handsome, ruggedly muscled, very nicely put together. She loved being with him, loved the way he made her feel, as if she were unique in every way, exciting in her slightest movement. So cherished, and so thoroughly explored, tempest and tenderness in one exciting touch. She had been falling in love with him the night she'd met him. She'd eaten her heart out when she'd lost him. And she'd tried to tell herself that she was an idiot, wanting him through time and distance. But she had fallen in love with him, and time and distance be damned; what she felt now was pure wonderment. He was beautiful to her, from his tousled black hair to his taut buttocks, relaxed penis, muscled legs.

He turned, and she closed her eyes, not wanting to be caught observing him.

He kissed her forehead, left her side, dressed.

Tangled in myriad emotions, unwilling to let them all show, she allowed him to go. Then she opened her eyes to the weak shafts of sunlight filtering in.

She sat up, absently rubbing her arm. He must have really knicked himself shaving, there was dried blood on her arm. Seeing his robe thrown at the foot of the bed, she reached for it, stroking her hand fondly over the shoulder and collar of the maroon garment. It was slightly damp, slightly stiff.

She frowned. Peered at it more closely. And felt her stomach turn.

Blood.

Not just a spot or two.

The front of his robe seemed to be covered with it.

CHAPTER FIFTEEN

HAD HE HIT a damned artery, for God's sake?

Despite herself, she shivered, and she forced herself to reconsider every dumb horror movie ever made.

The women always tended to be such fools. Believing in men. Falling for vampires. Monsters. Seeing what they wanted to see, trusting...

She cared about him, had been in love with him, was falling all over again, or had never fallen out of love with him. She believed in him. If you loved someone, it wasn't foolish to have faith in him. She did know him. He was an honest man who knew right from wrong.

But his wife had died mysteriously. Here.

And last night, he'd been covered in blood.

Stop, she told herself. Brett had been slightly bloodied, as well. And to the best of her knowledge, they'd both left only their own blood, so what difference did it make? No one else was running around wounded or lying around dead. After Dianne's drama in the crypt, there'd been no screams in the night, no cries of foul play.

Sabrina didn't even know what she was worrying about.

She lay still, tired, closing her eyes again. Then a pounding on her door jolted her out of her daze, and she flew up into a sitting position.

"What?" she cried out.

"Hey!" It was Brett, calling to her. "It's me. Are you decent? I know you're alone—the king of the old castle is downstairs sipping coffee." He paused. "I'm glad you were so concerned about me earlier," he added plaintively. "Hey, Sabrina, come on out. Speak to me. Tell me you're alive and well. I'm alive and well, no complications from the bump on my head or even that little cut on my finger. It's nearly noon, Sabrina, and we're supposed to be in the great hall for a tell-all. Aren't you coming?"

She leaped out of bed. "Brett, I need to shower and dress. I'll be right out." She sped to the bathroom.

She wouldn't miss this tell-all for anything in the world.

In ten minutes she had showered and was ready. Brett had waited for her; he was leaning against the hallway wall, sipping a cup of coffee, when she came out of her room.

"Well, it's about time," he complained.

"I was very fast."

"I was about to desert you, since my coffee cup is nearly empty. I need more caffeine. Hell of a night. Frankly, you look bushed. I'm jealous as hell."

"Right, because you spend so many lonely nights yourself?" she queried skeptically.

He grimaced. "All right, not so many. But I'm seeking consolation for the fact that I lost you."

She shook her head. "Did you get any sleep? And how is the bump on your head, really?"

"Just a little sore. And yes, I got some sleep. Did you? Oh, never mind. Silly question."

"Brett…"

"Sorry."

"How's the finger?"

"Oh, a little tender, that's all. Want to kiss it and make it better?"

She sighed.

He grinned. "Sorry, I guess I can't help myself. Truce? I really do want to be friends. Of course, if you change your mind and want more—" he leaned closer to her "—or if you're ever afraid that your rich, lordly lover is planning on tossing you off a balcony—"

"Brett!"

"—feel free to call on me."

"Brett, I thought Jon was your friend."

"He is. But all's fair in love and war and mystery."

They had reached the bottom of the stairs and stood at the main entry. Through the long, narrow windows Sabrina could see that the snow was piled high and the day was gray, with a hint that the storm could start up again at any time. It was actually rather beautiful, in a bleak sort of way.

Kerosene lanterns continued to burn from their wall fixtures, but with a little struggling sunlight seeping in as well, the castle seemed much brighter.

"Coffee, dear, is that way," Brett said, propelling her toward the great hall.

Jon was seated at the head of the table, coffee in hand, deep in conversation with Joe and Thayer. Jennie Albright, as calm and competent as ever, was busy setting the Sterno aflame under the chafing dishes. On one side of the table Dianne and Anna Lee were discussing the pros and cons of body piercing, while on the other Joshua, Camy and Reggie were lamenting the lack of artistic talent demonstrated in a new museum of the macabre in London.

"I still insist that there is no such thing as a female serial killer," Thayer was saying as Brett poured himself more coffee and joined Jon's grouping.

"Well, what does one call a woman like Countess Báthory?" Joe asked. "She killed dozens of young women, hundreds, perhaps."

"And there's that prostitute who began offing johns in Florida," Jon reminded Thayer.

"Okay, she may come close to the profile of a true serial killer," Thayer said. "The point is, the typical serial killer is a sexual killer. Predatory—and male. Seeking sexual fulfillment through violence."

"It's true that most of the sociopaths the criminologists and behavioral scientists and FBI profilers have studied have been men," Jon said, "but—"

"But I would certainly call that wicked old Countess Báthory a serial killer," Anna Lee said, sliding into the argument. "She killed all those poor girls for their blood so that she could be more beautiful so that she could have more sex."

"Actually," Reggie interjected, "I read that Countess Báthory played with her victims before she killed them, as well. If that wasn't sexual…"

"In a different way," Thayer insisted, but he seemed a little quieter, as he'd been thrown a new twist to an old argument. He had been a hands-on cop, not a scholar, but he still knew plenty.

Joe jumped to his defense. "Male killers of the kind Thayer's discussing can only get off on feelings of control, domination and power. Countess Báthory lived hundreds of years ago, so it's unlikely we'll get any real insights into her murderous activities. In part, she probably simply believed she was above everyone else and had a right to kill peasant girls for her own sport."

"One way or the other, she was definitely a monster," Dianne agreed with a shiver.

"Careful," Brett warned, "V.J. will be down Joshua's throat for fashioning her into the beautiful Blood Countess if she hears us bashing the lady with too great a fervor."

"Where is V.J.?" Sabrina asked.

"Not down yet," Jon said.

"The point is, the historical Countess Báthory isn't the same as the serial killers we track today," Joe continued.

"Not the same as a Bundy, a Dahmer, a Gacy and so on," Thayer assured them. "Trust me, please, on this one. I know."

"The cop speaks," Anna Lee murmured.

"From what I understand," Jon interjected, coming politely to Thayer's defense, "our ex-cop is basically right. Psychologists are always arguing heredity and environment in the creation of killers, but there does seem to be a relationship between testosterone and violently aggressive behavior. Damaged males who feel they've been degraded, violated, put down, et cetera, tend to become violent, while studies show that women turn the loathing against themselves and are more likely to commit suicide or become victims themselves when their self-esteem is low."

"But women do kill," Anna Lee said.

"True, some do," Joe said lightly, looking right at her.

"So, Thayer, why do females kill, then?" Dianne demanded.

Thayer looked at her soberly. "Passion."

"Passion!" Dianne protested. "Always?"

"I'd say they kill out of fear more often than not," Sabrina suggested. She'd poured herself coffee but hadn't joined the others at the table. Leaning against the buffet, she looked at them all as they turned to stare at her.

She shrugged, looked at Brett, and then at Jon. He was watching her curiously. "Say that someone's driving a woman mad, and the opportunity comes by for her to do something about it. A crowded subway…a little shove. Or busy street and a car speeding along…only seconds to think! Do I push gently, just give a little shove…?"

The room was silent as they all stared at her.

Except for Thayer, who hadn't heard any deeper implications.

"Sure," Thayer agreed. "Some murders are so simple, it's pathetic. A husband freaks out because his wife has made leftovers three nights in a row. He yells, she snarls—boom. Blown away—assuming he has a weapon handy. Women—the husband is abusive night after night, day after day. Breaks her arms or blackens her eyes, digs, digs. She's no good, she does nothing right. He screams about the lamb at dinner, tells her the mint sauce sucks and isn't fit for swine. He drinks like a fish, comes in every night at two in the morning smelling of stale booze and rotten cigars and wants sex. She can't feel, can't think anymore. She's just scared all the time. Finally, one day, megabelly sticking out from under his ugly, stained T-shirt, he sits feet-up on the recliner, belching for another beer while he watches a football game at a million decibels—she freaks out. She doesn't bring him another beer—she comes in, shotgun blasting."

"He's gross and disgusting," Dianne said, smiling. "Is the woman charged with murder, acquitted for self-defense or given a medal for ridding humanity of a danger to the human race?"

Light laughter filled the room. It was a pleasant sound.

Despite the serious subject matter, they finally sounded like a group of mystery writers having fun discussing their interests, as it should be at a retreat.

The retreat Jon had intended, with a finale that benefited children, Sabrina thought. She suddenly felt a deep sadness that something had so altered the proceedings.

And yet...sad or not, there still seemed to be an underlying touch of evil here.

Who was telling the truth? And who was masking something beneath the surface?

Thayer was too involved in the discussion to notice anything evil, said or unsaid, at the moment. He grinned, responding to Dianne. "Naturally, you know that there's always a motive to murder."

"Even if murder is casual?" Anna Lee asked. "Like someone pushing a stranger standing on a subway platform onto the tracks?"

Thayer nodded. "There's insanity—that's a motive in itself. The guys who hear voices. The paranoid who believes people are after him. There's always a motive." Thayer shrugged. "We've always had monsters. It just seems we have worse ones today—bastards who get a kick out of pain and can only feel pleasure and release through torture and killing. It's great that forensic science is coming so far. One tiny fiber, one microscopic drop of blood or skin cell, DNA matching—it's terrific."

"Of course, you still have to have a suspect," Joe reminded him.

"Sure—hey, it's terrifying to realize how many crimes go unsolved!"

"Well, thank God people do love a good crime solved, or we'd all be out of business," Anna Lee said. She smiled suddenly, glancing around at the group. "Speaking of which, aren't we all supposed to be admitting our own most horrible sins today—and discovering what trickster is sending people to the wrong places?"

"Susan will make mincemeat of us all, no matter what," Joe said unhappily.

Anna Lee shrugged. "We'll simply tell her that if she dares print a mean word, we'll do an Agatha Christie on her—we'll every one of us kill her with a rope, knife, gun, poison, garrote, et cetera, if she doesn't mind her manners."

"Speaking of Susan, where is she?" Jon asked.

"Haven't seen her," Joe told him.

"Nor have I." Dianne shrugged.

"She's really, really mad at all of us," Thayer said with a grimace.

"Has anyone seen her?" Jon asked, looking around the table.

"Not since last night," Anna Lee said.

"Come to think of it," Thayer said, "I haven't seen V.J. or Tom, either. Tom was standing guard for Susan while she bathed last night, remember?"

"Maybe they're all still sleeping?" Dianne suggested.

"Well, Tom and V.J., maybe. But Susan?" Brett said skeptically. "I mean, Tom and V.J.—"

"We're supposed to confess our own sins, not go around casting accusations at others, young man," Reggie declared, chastising him sternly.

"Sorry, I just meant that—"

"Meant what?" a new voice demanded.

Tom Heart, freshly showered, dressed in perfectly pressed gray wool trousers and a matching sweater, walked into the room. He helped himself to coffee, then realized that everyone was looking at him.

He lifted his coffee cup. "What's up?"

"We were getting worried," Jon said.

"Why?" Tom asked innocently.

"Because it's getting late, and we didn't see you," Anna Lee said. "Or V.J."

"Victoria—V.J. said she'd be right down. She was finishing dressing when I…tapped on her door. And here I am. So why the long faces?" Tom asked.

"Tom, no one has seen Susan," Jon said.

"And you're all depressed about that?" he inquired incredulously.

"We're worried about her," Jon said.

"Well, she was fine last night," he muttered. "She came out of the shower yelling that I was supposed to have been standing guard in the hallway instead of in her room."

"Sounds like Susan," Dianne murmured.

"Well, then what?" Jon asked.

Tom looked uneasy. He shrugged. "V.J. was in the room—she had happened by, and we were talking. Susan was totally obnoxious. She called us a couple of perverts and said that we were sick and after her."

"Oh, this is getting good already," Anna Lee purred. "What did you do?"

"I told her to go fuck herself, and V.J. and I walked out and—" He broke off.

"And what?" Dianne pressed.

"And—and we went our separate ways," Tom said firmly.

But he was lying. Sabrina was convinced that he was lying.

"Wow, Tom! What happened to your hand?" Anna Lee asked suddenly, rising and walking over to him.

"My hand?" Tom said, and then he glanced at his palm and saw the long cut, suddenly oozing new blood, to which Anna Lee was referring. "Oh...that. Looks much worse than it is."

"Paper cut?" Reggie drawled skeptically.

Tom gazed at her, shaking his head with a rueful smile. "I broke one of those old kerosene lamps of yours, Jon. Sorry, I'm sure they're real antiques."

Jon waved a hand dismissively. "I have more lamps. But that does look like a nasty gash."

"Tom, where did you say V.J. was?" Sabrina demanded.

"She didn't answer her door last night," Brett said.

"What the hell were *you* doing knocking at her door?" Tom demanded angrily.

"Trying to find someone adventurous—and hungry—with whom to roam down to the great hall," Brett said indignantly.

"Is that all?" Anna Lee asked teasingly. Then she smiled at the group. "After all, we're on to a new game here, right? Kind of like kiss and tell. We confess our sins, and we figure out who killed Cassie—if she was killed, of course, since the official ruling was accidental death."

"I don't have anything to confess regarding V.J.," Brett said with an edge of anger.

"Not concerning V.J., maybe," Anna Lee said sweetly.

Joe leaned back. "Now wait, if we're looking for motive, V.J. hated Cassie. They never got along. Cassie was mean and crude to her, and V.J. never hesitated to say what was on her mind, either."

"V.J. didn't kill Cassie!" Tom scoffed.

"Ah, Tom, dear," Anna Lee said. "*You* might have

wanted to kill dear Cassandra. She wrote ugly things about you, implying you were having affairs all over the place. Let's see, you are separated now, but not divorced yet. Cassie could have cost you a big—capital *B-I-G*— settlement, right?" she queried.

"Anna Lee, we're confessing things regarding ourselves, remember?" Jon said firmly.

Tom lifted a hand to Jon. "It's all right, it doesn't matter. I didn't kill Cassie. I know the law, and my obligations, and I don't hate my almost ex-wife, nor do I begrudge her half the income I made, because we both took a chance on my writing. I already give Lavinia all but blood, yet I give it with an open heart."

"Oh, is that the perfect man, or what?" Anna Lee said. "I still say you had motive."

"Since motive can be almost anything, I think we've all got something that could qualify as motive," Jon said dryly.

"Not me," Dianne said softly.

"No?" Anna Lee queried. "Oh, Dianne, darling, no, I'm afraid you're not out of this at all. Let's see, Cassie was your mother, but she spurned you. She wouldn't acknowledge you to the world, you were a problem, a bother, someone who made her *old*. Perhaps you freaked out yourself, and she happened to be at the balcony and—"

"What a wretched pile of bull!" Dianne cried angrily. She circled the table, hands on her hips, glaring furiously at Anna Lee. "For you to say such an awful thing, when all you ever wanted was to cause trouble. You have the morals of an alley cat. You couldn't have Jon, so went for my mother. And God knows who else. You like to cause chaos wherever you go. You're desperate for attention, so you have to be outrageous. You have to intrigue the public with your exploits because you can't write your way out of a paper bag!"

"Ouch," Anna Lee murmured. "How did I ever miss the fact that you were Cassie's daughter?" She didn't, however, seem particularly concerned. "Well, now we all know where I was sleeping, but there's more to the story, boys and girls. Shouldn't we all fess up?" She swung around and stared at Joe. "Have you anything to say?" she asked him.

He lifted his hands, shrugged sheepishly. "I—I was caught between them," he said unhappily.

Jon rose slowly and leaned against the mantel. The sound of a pin dropping would have been like thunder, everyone had gone so silent. Yet Jon seemed calm, as if he weren't learning anything new at all.

Joe cleared his throat. "I was really mad at Cassie," he explained. "Yet no matter how mad I was at her—and I lost a chance at an important anthology because of her—I was still fascinated by her. She was married to Jon, so I kept my distance. But Anna Lee was having a good time knowing that I had my own little fantasy love-hate relationship going with Cassie. Anna Lee must have been in a rustic mood at the time, for she decided to forgo her caviar tastes and seduce me. And then…"

"And then what?" Jon asked, looking at Anna Lee.

Anna Lee shrugged, then a strange flash of pain went through her eyes. "Jon, you wouldn't see the truth. You wouldn't divorce her. I was only trying to show you what kind of a woman she was."

He crossed his arms over his chest. "You were trying to show me what kind of a woman my wife was?"

Anna Lee ran her fingers through her beautiful hair.

"You wouldn't listen when I told you she was well enough to be sleeping around."

"Anna Lee, I knew Cassie, and I knew what she was doing, and I was at the end of the line with her, but in my saner moments, I knew she was running as fast as she could because she was trying to outrun cancer. I didn't always care what she was doing, except when she tried to hurt other people—something it seems she had a lot of help doing." He spun on Joe suddenly. "So finish your story."

Joe was so red he was almost purple.

"I—I—only once—we—I—"

"Oh, Joe, spit it out!" Anna Lee demanded, amused. "We had a ménage à trois!"

Joe put his head down. "I'm so sorry, Jon. I was so… It's just that…" He looked up at Jon. "You're a wealthy, respected, powerful, good-looking man. I've always looked like a bear with a hangover. They were suddenly both teasing me, and wanting me…and then," he added softly, staring accusingly at Anna Lee, "and then laughing at me."

Anna Lee shrugged, evidently not terribly penitent about her sexual exploits. "We were all adults, Joe. And we weren't laughing at you. You must have just felt that way."

"Inadequate?" Dianne queried softly. "Put-upon? Maybe even used?"

"Oh, no," Joe protested, "I'm not taking that kind of a rap! No, I didn't feel abused, no, I never felt murderous because women had humiliated me, or anything of the kind!" He stared at Anna Lee. "Besides I couldn't have been that bad in bed. Anna Lee comes back now and then when she's in the mood."

Brett was suddenly standing, hands on his hips, staring at them both. "I don't believe either of you!" he cried out. "Cassie wasn't like that!"

Jon stood behind him, setting a hand on his shoulder. "Brett, she was."

"No. You're both making this up, and why, I sure as hell don't know! What, for a great story? Something to make you both look so sick and miserable that you couldn't possibly be guilty? You're making this up, I swear. I knew Cassie—"

"Brett!" Jon said more firmly. "You didn't know Cassie. You just thought you did. You knew what she wanted you to know, you thought what she wanted you to think. You fell into her trap, you cared too deeply."

"No!" Brett said. Suddenly he sank back into his chair, his fingers against his temples. "No, I..." Then he looked up again. At Jon, then over at Sabrina, in a way that made her heart seem to bleed. He looked at Jon again. "I was so jealous of you. I had been married to Sabrina. And she never admitted to even knowing you, let alone sleeping with you. And yet whenever your name came up, she would look a little sad...and I just *knew* that you two had had an affair and that—and that no matter what a good, loyal wife she was determined to be, I was being compared to you. And I came up short. And right after the divorce, I couldn't believe that my own behavior had caused her to leave, and so...so I wanted to get even with you. I blamed you for my divorce—it was as if you had seduced my wife. So... I set out to seduce Cassie. And she cared about me in her way. I know she did, because, because..."

"Brett," Jon said with a soft sigh, "you cared about her because it was easy to care about Cassie. Even after she stopped being alluring to me, I cared about her. She was in pain, she was desperately running. She wanted so badly to be beautiful and young forever. She needed to be loved, she was afraid to be alone and afraid to die. She was a smart woman, well educated, her insights were often good, and she could be charming and at times even gentle and caring."

He hesitated, looking at Dianne. "She did know what she had done to her own daughter, and she donated huge sums to societies for orphans and sick children. She wasn't a horrible person. I did know her—I knew what she was doing. It just didn't matter. That I had married her to begin with was what was really wrong. We'd known each other for years. She'd gotten me my first agent, shown me a lot of the ropes. She was a beautiful woman, and we had lots of fun. We were on again, off again. Then she got sick. And she didn't want to be alone. And we decided to give it a try. Marriage between us was probably doomed from the start. But she was a friend. And I did care about her."

Jon paused, then lifted his hands suddenly, a wry smile curling his lips. "Okay, so who here *didn't* sleep with my wife?"

"Well, dear boy, I most certainly didn't!" Reggie exclaimed indignantly.

Jon smiled. "Should we have a show of hands? The yeas and the nays?"

"I'm a nay," Tom asserted.

"Me, too," Camy declared.

"Nope," Thayer said.

"Not me, either." Joshua, silent up until now, leaned forward in his chair.

"I wasn't here," Sabrina murmured.

"Well, we're missing Susan and V.J., so we'll have to ask them later," Jon murmured dryly.

"Do you think we've all bled enough today?" Anna Lee asked abruptly. Her voice was so changed that Sabrina stared at her, wondering if her casual bluntness regarding her sexual exploits wasn't partially show. Was she bothered by the things she had done?

Motives could be so strange. Brett had set out to hurt Jon, because Jon had inadvertently hurt him. Anna Lee had loved Jon, so she had seduced Jon's wife. Joe had fallen in love with Cassie and been swept into Anna Lee's intrigue. And as to the others...

Cassandra had held things over all their heads. Evidently she'd liked to threaten people. She'd believed she could ruin Tom Heart, destroying his career and his marriage. She'd fought openly with V.J. What about Thayer, Reggie, Joshua and Camy? And would Dianne have been so hurt by what her mother had done that she might have committed murder?

"Jon?" Anna Lee continued, pressing the issue.

He lifted his hands. "We're no closer to any answers, are we?" he said softly.

"Not true," Brett said. "We know who was—and wasn't— sleeping with Cassie."

Jon smiled ruefully. "That doesn't tell us who killed her."

"If she *was* killed," Anna Lee said. She leaned forward. "Jon, maybe we should just leave it be."

"But what about all these crazy, misleading game instructions going out to people? Who's the one playing tricks to scare us?"

"Dianne!" Anna Lee announced.

"Once!" Dianne cried. "Only once, when I wrote the notes for you to come to the crypt."

"So what about Susan's note?" Jon demanded.

"Dianne, if you did it, please, for the love of God—" Anna Lee began.

"I didn't write Susan's note!" Dianne said irritably. "I'm not going to confess here to what I didn't do."

"Susan is simply crazy," Brett said irritably. "Let's go by process of elimination. I wasn't here, so I'm innocent. Sabrina wasn't here. She wasn't even here when the tragedy happened. Joshua wasn't here, Jon wasn't here—"

"Any one of us could have written a note before leaving," Jon said firmly.

"But if we weren't here, how could we have tormented Susan in the chamber of horrors?" Brett asked.

"Accomplice!" Thayer said softly.

"If Susan was really tormented at all," Tom said. "She's such a dramatist, and she thrives on attention."

"Please, Jon," Anna Lee said, "I've a pounding headache. Could I go back to sleep for a while?"

Jon lifted his hands. "Of course," he murmured. He looked around the room. "We'll meet for supper-cocktails in the library. We can keep playing the game, but the case we solve may be about ourselves."

"But, Jon, what if there's nothing *to* solve?" Camy asked. "What if Cassie's death was just a tragic accident?"

"Well, if that's what we discover—and hopefully it will be so—we'll still have solved the case," he said.

"Well! If we've gotten past the mudslinging and the fess up, I'm for cards in the library," Reggie said hopefully.

"Bridge?" Tom asked.

"Poker, dear boy! Poker!" Reggie said.

Joe laughed. "I'm in."

"Me, too," Thayer agreed.

They all rose. Anna Lee left the room quickly, ignoring the rest of them. Reggie, Joe and Thayer started toward the library. Sabrina began heading toward Jon, but she saw that Camy was talking with him, apparently upset. Brett hovered near, as if he, too, were anxious to get in a word with their host.

Sabrina started to leave the room. Tom Heart blocked her way, his injured hand wrapped in a napkin. "Cards?" he said.

She shook her head, suddenly uneasy. "No, Tom, thanks. I didn't get much sleep. I'm going up for a nap. Maybe I'll join in if you're still playing later."

"Sure."

She slipped by him. Anna Lee had already disappeared up the stairs. Sabrina headed quickly up behind her, started for her own room and then paused.

She walked across the hall to V.J.'s door.

"V.J.?" she queried softly. No response. She tapped lightly on the door. "V.J.?"

Still there was no answer, and she knocked harder. "Damn it, V.J., you're making me nervous here!"

There was still no response, so she hesitantly set her hand on the doorknob and twisted.

The knob turned. V.J.'s door wasn't locked.

Sabrina inched the door open. "V.J.?"

Nothing.

She pushed the door fully open and stepped into her friend's room.

And saw V.J.

She was stretched out on her bed, dressed in a simple, elegant dress. No frills or lace for V.J. Her head was upon her pillow; her hands were folded upon her chest. She was laid out as neatly as a corpse in a coffin for a viewing. A thin red line encircled her neck.

"V.J.!" Sabrina shrieked, and flew across the room to her friend.

CHAPTER SIXTEEN

JON BEGAN TO wonder just what kind of can of worms he had opened.

"I don't understand any of this, Jon, and if I had managed things better—" Camy began.

"Camy, anyone could have written notes—"

Joshua had come up behind her, his aesthetic eyes dark and disturbed. "Camy, I'm supposed to be helping you keep an eye on things—"

"Joshua, you're an artist and a friend. I'm the one who works for Jon."

"Camy, Josh, you've both done great work for me. There's nothing more you could have done. Please—"

"Jon, we need to talk, really talk," Brett said, barging past the two.

Jon lifted his hands, palms up. "Camy, you didn't do anything wrong. Quit worrying. The game was great, clever, you and Joshua were doing wonderfully, but with the storm, the darkness and everything going on, maybe we just can't play it anymore."

"Jon, I need to speak with you," Brett insisted.

Jon turned to McGraff. "Brett, I'm not angry. Honest. I understand what you did, and why. It's all right."

"Damn it, Jon, it's not all right. Friends don't screw friends."

"Well, Brett, literally, it wasn't me you screwed."

"Oh, God, Jon."

"Sorry, Brett. Couldn't resist that. But I'm dead serious—it just didn't matter anymore."

"Jon, she was still your wife."

"Brett, it's over. I don't feel anything—no anger, no pain, nothing. Try to understand that there was just too much pain going on at the time with everyone. And try to see that it's all right because I've said it's all right. And I need to get by you and get outside."

"Outside?" Camy protested. "But the cold and the snow—"

"Won't hurt me now," Jon interrupted. "It will feel great. Excuse me," he said. Then he hesitated, turning back to Brett. "How's the head?"

"The head?"

"Your injury."

"Oh!" He felt his temple and shrugged. "Just a little sore, I guess. It's all right."

"Good."

Jon started toward the door, eager to feel the cold, clear air outside. The sun wasn't exactly pouring through the clouds yet, but at least the light outside was natural and the air would be fresh.

He didn't make it to the door. Joe stopped him. "Jesus, Jon, you've been a good friend, and I'm sorry, honest to God. It was only once, you know, and there wasn't really even any…you know, not with me and Cassie. But what I did was wrong, I admit it, and I'm sorry. You've been a stand-up kind of friend, and I was a fool."

"Joe, I need you to try and understand this. I knew what Cass was doing. I didn't always know with whom, but I didn't care anymore. She used people because she hated these Mystery Weeks of mine—she was even trying to get me to leave when she died. So quit worrying. But if it makes you feel any better, if I ever marry again and you so much as look at my wife, I promise to beat you to a pulp."

Joe half smiled.

"Joe, honest. It was over between the two of us, okay?"

With his grizzled face and sad eyes, Joe looked at him steadily. "No, I don't guess it can ever really be okay, because I don't know if I can forgive myself."

"Joe, for the love of God, *I* forgive you. You have to forgive yourself. It didn't matter then, it doesn't matter now. Unless, of course, you pushed Cassie off the balcony?"

Joe's eyes widened. "No, Jon, I swear, I never went near Cassie that day. I wouldn't have hurt her. I never would have hurt her…"

"Yeah, well then, let me by, will you?"

Joe stepped aside. Jon could hear some of the others gathering in the library across the way and he hurried toward the castle doors. He paused at the coat-tree for his jacket, patting the pocket and finding a pair of gloves.

Snow had piled up, so he had to slam his shoulder against the door to open it.

He stepped out quickly. It was damned cold. But the cold embraced him, the air was fresh and the castle grounds were encased in a crystal glaze that was as beautiful as it was deadly.

He walked along the snow-covered gravel path, sinking at least a foot with each step. Walking out toward the stables, he saw old Angus MacDougall with a shovel.

"Mornin', sir!" the groom called out.

"Mornin', Angus. Are you and the horses doing all right in this?"

"Aye, sir, that we are! I've got the stables warm as toast, burning wood in the stove. In fact, if you get too cold in that lofty castle, sir, you come on over and join me. Ah, me boys will surely be along within the next few days, and we'll have the place shoveled up fer ye, Mr. Stuart."

"Sure, Angus. Got another shovel? I'll set to the pathways with you now myself."

Within minutes he was shoveling snow, and it felt good. Good to move his shoulders, to use his arms, to feel the movement of his muscles.

SABRINA HAD NEARLY reached the bed when she heard the voice, deep, husky, menacing.

"What the hell do you think you're doing?"

She came to a stop and spun around.

At first she couldn't see who had come into the room. Mere slivers of light penetrated the narrow windows, and for a second she couldn't place the voice. Then she realized who it was, and she remained frozen in place, her heart thundering.

"What am I doing?" she retorted with a show of fury, her heart pounding a million miles an hour. V.J. lay on the bed. He stood in the doorway, blocking it.

There was no way out.

"What are *you* doing?" she demanded. "V.J. is… V.J. is…"

He started moving toward her.

STRANGE MORNING, JON THOUGHT as he worked. The simple manual labor of shoveling—so often nothing more than a royal pain in the butt—felt really good. He could think and shovel mechanically. And expending his tension was good—it just might keep him from sending a fist, or his head, into a wall. He had suspected many things. Now he knew them for facts. And actually, he hadn't been lying; none of it really mattered. It was strange to think back. He'd been so young when he'd first met Cassie. Oh, he'd had his share of relationships, had his heart broken a few times and broken a few hearts in turn. Then he'd met Cassie. She'd known the ropes about life, about publishing. She'd been fun, wild, and when she'd been busy, he'd seen other people.

He'd met Sabrina.

He'd known that love at first sight was unlikely, that emotions needed to be explored, but he'd loved every little thing about her. Her naïveté, her charm, her strange wisdom. He'd loved touching her. And he'd thought that he'd been equally good for her. But she'd left, and no matter what he'd tried, she'd refused to see him.

That's when Cassie had come to him, with cancer, and she'd been so afraid, hadn't wanted to be alone. He'd been wrong to marry her, because he hadn't really loved her that way, and maybe her knowing that had caused her outrageous behavior. They had just kept hurting one another, and it was damned sad, because he had meant to be strong for her, meant to be, if not the husband and lover she had hoped for, the friend she really needed. But the games had become too much.

"Hey! Got more shovels?"

Jon looked up. Thayer was outside, flexing his arms.

"Sure. Angus, we've got more shovels, right?"

Angus nodded happily.

Thayer started shoveling; a few minutes later, Joe joined them, as well.

Then Brett appeared. He watched for a while, then he started shoveling, too.

Pathways quickly came into being. Then Reggie appeared. "So there's where you boys go when you can't ante up!" she called from the castle steps.

Brett saluted her. "Come on out and shovel, Reggie."

"Don't you dare!" Jon warned her firmly.

Dianne stepped out behind her, followed by Camy.

"Maybe Reggie's a bit—" Joe began.

"Don't you say it!" Reggie warned.

"I wasn't going to say old—I was simply going to say mature!" Joe protested.

"The hell you were!" Reggie chastised.

"Dianne's young and strapping. Come on out here and work, woman!" Joe challenged her.

She was dressed for it—in black pants, black boots, heavy black sweater. She walked out into the snow, heading toward Joe, who was ready to hand her his shovel. But as she reached him, she smiled, bent down to pick up a handful of the white fluffy stuff, and pelted him right in the face.

"Hey, man, she got you!" Brett called out.

Joe wasn't about to take it lying down. He squatted, whipping up huge snowballs to cream first Dianne and then Brett.

Jon started to laugh. He was hit in the shoulder. Dianne had turned her attack on him. He started to throw a snowball back at her and felt a thud on the back. Spinning around, he saw that Camy was slinging snow, as well. The white stuff began soaring everywhere. In minutes the group had grown. Anna Lee—so desperate to run up and take a nap—was back. Joshua had joined in.

And it was, in fact, hard to tell who was who anymore, they were all so covered in snow.

Even old Angus got in on it. He had a mean curve and was dishing out more than he was getting.

In the midst of the fight, Jon began to look around. Where was Sabrina?

Almost everyone seemed to be there.

Except Susan, V.J., Tom and Sabrina.

Susan, V.J., Tom.

And now Sabrina.

Jon began to dust himself off, running toward the house.

"V.J. IS SLEEPING," Tom stated with annoyance.

"Sleeping!" Sabrina exclaimed.

"Yes. She's tired. Why are you trying to wake her up?"

Sabrina looked from Tom to V.J.—the way her friend slept, like a corpse laid out in a coffin, hands folded over her chest. She started toward the bed again, not trusting Tom's words.

If V.J. was dead, Tom had killed her. And now she was alone with Tom. And there was no way out…

"Why do you want to wake her up?" Tom demanded again, irritated.

"The red…on her neck…" Sabrina heard herself say. Stupid! She should have turned, walked away, gotten help. Let Tom think that she believed V.J. was sleeping.

"The red on her neck?" Tom said.

He frowned, striding into the room. Sabrina shrank back from him, going to the opposite side of the bed to keep something bulky between them. Yet when she looked down, she realized that V.J. was merely wearing a cameo at her throat, on a red satin ribbon that nicely accented the color of her navy-and-red dress.

Her chest was rising and falling.

Her eyes suddenly opened. She saw Sabrina on one side of her, and Tom on the other. She jerked upright. "Good God, what is going on here? Does a woman have to suffer an audience when she wants to take a nap?"

"I don't know what Sabrina was doing!" Tom exclaimed, throwing up his hands. "She came in here to wake you up!"

V.J. frowned, looking at Sabrina. Sabrina shrugged with a rueful smile. "I was worried about you."

V.J. stared at her blankly, then smiled. "Oh, I guess I missed the confessions. I'm sorry. I was dressed, I was ready… I just stretched out to catch a few winks, and I guess I went out like a light."

"Sabrina!"

Sabrina jumped, startled to hear her name bellowed with such ferocity from down below.

"Sabrina!" Again, closer.

She turned from V.J. and hurried to the door just in time to see Jon throwing open the door to her room. She stepped into the hallway.

"Jon!"

He spun around. She saw the naked concern in his marbled eyes as he stared at her down the length of the hallway. She was suddenly ecstatic. V.J. was alive, Jon was in love with her and all of their fears were unfounded.

"Jesus, I was worried!" he said, walking down the hallway to her, a smile on his lips.

She smiled, too, because he was ready to embrace her. But he was covered in snow.

"You're all wet!" she exclaimed.

He nodded—and took her determinedly into his arms. "We were having a snowball fight, and I realized you were missing. And V.J. was missing. And Tom."

"I seem to be missing everything," V.J. said dryly, stepping into the hallway.

"She was sleeping. Sabrina barged right in, acting as if she were certain I had throttled V.J.," Tom said, shaking his head. He slipped his arms around V.J.'s middle, and his voice became husky as he spoke. "Don't you know? I could never hurt V.J. I'm in love with her."

Sabrina was silent. V.J.'s husband had passed away, but wasn't Tom still a married man?

As if reading her mind, Tom said, "My wife and I are separated, amicably. And when the divorce is final, V.J. and I are going to be married, and we're going to spend the rest of our lives, however long that may be, together."

Sabrina found herself smiling, stepping away from Jon to place a kiss on Tom's cheek. "Good for you." She gave V.J. a big hug.

V.J. was blushing slightly. "I guess I dozed off again this morning because I'm not as young as I used to be. And last night Tom and I were up for hours and hours, talking and…well, you know, talking and—"

"Oh, my God, the old folks were shagging away!" someone announced from the other end of the hall. Brett, hands behind his back, was walking toward them.

"Brett…" Tom began angrily.

"No, no, dear, I'll take this one," V.J. said gaily. "Brett McGraff, don't you dare call us old folks. *Reggie* is old. We're merely on the downside of middle age," she huffed. "And just what are you doing here anyway?" she asked.

"We had this perfectly good snowball fight going, and all of a sudden I see Jon here realize that he's been away from Sabrina for more than ten minutes. I figured she was snug and warm in the castle, so…"

"So?" Jon demanded, hands on his hips, a brow raised, a slight curl to his lips as he took a step toward Brett.

Brett grinned like a cat. He drew one hand from behind his back and threw a snowball at Sabrina.

Perfect aim.

It caught her on the chin, and snowflakes danced around her.

"Jon!" V.J. said. "Are you going to let him do that to her?"

"Certainly not," Jon said.

"Oh, I can take care of myself on this one," Sabrina announced, already heading toward Brett.

Brett turned to run. As he did so, he said, "We missed you, too, V.J.!" And he caught V.J. with the snowball he had carried in his other hand.

They all tore after him.

Brett was fleet, and he made it out of the house. But once there, he was in trouble. The others, who had still been pummeling one another, saw the attack on Brett and joined in. Within seconds he was unable to return fire. He was laughing, down on his back. V.J., her dress sodden, knelt on one side with Sabrina on the other, all but burying him in snow.

Laughing, Sabrina realized that Jon was standing back a little, amused by the whole thing.

"Jon!" Brett whispered to the two women. "I'm mush already. Get Jon!"

And so they did. It was fun to see his expression change as they turned their focus on him.

He sprinted a good distance away and kept up a steady barrage of return fire for an admirable amount of time.

Old Angus was the one who finally helped them get him. "Back him against the stables yonder, bur-ry the boy!" he suggested.

So Jon, too, wound up flat in the snow, Sabrina straddling him. He was laughing so hard he couldn't ward off her snow assault—but then he suddenly shifted, rolling, and Sabrina was the one on her back in the snow, pelted by handfuls of the soft, light, fluffy stuff.

"Cry uncle!" he warned her.

"Never!"

More snow. "Cry uncle!"

"Not on your life!"

She was nearly buried alive. "Come on now, give in, cry uncle!"

"Never, never, never—uncle, uncle, uncle! You will get yours!" she told him.

He smiled and answered softly, "I'm counting on it."

He stood, drawing her to her feet. The entire crowd was completely soaked, except for Reggie, who had apparently been issuing battle instructions from the castle steps. Laughing, they stamped their feet and shook themselves off.

"That was great fun. Maybe we should all be snowbound more often!" Dianne said.

Smiling, friendly, natural, she looked her age—just barely an adult, young and fresh and enthusiastic. Sabrina found herself thinking that Dianne might be capable of a few macabre pranks, but never murder.

But then, everyone in the group was laughing, having fun, with a strange innocence.

Yet even as she considered how innocent they all seemed, she noticed that there was blood in the snow by her feet.

"Someone is bleeding," she said.

"Tom, your hand—maybe you've split it again," V.J. said.

"Don't think so," Tom said, stretching out his palms. "Nope. My hands are freezing, but no blood. It's probably congealed!"

"We should all get warmed up—only half of us were wearing gloves," Jon said. "Someone has cut himself— or herself—good. Is everyone all right?"

"Your cheek is bleeding," Dianne mentioned to him.

"Old shaving wound," he said.

"Brett, how's that finger you cut?" Sabrina asked.

"I don't think I'm leaking blood," he said. "But then, I've actually got several wounds, you know."

"Yeah, right!" V.J. exclaimed. "Poor, poor boy!"

"Maybe it was me," Thayer said, rubbing his chin.

"You cut yourself shaving, too?" Anna Lee asked.

"Yep. It was like a gusher—caught myself right under the chin," he announced.

"Maybe we should all attend a barber's convention next time," Joe said sorrowfully. "I did a number on myself yesterday, as well. It was the shaving by candlelight, I think."

"That looks like more blood than a shaving knick," Sabrina murmured.

"Whoever is injured will surely find his or her wound," Thayer said.

"We need to get in and warmed up before someone suffers real frostbite," Jon said.

"Have we got enough wood to keep the fire in the library burning?" Thayer asked him.

"Yep," Jon said. "There's a storage room in the dungeon. Want to lend me a hand?"

"Sure."

"I'm for a hot shower," V.J. told them. "You men just go ahead and be men and make the place nice and warm and cozy, and we ladies will be down shortly."

They all moved into the castle, Jon and Thayer and Joe heading straight for the stairs to the dungeon.

Sabrina started to follow Reggie on in, then noticed that Joshua had lingered behind and stooped down to see the blood in the snow.

"What's the matter?" she asked him.

Startled, he looked up at her. "Nothing," he said, and gave her a slightly baffled look. "I just hope that whoever is hurt realizes it soon. This is a lot of blood."

"Maybe it just looks like more than it is. Why would anyone want to hide an injury?"

Joshua grinned at her. "I don't know—tough, crime-writing guys. Maybe they don't want to look like sissies. Me, on the other hand…well, my hands are my life, my work. If I have a paper cut, I nurse the damn thing."

Sabrina laughed, then sobered. "Joshua, when Brett was thrown, you went back and kept looking around where he fell, as if something was wrong."

"Well, something was wrong. Brett had been thrown, and he'd hurt himself."

"No, no, I mean…"

He hesitated, his eyes blank for a minute, then he shrugged. "It was nothing, really. I just needed to look. The artist's eyes, you know." He shrugged again.

But Sabrina thought he was lying. There was something. Something he didn't want to tell her.

"Well," he said, rising. "You should be doing the lady thing in the shower while I go do the manly man thing with the wood in the basement." He grinned.

She smiled in return. "I can help with the wood."

"Nice of you to offer, but you don't think that six strong guys can bring up enough?"

"Well, I was trying not to be sexist."

Joshua shook his head. "Do it V.J.'s way. Be sexist when it's convenient. Go warm up. Your lips are blue, and your teeth are chattering."

Sabrina took him up on his advice. She saw V.J.'s door closing as she reached her room, and down the hallway, Dianne's door closed, as well. On a hunch, she walked across the room to Susan's door and knocked. "Susan?"

No answer.

"Susan, it's Sabrina. You can't stay angry with all of us forever. Please, come out?"

There was no reply. She twisted the handle. The door was locked.

She exhaled thoughtfully. Evidently Susan was still royally pissed off. And it seemed that there was nothing she could do. She turned and slowly walked to her own room.

Brett came up behind her.

"Save water, shower with a friend?"

"Brett!"

He grinned and disappeared into his own room.

Sabrina went in and headed for the shower. Once again she was grateful the hot water was holding out. It felt wonderful on her hands. She had idiotically, rushed out without gloves. She was probably lucky she didn't have frostbite. She might have been the one bleeding all over the snow. The snow fight, however, had been fun.

Except for all the blood she had seen afterward.

She frowned as the water cascaded over her, wondering why the blood bothered her so much when no one appeared to be seriously injured.

There had just been so much of it.

Still, everyone seemed to have a cut. And every man here seemed to have forgotten how to shave.

Including Jon.

He hadn't just bled a little bit. His robe had been drenched with wet, sticky blood.

From a shaving cut?

And despite herself, she couldn't help but be haunted by the thought that...

He had lied to her last night. And if he had lied to her last night...

Might it all be a lie?

CHAPTER SEVENTEEN

WITH PLENTY OF wood piled by the hearths in the library, and the great hall, Jon went upstairs to shower. He stopped by Sabrina's room, but she wasn't there. His heart started pounding, and he berated himself, wondering why he should feel fear every time he didn't see her. Of all of them here, Sabrina was the least likely to be in danger. She hadn't been here when Cassie was killed. She hadn't been part of any sex or revenge games. She wasn't a danger to anyone.

Hearing Sabrina's laughter from V.J.'s room, he sighed in relief. Apparently the two women were deep in pleasant conversation. He went on to his own room, wondering why nagging suspicion still plagued him. Dianne had been certain that someone had killed her mother. Jon had never felt more uncertain about anything in his life. Had Cassie been killed? Or had it been a tragic accident?

Strange things had happened here since this week began, yet what, exactly, did they mean? Anyone—not necessarily guilty of murder—might have wanted to torment Susan Sharp. She had tortured all of them at one time or another, and she could be, even as a female, such a pompous prick. There was also the note he had received. But again, maybe someone not guilty of murder had sent him the note just to make sure he paid—either for Cassie's death or for just not loving her enough. The gunshot in the hallway, however, was not so easily explained.

But what did these odd events add up to?

Nothing! he prayed.

In his own room, because he seemed to be growing paranoid, he made sure that the door to the secret passage was secure. It was. Then he showered and attended to other details of running the castle.

It was early evening when he walked back down to the library, and once again it seemed that he was hosting a group of pleasant, normal, *innocent* men and women.

A poker game was in full tilt. Reggie was winning, taking pennies, nickels, dimes, quarters and the occasional dollar bill from Joe, Tom, V.J. and Thayer. Joshua, Sabrina, Brett, Anna Lee, Camy and Dianne were involved in a game of *Uno*.

Only Susan Sharp seemed to be missing. Again.

"Hey, Jon!" V.J. said, smiling as he came into the room. There was a new glow about her now that she and Tom were out in the open about their feelings.

"Jon, join us!" Reggie said.

"She'll fleece you!" Brett warned. "Come play *Uno*. It's more cutthroat but cheaper."

"Brett, pay attention. Draw four cards," Anna Lee said.

"Oh! You monster! You did that to me?" Brett cried.

"You don't know the half of it, honey," Anna Lee returned in a mock Mae West voice.

"Reverse!" Sabrina announced.

Jon caught her eye as she glanced up at him. There was something different about the way she looked at him. He frowned.

Had all this sordidness finally become too much for her? No, it wasn't like Sabrina to judge. And yet...

She was looking at him differently.

Guardedly.

"Aargh!" Brett cried. "Help! These women are out to get me."

"Uno!" Camy announced.

"Someone get that woman," Dianne commanded. "She's about to win!"

"Well, that is the point of the game, isn't it?" Camy asked. She smiled and looked at Jon happily.

"That's the point of the game," he said lightly. In a way, it was nice that Susan wasn't around, saying things that hurt people and stirring up trouble. Still, at this point, he was beginning to get worried.

"No one has seen Susan yet?" he asked.

"Nope," Thayer said, studying his cards. "But she left us a note."

"Left a note? Where?" Jon asked with a frown.

"Out!" Camy cried. She rose from the round oak game table and walked to the mantel. "Jennie found this when she came to set us up with drinks." She grimaced. "Want me to read it?"

"Go on—do. Jon will enjoy it as much as the rest of us, I'm sure," Joe said dryly.

Camy read aloud.

"To all you murderous, pathetic little pricks—leave me the hell alone. I don't wish to see or talk to any of you, and don't begin to imagine that any of you could ever suck up to me again after what has happened here. You're sick, all of you. I warn you again—while we're stuck here, stay away from me!

Otherwise, I will prosecute, and if I can't land your sorry asses in jail, I'll see to it that none of you ever writes for a legitimate publisher again.

Susan."

Camy looked at Jon apologetically.

"She sure does sound pissed off," Dianne murmured.

"Bully for her," V.J. said.

Tom shrugged. "I say what I said before. Fuck her."

"Really," Brett said, "who the hell does she think she is? I've never heard anything like it! Threatening us that way. As if she has the power to keep all of us from ever writing again."

Joe played a card. "Funny, you'd think Susan would know better. She might stick a few knives into us, the way Cassie could, but she'd never in a thousand years convince a publisher not to go to contract with an author who was bringing in the bucks."

"All right, all right," Jon said. "We've established the fact that Susan is a bitch. But I'm still worried about her."

"Jon," Sabrina said, looking up at him. Blue eyes liquid, hair streaming gold in the firelight, she was wearing a royal blue knit that clung to every curve of her body. He could pick out the subtle scent of her perfume, and he suddenly wanted to forget the hell about Susan Sharp and everyone else, as well.

Except that there was that something different about Sabrina now...

"I knocked on Susan's door," she said. "I tried to talk to her. In fact, I carried on something of a conversation with her locked door. I don't think I've done anything to make her angry with me, but she wouldn't respond at all."

"Well, she can't stay holed up in her room for days," Jon said impatiently.

Brett looked up. "Why not?" he asked hopefully.

"Please, let's just leave her?" Dianne asked.

"Maybe she'll eventually starve to death," V.J. commented happily.

"No, she won't," Dianne told her. "She wrote another note, 'To the servants,' ordering that a tray be set in front of her door twice a day until this wretched, snowbound event comes to an end."

"Jon, it sounds as if she's really fuming and doesn't want to be disturbed," Joshua told him.

Jon lowered his head, smiling slightly. They were all more than willing to leave well enough alone where Susan was concerned. He looked up again. "Sorry, guys. I'm still worried. We've got to go check up on her."

"Oh. Let's not," Reggie said.

"Well, I'll check on her, then."

"Oh, we'll all go," Thayer said. "I'm out of nickels anyway, thanks to this old card shark."

"Card shark, yes, but I'm the only one who gets to call me old!" Reggie warned him. "But wait, Jon, let's enjoy our dinner first, and then we'll go and eat some crow with Susan. It will be easier on a full stomach."

Jon arched a brow. With a mischievous glint in her eyes, Dianne abruptly dropped to her knees, clasping her hands as if in prayer and looking up at him entreatingly. "Please, please, sir, just dinner. Let us have dinner in peace."

"Come on now, Dianne," he said, laughing. But then Joe Johnston was down on his knees as well, "Oh, yes, yes, please, sir, just give us some supper…in peace."

"Really, if you think—"

"Puh-lease!" Anna Lee added dramatically, kneeling, too. Laughing, Camy, Joshua and Brett joined the other supplicants on the floor.

"Dinner," Jon said firmly, shaking a finger at them, "but no more delays."

"Oh, thank you, thank you, sir!" Brett cried.

"Get up, the lot of you," Jon said, chuckling. "Dinner—and then we go upstairs and talk to Susan and at the very least make sure that she's all right."

He turned around and strode into the great hall.

Jennie was seeing to the Sterno fires beneath the chafing dishes. "We are getting quite inventive, sir!" she told Jon cheerfully. "Everything tonight was cooked upon the open flame. Well, except, of course, the salad, and that wasn't cooked a'tall! But we've lovely steaks and chops. No electric, but the snow itself is pr'sarving our food."

"Thank you, Jennie," he told her.

His guests remained in high spirits as they filled their plates and sat down by candlelight. A fire burned merrily in the hearth. Sabrina was quietly elegant, smiling, laughing, responding to the comments around her—but not to him. She wasn't exactly ignoring him, but she was somehow avoiding him, even though she was sitting beside him. What the hell had happened? he wondered.

Then he found himself wondering, as well, what would have happened if she hadn't disappeared years ago? Might they have stayed together then, eventually married? Hosted these parties, both enjoying them? Sabrina complemented the castle, and, he thought, she complemented him. She brought out the best in him. And if they had somehow stayed together, wed, would Cassie still be alive, a guest here tonight?

And would Sabrina be looking at him differently, as she had earlier, before...

Before what? He was baffled.

Sabrina suddenly looked at him and smiled, though her gaze still seemed guarded. Her blue eyes were dazzling, caught by the firelight. "What are you thinking?" she asked him, under cover of the chatter and laughter.

"That I wish you'd never run away. Maybe we could have changed fate."

She flushed slightly, looking down at the table. "Maybe you see more in me than is really there."

"What do you mean?" Jon protested.

"Well," she said quietly, "I'd like to think I have some strength, the courage of my convictions. But when Cassie came to you that day—"

"What?"

"I folded like an envelope," she said ruefully.

"But that was a long time ago. And it's my turn. What are *you* thinking?"

"Nothing, really." She looked away.

"You're lying."

She shrugged.

"Tell me."

"Nothing...really."

"Something, really."

She shook her head slightly. "There's just suddenly... so much blood around!"

"Really?"

She looked at him steadily. "Yes."

He arched a brow.

"There was blood all over your robe."

"I told you, I cut myself shaving."

"Then it looked as if you cut your throat shaving."

Startled, he sat back. "What is it you think I've done?" He lowered his head, closer to hers, lest the others hear their conversation. "My wife wasn't stabbed to death— she went over a balcony. And to the best of my knowledge, we've no other corpses around, other than the long-buried ones in the crypt."

Sabrina didn't answer. She was looking at Anna Lee, who was studying them with a frown.

Anna Lee smiled when she caught Jon's eye. "You know what's a dreadful shame?" she queried generally.

Before Jon could answer, Brett did. "Yes. We didn't get our host to confess to any deep, dark sins."

Anna Lee laughed. "That's not what I was referring to, but, yes, well, there's that, too, of course."

"I had no sins!" Jon said lightly, lifting his wineglass to Anna Lee.

"Bull," Brett objected. "Cassie told me you were seeing someone." He flushed when the words were out. "Sorry, I, uh…" He stiffened in his chair and shrugged, then couldn't seem to resist asking, "Who was it?"

Jon sat back. "It wasn't—"

"It wasn't me!" Reggie announced, fluffing her hair.

"Nor me!" V.J. assured them, laughing.

"Not his stepdaughter," Dianne said dryly.

"Well, I was trying, but it wasn't me," Anna Lee murmured.

"Susan?" a number of them said in unison.

"No!" Jon protested. He shook his head, sipping his wine again, glad to see that Sabrina seemed amused rather than horrified. "I wasn't seeing anyone here at all."

"But someone, somewhere," V.J. guessed. "Who was she?"

Jon gave in. "None of you know her, and it was only

an occasional thing, as we both traveled frequently. Her home base was Edinburgh, but we met in the States. She's an interior decorator, and she'd done some work for me in New York. Are you all happy now, or do you need more specifics?"

"Well, I'd love to hear every last detail!" Anna Lee teased.

"I think he's making it all up, protecting someone here!" Joe announced.

"Well, we've all denied it," V.J. said. "I had a husband at the time, and that was it for me. I haven't young Anna Lee's stamina. Sorry, no offense meant, Anna Lee."

"None taken," Anna Lee said dryly.

"He wouldn't dream of touching his stepdaughter," Dianne said, gazing at Jon. "Even if his stepdaughter might have been willing," she added softly.

"Don't you all go looking at me!" Reggie declared.

"I wasn't here," Sabrina reminded them quietly.

"So that leaves..." Joe began.

"Susan!" Tom said again, making a face.

"Right. Why would he be protecting Susan? Who in his or her right mind could think that Susan needed protection?" Thayer demanded.

"Ah, but maybe Jon wasn't behaving quite so innocently. Perhaps there was some forbidden affair, the castle laird's seduction of some sweet young thing from the village who came in to cook or clean," Joshua suggested, teasing, his eyes dancing. They all laughed.

"Indeed! We should check out the chamber of horrors for some young, innocent, unknown face!" V.J. suggested, waggling her eyebrows.

"You may look wherever you wish," Jon said. "But since it wasn't my 'sins' you were really after to begin with, Anna Lee, just what were you referring to when you said it was a dreadful shame?"

"Oh, just that we never solved the whodunit. It was really great fun, and so well-done. Who did kill your brother, Demented Dick?"

"Let's solve it now," V.J. said.

"We don't have half the clues. We didn't play the game," Thayer protested.

"Then we'll just talk it through, lay out the suspects and the clues, and we'll each make a determination!" Dianne said. "Jon?"

"Sure, why not?" he said.

Sabrina leaned forward. "Two of us are guilty, right?"

"Well, I'm innocent, seeing as how I was killed in chapel," Brett murmured.

"Right," Sabrina said. "Mr. Buttle, the Butler, was killed—probably because he saw something."

"My guess," Brett said, "is that it was Thayer's character, JoJo Scuchi, who killed Demented Darryl—because of an affair gone awry. Or... JoJo Scuchi was having an affair with Susan's character, Carla, the call girl with the clap, and he killed Demented Darryl for having given her the disease!"

"As demented Dick's and Demented Darryl's dad, I'm innocent," Tom Heart said. "I'm certain of that."

"And as Tilly Transvestite, I know that I'm innocent, as well. Number one—I'm not sure how, but I'm their mother. And I'm just too weird and caught up in my own psychological problems to kill others," Joe said with certainty.

"I think the Duchess—Sabrina—did it," Dianne surmised. "Demented Darryl tried to ditch out on back payments he owed her. She's been pretending to be a dignified duchess, when we all know that she was the queen of sleaze. The butler knew about her transactions. He'd seen too much, and he had to go."

"Sabrina was in the chapel when Brett bought it, remember?" V.J. said.

"So we're back to her needing an accomplice," Joe stated.

"Okay, Camy," Jon said, looking at his assistant. "We need a few more clues from the game. Are there two murderers?"

Camy glanced at Joshua, evidently sorry to part with information and give up the game. He shrugged at her. "Well, tell them."

"Yes, there are two murderers. I'll give you that much. You all figure out the rest."

"Give us this, too, please," Sabrina persisted. "Brett—Mr. Buttle—is dead, and therefore innocent. And I don't think that Carla, the call girl, is guilty, either. I think that her character was supposed to be the next to go."

"Maybe," Camy said.

"But Susan's character isn't the murderer," Jon stated. Camy shook her head. "No, she's not."

"And my character is innocent, too. Mary, the Hare Krishna—she's innocent, right?" Dianne demanded.

"A Hare Krishna? You're daffy, not guilty," Joshua teased.

Dianne smiled at him. Josh smiled back. Jon wondered if his stepdaughter didn't seem to be growing more and more fond of the artist.

"Well, we're eliminating suspects, at least," Tom said.

"As Tilly Transvestite, the dear boys' mum. I am innocent, aren't I?" Joe asked. "You don't need to answer, Camy. I can see by your face that it's the truth. After their miraculous births, I surely wouldn't do in one of my children."

"You are in the clear," Joshua said with a shrug.

"And that's it, the last clue we're giving you tonight," Camy said. "Joshua, no more hints!"

"But the game is over, isn't it?" Sabrina said quietly.

"Yes and no," Reggie argued. "We don't know who is guilty, but we do know who is innocent. I would personally like to work on it a little longer. What do you say?"

"Well, you know, the game isn't really over," Camy said, "since no one knows the truth at all."

"I'll say!" V.J. murmured.

Reggie looked sternly around the table. She fluffed her gray hair. "I want to solve this. I can't help it. It's in my blood!"

Despite his unease over Sabrina's comments about the blood on his robe—there hadn't been that much—Jon found himself laughing. Reggie was one great old broad.

"Okay, let's leave it at this," he said. "The innocent? Mary, the Hare Krishna. Mr. Buttle, the butler—he's a goner. Carla the call girl and Tilly Transvestite. That leaves us with Sabrina, the Duchess, Reggie, the Crimson Lady, V.J. as Nancy, the naughty nurse—"

"*Very* naughty nurse," Dianne teased.

"Hush, young woman!" V.J. admonished.

"V.J., dear, you've already given us one confession, and we don't want any protestations of innocence now, thank you," Reggie said playfully.

"Besides, just like the rest of us," Dianne drawled, "V.J. could be lying."

"She could be," Jon said. "And Anna Lee, as Sally Sadist, could still be guilty, along with Thayer as JoJo

Scuchi, Sabrina, the Duchess, running her covert operations, and, of course…"

"Who are we missing?" Joe asked with a frown.

"Me," Jon said simply. "Demented Dick. I think I'll be guilty till the end, don't you?" he asked lightly, gazing at Sabrina.

She looked away.

"Everybody happy with the way we've ended things for tonight?" he inquired.

"No," Reggie said. "I want to solve a mystery."

Jon pounced. "Good. So do I. So let's go talk to Susan."

"Susan isn't a mystery," Dianne complained. "Just a bitch."

"We had our peaceful dinner," Jon said firmly. "And now…" He rose determinedly. The others looked unhappy, but he knew they would follow suit.

He left the great hall and started up the stairs. He was aware of Sabrina's scent as she fell in slightly behind him, of Tom murmuring something to V.J., of Brett bemoaning the fact that the evening had been going so nicely and now they were going to go and spoil it all.

He reached the second floor and Susan's room. They were all silent. He rapped sharply on the door.

"Susan!"

No answer.

He looked at the others, rapped hard again. "Susan, it's Jon. I'd like to talk to you, just to make sure you're all right!"

Again, no answer.

"I told you!" Sabrina whispered. "She doesn't want anything to do with any of us."

"She thinks we're all monsters," Anna Lee said.

"Well, on that score," Brett considered, "she just might be right. I mean, we can be pretty horrible."

"Speak for yourself!" Reggie told him.

"I think he is speaking for himself," Anna Lee teased.

"Hush, woman," Brett commanded.

"Hush, all of you," Jon said sternly. "I can't hear if she's giving me an answer or not. Susan!" he called out again.

"Let's just leave her," Dianne pleaded.

He shook his head. "No, Dianne, we can't." He rapped his fist against the door with determination. "Damn it, Susan, if you don't answer me, I'm coming in!"

Still Susan didn't reply.

"Do we break the door down?" Thayer asked.

Jon smiled. "No, we use the master key. Susan!" he called, giving her one more chance, in case she was in the bathroom, or naked, or doing a mud facial, or something equally personal.

She'd kill him.

What if she had on head phones or something of the kind and simply couldn't hear him? He'd be invading her privacy. And maybe she did just hate the hell out of all of them and want to be left alone.

But he was worried.

Totally, completely uneasy.

This just wasn't right.

What if she had hurt herself? What if she had fallen, cried out for help, and none of them had heard her? What if she had slipped in the shower? What if she lay, injured and bleeding, on the shower floor, her blood trickling with water down the drain?

There were too many what-ifs to be concerned about her right to privacy.

He felt a sudden shiver rake his spine, an unpleasant sensation that made him more and more concerned that something was really wrong.

Sabrina was upset about blood.

Too much blood, she'd implied.

There hadn't been that much blood. But it had been on his robe. What the hell did that mean?

Was there a killer among them? In his mind's eye, he could suddenly see the worst. The killer had gotten to Susan, and she was lying on her bed, blood dripping down the sheets from the stab wounds that perforated her body.

He frowned, looking at the others.

"We've got to do it."

He turned the key in the lock and opened Susan's door. And, stepping into her room, he looked around.

A collective gasp sounded behind him.

And he saw what was there.

CHAPTER EIGHTEEN

NOTHING.

No body upon the sheets.

No endlessly running water.

No blood.

No grisly scene.

Nothing at all. No sign of Susan whatsoever.

"Well, where the hell is she?" V.J. demanded.

"Susan?" Sabrina called. She glanced at Jon, then walked farther into the room, pushing open the bathroom door, which already stood ajar. "Susan?"

"She simply isn't here," Dianne said flatly.

"Well, where the hell could she be?" Joe asked impatiently.

"She's probably been tiptoeing around, spying on us, trying to see how we reacted to her disappearance so that she could really do a number on us all," Anna Lee said.

"It's a big castle," Sabrina said. "She could be anywhere."

"That's just it. She could be anywhere," Jon said.

"Why are we so worried about her?" Tom demanded irritably. "Let's let her wander around and fume and be a bitch. I tried to be decent to her. I stood guard while she showered, and she went ballistic at me anyway, calling me and V.J. perverts for bursting in on her privacy. I'm sorry, Jon, but I've just about had it with her. She's beginning to make Cassie look like a goddamned saint."

They all stood very still, looking at Tom, who was seldom so passionately angry or bitter.

V.J. slipped her hand into his. "But, Tom, maybe she's hurt."

"We can only hope," he muttered.

"You don't mean that," V.J. said.

He sighed and threw up his hands. "All right, let's go search for her, Jon, if that's what you want."

"We should divide up, I think," Thayer suggested.

"Yes, I think so," Jon agreed. "We'd be ridiculous, all of us trooping behind one another around the castle, crashing into each other."

"I'm not going anywhere alone," Dianne said determinedly.

"No, of course not," Jon said impatiently. "We'll go in groups of two or three." He paused. "Reggie, maybe you should lock yourself in and—"

"Jon Stuart, quit acting as if I'm an invalid or so old that I should be stuffed!" Reggie protested.

"All right, then—" Jon began.

"Reggie, we just don't want you getting hurt," Dianne said gently.

"V.J. is almost as old as I am," Reggie insisted.

"Not nearly!" V.J. protested, appalled.

"Ladies, ladies!" Brett said.

"How do we split up?" Camy asked.

"Well, let's see," Jon said. "Thayer, Joe and I will take the different dungeon areas; Tom, you and Brett can check the first floor and then help V.J., Sabrina and Anna Lee search the rooms up here. Dianne, maybe you and Reggie can provide a liaison point for us in the great hall."

"I'll help you in the crypt and the chamber of horrors," Joshua said. "I know the area well."

"I'll help, too," Camy offered.

"No, Camy, why don't you hang out with Dianne and Reggie in the great hall. Or, better yet, you could go up to the attic and tell Jennie that Susan has disappeared and have her search up there."

"You know," Joe said, "being Susan and stubborn and ornery as a bull, she might have just taken off out of here, leaving us to worry about her."

"How?" Jon asked. "We're snowbound."

"Maybe she took a horse?"

"If there had been a horse missing from the stables, Angus would have said so."

"Maybe she sneaked out since we came back in," Joshua suggested. "The weather has improved a lot."

"It's a possibility, but I doubt it," Jon said. "Susan was never suicidal. The snow is deep, and it's a very long way even to the village. And if I remember right, Susan is not overly fond of horses. Tom," he said, reaching into his pocket, "here's the master key. Let's start searching, shall we?"

He stared at Sabrina, then turned and led the way down the stairs.

SABRINA DIDN'T WANT to be a doubting Thomas. The way Jon had looked at her made her feel terrible. His gaze had gone cold, hard, his eyes like marble defenses that kept her from his heart or soul. She didn't want to throw him away again...

But she didn't want to toss aside her own life, either. Logic argued that she had to be mistrustful. She didn't want to be a fool. And the more she thought about it, the more bothered she was. There had been blood on Jon's robe, much more blood than there should have been.

She was afraid, as well, that his robe still lay on the foot of her bed, that the others would see it—and the blood. She was afraid, yet she wanted to protect him at the same time.

"Well, how should we do this?" Brett asked.

"Stick together and go room to room," V.J. said. "You're welcome to rip mine apart first."

"Are we supposed to think that one of us has Susan hidden under a bed?" Brett demanded. "Not me, thank you. I have been known for some rather shameful sexual exploits, but I have never sunk so low."

"Well, that's questionable," V.J. murmured.

"Children, children, no squabbling," Reggie said.

"You and Dianne get to the great hall, where you're supposed to be. Camy, head on upstairs and see Jennie and the girls, and we'll get started here," Sabrina said.

"Right," Camy said. She, Dianne and Reggie started out. V.J. walked to her door and opened it. She strode into the room with the others behind, going so far as to lift the bed skirt. "No Susan, you will note."

Anna Lee walked into the bathroom, pulling back the shower curtain. "Susan?"

"She's not here," Brett said. "Not unless V.J. managed to dismember her and so totally roast her in the fireplace that there's nothing left of her but ash."

V.J. stared at him.

"How dare you—" Tom began.

"I was just teasing!" Brett protested. "I mean, it's obvious that Susan isn't here."

"Let's move on," Sabrina suggested.

"Jon's suite is at the end of the hall. Let's start there and work back this way," Tom said.

"Sure."

The five of them headed down the hall, Tom in the lead.

Sabrina hadn't been in Jon's room before.

She liked it very much.

A four-poster, king-size bed on an elegant dais domi-nated the main room, which was done in shades of deep blue and crimson. Antique tapestries and family arms adorned the walls.

There was nothing left of Cassie here.

There were two dressing rooms. One contained Jon's clothing. The other, exceptionally large, he apparently used as his office. The room overlooked the courtyard and had a doorway to the balcony; it was complete with word processor, printer, fax, phone, copier, shelves and files. Books he was currently using for research were piled atop his desk, along with notes and memos. Sabrina found herself wanting to touch his swivel chair, riffle his papers, delve into his very thoughts.

"Check this out!" Anna Lee said. She was standing at the door to the bathroom.

"Why? Is Susan hanging in the shower?" Brett demanded.

"No, just look at this place!" Anna Lee said.

They walked over to see.

"God, it's divine!" Anna Lee gushed.

It was. It boasted a huge whirlpool, sauna, shower, beautiful fixtures, black, gold, red, and white tiles, hand-some mirrors, and fluffy towels on warmers.

He had lived here with Cassandra, Sabrina thought. It was wonderful, rich, and she could just imagine having all this with someone she loved. Except...

Cassie had gone off the balcony just steps from this place...

"You mean, you haven't seen this bathroom before?" Brett quizzed Anna Lee.

"No. What would I be doing in Jon's bathroom?" she inquired, puzzled.

Brett stared at Anna Lee. "You were sleeping with Cassie, right?"

Anna Lee stared back at him, her hands on her hips. "Yeah, right. But she came to me." She hesitated a minute, biting her lower lip. Then she sighed, her shoulders drooping. "She wouldn't see anybody here. It was...kind of sacred to her, I guess."

As Sabrina stared at Anna Lee, V.J. began to hustle them along. "Well, come on, let's make sure Susan isn't stashed here anywhere and move on. Tom, let's be thorough. Check under the bed. Girls, look everywhere."

They went through the master suite again, then they all stared at the balcony doors.

Evidently no one wanted to walk out them.

Sabrina sighed. "I'll do it."

She stepped outside.

The night air seemed frigid, and she wrapped her arms around herself. The wind had risen again. It was keening. If Susan had decided to take off and leave the castle, she was surely an icicle by now.

There was nothing on the balcony. No one. And yet, of course, it was from here, the exact place where Sabrina now stood, that Cassie had plummeted to her death. Sabrina was disturbed by the sensation sweeping through her, a sudden, uncanny fear that someone was ready to push her. She spun around.

The others were where they had been. Waiting for her.

She remembered that somewhere in this room was a door to a secret passageway.

Maybe there were other secrets.

Maybe someone *was* watching her.

And maybe she was losing her wits.

"No one here. Let's move on, huh?" she said.

"Yeah, right, let's," Tom said.

"Dianne's room is next," V.J. announced.

"I'll just run down the hall to the top of the stairway and shout down to Reggie and Dianne and see if they have any messages from the boys down below," Anna Lee said.

"Okay," Tom agreed.

Four of them stepped into Dianne's room.

Dianne was not a neat freak. Her dressing table was strewn with brushes, combs, makeup and assorted toiletries. Her notepad computer was set up on a table by the window.

Clothing was scattered on the bed and chairs; shoes littered the floor.

"Susan couldn't possibly be in here," Brett said. "No room for her."

"I'll look in the bathroom. You boys check under the bed," V.J. told them.

Brett lifted the bed skirt. He suddenly yelped, and the others came crashing around him.

"What, what?" Tom demanded. "Brett, are you all right? What did you find?"

Brett drew himself up from his position by the bed. "Her dildo bit me."

"Oh!" V.J. cried in aggravation, belting him on the shoulder. "Will you be serious!"

"Actually, I was trying not to be so serious," Brett told her. "V.J., I am positive that Dianne isn't hiding Susan in this room!"

"But maybe Susan is hiding herself for some reason,

slipping from room to room, place to place," Sabrina suggested.

"Let's keep going. At this rate, it will be the end of the week before we get anywhere at all!" Tom said, disgruntled. "And I want to get some sleep."

"Sleep? Oh, bull. The cat's out of the bag. You want to get back into the sack with V.J.!" Brett said.

"McGraff, you bloody—" Tom began, but V.J. stepped in, a hand on his shoulder.

"Tom, be understanding. Brett is merely jealous. He's not accustomed to being the only one without companionship. Poor dear, night after night he lies there, twiddling his thumbs—and whatever else—while right next door the love of his life is—how did he put it?—in the sack with someone else."

"Low blow," Brett protested.

"Then learn to be nice," V.J. warned.

"We need to keep going," Sabrina reminded them.

"All right, love of my life, let's move on," Brett said.

They moved on.

Joshua's room revealed art tools, a covered easel, a work in clay. But no Susan. Camy's room, with her big desk and tons of paperwork, was kept neat and tidy. But no Susan appeared.

Anna Lee rejoined them. Nothing had been reported from below.

They looked into Joe's room—a total disaster. Thayer's room, regimental, his toiletries sparse, his clothes neatly hung. Tom's room, neither as haphazard as Joe's nor in such precise order as Thayer's. Still no Susan.

Anna Lee's proved a very personalized room, the scent of her perfume on the air, scarves here and there, jew-

elry in a tangle on the dresser, clothing draped gracefully about. No Susan.

Sabrina led the way into her own room, anxiously
looking at the foot of her bed for the robe Jon had been
wearing. The one covered in blood.

It was gone.

She didn't know whether to breathe easy or feel a
greater sense of panic.

The others weren't commenting at all, just walking
around, looking.

Anna Lee checked under the bed; V.J. searched the
bath. Tom went out on the balcony.

"This is ridiculous," Anna Lee said. "Obviously, no
one is hiding Susan in his or her room."

"I agree," Sabrina managed to murmur, sitting at the
foot of her bed. "But maybe Susan is playing a trick on
us, trying to hide."

"And if she is, she can hear us coming from room to
room," V.J. said.

"But could she keep disappearing, just one step ahead
of us all the time?" Sabrina asked.

"Who the hell knows what Susan is doing?" Tom demanded irritably.

"And," Anna Lee said, "the place is riddled with secret
passages. The Scots have always been ornery—and Jon's
family, being Stuarts, were into protecting the Stuarts,
hiding the young prince Charles II, and, I understand,
losing a few heads themselves when they supported the
Jacobites. They hid priests and ministers, outlaws and
so on. Maybe Susan knows more about the castle than
we do."

"Well, Jon certainly knows the place," Brett said. "It
is his castle."

"Hmm," Anna Lee mused. "But I did some research on so-called haunted castles in York once, and there were lots of instances where the 'hauntings' were caused when someone other than the owner knew about secret passageways and the like. Maybe Susan has discovered some deep, dark secret about the place. Better yet, maybe she's walled herself up within it somewhere."

"Now that would be fitting. Susan has never appreciated the genius of Edgar Allan Poe," Tom said.

"We've only got one room left—mine," Brett said. "Then I, for one, am going down for a drink. Then I'm coming back up to bed. Sadly, V.J., yes, alone. But I'm tired, so I'll accept my fate."

"Onward," V.J. said.

They entered Brett's room, together. Standing in the middle of it while the others walked around, Sabrina stared at the wardrobe, remembering how afraid she had been the night before.

Brett had been gone. Jon had been gone. Everyone, it had seemed, was walking the halls.

Shaving—in the middle of the night.

Or cutting themselves on lamps or the like.

But she had stared at the wardrobe, afraid, thinking that there might be someone inside it.

Someone ready to jump out at her.

Or someone unable to do so. Someone who lay cut, slashed, still bleeding...

"Under the bed?" V.J. asked Tom.

"Nothing."

"Bathroom's empty," Anna Lee said.

Sabrina suddenly felt her heart pounding. The wardrobe still haunted her

She walked toward it.

"Sabrina!" Brett said sharply.

She ignored him and threw open the wardrobe.

IT WAS HIS CASTLE. The crypt contained his dead relatives.

Jon had never been afraid of the dead. Years and years ago, when he'd been a young child, his father had reassured him after he'd seen a horror flick. Don't ever be afraid of the dead, son. They're the safest people around, they can't do you harm anymore. Ever. Sometimes, son, you do, however, need to be afraid of the living.

Jon believed in God, in a supreme being, but he didn't believe that God had people come back as spirits to haunt the living. He wasn't superstitious. He'd never felt the least fear while walking any part of this, his family's ancient castle. He'd loved it since he'd come into his special inheritance. There was no part of the brick, stone, mortar or wood that had ever made him uneasy.

Until tonight.

The chapel was evidently empty. Nevertheless, they combed the pews, looked behind the altar, peered through all the shadows.

They walked the bowling alleys, even checked the mechanisms for the pins, and approached the pool area together.

"Well, she didn't drown," Thayer said as they gazed into the water.

"Nope, apparently not," Joe agreed.

"Did you look in the men's room?" Jon asked Joshua.

"And the ladies', too. Restrooms are empty," Josh reported.

"Well, the crypt is next, I guess," Joe said. He actually sounded uneasy.

"Yeah, I guess." Big, tough ex-cop Thayer sounded uneasy, too.

Jon led the way. They came in with kerosene lamps, lifting them high to dispel the gloom around the tombs. They methodically began to walk along the rows of the dead.

"Susan isn't here," Jon said at last.

"I never thought she would be," Thayer said gruffly. "She's got a big mouth, but she can be your basic chicken. Dianne might have the balls to come down here alone and pretend to be her mother's ghost, but Susan wouldn't be caught dead in a place like this."

Silence followed his words.

"Dead, you have no choice," Joshua finally said. He turned to Jon. "There is no sign of her whatsoever, Jon. As furious as she was, maybe she did take off into the snow. Maybe she did make it down to the village, and maybe she's sipping a hot toddy and watching the latest flick on the telly."

"Yeah, maybe," Jon said. But he didn't believe it. Not for a minute. "Let's move on to the chamber of horrors."

"Oh, yeah, let's, can't wait," Joe said.

The words broke the ice. The four laughed, recognizing their false machismo and owning up to a certain unease.

Joshua led the way into the chamber.

The others began to walk around.

Jon stood by the entry, staring down the rows of frozen tableaux. Nothing looked out of order. Nothing at all.

It was very cold. The temperature was supposed to be kept cool here to preserve the wax figures, and with the power gone, the rooms were shut down completely. But the cold wasn't what bothered him, though he couldn't quite say what was.

He walked into the room, moving among the tableaux. The others moved about as well, lamps held high.

"Susan, here Susie, Susie!" Joe called.

"Come out, come out, wherever you are!" Thayer added.

Their words seemed to ricochet off the stone walls. The men took different aisles, crossed each other's paths. It was eerie, the way the wax figures stared down at them.

So very real.

Joshua was standing in front of the tableau of Lady Ariana Stuart being tortured on the rack.

"I am good," Joshua said, realizing that Jon stood by him. "Damn good." He shrugged. "Either that or it's a dark and stormy night, the lighting sucks, I'm a scaredy-cat and I'm beginning to see my own work come alive."

Thayer came up to them, clapping Joshua on the shoulder. "You're good. You're that damn bloody good. V.J. over there looks as if she's about to have us all for supper. I hate to admit it, but this place is giving me the chills. Cold as a witch's tit in here. Jon, think we can go back up? Nothing's stirring down here."

"We've walked every aisle," Joe said, reaching them. Despite the cold, little beads of sweat had broken out over his brow. "No one is here."

"So where the hell do you think she is?" Thayer asked.

"I don't know," Jon said, moving at last to exit the chamber. The others managed to squeeze out ahead of him. He almost smiled, but as he closed the double doors as they left, he felt a curious chill along his spine, and he paused, reopening the doors and lifting his lamp one more time.

Nothing. And yet something subtle was plaguing him.

He didn't know what. But something was just slightly wrong. He had a sense of...

He didn't know what.

He closed the doors, shaking his head impatiently. And he followed the others up the stairs to the ground floor and the great hall.

Dianne was playing solitaire, a huge glass of wine in front of her.

Reggie was sitting at the table, drumming her fingers, looking entirely peeved. Camy, too, sat at the table, her head resting upon her folded arms. She looked up when the men came in.

"Jennie and the girls say they haven't seen hide nor hair of Susan," Camy said.

"Nothing down below," Thayer said cheerfully.

"And nothing here except for three tired, bitchy broads," Reggie informed them.

Jon smiled. "Anyone for a drink?" He started to pour himself a whiskey.

That's when they heard the shriek from above.

SABRINA SCREAMED, JUMPING BACK as a head bounced out of the wardrobe at her.

Long hair splayed everywhere.

"Sabrina! It's a mannequin head—and a wig!" Brett said, coming up behind her, slipping an arm around her.

It was.

A white plastic head, a black wig.

"Hey, honey, it's okay!" V.J. told her.

Sabrina felt like an idiot. It was, indeed, just as Brett had said. She stared at the wardrobe. Why the hell had she gotten in into her mind that something awful was going to be found in that wardrobe? It was simply so

stuffed with clothing that opening it had caused the head
to bounce from a top shelf.

As she stared at it, still trembling, the others burst into
the room, Jon in the lead, Thayer behind him, Joshua,
Joe, and even Dianne and poor Reggie, puffing away to
keep up.

"What? What is it? What happened?" Jon demanded.

"Nothing, nothing," Sabrina said quickly. "I just
scared myself silly."

Jon walked over to the fallen foam head and picked it
up and the wig. He looked at Brett. "Not yours, I take it?"

Brett shook his head. "Not my color."

Jon walked to the wardrobe, surveying the contents.
"I hadn't realized these things were here," he said.

"They were Cassie's?" V.J. asked.

"Yeah. Sorry, Brett, we didn't leave you with much
space for your things."

"My needs are few and simple," Brett said.

"Yeah, right!" V.J. exclaimed with a laugh.

"Well...no sign of Susan, right?" Tom said to the others.

"Not a single hair off her head," Joe answered.

Jon stopped in front of Sabrina. "Are you all right?"
She nodded. "I just feel like a fool."

"We're all on edge."

"And you were fixing drinks, remember?" Thayer reminded him.

"Yeah," Jon said, his eyes still curiously dark on Sabrina's. He turned then and left the room. Everyone traipsed
after him.

Joshua helped him mix drinks. "Believe it or not," he
commented, "we're finally running low on ice."

"I don't need ice," Joe told him, and he helped himself to two shots of bourbon.

Sabrina opted for a Tia Maria. As she accepted a glass and moved away, Jon said, "We've still got to find Susan."

"But not tonight!" V.J. told him.

"No, I suppose not," Jon said with a sigh. He glanced at his watch. Sabrina looked up at the clock over the mantel. Nearly 1:00 a.m.

"Joshua, Thayer, tomorrow we'll take the horses out and see if she did wander off somehow. Within another twenty-four to forty-eight hours, the roads should be cleared, and the electricity and phones should be back. But if she's out there…" he began unhappily.

"If she's out there without heat and shelter, she's already dead. And we'd probably freeze to death looking for her if we tried it now. And we'd never see a damned thing in the dark anyway," Joe said.

It was true, Sabrina thought. They were done for the night. Jon knew it; he just didn't seem to like it.

"Well, then, everyone, let's call it a night, shall we?" He looked at Sabrina.

She drew her eyes from his, not wanting to face him. *The robe was gone!* she wanted to shout. *Your robe, with the blood all over it.*

She started for the stairs instead.

AN HOUR LATER the old castle was silent except for the creaks and groans that haunted its ancient stones and timbers every night.

Sabrina paced her room.

They were all locked in, weary, in need of a night's rest.

She waited. Afraid that he would come. Afraid that he would not.

They had searched the whole castle.

Except for the secret places. The places only Jon knew. She wanted to shout at him, and she wanted to run away. Except that…he didn't come.

Then, when she had walked toward the balcony, she suddenly felt his presence, and when she turned, he was there.

She kept her distance, staring at him. Tall, imposing, handsome, sexy, he was in a different robe, dark hair damp, with a fluff of hair showing at the V of his lapels.

He watched her gravely. "Do you want me to leave?" he asked.

"Your robe was gone," she stated. "The one with the blood all over it."

"My housekeeping staff is very good," he told her.

"Ah…you didn't make sure it was removed?" she asked him.

"No," he said, walking toward her. "Did you find a bloody corpse anywhere, and you're simply not sharing that information with us?"

Her eyes fell. He was in front of her. She could smell his soap, his aftershave, something more uniquely him. She felt an instant melting sensation within, and she knew that she wanted him. And if he touched her…

"Where have you been?" she demanded suspiciously.

He tilted his head. "Trying to make a thorough search of the place. I've just been through all the hidden passageways."

Logical. She had been thinking herself that the passageways should be searched.

However…

He had done so alone.

"Are you afraid of me?" he asked her.

"Should I be?"

He shook his head, looking at her. "No," he said firmly.

She bit her lip, not moving.

He turned around and started to leave.

She might be a fool, but she couldn't bear it. "Jon!" she cried, and she raced after him. She threw herself against his back, her arms encircling him, her chin resting against his robe. He went still for a moment, then turned. And as he did so, she fumbled for the belt of his robe, tugging it free. She buried her face against his chest, slid her hands along his ribs, over his hips. He was naked beneath the robe. The brush of her fingers brought him to an immediate erection, and she cradled it with her hands. She looked up at last, ready to meet his lips as he lifted her chin and kissed her.

She sank against him, kissing him everywhere, barely aware of his guttural moans as she slid down his torso and closed her mouth around him. He cradled her nape, fingers tangling into her hair; then he was drawing her up, lifting her, pressing her down on the bed. And he was everywhere then, bathing her with the hunger of his lips and tongue. He allowed her no inhibitions, granted no mercy. He delved into her most intimate places, slowly, with fire, until she thrashed beneath him with a violent frenzy that brought him atop her, staring down as he slowly penetrated her, watching her eyes, feeling himself sink within her, feeling her sheath him. Then she closed her eyes and felt the searing exhilaration of his passion as he began to move with an ever increasing pace within her.

When it was over she lay spent and exhausted in his arms, thinking that she loved him desperately.

And wishing that she did not.

He didn't speak. He kept his arms around her.

Thus entangled, they slept.

ALMOST TWO HOURS later Jon awoke with a jolt.

He sat up and looked around. For a moment, he was confused. What had awakened him?

Then he realized that he'd had the uncanny feeling of being watched.

He gave himself a shake.

Sabrina slept on, sweetly, beautifully at his side, her naked body curved to his.

And still...

There was nothing. No strange sound in the night. No strange scent. Just a feeling that they hadn't been alone, that someone had stood there, watching them sleep...

He rose, donned his robe and slipped into the secret passageway.

REGGIE WAS OLD but not dead. Yet.

And they were all missing something, the fools.

When she was certain that everyone was asleep, she rose. She buttoned her velour robe warmly about her and donned her comfy yellow slippers. She had a really good flashlight, and she reached for that.

Thus armed, she left her bedroom.

The hallway was silent.

Dead silent.

There weren't going to be any clues on this floor, she was convinced. She went down to the main level, glancing into the dimly lit great hall, then the library.

Not a creature was stirring, she thought. Except for maybe a few mice, she decided with some humor. And maybe a few great big rats! It was a very old castle.

In the great hall, she plucked up one of the heavy candleholders from the table. Brass bludgeon in one hand, flashlight in the other, she was ready to take on the world.

Not that she thought she needed to take on anyone. Even monsters had to sleep. She just wanted to be prepared.

She journeyed down to the level below.

The pool rippled in the dim light. The bowling alleys were silent.

In the chapel, she crossed herself.

In the crypt, she prayed for the dead.

In the chamber of horrors…she met the murderer.

She was deep into the room, looking…for what, she didn't know. She liked mystery, loved mystery, and she intended to solve this one.

She did.

And then…

She heard something. A slight sound. And she turned. And faced the killer.

She never screamed. Nor did the killer even touch her. She didn't give the murderer the satisfaction of killing again.

The explosive pain in her chest ripped into her with the power of an atom bomb. Thankfully, the agony was fast. She couldn't breathe. She stared; she felt her eyes popping.

Then she fell.

She heard the killer's laughter, and she knew she was dying.

The killer thought she was *already* dead.

But not yet…

Not yet.

CHAPTER NINETEEN

Sun streamed through the window.

Sabrina awoke slowly, aware of dazzling rays of light penetrating the room. She was aware, as well, of the warm body beside her, and she twisted, glad that Jon was with her. Yet, as she turned, she saw that he was awake already, staring up at the ceiling with a frown.

The frown left his face when he realized she was studying him, and he turned to her. "Hi."

"Hi yourself."

"You made it through the night," he told her softly.

"Yes. Meaning…?"

"Well, you don't really trust me, do you?"

"Yes…it's just that…"

"There was blood on my robe." He shrugged. "Well, we should be out of here soon. We can have a forensics expert check it out."

He sounded bitter. She didn't want him to be bitter.

"You'll admit, there's a lot of unusual stuff going on around here."

"A lot of mysteries to be solved. People are confessing to all kinds of things, but we still seem to be missing one simple truth."

"What really happened to Cassie? And now, of course, where the hell has Susan gone?"

She sat up, hugging sheets and knees to her as she

looked at him. "I was actually really tired and slept through the night. Were you here all night, or did you disappear?"

He arched a brow, hesitated, then admitted, "I disappeared for a while."

"Oh?"

He nodded. "Remember how you told me that you thought someone had been in this room watching you, and I told you that it hadn't been me?"

"Yes, of course. I never saw anyone, though. It was just a feeling."

"Well, I woke up with that same feeling."

She arched a brow at him. "It is your castle, and you're the king of it, remember? Who else could have been in here?"

"I don't know. But I didn't like the feeling. It was very uncomfortable."

"So you went running around in the dark to see if anyone else was up again, right?"

"Yeah, more or less."

"Well, were other people up, running around the castle?"

He nodded grimly.

"Who?"

"Well, actually, you were one of only two people to sleep through the night."

"Oh?"

"As I left here, Anna Lee was just coming from Joe's room."

"Why?"

"I don't know, and I didn't ask."

"Go on."

"Camy was up working, and V.J., Tom, Brett, Dianne

and Joshua were in the great hall, chowing down on midnight snacks. Apparently, you and Reggie were the only people sleeping. I seem to be hosting a party of night owls."

"So you all had a party without Reggie and me, huh?"

He nodded, then grinned. "They decided that I was the killer."

She felt her heart pound against her chest. But they were talking about the game, of course. "Are you the killer?"

"I can't tell you. We decided not to admit or deny anything until we were all together again."

"But when—" she began.

"Later, this evening. I've got to get up and get going. I'm going to take Joshua and Thayer with me and see if we can figure out if Susan did try to leave here. Though why she would leave notes to people if she meant to walk out into mountains of snow…"

"Why would she?" Sabrina asked.

"I don't think she would."

"Then where could she be?"

"I don't know. And I admit I'm growing more and more afraid of finding out. Still, after searching the castle last night, it only makes sense to ride around the general area and look for her. So I guess I should get up, huh?"

She nodded. He kept staring at her. She laughed suddenly and moved into his arms. It seemed a unique opportunity, waking up beside him. One not to be wasted. To just slide into his arms and make love was a temptation not to be resisted.

Yet afterward, he didn't linger. He rose, showered quickly, kissed her, walked away, came back, kissed her once again, then hurried out by way of the secret passage. When he was gone, she bounded to her feet, showered and dressed in jeans, a cashmere pullover, boots and a heavy jacket.

She hurried downstairs and found that she was the last to arrive in the great hall. Despite their lack of power, Jennie Albright was still whisking up wonderful meals. As Camy handed her coffee, she saw that the others were already dining on eggs, ham, salmon, crispy potatoes, and toast cooked in little metal baskets that went over the open fire.

"You look as if you're ready for the outdoors," Brett told her.

"Yeah, I am. Cooped up too long. I want to take a walk down to the stables."

"You're not coming with us," Jon told her.

She arched a brow. "Why not?"

"Because Joshua and I know where we're going, where to ride, where it's dangerous and where it's not."

"I know how to ride."

"But you don't know this terrain."

"What about Thayer?"

"I spent a lot of time riding last time I was here," Thayer told her apologetically. "Before..." He looked away uncomfortably.

"Before Cassie was killed," Jon said bluntly. "Let's go," he told the others, and they left the great hall.

Sabrina watched them go. Brett came up behind her. "He's afraid for you."

"Why?"

"That's easy, isn't it?"

She turned around and looked at him. Brett smiled. "He's in love with you," he said. He shrugged. "Anyway, want to build a snowman?"

She hesitated for a moment. "Yeah, sure, why not."

The went outside. The air remained icy, despite the sun, but still, it felt good. Once again the others began wandering out. V.J. and Tom remained by the doors, but Camy, Anna Lee, Dianne and Joe came out and joined them in creating a huge snowman. Then when Dianne missed while in the process of adding a wad of snow to their creature's midsection, sending the snow all over Brett, their artistic endeavors deteriorated into another major snowball fight.

Finally, though, Sabrina realized that she was way too cold. And looking up, she saw that the sun had fallen, and they were heading into late afternoon. "Hey, we're going to be frostbitten Popsicles if we don't get inside!" she called.

"I think my nose is already gone. I can't feel it!" Dianne claimed.

"Mine was too big anyway," Joe said. "But I need my feet, and I can't feel them anymore, either!"

Laughing and drenched, they returned to the house. By then, V.J. had gone in. She was pacing in the entryway. Sabrina smiled at her. "I'm soaked!"

"That's what happens when children play," she said, but she looked distracted.

"What's the matter?"

"Reggie hasn't come down yet."

"Well, I'm going to take a shower and change. Walk up with me and see if she's in her room."

"All right."

In the hallway, they parted, Sabrina heading for her room, V.J. walking down the hall to Reggie's. Sabrina heard V.J. knocking, but then closed her door.

Well aware that the hot water wouldn't last forever—

and that several of them were thawing in it right now—
Sabrina showered quickly. As she wrapped a towel
around herself, she heard a banging at her door. "Yes?"
she called out.

"It's me. V.J."

Sabrina opened her door, and V.J. walked in, tense
and worried. She was carrying a kerosene lamp, and she
lit it as she spoke. The shadows were taking them from
afternoon to evening.

"Reggie isn't in her room," V.J. said.

"What's going on?" came another voice. Brett, freshly
showered as well, had just come into the hall and stood
at Sabrina's open doorway.

"I'm worried about Reggie," V.J. said.

"Hang on, I'll get dressed, and we'll start another
search party," Sabrina said.

She grabbed her clothing and hurried into the bathroom. Brett had followed V.J. into the room, and the two
were talking.

"I mean, Susan might choose to disappear, but not
Reggie," V.J. announced firmly.

"V.J., calm down," Brett said.

As Sabrina zipped herself into dry jeans and stepped
from the bathroom, V.J. was shaking her head. "You don't
understand. Reggie pretends to be so tough, but she's on
all kinds of heart medication."

"Does Jon know that?" Sabrina asked.

"Jon always seems to suspect when something is
wrong, but Reggie's so stubborn. I think she lied like
crazy to Jon, telling him she was in wonderful shape
so he wouldn't leave her out of things—which he would
have if he thought she was failing in the least. But I know
something has happened to Reggie. I just know it."

"All right, where might she be?" Brett asked.

"Well, she's not in the great room or the library or her room," V.J. said.

"I guess we go downstairs. To the dungeon," Sabrina said. She wondered why she was more and more loath to do so.

"Let's go," Brett said.

V.J. and Sabrina followed him out into the hallway. Joe, also freshly showered, was coming from his room. "What's up?"

"We can't find Reggie," V.J. said. "Want to help us on another hunt?"

"Sure. Where's Tom?"

"In the library. He probably thinks I'm with Reggie now," V.J. said.

"Well, let's get Tom and start searching again," Joe said.

"Sounds good," Brett agreed.

They went down to the library. Tom and Dianne were playing gin rummy at a table by the fire. Sabrina noticed the way Tom's face lit up when V.J. entered the room, and she wondered how either of them had ever managed to fool anyone for as long as they had.

But then, seeing the expressions on their faces, Tom frowned. "What's wrong?"

"I can't find Reggie," V.J. told him.

"We're going down below on a hunt," Joe said.

As he spoke, they heard the front doors open. Sabrina walked to the library door, looking toward the main entrance. A great blast of cold air came sweeping in along with Jon, Joshua and Thayer. They looked worn and freezing. All had red noses and runny eyes.

"No luck?" Brett asked, though the answer was obvious.

"No luck," Jon said, unwinding a scarf from around his neck. "You can see down the cliff, though, that the road crews in the village have dug through some of the major blockages. We could be out by tomorrow." He sounded relieved.

"Damn, I gotta get to the fire!" Thayer exclaimed, making his way through to the library. "This is terrible. I may have to sue. I think my balls are frozen."

Sabrina smiled as he hurried by her. Then she met Jon's eyes, and she saw the hard, dark concern in them.

"What's going on?" he asked carefully as he looked at her.

"V.J. is worried. We can't find Reggie."

"Jesus! Reggie?" he repeated.

"Yes, we were about to go down below and see if she's there for some reason."

"Damn!" Jon swore. He drew off his coat and gloves, dropping them on the hall tree. Heedless of the snow he tracked in he headed around the main staircase to the second set winding down below. Sabrina followed him, Brett at her heels and the others close behind him.

He picked up one of the lamps from a wall fixture as he hurried down the steps. "Reggie! Shit!"

"Jon?" V.J. called anxiously. "Is there something wrong, something you know?"

He paused briefly, turning back. V.J. nearly plowed into him. "Yes, there's something wrong. I should have known Reggie better. We asked her to sit in the great hall while we were looking for Susan, and I think she was insulted. She might have decided to do her own search after we went to bed. She just won't realize her age!"

V.J. went white. She was right on Jon's heels as they hurried on down the rest of the steps.

"I'll take the chapel," Joe called.

"I'm with you like glue," Dianne told him.

"Crypts," Thayer offered.

"Crypts, fine. I'll do the tombs with you," Tom said unhappily.

"Brett, try the pool, the bowling alley," Jon said, already heading into the chamber of horrors. Sabrina and V.J. were on his heels.

"Oh, Jesus, dear God!" Jon breathed as they walked into the chamber.

Because there was Reggie. Crumpled on the floor, right in front of the tableau of Lady Ariana Stuart and her torturer.

"Reggie, Reggie!" He was instantly down on his knees, carefully testing her pulse, her breathing.

"Reggie!" V.J. shrieked, dropping down beside her.

By then, the others had come hurrying in.

"Oh, God, she's dead," Joe said.

"Was she cut? Shot? What?" Thayer queried.

"No... I think it was her heart," Jon said. He still knelt by her. "Reggie, Reggie..." The emotion he had borne the writer was evident in his voice as he leaned over her again.

"She's dead, oh, God," Dianne breathed.

V.J. looked at Jon. "CPR," she said.

He shrugged. Reggie was dead. But...

V.J. bent over Reggie's face, counting, giving her oxygen, while Jon worked her heart. Suddenly, there was a strange look in his eyes. "Wait... I think...oh, God, there's a pulse. Faint as hell, but she may be breathing. V.J.! Damn! She may just be breathing!"

"We've got to be talking serious brain damage here," Dianne said. "Maybe we should just—" She broke off, because V.J. was glaring at her. "Just let her go," Dianne finished very softly.

"She may pull out of this," V.J. insisted.

"What?" Tom exclaimed.

"She may only be in a coma. She may be in shock." V.J. said impatiently. "If we can just keep her warm…"

"Let's get her upstairs," Jon said.

He lifted Reggie as if she were a small child. He carried her up both flights of stairs to her room and laid her gently on the bed. V.J. adjusted pillows, took off her slippers, began chafing her hands. Jon covered her in blankets. He hovered over her.

By then, Camy and Anna Lee had both come from their rooms to see what had happened.

"What's going on?" Camy asked.

"Reggie…" Joe began.

"Reggie's dead!" Anna Lee announced.

"No…just mostly dead," Brett said with a sigh.

"I'm going to have to go down to the village, get help up here now," Jon murmured. "It's her only chance. V.J.— you'll stay with Reggie?"

"Of course."

"But not alone. Three people with her at all times," Jon said.

"I'll take first shift," Dianne offered.

"Just keep three people with her at all times. And the rest of you, lock yourselves in or hang together."

"Jon, I can come with you," Joshua told him.

"No, I'll go faster alone," he insisted.

He turned, leaving the room. His eyes fell on Sabrina as she stood just outside the doorway, watching.

He mouthed the words "Lock yourself in!" and swept on by her.

She heard his footsteps as his long strides took him swiftly down the hall.

She hesitated, then followed him.

When she reached the main floor, he was nowhere to be seen, but he hadn't yet taken his coat from the hall tree. She frowned, puzzled, then realized that he had gone back down below.

JON HURRIED BACK down to where he had found Reggie. In his concern to grasp at any hope of keeping her alive, he had ignored something right before his eyes.

Something that hadn't registered until she had been laid out on her bed.

A kerosene lamp remained where he had left it when he had knelt down next to Reggie. It spilled its light across the floor.

Reggie's hand had lain in a little pile of dust and straw that had spilled from the tableau.

And he searched for what had nagged at him, he found it. Yes. She had tried writing in the dust. It was difficult to read—it might have just been hand spasms. But no. There were definitely letters there, formed in the dust. *R... I... P... P... C*—no, *E. RIPPE... R.* Ripper.

He sat back on his haunches, frowning, then looked toward the tableau of Jack the Ripper.

He stood, realizing what his previous sensation down here had been. It smelled like...

When an animal got caught inside and died. It was cold down here, very cold, but still...

Shit.

He started walking to the tableau. There was Jack the

Ripper in his stereotypical cape and black hat. And down below him was his victim. Mary Kelly.

Not Mary Kelly.

Susan!

Dead and decaying, dressed in the clothing that had adorned the wax figure. It was real blood, not paint, that now caked the slashed throat of the victim.

Her eyes were open and staring.

There was no mistaking her condition. No hope, no chance.

Susan was dead.

"God!" he breathed aloud, and the stench and the horror of it all suddenly gripped him. He doubled over so as not to be sick. And as he did so, he realized that he was hosting a killer far more dangerous and psychotic than he had ever imagined.

There was no question now that Cassie had been killed. And that Susan had known something...

That had cost her her life.

"Fool!" Jon charged her corpse, gritting his teeth. "Susan, why didn't you just tell us the truth? Why did you play games?" He was angry with her. He was horrified. She had played with cravings to be powerful, and she had paid with her life.

"Jon?"

He heard his name called. Sabrina. Oh, God.

"Sabrina, no!" he called.

But she was there, hurrying to him.

And staring.

At Susan's open eyes. The dried blood around her throat. The horror...

And then she looked at him. And there was terror in her eyes.

CHAPTER TWENTY

"OH, JESUS, OH, GOD!" Sabrina exclaimed. She backed away, suddenly aware of the stench of blood, of death.

She opened her mouth to scream. "No, no!" Jon commanded, his hand clamping hard over her lips. Hard, smothering.

No, no.

She'd been a fool. He *was* a murderer.

"Damn it!" he whispered to her furiously. "Don't be ridiculous. I didn't do this. I only found her now because Reggie must have had a heart attack stumbling upon the truth down here herself. She left us a clue. *R-I-P-P-E-R*, written in the dust. I've got to get her to a hospital, get help up here and get the rest of us out. She knows who the killer is. Reggie knows, do you understand?"

As he spoke, Sabrina could still see Susan. See her throat. However had they missed this? That the vicious slash, and the blood, were real? How had they not seen it before?

Because the wax figures were so good, so real. You had to be right on top of this, you had to be *smelling* this to realize. Nothing had been different here, nothing at all…except that wax had become flesh, and paint had become blood.

Jon hadn't done it. So he said. But if he had done it, he could strangle her here and now…

His hand was easing from her mouth. "I've got to get moving."

"What are we going to do? Tell the others?"

"We have to. If we don't let everyone know that we're aware Susan is dead, Reggie alive becomes even more dangerous to the killer."

He took her by the hand, and they rushed up the steps. Jon burst into the library. V.J., Tom and Dianne were absent, upstairs in Reggie's room. The others were all present.

Jon looked around at them. "We've found Susan," he said simply.

"Is she—?"

"Dead," Jon announced.

Anna Lee stood uncertainly. "Not another heart attack?"

"No. She was murdered. Her throat was slashed."

"Where?" Thayer demanded. "Why didn't we find her body before?"

"Because she's in the Jack the Ripper tableau," Jon said.

"Lord!" Joshua exclaimed. He had been drinking tea by the fire. He set down his cup, stood and raced for the stairs.

"Wait!" Jon called, following him. "Wait, Josh, don't touch her! I'm going to get the police in here!"

But Joshua was on his way down the stairs, Jon and Thayer right after him. Joshua reached the tableau and touched Susan before they could stop him. They pulled him back, and he let out a horrible, keening sound. "Oh, my God, oh, my God…"

Sabrina had followed but remained in the doorway. Anna Lee, at her side, started to cry. "Oh, God, oh, hell, oh, God, oh… I'm going to be sick."

She turned around, hand clamped over her mouth, heading for the ladies' room.

"Don't! Don't touch her! No one touch her!" Jon said forcefully. "Joe, Thayer, help me get Josh out of here. Camy, get Anna Lee. Everyone, out of here!"

He ushered them all out and closed the doors. Sabrina was still feeling sick herself. She met his eyes, and he reached out a hand to her. She hesitated just briefly, then took it.

Camy had an arm around Anna Lee. Together, they headed up the steps. They moved into the library like automatons.

Jon poured Anna Lee a drink, handed it to her. He looked at Camy. "You all right?"

She nodded. "I need a brandy, but I'll get it. We'll all get drinks."

"Get your drinks, and lock yourselves into your rooms. Now. Before I go," Jon told them.

"What about V.J., Tom and Dianne?" Joe queried.

"They're together. V.J. can't be guilty. I would never have noticed Reggie's faint pulse if it weren't for her," Jon said.

"But what about Dianne?" Joe asked.

"Whoever killed Susan killed Cassie. You can make up whatever scenarios you want, but Dianne drove me crazy to do this Mystery Week again. She isn't a killer. She certainly didn't kill her own mother. So the rest of you get to your own rooms and lock yourselves in."

"Can I lock in with Joe?" Anna Lee asked softly. "If you'll have me," she said to Joe.

Joe smiled. "Sure, you know I will."

"Everyone up," Jon said.

They started up the stairs, paired off. Jon asked Joshua

to explain the situation to Tom, V.J. and Dianne, and directed Camy to go up and tell Jennie and the girls to keep themselves locked in, as well.

Joe and Anna Lee walked, hand in hand, to Joe's room.

"Guess you don't want me guarding Sabrina?" Brett said hopefully.

"Guess you'd better both just lock your doors," Jon said.

Brett stopped Sabrina. "You know I'm not a killer. A womanizer, yes. But not a killer. If you do need help while hero-man is away…" He left it at that and went into his own room.

Jon came into Sabrina's room with her. He wedged a heavy chair in front of the panel leading to the secret passageway, then hit a brick in the fireplace that caused another brick—with a drawer behind it—to pop out. A small pistol lay inside.

"Know how to use a gun?" he asked her. She shook her head. He picked up the revolver and demonstrated. "The safety is off. Grab, aim, pull the trigger. Aim, pull the trigger. It's a six-shooter."

She nodded, moistening her lips. He set the gun back in the drawer and shoved the stone back into place.

"Open it for me," he told her.

She did.

He nodded, then drew her into his arms and kissed her hard. "I'm sorry, so damn sorry!" he said after a moment. "I should have ended this whole week long ago."

"And let a killer get away? To kill and kill again? This killer is psychotic. Maybe he can be caught now."

"And Susan is dead, and Reggie may die."

"God forgive me, no one deserves a brutal death, but

Susan obviously knew something, and she should have told us all what it was. And Reggie—"

"Reggie is one of the finest people I know," he said.

"And she may live."

"As may we." His eyes studied hers. "This isn't a great time, but you do have a way of disappearing on me, and so let me at least get the question in. Will you marry me?"

She opened her mouth to reply, but he set a finger on her lips. "Don't answer yet. Wait until I get back."

"Oh, God, it's so late. It's freezing out there. You'll——"

"It's all right. I could see all the road clearing that's been done below. Damn I just knew Susan hadn't gotten that far. She hadn't gotten far at all," he said bitterly. He kissed her once again. "I love you, you know. I have since I met you."

She smiled. "I love you. And maybe Brett did have a right to seduce Cassie. You did ruin all other men for me."

"You know I'm not a killer, right?" he said, brushing her cheek.

She nodded.

"But you know that someone here is."

She nodded again. "I'll keep the door locked against everyone. And I know where the gun is." She shuddered a little.

He gazed at her, kissed her, drew away. "I've got to go."

He didn't look back. He left the room, ordering her gruffly to lock the door.

She did so.

His footsteps faded, and the castle became silent.

For a while, she paced. Then she sat. Tried to read. Time seemed endless. She looked at her watch, certain that hours had gone by.

Thirty minutes.

It would take forever for Jon to get back.

She started pacing again, then hesitated, certain she had heard a sound. She had. A scraping sound. Very soft. Almost indiscernible. She walked to her door, laid her ear against it, closed her eyes, listened.

A squeak. A scrape. Like a door sliding open.

She realized that the sound wasn't coming from outside the room, but inside.

She spun around. And she knew why she had felt she was being watched before. She knew why Jon had felt the sensation.

There was a second false panel, on the other side of the room, flanking the right side of the balcony. It was open, and Brett stood there now.

His face was chalk white. Drawn. She watched in horror as he started walking toward her.

"Brett… Brett…what…?"

So it was Brett! He was the killer! Oh, God! She had to scream, get to her door, get help…

JON HAD HIS horse saddled in the stables when he felt a touch on his shoulder. He spun around, mentally bracing himself, aware that the murderer could have followed him to stop him.

But it was old Angus. "Sir?"

"I've got a dying woman in there, Angus, and something worse. A murderer."

"Yer wife's killer, sir?"

He looked at Angus and nodded slowly.

"We'll get him, sir. We will."

"I have to ride out, Angus."

"Sir, there's something you should know first," Angus told him gravely, a very slight smile playing at his lips.

SABRINA NEVER GOT the chance to scream.

Brett pitched forward into her arms, crying her name. "Sabrina!"

His eyes closed. And she realized that he was covered in blood from a wound in his back.

"Brett!" Stumbling beneath his weight, she got him to her bed. Frantically, she tried to staunch the wound. He was unconscious. She was so involved with her frenzied efforts that she didn't see or hear anything at first as she wadded a pillowcase, her nightgown and then bedcovers to bind his wound.

Then she heard the sound.

And she realized that someone had come in after Brett.

Someone in a cloak and a top hat, wielding a huge knife that dripped blood.

Standing at the foot of her bed.

She couldn't see a face, just a scarf tied over the nose and mouth, the hat brim pulled low. The figure blocked her exit. And it was moving toward her.

She could scream, but she'd never get help in time.

There was only one way out. The secret passage.

And she had no idea where it led.

No choice.

She screamed as loudly as she could for good measure, then sprinted toward the open panel and the passageway.

JON REENTERED THE castle by way of the basement storm doors that led through a short passage to the furnace, the water system and then into the chapel.

Among the old vestments there he found a large black

hooded cape. Wrapped in it, he made his way back into the chamber of horrors. He surveyed each tableau, deciding where he should wait.

He turned.

And from the corner of his eye, he saw movement.

A wax figure was moving. The torturer from the Lady Ariana Stuart display. The figure suddenly jumped out at him.

Wielding a knife.

He caught the figure's arm. They grappled to the floor, exchanging blows. The knife rose and fell. Jon moved quickly, yet felt a slash against his thigh. He gritted his teeth at the pain, praying he wasn't losing too much blood. The killer was aiming at him again. He shielded himself with a blow to the creature's arm and got in a good shot to the jaw. The knife flew across the floor. The killer rose, ran after the knife, turned.

Footsteps. Someone was coming. From somewhere within the walls of the castle.

The accomplice?

If he was attacked by two of them...

He heard gasping, crying, screaming. Someone running from someone in pursuit.

Jesus!

He swung his fist again.

DESPITE THE DARK and her staggering, desperate terror, Sabrina knew where they were headed.

The dungeon.

It was still dark where the winding stairs ended, with nothing but hard wall in front of her. In a panic, she began beating at it.

Miraculously, a panel gave. She burst out from the passageway...

And into the chamber of horrors.

Jack the Ripper was gone. Susan still lay dead.

She heard movement behind her. The killer. Jack the Ripper, come to life!

"No!" she screamed, and she turned to run. He caught her by the hair, spinning her back around. She struggled desperately, fighting, scratching. She heard a grunt, a groan.

He forced her against a tableau. She saw her own face as she was pressed downward. Saw more rope as the killer struggled to reach it, bind her so that he could kill her at his leisure...

She screamed and screamed...

And realized that the torturer above her was alive, as well.

Jon.

He suddenly leaped down upon her assailant, and the two went flying across the floor, battling intensely.

A knife went flying. Sabrina scurried to retrieve it, but it slid into the straw beneath the wax tableau. Jon and the figure pummeled one another with their fists. Sabrina scrambled through the straw, gave up the search and looked for something else with which she might attack the killer.

Then she heard a sickening crunch.

One of the cloaked figures went down. The other turned to her, drawing back his cowl.

"Jon!"

She cried his name and went racing toward him. He caught her in his arms. "Oh, God, oh, God!" At first, she just kissed him. Then she drew back. "But who...?"

"Joshua," he said softly.

"Joshua killed Cassie?" she said incredulously.

"No!"

The downed figure struggled up to his elbows. Joshua's handsome face was sporting mean bruises. His eyes were both blackening; his nose was crooked and swollen. Talking was obviously an effort. He was winded, broken.

"No, I didn't kill Cassie," he said. "But…"

"Camy killed her," Jon finished. "And you killed Susan to protect her."

Joshua laughed, then choked. "No, Camy killed Susan, too. And Reggie…but…" He looked up, tears in his eyes. "You've killed Camy, haven't you? That's her, in that pile at your feet, Jon."

Sabrina thought Joshua had lost his mind. Then she realized that he was talking about a crumpled form at the feet of the wax figure of Jon on display.

"There—that's Camy. Where I immortalized you in wax, right, Jon?" Joshua asked.

"She isn't dead. She's unconscious."

"But it doesn't matter, does it? She might as well be dead. We'll be locked away forever."

Staring at him incredulously, Sabrina asked, "Why, Joshua? I don't understand."

"It's kind of hard for me to swallow, too," Jon said dully. "I trusted both of you. With everything. With my life."

"At first…it just happened," Joshua said. "Because Cassie meant to have Camy fired, and ruin everything between Jon and me. You see, I am good." He smiled awkwardly. "But you know, art is like writing. Good doesn't necessarily mean fame or fortune. All my renown came from Jon's interest, no matter how good I was." He grimaced with pain and looked at Jon steadily. "Camy told me she killed Cassie by accident. But since then... there have been other accidents. A girl I was friendly with in the village went over the cliff last year and—" He broke off, shrugging. "Then...you were right about the bullet in the hall, Jon. Camy did it. I told her she was being crazy. She said it was part of the game. Then she shot at the horses when we were riding. I don't know if she meant to kill either of you or Brett, but the rearing horses would have been blamed for any deaths. She wrote the note to you that she lied about, accusing you of being the murderer, to create trouble among all of you. To deflect attention."

Joshua frowned, his pain evident once again. "How did you know, Jon? How did you know to come back? How did you suspect that Camy and I..." His voice drifted off; he lifted his shoulders. "I thought that we might just get away. Obviously, with all the forensic techniques available now, someone might have discovered who killed Susan. But it wouldn't have mattered. We would have disappeared by then. Gone to Mexico, Guatemala, Africa—somewhere. But then Brett there just had to play boy wonder and get nosy. He came back down. He found Camy and me here. I had to try to silence him. But how did you know what might be happening here, Jon?"

"Angus had seen you two together, Josh. You and Camy."

"Why didn't you leave?" Joshua asked pathetically as he used the wall to slowly pull himself up off the floor. "Why didn't you leave to get help for Reggie?"

"Angus's son had finally made it up to the castle to help his father, and he rode down to the village for me," Jon said. "And when Angus told me that he'd seen you two together—often and secretively—I began to fear that something worse would happen if I left."

"Something worse is still going to happen!" a voice suddenly said heatedly. Sabrina and Jon spun around. Camy, whose ostensibly unconscious form had lain at the feet of Jon's wax image, was up. She fumbled in her cloak pocket and produced a gun. "I know how to use this—I made a point to learn. A woman frequently alone in an old castle in the wilds… I needed to be armed, to protect myself, you know," she said. "Damn you, Jon, you just couldn't let the bitch die! I really never wanted to hurt you. You knew that Cassie was a monster, and Susan was even worse, and—"

"What about the village girl?" Jon asked her softly.

Camy looked as if she was about to lie. Then she shrugged. "She was in the way. I don't like competition. Joshua thought she was beautiful. Get up, Joshua. I'm sorry, Jon, but you've got to die now, too."

Jon stared at her, then folded his arms over his chest. "No, I don't think so. Joshua knows now that you're psychotic. He's not going to help you. And I'm not going to let you kill me."

"You can't kill us all, Camy!" Sabrina protested.

She looked at Sabrina and laughed. "Honestly, I'm sorry you just had to get so involved. You seem fairly decent. And old Reggie, if she just hadn't been such a nosy old puss! Still, it was fun to haunt you. You all think you're so clever. Jon thought he knew all the hidden passages in the castle, but I was the one who knew them all. And used them. Yes, it amuses me to watch people. I even watched you sleep. I thought you were the smart mystery authors, but I was the one with the power, the power of life and death, over you. It was tremendously amusing to use Jon's robe to clean the blood off me after I'd offed Susan. You were so intriguing. So desperately in love— and feeling such a fool that you might be in love with a wife murderer! Weren't you still suspicious of him, right up to this very minute?"

"No," Sabrina said. "No." She crossed her arms over her chest as well and announced, "No. We're getting married."

"You're getting dead!" Camy said, and started laughing.

"Camy, you are a monster," Jon said. "Sabrina, we are getting married?"

"As soon as possible. Life is too short to waste any time," she told him.

Camy, disgruntled that they seemed to be ignoring her, exclaimed, "You don't know how short!"

"You are the one and only real monster, Camy, and you've played havoc with my life long enough!" Jon announced. He limped toward her.

"Keep your distance, Jon. I'll shoot you."

"Then do it! And you'd better aim well!" he said furiously. "Shoot to kill, because if I get my hands on you—"

"Wait, Jon! Camy, we've got to stop. We're done—" Joshua began, but Camy was grimly taking aim.

"No!" Sabrina shrieked.

The gun went off.

"Jesus!" Sabrina swore.

Camy had shot Joshua. With a bullet in his shoulder, he slammed against the wall, sinking down to the floor.

Sabrina started toward Joshua, and Camy turned the gun on her, firing. She missed. Sabrina dived to the ground while Jon rushed for Camy.

Camy fired two haphazard shots, diving behind one of the tableaux as she did so.

"Jon!" Sabrina shrieked, rising.

"Stay down!" Jon commanded.

She couldn't stay down. Jon knew as well as she did that they should make Camy keep firing wildly until she was out of bullets.

And Sabrina had to pray that the gun was a six-shooter.

Sabrina started to streak across the room again. Camy fired again. Missed.

One bullet left.

"Damn you, Sabrina, stay down!" Jon commanded.

At the moment, she did. They were all hiding among the wax tableaux, no one knowing exactly where anyone else was.

Then Camy suddenly rose from right behind Sabrina. She smiled, taking aim. "I kill you, and Jon is just as good as dead," she said softly.

Her finger started to move on the trigger.

But Jon suddenly rose from behind Lady Ariana Stuart like a wave, a force of nature, a vengeful phoenix rising from ashes. He came hurtling across the room, tackling Camy at the ankles.

Camy shrieked, trying to aim and shoot.

But she teetered. Falling, she tried to take aim at Jon.

Her gun exploded.

So did a second weapon from somewhere else in the room.

Camy went limp, her eyes open, staring. Dead.

Brett, white as a ghost and still festooned in Sabrina's makeshift bandages, stood wobbling at the entry from the hidden passage.

"Jon?" he said quietly. "Jesus, am I too late?"

"Just a flesh wound or two," Jon said, rising, his hand on his upper arm.

"I know you're a fighter, buddy," Brett told Jon. "And you might have disarmed her, but I couldn't risk losing my best friend." Brett smiled, then crumpled to the floor.

Jon walked to Sabrina, reaching to help.

Camy lay dead. Joshua was wounded or dead. Brett was on the floor, passed out cold. She and Jon were alone among the carnage.

"It's over," he said softly. "Jesus, it's over," he repeated. "See if Joshua is alive, if he has a chance. I'm going to get Brett upstairs, stop the bleeding again, get him stabilized. Amazing, isn't it? He did just turn out to be my best friend." He knelt by Brett, carefully lifting the other man.

Then he looked up at Sabrina. "Did you really believe in me?" he asked.

"Always, in my heart."

"But you were suspicious."

"Logically, in my mind. But…"

"But what?"

"My heart would never listen," she told him.

He smiled and, limping, led the way out of the chamber of horrors.

EPILOGUE

"JON!"

He heard his name called, and he looked back.

There she stood, on the balcony. Calling to him.

He paused, smiled and waved back.

It had been two years since the night the medics and evacuation team had rushed up to the castle and the police had followed.

Both Reggie and Brett had made it. Jon's own wound had healed easily, leaving only a tiny scar. Joshua had died on the operating table.

The media had hopped on Joshua Valine's death, having a field day with the pathology of the unusual artist. His work garnered great publicity and attention—posthumously. But the gossip made Jon sad. Joshua had been guilty, but more of falling in love and refusing to think with his mind instead of his heart. He had become an accessory to brutal acts, though, and Jon often wondered if the artist could have survived year after year in jail. Camy's bullet and Brett's determination to protect his host and friend had written *finis* to the case before it ever went to a court of law.

Sabrina had left with the medical team that night to be with Brett—as a friend. And as soon as the police had finished with him, two weeks after the event, Jon had taken off from Lochlyre Castle, as well. He had needed to get away. To come to terms with everything that had happened. And he'd needed to do it alone.

Then, at last, he'd managed to go after Sabrina. And it was only with her that he'd broken down. He thought he had forgotten how to cry, and he hadn't realized that he'd blamed himself for Cassie and for Susan and for all the pain suffered in his castle. But that first night back with Sabrina, he'd begun to forgive himself. And to fall in love all over again.

They were married quietly, with her folks, her sister and brother-in-law and baby nephew in attendance. He'd never been happier.

On their first anniversary, they were gifted with the birth of a son. And soon after that, Sabrina had insisted that they leave the States and come back here. To Lochlyre Castle. The castle wasn't evil, she reminded him. Only some people were. She loved the estate, and vowed that it should be a place of happiness. That they could make it so.

And she had.

"Jon!"

"What?"

"You're just staring at me."

"Well, you called me."

"I got a card from V.J. and Tom. They're in Spain, and they want to come here for a week to visit."

"Great! Tell them to come!"

He was surprised at the happiness he felt. He did love his castle. And, thank God, others wanted to come back, as well.

"V.J. says we need to host another Mystery Week sometime soon."

"We'll think about that one, okay?"

"Okay!"

Sabrina's eyes were dancing in the sunlight. The breeze stirred her hair, making it flow around her face. She looked gorgeous, seductive, on the castle balcony. He'd gotten rid of the Poseidon statue, and the courtyard was planted with a vast variety of flowers.

She smoothed her hair back. "Jon…"

"Was there something else?" he asked.

"Yes!"

"What?"

"The baby is sleeping…"

"Yeah?"

"I thought you might want to come back for a while…"

He grinned, waved and started back to his castle. It was exactly where he wanted to be.

* * * * *

We hope you enjoyed reading

SHADOWS IN THE NIGHT AND NEVER SLEEP WITH STRANGERS

by *New York Times* bestselling author

HEATHER GRAHAM

HARLEQUIN

INTRIGUE

EDGE-OF-YOUR-SEAT INTRIGUE,
FEARLESS ROMANCE.

HIHG1117

She had died here. Temporarily, anyway.

But she was alive now, and Jodi Canton could feel the nerves just beneath the surface of her skin. With the Smith & Wesson gripped in her hand, she inched closer to the dump site where he had left her for dead.

There were no signs of the site now. Nearly ten years had passed, and the thick Texas woods had reclaimed the ground. It didn't look nearly so sinister dotted with wildflowers and a honeysuckle vine coiling over it. No drag marks.

No blood.

The years had washed it all away, but Jodi could see it, smell it and even taste it as if it were that sweltering July night when a killer had come within a breath of ending her life.

The nearby house had succumbed to time and the elements, too. It'd been a home then. Now the white paint was blistered, several of the windows on the bottom floor closed off with boards that had grayed with age. Of course, she hadn't expected this place to ever feel like anything but the crime scene that it had once been.

Considering that two people had been murdered inside.

Jodi adjusted the grip on the gun when she heard the footsteps. They weren't hurried, but her visitor wasn't trying to sneak up on her, either. Jodi had been listening for that. Listening for everything that could get her killed.

Permanently this time.

Just in case she was wrong about who this might be, Jodi pivoted and took aim at him.

"You shouldn't have come here," he said. His voice was husky and deep, part lawman's growl, part Texas drawl.

The man was exactly who she thought it might be. Sheriff Gabriel Beckett. No surprise that he had arrived, since this was Beckett land, and she'd parked in plain sight on the side of the road that led to the house. Even though the Becketts no longer lived here, Gabriel would have likely used the road to get to his current house.

"You came," Jodi answered, and she lowered her gun.

Muttering some profanity with that husky drawl, Gabriel walked to her side, his attention on the same area where hers was fixed. Or at least it was until he looked at her the same exact moment that she looked at him.

Their gazes connected.

And now it was Jodi who wanted to curse. Really? After all this time that punch of attraction was still there? She had huge reasons for the attraction to go away and not a single reason for it to stay.

Yet it remained.

Don't miss
ALWAYS A LAWMAN,
available December 2017 wherever
Harlequin® Intrigue books and ebooks are sold.

www.Harlequin.com

HIEXP1117

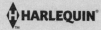
HARLEQUIN®

INTRIGUE

EDGE-OF-YOUR-SEAT INTRIGUE, FEARLESS ROMANCE.

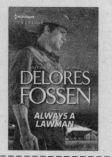

Save **$1.00**
on the purchase of ANY Harlequin® Intrigue book.

Available wherever books are sold, including most bookstores, supermarkets, drugstores and discount stores.

Save **$1.00**
on the purchase of any Harlequin® Intrigue book.

Coupon valid until February 28, 2018.
Redeemable at participating outlets in the U.S. and Canada only.
Not redeemable at Barnes & Noble stores. Limit one coupon per customer.

52615232

5 65373 00076 2 (8100)0 12317

® and ™ are trademarks owned and used by the trademark owner and/or its licensee.

© 2017 Harlequin Enterprises Limited

HIDFCOUPII17

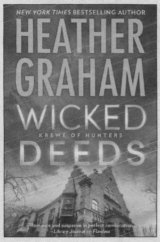

THE WORLD IS BETTER WITH

Romance

Harlequin has everything from contemporary, passionate and heartwarming to suspenseful and inspirational stories.

Whatever your mood, we have a romance just for you!

Connect with us to find your next great read, special offers and more.

 /HarlequinBooks

@HarlequinBooks

www.HarlequinBlog.com

www.Harlequin.com/Newsletters

⊕ HARLEQUIN®

A *Romance* FOR EVERY MOOD™

www.Harlequin.com